VEGAN COWBOY

To Michael,

♡ for all beings,

Carol

Carol Treacy

First published in 2014 by Carol Treacy

ISBN-13: 9781499626490
ISBN-10: 1499626495

Printed in the United States of America

Cover design by Sue Slutzky

For Charlie

FORWARD

When I was thirty-four, I became a vegetarian. Two books influenced my decision: *Animal Liberation* by Peter Singer and *Diet for a New America* by John Robbins. Once I opened the door to the food animal world, not the one portrayed by the factory farming industry via ad campaigns and our government's collusion in perpetuating the myth, I could never close it again. It is a world that I pray will one day be eliminated.

Many people believe that being a vegan means making sacrifices, living with less food and clothing choices. It's actually the opposite. Opening my heart to all animals and showing them compassion is a feeling of liberation and joy. Every time I eat a plant-based meal, I feel like I'm celebrating life. It's not about sacrifice at all, but the growth of the human spirit, looking beyond our conveniences and tastes for the preciousness of life, all life.

All the factory farm and slaughterhouse information in *Vegan Cowboy* is factual and some of the stories of the rescue animals are based on real events.

1

It was another disappointing date. Like the one before and the one before that, which was almost a year ago. Few and far between. From bad to worse, Rae O'Brien approached the dating scene with an objective eye, not a critical one, but she was let down every time. Her son, Carson, said she was too picky, but that wasn't it. She was sizing up her dates with her gut reaction. So far, her gut needed bicarbonate. When Rae was younger, the cavalcade of sub-par suitors would have had her on the phone for hours with friends, thoroughly dissecting the dates with the precision of a medical examiner. But now, they're laughed off and checked off as another dud on her mental chalkboard. At fifty-eight years old, Rae was more than happy to spend her life without a partner. Her ninety-year-old father stopped asking Rae if she was dating anyone six years ago. She wasn't sure if it wasn't important to him anymore, he didn't care or he forgot that she was single. If her mother were alive, she would have given Rae a pitied look, the 'I tried my best to convince you that getting married and having children was the only road to take' look, even if that highway was covered in glass shards, thistles and an occasional tulip. Rae did turn onto that thoroughfare twice, hands firmly gripping the steering wheel. She followed the map to the letter, driving the first five and a half miles with Eric O'Brien. Husband number one was whip-smart, handsome, charming and exceptionally witty. Funny was his second language; however, alcohol was his first and he was fluent in cocaine. Rae divorced him when she realized that she would always take a back seat to his addictions.

Despite objections from her therapist, Rae plunged head first into a serious relationship with Stuart Tenman only three months after leaving Eric. Her heart was aching. She erroneously believed that giving it away instead of holding onto it and nurturing it, was the right thing to do. And it made her parents happy. After all, she was entering her thirties, newly single and childless. Stuart was a good man, responsible and financially stable, but too many critical differences in their personalities turned a seemingly decent marriage into an intolerable one. It wasn't until their son Carson was six years old that Rae's desire to be happy won over her need for financial security.

Rae was forty-two when she embarked on her life as a single mother. Convinced she would meet her life partner, she signed up for nearly every online dating service that coursed through the internet: kissme.com, greensingles.com, match.com, veggiepeople.com, even conscioussingles.com (as opposed to unconscious singles?). Despite the seemingly endless line of men, Rae never came close to getting married. Carson was peripherally responsible, as his tendency toward amazingly obnoxious behavior wasn't tolerated well, especially with men who didn't have children of their own. He could scare a date away with his persistent whining and constant motion in record time.

Dates and short-term relationships piled up like so many dirty clothes waiting to be washed. Rae's undying belief that Mr. Right was right around the corner devolved into a comfortable life of living free from compromise. Instead of reaching for a lover's hand to hold, Rae held Pierre, her adopted tuxedo cat. Changing the litter box became preferable to changing the position of the toilet seat from up to down. Rae didn't even miss having sex. If the need struck, though, a warm male body was easily replaced with a silicone faux body part.

Rae glanced at her watch. It was 8:45 in the morning. She had plenty of time to walk to work. It was only a mile away and on a day this beautiful, it would have been a crime not to exercise and take in the morning air before getting stuck in a stuffy office for eight hours. She crossed Bodega Avenue, one of the major arteries in Petaluma, to Baker Street.

Every time she looked at the street sign, she heard the iconic song by Gerry Rafferty, 'Winding your way down on Baker Street, light in your head and dead on your feet...' She could almost hear the inimitable saxophone solo. She made a mental note to find the song on YouTube, knowing full well that her mind could never retain a task to be performed later in the day or even early evening, so she made a mental note to put a pad and pen in her purse for moments like this. She hoped she'd remember. Rae walked at a fast clip. She was used to it because past boyfriends and husbands were always at least ten inches taller than her and her 5' 1 ¼" frame had to keep up. Most of the men preferred to walk ahead of her rather than slow their pace. Their rude behavior gave birth to her quick stride. Along with Kundalini Yoga, it helped keep her in decent shape, so for their lack of decency, she was thankful.

Rae did not like her job. It was not fulfilling or interesting. It wasn't a bustling office, where she could engage in lively conversation or a small office with a tight-knit staff. She worked with one person, the owner. In three years, Rae had yet to receive a bonus or a raise. She had no one to blame for the situation but herself because she was too damn lazy to find a place of employment that she might actually enjoy. And at this point in her life, Rae wasn't sure what occupation would ideally suit her. She would mentally throw out ideas like clay pigeons and then expertly shoot them down. Even her keen interest in the animal rights movement couldn't propel her into volunteering at the local animal shelter or a regional activist group. She preferred having her free time unencumbered by obligations. As a result, her 'inner tyrant' was merciless, chiding her for being lazy, apathetic and selfish. Donations to animal rights groups didn't count. Rae blamed menopause for shirking her duties as an able-bodied citizen but her inner critic, who she aptly named Cruella, didn't buy it. Someday, Rae knew she would grow tired of the verbal lashings and heed Cruella's urgings, but not now. The pall she felt overshadowed any passion she had for helping the animals, except for her vegan lifestyle which she embraced fervently.

Rae finally arrived at the offices of Moore & Company, a financial services business. She audibly sighed as she opened the doors to the nondescript building, walked up three flights of stairs and reluctantly entered Suite 302. If it weren't for bad interior design, there'd be no design at all. The furniture was mismatched, an ancient light blue and purple striped loveseat sat opposite two dark red leather swivel chairs. A rattan coffee table displayed copies of *Financial Times* next to a bouquet of artificial blue roses covered in a thin veil of spider webs. Framed prints dotted the walls indiscriminately. There was no symmetry to them at all. A black and white photo of Yosemite was separated from a 'starving artists' oil painting of still life by a fake Tiffany wall sconce. Below it was an unframed, oversized sun-faded print of lilies in a vase. The dark grey carpet was stained and one wall was painted Kelly green.

When Rae was the first to arrive, she turned on the lights, prepared the coffee and opened the blinds for the six floor-to-ceiling windows behind her desk and the desk of her boss, Zoe Moore. The outdoor light flooded the large room and the view of the Petaluma River was spectacular. Both women preferred the natural light to the overhead florescent ones but for reasons unknown to Rae, when Zoe arrived first she would turn on the lights, make the coffee and open the blinds to the three windows behind her desk. She had no reason not to open the window blinds behind Rae's desk other than to assert her authority. At least that was what Rae believed. Avoiding confrontation at all costs, Rae never wanted to ask Zoe why she only tended to her own blinds but one day, as she opened the window coverings, she said jokingly, "Hey, I like my blinds open too." Zoe didn't respond, a silence to which Rae was all too familiar.

Today, Zoe was at her desk and, as expected, Rae's blinds were shut. The contrast of Zoe's desk bathed in sunlight to Rae's dark, cellar-like work area was apparent. The irony wasn't lost on Rae. Her anger started to rise, then she felt childish for being upset. With grave injustices happening every second of every day, most people in crisis would welcome closed blinds over starvation, chronic pain and disease.

Zoe grunted hello, barely looking up from her computer. Rae returned the salutation and then opened up the blinds, causing them to slap together. The cracking sound barely registered with her boss. Rae sat down at her desk and turned on the computer. She watched the screen come to life, the Moore & Company logo as wallpaper stared back at her, just as dull and boring as the rest of the business. The thought of spending another day surrounded by financial reports, investment portfolios and securities made her want to tear out of the office and never look back, but that wasn't possible. At least not in Rae's world where a mortgage payment patiently waited for her every month as did the other bills for amenities that kept her comfortable, like running water, electricity and food. She sometimes day dreamed about selling her home and moving to Nelson, British Columbia, where the 1987 movie *Roxanne* was filmed. Ever since she watched Steve Martin and Daryl Hannah walk down the main street with its historic brick buildings and quaint shops, she was in love with this town of 10,000. She had been living with Stuart Tenman for a couple of years when she casually suggested that living in Nelson could be fun and maybe a change of scenery would enliven their relationship. Stuart quickly replied that she couldn't take the harsh winters in Canada. "You're a Southern California girl, Rae. You'd freeze your butt off. Besides, it would be almost impossible to find a job in the City Planner's office. Maybe we could vacation there, if it's not too expensive." Rae had to agree that, unless she was bundled up resembling a sated tick, her fingers and toes would go numb, making her miserable. Still, Rae wondered if she could hack living in another country, away from friends and family and the familiarity of Northern California. The internet had plenty of information on Nelson and sometimes Rae would google images of the town, admiring the hillside homes sharing the mountainside with red, yellow and orange foliage. She imagined hiking in the dense forests and sailing on Kootenay Lake.

Zoe and Rae were around the same age but where Rae was slender, Zoe was on the verge on anorexia. Her fear of gaining weight led her to adopt severe restrictions in almost every food group. If Rae dared to bring in a snack and it had even a tiny crunch to it, Zoe would glare at her. At first, Rae found it intimidating, but after a year of employment she enjoyed bringing in chips, popcorn and Dr. Kracker's extra crispy seeded bites. On more than one occasion, Rae would leave her desk for only a minute or two and discover that Zoe had pilfered her snack. Rae had to laugh at the absurdity of it all.

Rae had taken the job as office manager because she had been laid off from the Marin Scope Newspaper Group as an account executive five months earlier. In a state of panic, she went onto craigslist and searched for job openings in Petaluma to avoid commuting. She wasn't required to know about the business of finance, which was opportune since Rae's financial prowess peaked at checkbook balancing and even that wasn't her forté. Her extensive knowledge of computers and Microsoft Office landed her the position. She was efficient, had excellent follow-through and her sales training made her the ideal receptionist, making every caller feel like they were the only person she was hired to assist.

It was another day of answering phones, invoicing clients and assisting Zoe with reports and spreadsheets. She also began the annual process of picking out Easter and Passover cards for their clients. The internet made it easy to peruse hundreds of card designs without leaving the office and schlepping to the local stationery store. Zoe asked Rae to choose three different cards for both Easter and Passover so she could make a decision. Rae attached her choices in an e-mail with an asterisk next to her two favorites. A few minutes later, without discussion, Rae received Zoe's reply with her decision: Rae's preferences were not part of the order. At 5:00 p.m., Rae was released from the four boring walls and boss that kept her captive since nine that morning. She practically sprinted out the door.

2

Walking home was a welcome respite and Rae reveled in the warm weather, odd for March. Usually the ever-present cloud cover threatened to rain on the city named by the Miwok Indians, a tribe of two thousand in the 1700s. By the mid-1800s the tribe was reduced to eighty as a result of Anglo-American diseases and their assimilation into the ranching communities that took over the town. Today's Petaluma held little resemblance to the days the Miwok lived on the land. Every fast food restaurant claimed a spot on Washington Avenue. They were neighbors with auto parts stores, tire companies and other assorted businesses whose architecture resembled mini tilt-ups, barely concealing their distaste for architectural integrity. Rae stopped counting the number of home builders that razed the hillsides and erected pseudo-fancy tract homes, passing them off as unique and well-constructed. As a result, the city teemed with residents and congested the streets and parking lots that were designed for a smaller population than 55,000 and counting.

As she crossed the street, Rae heard the rev of an engine and then the squeal of tires as a car came to a screeching stop next to her. Rolling down the window, Rae saw a handsome boy with steel blue eyes and the beginnings of a goatee.

"Need a lift, Madre?" Carson asked as he sat low in the driver's seat of his 1989, cherry red BMW 319. He bought the car from a private party, failing to getting it checked out by a mechanic, which was ironic because Carson worked for an auto repair shop. He had given it a cursory look, declared it fit to drive and handed over four thousand dollars in cash to a very happy seller. Two months later, the car required a new transmission, rear axle and four new tires. The heater didn't work and the wipers functioned sporadically.

"Sure, thanks son."

Rae slid into the car, getting her pant leg stuck on the seat's peeling vinyl. The car smelled like French fries and marijuana. She was about to grab the door handle but Carson stopped her.

"Don't touch it, it's broken!" He leaned over her and pulled on the partially closed window, shutting the door. Gunning the engine, he shot off from the curb. Rae was going to say something, but held her tongue. Last time she asked him to slow down, he went faster.

"How was school?"

"Sucked."

"Well, you have less than four months before you graduate and it'll go by fast. Are you going to work at Schuster Brother's full-time in the summer?"

Carson shifted gears, giving the engine more gas than it needed. "They want me to but I think I'm going to chill and just have fun for a while. Par-tay 'till I drop." Before Rae could respond, he turned on the radio and death metal blasted out of the dashboard. Rae expected blood to shoot out of the speakers.

Carson screeched around the corner and turned up their street. He pulled into the driveway and came to a fast stop. "Thank you?" Rae said.

"Don't be such a wuss. You know, someday I'm going to get you to ride on the motorcycle with me."

"Not going to happen," Rae said. "Never. Your friends won't even ride with you. You need to be more careful. Didn't you learn anything in that safety class you took with your dad?"

Carson said, "Sure. If you're going to drive fast, drive safe and watch for cops." He got out of the car and headed for the backyard. "Later, Madre."

"Later, son boy."

Rae was greeted at the door by Pierre. Rita the Manx, a tail-less breed of cat, sat in the dining room staring at Rae with her huge green eyes. She always had a look of fear, like Rae was going to shoot her. Rae found the nine-year-old tabby at the Sonoma County Humane Society shelter two years ago. She had been living in a small cage for a year, sequestered from the other cats because she was too meek to defend herself against their bullying. Rae peered into the cage and locked eyes with Rita. She reminded Rae of a small cougar because of her tan, brown and black ticked coat and pink nose. The volunteer at the shelter cried when Rae said she'd adopt the diminutive feline. She told Rae that everyone there loved the sweet tabby and felt horrible that she was always passed up for adoption.

Within minutes, Carson came upstairs from his bedroom to the main house, grabbed a pizza from the freezer and turned on the toaster oven.

"Boner's coming over in a little while. He wants me to give him a tattoo."

"How are you going to give him a tattoo, or should I ask?"

"Electric toothbrush – I replaced the head with a guitar string."

"Tell me you're joking," Rae said.

"Can't do that, Madre."

Pierre jumped up on the kitchen counter as Carson unwrapped the pizza. He circled the empty box, peering into it then grabbed it and jumped off the counter.

"That cat is bonkers," Carson said.

"I know. Why do you call your friend Boner?"

"His name is Robbie Banner. Banner, Boner."

"Got it. I'd like you to finish your homework before Robbie comes over, okay?"

"Sure."

Rae took a block of tofu out of the refrigerator, along with a bag of broccoli. She set them down in the sink, opened the container of tofu and placed it in the tofu press, a device that squeezed the excess water out of the bean curd. Once the water was extracted, it was replaced by a marinade. The result was like going from a frog to a prince: the tofu absorbed the flavor and became super tasty. Carson smirked. "Are you going to make that with some tree bark and dirt?"

Rae shook her head. "You used to love tofu."

"That was before I discovered meat, which you should be eating, too, not tofu like some hippie."

"News flash. Vegans are healthier and live longer than meat eaters and the tofu didn't suffer, like the cow on your pizza, not to mention all the antibiotics and growth hormones pumped into food animals."

"If you fed me meat when I was a baby, maybe I'd be taller than five seven."

Rae turned to Carson. "First of all, both your grandfathers are five seven. Second, eating growth hormones in animal flesh may have increased your height, but you would have also been eating antibiotics and pesticides. Would that have been worth an inch or two?"

"Fuck yeah."

"And that, ladies and gentlemen, is why humans aren't the only beings on Earth, we just act like it."

"Uh, okay crazy lady." Carson went downstairs. Rae watched him go, shaking her head and seriously wondering where she went wrong. Actually, she did know why Carson eschewed the vegetarian lifestyle. After she divorced Stuart, who never quite embraced the vegetarian diet, she asked him to respect Carson's food choices and he complied. At six years old, Carson went to bat for the animals, explaining to friends how food animals were treated, even writing an essay on factory farming. But a few years down the road, Stuart began encouraging his son to eat meat. It started with salmon and progressed to chicken and then beef. By nine, Carson was a full-fledged omnivore and accused Rae of brainwashing him into believing that eating meat was bad. It was a pivotal moment in their relationship, since they had always been close. By the time Carson hit puberty, his distaste for Rae's food choices became more vocal. Rae knew it was because she was in the minority and vegetarians were viewed as outsiders but it didn't stop her from feeling the sting of her son's disapproval and disrespect. Her friends told her to ignore Carson's remarks. That he did it to upset her. That he was just being a typical teenager: abrasive, obnoxious, rude and annoying. On an intellectual level, she knew they were right, but she still mourned her son's vegetarian 'death.'

Rae washed and cut up the broccoli, then set it in the steamer on the cold stove. After changing into her yoga attire, she went into her spare room and picked out a yoga DVD from her extensive collection. Popping it into the DVD player, she unrolled her yoga mat and positioned herself in front of the television.

As soon as Rae recited the opening prayer, the day's anxieties started to dissipate. She didn't hear Zoe's droning voice or her son's disapproving rant. "Ong na mo guru dev namo" she chanted three times. By the third recitation, her breathing was deeper and she was more relaxed. For the next hour, Rae yawned her body open, inhaled energy through her eyes, feet and solar plexus, distributing it to every cell. Bow pose, Down Dog and Warrior Pose refreshed her tired muscles. When she was done, she said a long Sat and a short Nam. It means 'The truth within you.' For three years, she had been doing Kundalini Yoga almost every day. It kept her sane and centered and on track, for the most part.

After dinner, Rae brought her cup of peach-flavored green tea into the living room and took *Le Visage* out of the Netflix envelope. Not long after the movie started, Rae heard sounds of pain coming from Carson's room below. She paused the DVD and went over to the stairs.

"Is my son hurting you, Robbie?"

"It's cool," Robbie replied.

"Doesn't sound like it. Carson, I hope you had him sign a release form. The last friend you tattooed didn't and he had to pay for the amputation himself."

"She's joking, right?" Robbie said in slightly trembling voice.

Carson turned off the toothbrush/tattoo gun. "Very funny. Go away and watch your movie. Is it foreign or a documentary? Those are the only two you seem to love."

Rae said, "It's a foreign documentary on..."

Carson interrupted. "Don't care. Bye."

"Fine. Good-bye. Please keep the groaning to a minimum, Robbie."

Rae returned to the couch and Pierre immediately jumped into her lap. "Hey there, buddy. What's up?" Pierre looked up at Rae, his pupils large and round like mini-solar eclipses, his gold irises barely visible. They got like that at night, giving him a perpetually surprised look.

Pierre reached up and touched Rae's face with his paw. As he closed his eyes, his body eased into repose and his snow-white paw slowly moved down her face, resting on her chest. She stared at the sleeping cat. So soft, so trusting and innocent. Rae couldn't imagine causing him any harm, yet millions of cats suffer intolerable cruelty at the hands of humans. "I apologize for my species," she said. Pierre opened his eyes, changed position and fell back asleep, oblivious to everything except Rae's welcoming lap.

3

Fran Santiago couldn't take his eyes off of her. He always tried to sit in a seat that gave him full access to view her. There were other good-looking girls in his Communications class but this one was different. She had a vibrancy to her and that tattoo intrigued him; on her left arm it said VEGAN and inside the letters were animals. As soon as he had a chance, he was going to google the word and find out what it meant. He knew it had something to do with animals but that was about it. He also liked the way she dressed. Almost always in jeans with cowboy boots, a colorful shirt, earrings and she wore her long, dark hair back in a braid. Her shirt, the boots, even the jeans looked expensive. Fran looked down at his clothes. Cheap. He inherited the pants from his brother, Luis. The tennis shoes were from K-Mart. His watch was from CVS Pharmacy. He was outclassed but he couldn't help liking her. Songs were written about relationships between the rich girl and the poor boy from the other side of the tracks. He saw white girls with Mexicans all the time, especially in agriculturally-rich Sonoma County where a majority of the farmers used his people because they were cheap labor but hard workers. That's where Fran was headed, to the fields or construction sites with his brother and father, but the thought of using his hands instead of his intellect was so oppositional to him that he stepped outside the Santiago family tradition and applied for a scholarship to Sonoma State University. While his friends were barely scraping by in high school and partying hard on the weekends, Fran focused his attention on his grades. It was a lonely period in his life and he had few friends as a result, but he knew that his only path to higher education was through a scholarship. After three years of making the Dean's List, Fran was awarded a four-year scholarship to SSU. His parents were so proud they nearly went broke throwing him a graduation party.

Fran stole another sideways glance. It took all his will to concentrate on the professor's lecture and take notes. He watched as she pulled a tube of lipstick out of her purse and deftly applied it to her lips. The cherry red tint only added to her allure. Fran forced himself to look away from her so he could concentrate on the lecture.

Allie Bowden was completely unaware that she was being admired. She put the lipstick away and turned her attention back to the professor's lecture on the government's use and manipulation of the media. Communication, Power and Social Change wasn't her first elective choice but it was open and she needed the credit. Allie was always a good student. She didn't love school but she also didn't abhor it. She knew an education would open her horizons, so straight A's became her objective. Allie could have gone to any university she desired but she wanted to stay close to her dad. She lived with him on their ranch and even though he encouraged Allie to apply outside the Bay Area, she couldn't bear to see him living alone. It had been years since her parents divorced. Her mother had remarried a year later but her dad barely dated. He tried internet dating but that didn't last long. His dates were thoroughly impressed with him but his tastes were specific and no woman yet filled the bill. Even Lydia, his ex-wife, wasn't an ideal match for the compassionate cowboy. Allie saw that at the ripe old age of five but she couldn't verbalize it. Instead, she would take every opportunity to spend time with her father, whether it was curling up beside him while watching TV or following him around the cattle ranch like a mini-ranch hand, open to helping with whatever he needed.

"Dad, I'm home!" Allie yelled as she walked into the house.

"I'm out here," Granger yelled back and then waved to his daughter from the veranda. Allie strode across the terra cotta tile floor, her boots clicking as she walked. She plopped down next to her dad on the empty chaise lounge. Granger held out his hand and she grabbed it and squeezed it.

"How was college?"

"Riveting."

"Really?"

"No, but I thought you would like to know that you're getting your money's worth."

Granger said, "You know I don't worry about that."

"I know. So, what'd you do today besides tend to the menagerie?"

Granger smiled. When he did, he emanated such warmth and love. At fifty-eight, he was still handsome. His grey hair was slightly thinning on top, but not enough to notice. Allie used to call him daddy doe eyes because his large, dark brown eyes were soft and friendly.

"Lucy and Jake helped me shoe Tuscany. Too bad they're going to graduate next year. I bet they can't wait to leave sleepy Petaluma."

"They may decide to stay. Lucy told me that she and Jake really love it here. Can you blame them?"

Allie looked out over their land. 540 acres of rolling hills. A creek ran alongside the base of the mountain range and the terrain was dotted with oak trees and errant boulders that jut out of the land, looking like they fell from the sky, their locations were so random. Horses, sheep and cows grazed throughout the many valleys.

"Not at all," Granger replied. "But they're young and probably want to have their own place." Granger stood up and stretched. "Do you have a lot of homework? It's your turn to fix dinner but I don't mind if you have to get school work done."

"I don't have any homework tonight, so I'll wear the apron. I found this great recipe online while my philosophy professor was lecturing on deductive versus inductive logic. Gag me."

Granger laughed. As boring as some of Allie's classes sounded, he would have loved to go to college, but his dad wouldn't hear of it. Someone had to run the farm once he became too old and that someone was

Granger. There wasn't a discussion. The decision was made and forced upon a teenager who was too intimidated by his father to say no. His younger brother, Dale, flat out refused. He ended up going to Stanford and eventually medical school. As much as Granger would have loved to stand up to his dad, he didn't have the backbone. Granger wanted to become a veterinarian but his dad just laughed, telling him he wasn't smart enough to be a doctor. His lot in life was working with the cattle. He had to admit that he was good at it. He loved being around the animals, but not for the same reasons as his father's. He saw the animals as individuals. Some cows were more playful than others. Some of them liked to sit under the oak trees. Others preferred the open valleys. And one of his favorite steers, Rodney, enjoyed following Granger around the ranch. He reminded him of a large puppy. Very large.

Granger grabbed his beer and followed Allie into the kitchen.

"You want me to help with the prep?"

"Sure, Pop." Allie took some veggies out of the refrigerator. "You can dice the carrots and onions for me." She went to the cupboard and grabbed a bag of brown rice, lentils and a bulb of garlic.

"How about some music to cut by?" Granger went over to the stereo, popped in a CD and as Brahms' *Symphony No. 3* started to play, Granger grabbed a knife from the kitchen drawer and started chopping the onion.

4

Fran let himself into his parents' apartment. He said hello to his mother and gave her a big kiss then walked into his brother Dario's room and went straight to the computer. Dario was on his bed, reading.

"What are you reading?"

Dario turned the book cover toward Fran. "*The Catcher in the Rye.* I read that at your age. You like it?"

"It's okay."

"Did you know that in the 60s and 70s, *The Catcher in the Rye* was the most censored book in high schools and libraries in the United States?"

Dario looked up at his brother, "Why? What's the big deal?"

"Back then, books didn't have so much swearing in them, especially coming from the protagonist, a teenager."

Fran went over to his brother's computer and summoned the internet. On the keyboard, littered with snack crumbs, he typed the word 'vegan.' He got 22,800,000 results. Fran chose the Wikipedia definition. He clicked on the link and waited while the computer struggled to reach its destination. Finally, it appeared. As Fran read, his face dropped. A vegan eschews all animal products, including eggs and dairy, honey and the wearing of animal skins, including silk and wool. Some vegans will not eat white sugar, which has been processed using charred animal bones.

No meat, no dairy, no eggs. Fran was told humans would die without these vital protein sources, yet Allie looked amazing. Her skin was flawless, hair shiny and her body was incredible. Fran would never give up eating meat or cheese or milk and she would most likely want to be with someone who was like her. Fran reluctantly made the decision to forget about Allie. His social scene revolved around food. It would have been awkward enough that she was white, but introducing her to his parents and friends as a vegan would be a disaster. She couldn't go to barbeques with him or parties where they always had ribs, chicken, shredded pork or hamburgers. He'd always be concerned that she wouldn't get enough to eat. His stress level was high enough going to school and working.

Dario looked over Fran's shoulder at the computer screen. His eyes scanned the page. "You gonna be a vegan?"

"What? No way!" Fran replied.

"Then what are you looking it up for?"

"School." Fran got up from the computer and went into the kitchen where his mom was fixing dinner: fried chicken, tortillas, beans and rice. It smelled wonderful and Fran was hungry. His mother's hands were covered in flour but she made a point to go over to her son and kiss him on the cheek. Her English was broken but sufficient.

"You staying for dinner, Franny? I make a lot."

"Sure mom, but I'll have to head home after. Got a lot of homework."

His mom gave him a big, toothy smile. "Your papa and Luis will be here soon. Can you set the table?" Fran nodded.

Lornita dipped the chicken parts into the egg mixture, then the flour and placed them in the frying pan filled with oil. She watched Fran as he set the table. There was pride in her dark brown eyes. Her middle son was the first of her children to go to college, an accomplishment she only dreamed of for her boys. Luis had no desire to continue his education past high school. The family was surprised he graduated, Luis included. Dario, though, was a good student. He seemed to enjoy school and excelled in English Literature. He told everyone that he was going to college, just like Fran.

Lornita looked out the kitchen window. A scant fifty feet away was another three-story apartment building with the same architecture:

a no-frills rectangular box. Aside from the brown trim around the windows, little effort was made at adorning the light blue buildings. Diseased box hedges filled in the narrow strips of dirt on either side of the front doors. The leaves were sparse and most were brown or on the verge of turning. Most of the residents were Mexican and most were employed in the vineyards or janitorial services.

"My Franny is going to be president of United States."

"I'll settle for a bachelors degree in business, Ma, and take it from there." He hugged his mother and continued to set the table.

Fran looked at his mom as she stirred the pinto beans on the stove. She was about five feet tall and stocky. Her face was perfectly round with a small roman nose, sparkling hazel eyes and medium length straight black hair. She was only forty-two but looked older. She got up at 5:00 a.m. every weekday, took the bus to San Rafael, a city twenty miles south of Petaluma, and cleaned office buildings for a commercial janitorial service. It was hard work but she never complained. Lornita did it for her three boys. If they were free to choose their destinies, then she fulfilled hers.

5

"I miss my ass," Rae said. She and Darlene were in Rae's backyard, drinking a bottle of zinfandel. With a cascade of auburn curly hair flowing around her freckled face and lightly touching her shoulders, Darlene was striking. She took a sip of wine, licked her lips and said, "Did it go on vacation without you again?"

"Honey, it's on permanent vacation. In its place is a derriere devoid of muscle. When I do the yoga pose where I'm sitting on my feet in a kneeling position, it's heels on bone and it hurts!"

Darlene stood up and felt her behind. "Mine is still there, but for how long? You're one of my few friends in shape or so I thought. How old are you again?"

"Fifty-eight. And you are…?"

"A lot younger." Rae gave Darlene a dirty look. "Don't look at me like that. You were my age a long time ago. I got a ways to go before I start to atrophy. Thanks a lot for the preview." Darlene repositioned herself on the chair. "By the way, I have two tickets to see Yo-Yo Ma at Davies Hall next Friday. You want to go?"

"I don't know. Traffic on the freeway will be horrendous."

"Okay, first of all, I'll drive. Second, it's Yo-Yo Ma, one of the most amazing cellists in the world. The world. I got two tickets to paradise. How can you refuse? Say yes…please!"

"Fine. You drive and I'll buy dinner. Can we go to Golden Era? It's the vegetarian restaurant on Grove Street."

"Isn't that in a snarky neighborhood?" said Darlene.

"Yeah, but if we leave early enough, it'll still be light out so we won't get raped or mugged. I guarantee it."

"Okay, it's settled. Veggie food, no muggings, Yo-Yo Ma. I'll drink to that." They raised their wine glasses. "Maybe you'll meet a nice man at the concert. That would make it a perfect evening."

"I'll be happy ordering the sweet and sour faux chicken at Golden Era. Man optional." Rae said.

"Really? Is this another thing I have to look forward to when I'm your age?"

Rae nodded. "When all the estrogen and testosterone is drained from your body by menopause, you look at men like they're alien life forms. At this stage of my life, the only man who's going to knock me off my feet is going to be a slender, jeans and white t-shirt wearing cowboy who happens to be a vegan."

"That's an oxymoron, vegan cowboy." Darlene shook her head.

"If Clinton can become a vegan, anybody can," Rae said. "More wine?" Darlene nodded and Rae filled their glasses. Rae raised her glass and Darlene followed. "To my vegan cowboy, wherever he may be."

"Probably living in a mental institution suffering from an identity crisis."

"I don't think so," said Rae. "He's out howling at the moon with the coyotes. Let me just close my eyes and imagine the scene. I'll be right back." Rae sat back in the chair and closed her eyes. A smile slowly appeared on her face then she started howling. Darlene joined her. At first it was done in jest, but as the two continued to howl, it became visceral and unabashed. They only stopped when Rae saw her neighbor, Kevin, peek over the fence.

"I was about to call animal control. A little too much wine, ladies?"

Rae replied, "Nope, just got the call of the wild and had to answer. You want a glass of wine?"

"No thanks. I'd say enjoy your evening, but I believe you already are. Later."

Rae and Darlene both said good night at the same time. They decided it was enough wine and carnal enjoyment for the evening. Darlene let herself out the back gate and Rae went inside. She wasn't sure if it was the wine or the howling but she felt lighter, like her spirit was let off its leash for a few transcendent minutes. Carson came upstairs to the kitchen. He grabbed a pizza from the freezer.

"You and Darlene are nuts, howling like that. Do I have to have you committed, Madre?"

Rae laughed. "If I continue to work for Zoe, you might. She drives me nuts with her petty demands and selfish attitude."

"Why don't you quit?"

"I don't feel like looking for another job. I've had so many."

"Well then stop bitching." Carson popped the pizza into the oven.

"Hey now. Don't talk to your Madre like that."

"Whatever. Do you have twenty dollars? Boner and I are going to the movies later."

Rae said, "Yeah." She pointed to her purse hanging on the dining room chair. "I'm going to the city next Friday with Darlene. We're going to the symphony and dinner, so I'll be leaving right after work."

Carson took the twenty out of Rae's wallet. "Thanks."

"Aren't you going to ask who we're seeing there?" Rae said.

"Uh, the symphony?"

"Yes, smart ass but the famous cellist, Yo-Yo Ma, is performing, too."

"Sounds boring."

"Well, it ain't Rotting Zombies, that delightfully insane band that you like to listen to."

Carson started playing his 'air' guitar and singing one of the band's songs, "Got your hand in my crotch and I love it, I love it. Got my blood boiling hot, baby, love it, love it. Die for me. Lie for me..."

"Actually, that reminds me of Yo-Yo Ma. Goodnight, son."

Rae headed for the bathroom as Carson continued to sing. She was feeling pleasantly high from the wine when Cruella broke the serenity, plowing through her thoughts, urging her to stop procrastinating and find a sanctuary or a group where she could volunteer. Even if it was only for a few hours a week, it would get her involved with like-minded people and it could evolve into a paid position. She got into bed and grabbed her laptop from the night stand. Before appeasing Cruella, she decided to check her e-mail. Her Yahoo account defaulted on their home page, or as Rae liked to call it, the Distraction Zone. As she was about to click on the mail icon, she saw a photo of a cat on a motorcycle. The caption read, 'Tabby rides across country.' She clicked on the story and read about Joyce and her companion animal, Ducati. Back on the home page, Rae was about to click on the mail icon when she saw a photo of George Clooney and Stacy Keebler, his latest girlfriend. *George calls it quits* read the headline. Rae had to know what happened, so she clicked on the article and was once again transported into another mindless story. Ten minutes and a photo montage of the couple's relationship later, she made it to her inbox. Rae had a lot of new messages, not one from a friend. They were from non-profits wanting a donation or a signature on a petition, coupons from stores, the latest books from Amazon.com, and even a message from *Extra TV* about George and Stacy's breakup. Rae scrolled down, reading some of the messages, deleting some and unsubscribing from others. When she was done, she couldn't remember why she had gotten on the computer. Rae stared at the screen, willing herself to remember. Just then, Rita jumped up on the bed, followed by Pierre. They went over to the edge, sat down and looked out the partially opened window.

"Hey kitlins. Whatcha doing?"

Neither one acknowledged Rae. Rita curled up in a ball and Pierre started licking his tail. "Don't forget I rescued you two from the shelter. I saved your butts. The shelter. Volunteering. Yes!"

Armed with her memory back intact, Rae clicked on Google and searched for animal sanctuaries in Sonoma County. Considering the area was a big agricultural zone, the list was smaller than Rae expected. Ideally, she would have liked to find an animal sanctuary for rescued farm animals. She knew that volunteering for dog and cat shelters would be too emotionally taxing. The temptation to adopt homeless animals would always be there and she didn't have the fortitude to take in any more animals or children. She could manage Pierre, Rita and Carson. Barely.

Rae scrolled down to the Bird Rescue Center in Santa Rosa. It was about twenty miles away, too far to travel on the weekends. Another bird rescue was even farther north in Cloverdale, but closer to home was Wild Animal Rescue in Petaluma. Rae clicked on the link. The home page proudly featured two mountain lions that the facility was home to, rescued when they were cubs after their mother was shot by a hunter. Other rescued animals included a baby hawk, coyotes, raccoons, foxes, opossums, and otters. Interested in learning more, Rae clicked on the tour video. She was watching it when a 'word with friends' icon began flashing on the bottom of the screen. It was just enough of a distraction to pull her away from the wildlife center's website. Rae paused the video and clicked on the flashing icon.

Thirty minutes later, Rae finished watching the video. She made a mental note to call the facility and inquire about volunteering. Closing the laptop, she placed it on the nightstand then picked up the book she'd started reading a week ago.

Rae glanced at the left side of the bed. There was no one there to tell her not to read. No one pawing her to have sex. She didn't have to listen to someone snoring, keeping her awake or have someone complain when she threw the covers off because she was having a hot flash. She didn't have to compromise or endure being part of a stagnant relationship. She patted the empty spot and said good night to no one, then opened her book and began to read.

An hour later, Rae turned off the light and closed her eyes, but visions of sugar plums didn't dance in her head. Instead, she heard and saw different iterations of the same theme she'd been experiencing for years: pigs screaming as they were led to slaughter, elephants being gunned down by poachers, dogs being beaten to death, children abused. Depending on what Rae read in the paper that day or witnessed on the internet, the images would flood her brain. Before the parade of carnage and misery played too long, with closed eyes, she would turn her gaze upward and silently repeat 'love, peace, compassion' over and over until she fell asleep. Rae had learned that when her eyes looked up toward her forehead, her mind automatically switched into the alpha state. With the exception of a few days a week, she had to employ this technique to get any relief from the madness her mind conjured up.

6

At 6:00 in the morning, Granger's alarm went off, waking him from a deep sleep. He sat up in bed and looked out the picture window. As far as he could see, the rolling hills were covered in a light fog. In the foreground, meadow grasses and wildflowers dotted the hills. Wild irises were Granger's favorite. They sprang up indiscriminately, their delicate purple and white petals contrasting dramatically with the beige and chocolate brown colored scrub. A red fox moved silently in the grass. Granger watched it stalking its prey. It pounced, disappearing momentarily, then trotted toward the hills, carrying something in its mouth.

Granger splashed water on his face, brushed his teeth and then put on his running gear. He spent about five minutes stretching, then quietly went out the back door so he wouldn't wake the dogs. They slept in Allie's room and she didn't have to get up for another hour. After one last calf stretch, Granger took off. He decided to take the trail that led to Cougar Pond. He took some deep breaths, inhaling the cool morning air, mixed with rosemary and sage, two plants that were as common on the land as the Manzanita bushes and oak trees. He ran past the abandoned barn where he and his brother used to play. It had a hay loft and they would play cops and robbers for hours using cap guns, the ones where you had to apply the single cap to the catch. They would run themselves into exhaustion, sprinting up and down the stairs, throwing the 'bad' guy off the loft into a pile of hay. When they finally got too hot and sweaty to perform their game, they would race to Cougar Pond and jump in, feet first. The shock of the cold water against their sweaty skin was exhilarating. They'd swim and dive until their mom called them for dinner. The sound of the steel triangle could be heard a good quarter of a mile away.

Granger continued running on the trail. It hugged Cougar Pond and then headed up the hill. On his right, he looked at the spot where his dad taught him to ride a horse. It was one of the few happy memories he had with Evan Bowden.

An hour later, Granger returned to the house. Allie was finishing breakfast. He walked up to his daughter and stopped short of hugging her. "You know I'd like to give you a big hug, but I'm a sweaty mess."

"Got it, Pop. I have three classes today, so I'll see you around two." Allie gave her dad an air kiss and with that she was off.

Hammerhead, a mutt, and Fin, the sheltie terrier, greeted Granger. Both dogs were rescues. Hammerhead was found wandering around the ranch, most likely left behind when his 'people' moved. They guessed he was around two years old when he came running up to Allie, nearly knocking her down in his enthusiasm to find a person after encountering one too many cows. His right ear was half chewed, suggesting that he had a run-in with a coyote or fox. That was five years ago and he was still the most affectionate dog, constantly showing gratitude to his adopted family. Fin was a different story. Every ranch seemed to have a sheltie terrier. They were bred to herd cattle. Granger grew up with Frank and he lived to the ripe old age of fifteen. He was sweet and trusting and very loyal. Fin was aptly named because he reminded Granger of a shark, at least that was the case when they first adopted him from the Petaluma Animal Shelter. It wasn't until they brought Fin home that they realized why he had been discarded. He had the temperament of a petulant child and didn't listen to anyone. He was rude and very disagreeable but with patience, guidance and Hammerhead's friendship, Fin began an evolution from cretin to cuddle bug.

One last stretch before Granger showered and fixed breakfast. He put his leg up on the patio rail and leaned over. As he got up, ready to stretch the other leg, he looked at the field and noticed one of the cows was lying on its side, moving back and forth. "Shit!" Granger said. He went into the house and grabbed his cell and as he ran out to the field, he speed dialed the veterinarian.

7

On her way to class, Allie saw a familiar face. A very handsome, familiar face. "Chris!" she yelled across the hall. Chris looked up and smiled. He came over and gave Allie a hug. "So this is where you've been since high school. Third year?"

"Yeah," Allie said. "When did you join the college crowd? I thought you left Petaluma for good."

"Nah. I went off to find fame and fortune in Los Angeles as a model, but got tired of the grind really quickly. Plus, I figured it wouldn't hurt to get a college degree and what better place than Sonoma County."

"Well, welcome back."

"Thanks. We should grab lunch some time. Play catch up."

"Sounds great," Allie said. "I'll give you my cell number." Allie tore off the corner of her Communications notebook and wrote down her number. She handed it to Chris. They hugged goodbye and Allie walked away with a huge smile on her face. She had a crush on Chris Welke since the fifth grade. She was sure he knew it but had never shown any interest in her until now.

When Allie got to her Communications class, the professor had already started lecturing. She quietly sat down and took out her laptop, accidentally dropping her notebook on the floor. Fran picked it up and handed it to her. She mouthed, 'thank you' and Fran nodded. Once again, he caught himself staring at her VEGAN tattoo. Up close, the intricacy of the skin art was amazing. He could see the hair on the chimpanzee and the pig's hooves were so realistic. When he looked up, Allie was smiling. She had been watching him the entire time. He smiled back, self-consciously. Once again, he was smitten.

Allie hadn't even noticed Fran until then. She had been taking notes and trying to concentrate but his eyes were so focused on her arm that she couldn't help but observe him. He had a nondescript face, but Allie found it pleasant. His eyes were almond-shaped and he had a small nose that gently sloped down. His lips were full and his chin narrow. When he smiled, he revealed perfectly straight white teeth.

The tattoo certainly drew a lot of attention. Allie got it on her tenth anniversary of being vegan. She wanted to make a statement. She lived veganism. She breathed it. Yes, it was a religion. It was a lifestyle. It meant everything to her, so it was only logical that she had VEGAN spelled vertically down her arm. It was the tattoo artist's idea to fill it with animals. It took a lot longer than she thought and cost a lot more than she had anticipated. The tattoo artist let her come back for each letter until it was done. And when it was, she couldn't have been happier. Her mother couldn't have been more upset. She cried and yelled and cursed at Allie for destroying her skin. Granger just shook his head and asked to see it. He must have stared at that tat for fifteen minutes, examining the detail and colors. He wasn't happy that she used her body as a canvas, but he couldn't deny the result was impressive.

Allie's thoughts went back to Chris. She got butterflies in her stomach when she recalled their meeting. He looked better than he did in high school. His cheek bones were more defined and his hair longer than his teen-age short-cropped style. She remembered that he was seeing Leslie Shropshire their senior year. Allie didn't like her. She was a poser, a WASP pretending to be a rapper/gangsta, but just looked silly. She couldn't understand what he saw in her, but high school's an experimental time, trying to rein in one's unpredictable hormones and learning to live with them. She hoped Chris would call.

8

It was the fifth outfit Rae tried on and she was ready to scream. She was convinced that her body changed on a daily basis. She was an involuntary shape shifter but instead of morphing into a wolf or eagle, she was devolving into a vole. Menopause turned her reliable internal world upside down and Rae knew it was only going to get worse. She had twenty minutes to get dressed before Darlene picked her up for their trip to San Francisco. It was April first and she had already been fooled. Her dad called and told her that he and his second wife, Jan, were getting a divorce. Rae must have sounded too thrilled because he quickly said 'April Fools' without carrying the joke any further. Rae lost her mother nearly fifteen years ago to breast cancer. After being married for forty-nine years, her father was devastated, yet despite that fact he informed Rae and her sister Ellen the day after the funeral that he had 'needs' and would be dating soon. Rae was convinced that he had secured a date for that day, but he didn't work that quickly. He waited three weeks.

Outfit number six worked but she would have worn it, even if it didn't. She was tired of trying on clothes and needed time to put the reject outfits away before the cats laid on them, dispensing copious amounts of hair. Rae could never figure out why cats would lay on anything that you put down on a table, chair, bed, carpet. It didn't matter. They wanted to lay on it. She had just finished hanging up the last shirt when Carson poked his head in the door.

"Where are you going?"

"I told you. Darlene and I are driving into the city for dinner and the symphony."

"Oh yeah," said Carson. "A night of sheer boredom. I'm going over to Boner's then taking a ride on the Buell to the coast."

"Please be careful. Your friends told me you ride like a maniac."

Carson laughed. "They're a bunch of pussies. I'm fine. Later."

"Wear your helmet and don't forget to feed the cats."

Rae heard a car horn. It was Darlene. She grabbed her purse, waved goodbye to Carson and headed out the door.

"Ready for a little Yo-Yo Ma?" said Darlene.

"I'm in the mood for a big Yo-Yo Ma and a bigger glass of Zin. Take me away, now."

"Bad day?"

Rae held out her arm and grabbed her underarm. "Bad body. It's not cooperating anymore. Before menopause, women have to deal with their periods and cramps and birth control, but when Hurricane Menopause hits it wipes out all that crappy stuff and leaves us with wrinkles and flab and a non-existent libido. I don't know which is worse."

"Being younger than you, much younger." Darlene paused and looked over at Rae who gave her the stink eye. "I can't tell you how excited I am to hit menopause. Is it really that bad?"

"Let's put it this way, a couple of months after my period stopped for good, I was lying in bed reading. It was warm, so I was just wearing my underwear and bra. I glanced over at the closet door mirror and for a split second I thought there was a very small baby on my stomach. I'm not kidding. I then realized, to my horror, that it was my stomach! I never had a flat stomach, but I also never had belly fat like that."

Darlene switched lanes. "Have you thought of hormone replacement therapy?"

"I've tried different natural remedies but they don't seem to work and I don't want to take anything prescribed by a doctor. I don't trust the pharmaceutical companies."

"Come on, now. They're not all bad. My friend's son is schizophrenic and if it weren't for the prescription drugs he's on, he'd be in a mental institution or living on the street."

Rae shifted in her seat and turned to look at Darlene. "Okay, I grant you that we need certain drugs but I also believe that doctors would rather prescribe a pill than try to cure a patient of an ailment or psychological problem and the drug companies are notorious for pushing their drugs onto the medical community. My cousin is a dermatologist and those assholes give her free drugs and take her and other doctors on extravagant vacations. Plus, the drug companies do a lot of testing on animals. Can you imagine the immense pain and torture they go through?"

"Geez, if I had known I was going to open a can of worms with an innocent question, I wouldn't have asked."

"Don't get all defensive on me. I agree that some medication is necessary. I just don't like the way pharmaceutical companies operate. Did you know that when the FDA bans a drug in America, the company sells it to doctors in third world countries? Nice, huh?"

"No, that's disgusting. You have some very valid points. Can we talk about something else?"

"Of course she said, realizing that her friend was bored with the conversation at hand."

"No, that's not it. Well, it kind of is, but I did want your opinion on something that happened at work."

"Hit me."

It was a good thing Rae was buckled in, because she was in for a bumpy ride. She loved Darlene, but the woman complained on end about the politics in her office. Going on twelve years, Darlene was one of the top account executives, selling advertising space in The Press-Democrat, Sonoma County's premier newspaper. Because of her seniority, she had a lot of the coveted accounts, so it was inevitable that the other AE's wanted to dethrone the 'queen.'

Nearly an hour later, they were driving across the Golden Gate Bridge. Rae gazed up at the dazzling work of art. Its burnt orange-colored art deco towers loomed above. The cables always reminded Rae of oversized harp strings. She never got tired of looking at it. It seemed to radiate the energy of the city.

"Did you know that the Golden Gate Bridge is the largest art deco structure in the world? Everyone thinks it's the Empire State Building but the bridge beats it by over seven thousand feet."

"Fascinating," said Darlene. "How do you know this rather obscure factoid?"

"I took an art deco class in college and was fascinated by the bridge. The professor compared it to the Empire State Building in size and it stuck with me. Of course, everything I learned in geography and geology has completely left my brain."

As Darlene turned onto Lombard Street, Rae's cell phone rang. She looked at the number and didn't recognize it, so she hit the end button. About five minutes later, her cell rang again. Same number. Rae picked it up.

"Hello...oh Hi Jarod. I didn't recog...what...very funny. April Fools... no I don't believe you...it's April Fool's Day, fool. Look, I gotta go...Fine, I'll call your mom. Yes, I have her number. Okay, I will. Bye."

Darlene said, "What was that all about?"

Rae took a deep breath. She tried to suppress the anxiety welling up in her chest as she searched for Victoria's number and then hit the call button. "That was Carson's friend, Jarod. He said Carson was in a motorcycle accident. I think he's doing an April Fool's on me. Shit, I hope he is. I'm calling his mom now." Victoria answered on the second ring. She confirmed Rae's worst fears: Carson lost control of his motorcycle on Bodega Avenue. She was at Santa Rosa Memorial Hospital waiting for the helicopter that airlifted him from the road. She promised to call Rae when he arrived.

Rae hung up the phone. She was clearly upset but also composed, since she didn't know the extent of Carson's injuries. By this time, Darlene knew from the conversation that she had to go back to Petaluma. She made an illegal u-turn and headed back towards the bridge.

"Goddamn it! All of Carson's friends said he drove like a maniac. Why wasn't he more careful? He was airlifted to the hospital. That's not good. Shit. That's not good at all."

"Do you want me to take you to the hospital?" Darlene said.

"If you could drop me off at the house so I can drive there, that would be great. I'm so sorry, Darlene."

"Yeah, you totally messed up my plans – are you kidding? Don't apologize. I'll drop you off and then follow you there. You should probably call Stuart and let him know."

"I'll call him when I know the extent of Carson's injuries."

Again, Rae's stomach turned. She forced herself to breathe. Maybe it was an April Fool's joke and Victoria was in on it. She didn't know her that well. Looking out at the ocean as they crossed back over the bridge, Rae watched a large sailboat pass underneath the bridge. She could see people on the deck, bundled up. They were totally oblivious to Rae's situation. She wanted to join them and forget about the impending visit to the emergency room.

9

Victoria called back a half hour later. By this time, Darlene was driving through Novato and they were about fifteen minutes from Petaluma. Jarod's mother was clearly upset. She was talking fast.

"Hi Rae. I'm so sorry. I got here as soon as Jarod called because I wanted Carson to see a familiar face when he was brought to the emergency room. He's lucid but on morphine. They have him in a neck brace as a precautionary measure. They just finished taking the x-rays and I'm waiting to hear what the doctor has to say. I'll call you as soon as I know anything."

"How does he look, Victoria? Did he break any bones? Does he have road rash?"

"He looks great on the outside. He told the ER doctor that he remembered the bike handles getting wiggly. After that, he woke up in the helicopter. The doctor suspects that he was ejected from the motorcycle and was thrown through the air. Someone found him in a ditch. Here's the doctor...yes, I'm talking to his mother...her name is Rae...okay. Rae, the doctor wants to talk to you. I'm putting him on."

"Okay. Thanks Victoria. I really appreciate you being there for Carson."

"Hi Rae. This is Dr. Frenlich. I just examined your son's x-rays. Thank goodness he was wearing a helmet. No broken arms or legs. Carson has suffered a bruise on the brain from the impact. It sounds worse than it is. It's like a bruise on the skin. We'll monitor it but I wouldn't worry. He broke three ribs and one them punctured his right lung, causing it to collapse. He has three crushed vertebrae in his lower spine. He was able to move his legs and feel his toes so there's no spinal cord injury. No paralysis. We'll be moving him to ICU as soon as they can set up the room. Do you have any questions?"

"Not right now. Thank you, doctor. I'll be there in about forty-five minutes. I'm going to call Carson's dad, so he may show up before me." Shaking, Rae hung up the phone and started crying.

"Carson broke his back. He has a collapsed lung and broken ribs."

Darlene said, "Let me drive straight to the hospital. You'll get there a lot sooner, okay?"

Rae nodded. She took another deep breath and with trembling hands called her ex-husband. They had been divorced for over twelve years but he still managed to unnerve her. He had a way of asking questions, dispensing advice and even answering the phone with a dictatorial tone in his voice. It didn't hurt that he was over six feet tall. There were few occasions when Rae was able to stand up to him, but she was more ashamed than proud of the way she handled their interactions. Under the circumstances, she was hoped he would be humble and cooperative.

Stuart answered on the second ring. "Hi, it's Rae."

"I know."

"This is not an April Fools. Carson was hurt in a motorcycle accident. I'm on my way to Santa Rosa Memorial Hospital. He was airlifted there about twenty minutes ago."

"Shit. I knew this day would come. I just knew it."

Rae gave Stuart an assessment of the injuries. She could tell he was as angry as well as upset. "I'll be there as soon as I can." After they hung up, there was a split second when Rae felt that Stuart was angry with her, too. She let it pass and focused on Carson.

Rae couldn't get to the hospital fast enough. She kept seeing her son crumpled on the side of the road, helpless. She wondered how long he had been lying there and who found him and called the ambulance. Finally, they arrived at the emergency room entrance. Rae jumped out and headed to the reception desk. Her heart was pounding.

"I'm here to see my son, Carson Tenman. Is he back here?" Rae started to walk toward the emergency room doors but the nurse stopped her.

"Hold on, please Mrs. Tenman. Let me get the doctor."

"It's O'Brien. Rae O'Brien. Can't I just go back there and see him?"

"I need to call the doctor. It will only be a minute."

"Excuse me. Did you say you're Carson's mother?" Rae turned around and standing in front of her was a man around her age. He had a look of concern and was more than stressed out.

"Yes, I am."

"I'm Granger Bowden. Carson had the accident in front of my ranch." He held out his hand and Rae shook it.

"You found him?"

"I did. It looked like he was thrown from the motorcycle and landed about thirty feet into an open ditch. I wanted to make sure he was okay but the doctors won't tell me anything since I'm not family."

"He broke his back and some ribs. His left lung collapsed." Rae almost started to cry but held it in.

"Is he...can he move his legs?"

"Thankfully, yes. That was so nice of you to come to the hospital. You don't even know Carson." Rae noticed that Granger had tears in his eyes. As he wiped his eyes, she could feel the emotions welling up in her again. Without thinking, Granger went over and hugged Rae. He felt strong and deeply comforting. Rae broke down as he continued to hold her. When her tears subsided, he let her go.

"I'm so glad to hear that he's not paralyzed," Granger said. "Some of his friends were here. I think one of them is Jarod. They went to get something to eat and wanted me to tell you that they'll be back."

Just then, the doctor came out of the emergency room and walked over to Rae. "Are you Carson's mother?" Rae nodded. "I'm Dr. Frenlich. I spoke to you on the phone. You can see Carson now."

Rae turned to Granger. "Thank you so much for being there, for finding my son and getting help. I really appreciate it."

"It was the least I could do. Would you do me a favor and just let me know how's he doing?"

"Of course." Rae took out her cell. "Give me your number." Granger recited it.

Carson was lying on a metal gurney, covered by a sheet. His clothes were sitting on a chair, cut off by the paramedics. In the corner, she saw his motorcycle helmet covered in mud. A large dent marred the left side. Rae shuddered to think what condition her son would be in if he wasn't wearing the helmet. She looked back at Carson. He had no outward signs of injury, except for a few scratches and smudges of dirt on his face and arms. He looked at his mother as she stood over him. "Mom," he said. Rae wanted to grab him and hug him tightly and never let him go, but instead she gently took his hand in hers and stroked it. The smart-mouthed eighteen-year-old looked so innocent and helpless. At least he wasn't in pain. The morphine took care of that, giving his eyes a glazed look as if he were in another dimension.

Dr. Frenlich came over to Rae's side. He spoke softly to Carson. "We're setting up your room in intensive care. As soon as it's ready, we'll get you in there and you'll be more comfortable." He turned to Rae. "Would you like to see the x-rays?"

"Can we wait until his father arrives? I know he'll want to see them, too."

"Of course. Let me know when he gets here."

Rae continued to hold Carson's hand. Through their touch, she tried to send her love and support. She remembered the time Carson was four years old. He had so much energy and this night he was particularly pumped up. Rae told him to stop running around but he just laughed. He took off toward the hallway, looked away for a second, and when he turned back, he ran into the wall corner. The impact was hard enough to knock him to the floor. When she got to him, a giant goose egg was already forming on his forehead. Stuart went to get a cold compress while Rae held the screaming child, rocking him back and forth. He eventually stopped crying and fell asleep in her arms. She blamed herself for not physically stopping him from running amok but looking at Carson now, she realized that you can only shield your children so much. They have a certain amount of free will at four years old and certainly do what they want at eighteen.

Emergency rooms are built for practicality and efficiency. The walls are a universally appealing off-white. Steel and metal seem to inhabit every piece of furniture and equipment. Even the staff had stethoscopes around their necks or metal objects in their coat pockets. The place smelled of antiseptic. Any sweet-smelling fragrance would get lost, gobbled up by the sterility. Rae had a vision of her wheeling Carson home. She longed to hear his heavy metal music blasting from his room; his friends laughing and swearing, talking about girls and tattoos and even motorcycles. She wanted to see him lying in his bed below the poster of Carmen Electra, her voluptuous body bursting out of a tank top and cutoff shorts. Instead, they were going to transfer him into a room where he'd be living for a while. Life support machines and monitors would be his roommates. It made her shudder.

Stuart showed up about fifteen minutes later. He acknowledged Rae with a nod and then went over to Carson and kissed his forehead.

"What the hell happened, Bud?"

"Don't know," Carson replied.

Before Rae could say anything, Dr. Frenlich approached Stuart and put out his hand. He introduced himself and then asked if he and Rae were ready to look at the x-rays. They followed the doctor into a small office. On the computer screen were images of their son's cranium, lungs and spine. Dr. Frenlich explained the extent of Carson's injuries.

"On the top left is Carson's skull. You can see the dark spot on his brain. That's the bruise he got when he hit the ditch. I wouldn't worry about that. It will eventually heal and he'll be monitored for any signs of a concussion. No one saw the accident and Carson doesn't remember a thing except his handlebars getting difficult to control. We suspect that he fell on his head and then landed on the base of his spine. Three vertebrae, L2, L4 and T8 were crushed. It's a miracle his spinal cord wasn't damaged. The impact also broke three ribs and one of them punctured his left lung. You can see where it collapsed. Any questions?"

Stuart said, "When he is going to have surgery for his back?"

"Our resident spine specialist, Dr. Ponterra, will be here shortly. He'll be able to answer that. Right now, you can go to the third floor waiting room outside ICU and we'll let you know when Carson's in his room."

Rae and Stuart thanked Dr. Frenlich and went back to be with their son. Stuart saw the helmet in the corner. He went over and picked it up, turned it around and touched the dent. It was about one and a half inches deep. Inside the helmet was a patch of dried blood and dirt. He was grateful for Carson's amnesia, otherwise he'd be reliving the trauma of being thrown through the air and landing on his head for a long time.

"We'll see you soon, kiddo," Rae said as she and Stuart went back into the ER waiting room. Carson's friends were still there and so was Darlene. When they saw Rae and Stuart, they went over and hugged them.

"How's he doing?" said Jarod. "They only let family in, so we haven't seen him."

"Yeah," said Pierce. "It sucks."

Stuart said, "Well, the good news is he's not paralyzed. That's the only good news. He crushed three vertebrae and his left lung is collapsed. He also has three broken ribs. Thanks for being here guys, even if you couldn't see him. We appreciate the support. They'll be transferring him to intensive care and that could take a couple of hours."

Darlene said, "I'd be happy to stay with you, Rae."

Rae replied, "I don't know what I'd do without you. Thanks."

Jarod turned to Pierce. "Why don't we come back tomorrow?" Pierce agreed. The boys said their good-byes and left. Rae, Darlene and Stuart went to the cafeteria to get something to eat before going up to the third floor. The mood was tense. It's hard to make small talk when your child is broken. Finally Stuart spoke.

"Ever since he got that motorcycle, I was waiting for this day. I even took the motorcycle safety class with him but our kid had to go fast."

"I know. Even his friends wouldn't ride with him."

Darlene said, "My brother had a motorcycle when he was sixteen and it was a miracle he didn't crash. These teenage boys think they're invincible."

Stuart bit into his hamburger. He chewed slowly, deliberately. He took a sip of iced tea. "The whole thing feels surreal." He finished his hamburger and started working on the French fries. "This never would have happened if you didn't let him get a motorcycle." Rae stopped eating and glared at Stuart.

"You're blaming Rae for the accident?" Darlene was shocked that he had the nerve to place any blame during the one time they should be united and supportive.

"Stay out of this Darlene," Stuart said. "If he lived with me, there's no way I would have let him get a motorcycle."

Rae was furious. "That would have worked out, right? Carson works at an auto garage. You don't think he would have bought a bike and then kept it somewhere so we couldn't see it? I know you're upset, but you have a lot of nerve blaming me."

Rae got up and left with Darlene in tow. She wanted to see Carson alone but knew that wasn't going to happen. So many things were going through her head. She didn't see the accident but that didn't stop her from imagining what it was like. She saw too clearly Carson laying on the gurney with morphine eyes, the dented, bloodied helmet, his torn clothing, the oxygen tube in his nose, knowing he couldn't move. She saw the motorcycle in the street. And now she could hear Stuart's words of blame. Was it her fault? Should she have stopped Carson from getting the motorcycle? Could she have stopped him? This is a kid who was caught trying to sell baggies of marijuana in middle school. At thirteen years old, he was expelled just six weeks shy of graduating. Did Stuart really think he'd listen to a directive from his parents forbidding him to own a Buell motorcycle, a bike that he'd wanted since he was fifteen? She knew Stuart was upset but when did he have the time in his grief to pin it on her? Twelve years. That's how long they'd been divorced and that's how long Stuart held it against Rae. He wanted to reconcile, go to counseling, and work it out. But for Rae, there was nothing to work out except dividing up their property.

"That's not fair, blaming you," Darlene said, breaking up the images in Rae's head.

"Doesn't surprise me. He has to place the blame with someone. Let's go to the third floor waiting room."

"Don't you dare blame yourself."

"I won't." But somewhere inside her conscience there resided a little guilt.

Rae and Darlene were sitting in the waiting room when Rebecca poked her head around the door. It looked like she got dressed in a hurry, wearing jeans and a wrinkled t-shirt. Her hair was up in a bun and her face was make-up free. She went over and gave Rae a long, heartfelt hug. "I am so sorry, my dear. Darlene told me on the phone what happened."

When Rae tried to respond, she broke down, causing a chain reaction with her two best friends. The three of them sat there and cried for a good minute, trying to speak in between the sobs. When it quieted down and all eyes and noses were dried, Rae said, "Thank you both for being here with me. I'd be a wreck without you."

"Day or night, we're here for you, right Darlene?"

"Absolutely."

Nearly an hour later, a nurse stuck her head in the door and told Rae that she and one other person could see Carson. Two guests at a time were allowed in ICU. Rae told the nurse that her ex-husband would be upstairs soon, making him the second visitor. She followed the nurse down the light green hallway to the ICU doors. The nurse pressed a button and the doors automatically opened. They passed a room where a man was asleep, his legs tied to the bed. One of his hands resembled a bowling pin, wrapped in a large bandage. Next door was Carson's room. It took all of Rae's control not to gasp. Carson looked so small, laying in a bed with steel railings and cloud white sheets. Three machines stood behind the bed, all with tubes leading into his arms and the right side of his neck. All beeped intermittently, lights blinking on and off. At the base of the bed, a bag was hooked to the side railing, its tube running under the covers. Another bag beside it collected blood from Carson's collapsed lung, the tube running up the side of the bed and disappearing into his chest. Rae knew they were keeping Carson alive but she still had an overwhelming desire to disconnect them all. Carson smiled as she approached his bedside. She kissed him. "I don't know about you, but I think you need one more tube coming out of your body."

"Very funny, Madre."

"How do you feel, sweetie?"

"Okay. Where's my bike?"

"Your bike is gone. Why would you care about your motorcycle? Look what it did to you." Stuart stood at the door. His anger was palpable. He took out his camera and started taking pictures of Carson. "I want you to remember what you looked like so you don't do this to yourself again."

Rae rolled her eyes but she stayed silent. A knock down drag out fight and raised voices wouldn't bode well in intensive care. She looked over at Carson. The look on his face was passive. He was in no mood to argue with his father, either. The morphine kept his brain in a soft fog. He could see his IV and felt 'things' on and in his body but that was it. He was told by the doctors not to move because his back was broken, so he stayed very still. For a kid that never stopped moving, except when he played video games or was stoned, lying in a prone position felt foreign to him. Little did he know that he would be dealing with this for months. He tried hard to remember what happened but the same scenario played in his head: he headed out Bodega Avenue on his Buell. About six miles from the house, heading west to Bodega Bay, he switched gears. The handlebars started to shake and the next thing he remembered, he was lying down and it was really loud. He looked up and two men in uniforms were on either side of him. One of them yelled over the sound of the propellers, telling him he was in a helicopter. He was thrown from his bike and was on his way to the hospital. He wondered what happened to his bike. He loved that bike.

"I'll let you spend time with your father and then I'll be back after dinner, okay?" Rae kissed him good-bye and walked out, averting her eyes from Stuart.

Returning from dinner, Rae and Darlene said good-bye to Rebecca. She had a solid hour drive home to San Francisco, but promised that she'd be back in a few days. With Stuart gone from the room, Rae and Darlene sat with Carson on either side of his bed. Even though he slept most of the time, he felt their presence and it gave him comfort.

10

Despite the traffic, Granger made it back to the ranch in thirty-five minutes. He parked his truck at the entrance to the driveway and walked over to the spot where he found Carson. The weeds were crushed and there was a crack in the ditch. Granger involuntarily shuddered. He couldn't imagine what that kid was going through right now. Granger had some accidents on the ranch but nothing serious enough to warrant being airlifted to the emergency room. He wondered if Carson's mother would call him. He liked her. She had a pretty face and a nice figure. He felt guilty for thinking about Rae when it was Carson who should be garnering his thoughts.

Granger pulled into the drive and saw that the veterinarian's truck was still there. He sighed. One more of his steers, Rodney, might not make it. Allie came out of the house upon hearing Granger's truck. She ran up to him.

"How's that kid? Is he okay?"

"He broke his back and some ribs but he's not paralyzed."

"That's awful! He's so young. I hate motorcycles. Why do guys love them so much?"

"One word...no two," said Granger. "Freedom and speed. I see Dr. Nicols is still here."

"Yeah," she said. "Rodney's not doing well. The doc gave him some medicine and wants to monitor him, so I've been entertaining the good doctor. The usual, iced tea and tortilla chips."

"Aren't you the quintessential hostess? I can take over from here. Thanks, sweetie." Granger put his arm around Allie and kissed the top of her head.

Dr. Alan Nicols was sitting on the patio. When he saw Granger, he stood up. Granger shook his hand.

"Hey doc. I hear Rodney's not up to snuff."

"He has an infection on his left flank. Because of his age, he needs to be monitored or the infection could run rampant. I was just going to check on him, then I'll get out of your hair."

"No problem. Why don't you stay for dinner? I was going to make burritos," Granger said.

"Thanks, Granger, but I have another appointment after this. Allie told me there was an accident in front of your place. Motorcycle?"

Granger nodded. "Young kid lost control of the bike. Broke his back."

"Damn, that sucks. I tell all my patients not to let me catch them on a motorcycle. Those things are lethal."

Allie said, "But all your patients are...oh, very funny Dr. Nicols."

Granger and the vet went out to the barn. The black and white Guernsey was on his side. As the men approached, he craned his neck and watched them approach. Granger went over to his favorite steer and cradled his head in his hands.

"What's going on, Rodney? Huh, boy? When did you get this infection?" He stroked Rodney's neck as he looked down at the steer's leg. The festering sore was about four inches wide. Granger was surprised that he hadn't observed it before but with fifty head of cattle, it was hard to check every one of them, especially when many stayed out in the fields. From the time an animal seems healthy to the point where they're suffering, it's lightning fast. In the wild, a sick or injured animal is prone to an attack by a predator if they're visible or make a sound, so they remain very still and silent, despite their pain. Even without the inherent fear of being attacked, domesticated animals display the same behavior. Granger hated to see his animals suffer. He and Allie named and recognized them all. From afar, they all looked the same. But up close, they were easy to identify. Sam was lopsided, due to uneven back legs. Jonathan's left ear folded back, resembling a black taco. Sponge had a black spot that resembled Sponge Bob Square Pants and then there was Miguel, whose tail was inordinately short.

Granger continued to stroke Rodney's neck as Dr. Nicols examined the wound. He applied more antibiotic salve and administered a shot. Rodney didn't budge. "The shot also has a sedative, so he should sleep through the night. Check on him tomorrow morning. See how his energy is."

"Thanks Doc." Granger got up, gently placing Rodney's head on the hay. "He's my oldest steer. Allie named him. You know he lets her ride him?"

Doc shook his head. "You're my favorite client, but you are one strange guy."

Granger laughed. "Thanks."

After Allie had gone to bed, Granger sat outside on the patio, reflecting on the crazy day. His thoughts returned to Rae. As he imagined her face, he saw a shooting star. It seemed to fall on one of the oak trees high on the hill. He wondered if it was a sign and then he felt guilty again for thinking about Rae when he should have been more concerned about Carson's welfare.

He took another hit from the joint, inhaled deeply and slowly let it out, watching the smoke swirl and then disappear into the night air. It felt so good to unwind. Granger could feel the tension leaving his shoulders. He moved his neck back and forth. It made some loud clicks and cracks. "Ah, the thrills of getting older." He took a drink from his bottle of Hop Stoopid beer. It wasn't as cold as he liked it, so he got up and grabbed another one out of the fridge, opened it and resumed his star gazing on the chaise lounge. What was it about Rae that he found so attractive? Aside from the fact that she was pretty, was there something deeper? Was she a kindred spirit? Despite their brief conversation, he felt a connection to her, especially when they hugged. He wondered what she thought of him. Granger laughed. What an absurd question.

She probably barely noticed him. Her concern was for her son, not some cowboy who happened to find him.

Granger closed his eyes. He didn't want to think about anything right now. The cool night air felt good on his face. He heard the faint howling of a coyote. There was a rustling in the bushes to the left of the deck. Granger guessed it was a bird or maybe a rodent. He didn't care. Live and let live. That's something his dad would never say. "Right, Dad?" Granger took another hit off the joint. A brown garden spider walked across the table. He watched it as it delicately maneuvered around the ashtray and beer bottle. It walked to the edge of the table then crawled underneath it. "Have a good evening," Granger said.

11

It was a balmy, overcast Monday. The day of Carson's surgery. Three days passed since the accident. Rae had been to the hospital every day and planned to be there for the surgery, but Stuart convinced her to go to work since he was going to be there all day and, unless a problem arose, there was no need for both of them to hang around the hospital while they were opening up their son's back. The surgeon said the procedure would take about eight hours, so Rae gauged that by the time she got off work, Carson would be out of surgery.

Slowly walking up the stairs to the office, Rae was physically and mentally exhausted, the toll of having a child in intensive care. For a brief moment, sitting next to Carson, watching him drift in and out of sleep, she wished she had a man in her life for moral support, someone she could lean on and hold onto at night for strength, but then her defenses kicked in, honed from past relationships, and she reasoned that they'd probably be more of a burden. She hit the mental reset button.

Walking in the office, she wondered if Zoe opened the blinds behind her desk, then caught herself. She was shocked that, with everything going on, she could still be so petty. Zoe was on the computer, her blinds up and Rae's still closed. Without looking up, Zoe said, "How was your weekend?"

"Except for Carson breaking his back, it was super."

"You're kidding, right?" It was a rare show of emotion.

Rae shook her head. "I wish I was. He was in a motorcycle accident Friday afternoon on Bodega Avenue."

She went on to tell Zoe what happened. "After work, I'm going back to the hospital. He'll be coming out of surgery by then."

"I'm so sorry Rae." She waited for Zoe to tell her to take off whatever time she needed or that she supported her 100% or if she needed any help once Carson came home, she'd be there for her. But that was it. She was so sorry. Rae looked up at the unopened blinds. Why wasn't she surprised?

The day felt unbearably long. Whenever her cell rang, Rae expected it to be Stuart with bad news but it wasn't. It was a friend or a family member. Her dad called to see if Carson was out of surgery five times. At 5:00 p.m, Rae turned off her computer, grabbed her purse and headed out the door. Zoe had left a half hour earlier for her massage. She wished Rae good luck.

It was a little after 5:30 when Rae parked her car in the hospital lot and practically ran up the stairs to the waiting room. Stuart and his best friend, Jeff, were quietly talking. An elderly couple was on the other side of the room, reading. Rae gave Jeff a big hug and sat down across from him. "So, any news?"

Stuart replied, "Yeah. They have about another hour or so. He's been in surgery for over eight hours, but no complications…yet."

"There's a positive attitude," said Jeff.

"I'm just saying."

Jeff looked at Rae and held up his glass of water and mouthed 'half empty.' Rae laughed. Boy, did she ever know it. She used to call Stuart 'Chicken Little' because he had such a negative outlook. The sky always seemed to be falling.

Rae took a seat opposite the men and grabbed a magazine. She tried reading it but her thoughts kept returning to Carson lying on the operating table, his back splayed open. Rods and screws attached to his bone. She cringed thinking about it.

Almost ten hours after Carson was wheeled into surgery the spine surgeon, Dr. Panterra, walked into the waiting room. They all stood. "First the good news. It went very well. Carson is in recovery and you should be able to see him in about fifteen minutes. We placed titanium rods on either side of his spine and they're held in place with twelve screws. The not-so-good news is that two of the screws are very close to his spinal cord. They're not touching but there's always a chance that any jarring of his back, like a fall, could cause a screw to penetrate the spinal cord, which could result in paralysis. Bottom line, Carson needs to be careful."

Stuart said, "What are the chances Carson will be able to have the rods and screws eventually removed?"

"He's eighteen, right?" Stuart and Rae both nodded. "There's a strong possibility that his vertebrae will heal to the point that the hardware can be removed. We'll monitor his progress."

Rae said, "Thanks Doctor. We appreciate all you've done." She shook his hand as did Stuart and Jeff. Dr. Panterra left.

Stuart took a deep breath. "I sure as hell am glad that's over with." He took Jeff and Rae into his arms and hugged them both.

While waiting for Carson to return to ICU, Rae called everyone and told them the good news. She left out the part about the two screws precariously close to his spinal cord. She'd save that for later. Rae surveyed the room. It seemed to have grown larger and the walls looked whiter than the first time she sat in the waiting room with Darlene and Rebecca. She felt buoyant. Since Friday, it was the best news she had received. Just then, Granger popped into her head. She decided to call and tell him the news. Finding his number in her cell phone, she dialed. Granger picked up the phone on the second ring. "Hello?"

"Hi Granger. It's Rae, Carson's mom. The boy who was…"

"I know who it is. How are you? How's Carson?"

"I'm doing much better, thanks. Carson just got out of surgery. They inserted the rods and screws in his back. Twelve screws, can you believe it? Anyway, he's in recovery now and we should be able to see him in a few minutes."

Granger blew out a sigh of relief. "I'm thrilled to hear it went well. I really appreciate you calling me. I thought you'd forget."

"It's not easy forgetting a rancher named Granger."

"I'm not really a rancher. About twelve years ago I…"

VEGAN COWBOY

"Is that Carson?" Rae said to Stuart. She saw someone being wheeled toward the ICU doors.

"Yeah. Let's go," Stuart said.

"I'm so sorry, Granger, but Carson is being taken back to his room. I have to go."

"Of course, of course. Thanks again for calling and tell Carson I said hi."

"Will do. Bye."

Granger smiled as he hung up the phone. He was thrilled that Carson's surgery went well and he was elated that he had a chance, even a short one, to talk to Rae.

Allie walked in the door. "Hey Pop."

"Hi darlin'."

"Uh, why do you have a dopey grin on your face? Did you just win the lottery?"

"I just heard from Carson's mom. His surgery was successful."

"That's great news! It's my turn to cook tonight, right?"

"Nobody's cooking tonight. Let's go out to dinner." Allie looked at her dad quizzically. "Something you're not telling me?"

"Me? Nope. Everything's hunky dory. Oh, I did forget to tell you that Rodney's improving. His sore looks a little better and he's eating. Still can't stand on it, though. Doc said that'll be in another day or two. So, where do you want to go for dinner?"

"Let's try that new Vietnamese place in the Trader Joe's shopping center."

"Great." Even if the food was bad, Granger would still consider it a good evening.

12

Stuart and Rae followed the gurney carrying Carson back to his room. He was awake but still groggy from the anesthesia.

"Everything went really well, sweetie," Rae said and gave him a thumbs-up.

"They told me. I'm glad that's over with."

"We all are," said Stuart.

The hospital orderlies gently transferred Carson from the gurney to his bed. Then they re-arranged his IV's, oxygen tube and catheter bag. His collapsed lung had greatly improved and they were able to disengage the tube from his chest. A nurse walked in with a cup and a small pink sponge attached to a stick.

"Carson, you've been in surgery for almost ten hours. Your stomach is empty, so you can't have too much water otherwise you'll get sick." The nurse looked at Rae and Stuart. "He's going to want water, but only let him suck the sponge. In about half an hour, I'll bring him a popsicle."

The nurse dipped the sponge, which was the size of sugar cube, into the cold water, and put it up to Carson's lips. He sucked it eagerly. "Can I have more?" The nurse gave him one more spongeful of water, then she said, "No more for another couple of minutes."

As soon as the nurse left, Carson turned to his mom and asked for more water but she refused.

Stuart said, "I guess you don't give Carson everything he wants."

"Please, not now."

"You're right," Stuart said. "I'm sorry. It's been a stressful day."

"True." She turned to Carson, "I'll be back in a while, honey."

Carson almost sat up. "Please don't go."

Stuart got the hint. "Jeff and I will grab a bite to eat. We'll be back in an hour."

As soon as he was out of earshot, Carson said, "Okay, Mom, now please give me more water. I'm dying."

"In a few minutes, Cars. I'm not going to be responsible for you getting sick. Besides being ridiculously thirsty, how do you feel?"

"See this button?" Carson slightly lifted up his hand. He was holding a small device. Rae nodded. "When I start to feel pain, I press it. Can I have more water, PLEASE?"

"One more minute." She sat down next to Carson's bed and put her hand on his arm. "When your dad comes back, can I borrow the button?"

"If you give me more water." Rae reached for the sponge and let Carson suck it dry. She did it once more, feeling guilty for not heeding the nurse's instructions, but Carson was insistent. Rae sat with her son in silence, holding his hand. Finally, the nurse came in with two cherry Popsicle halves, giving Carson one and offering the other half to Rae. Since Carson's arms were encumbered, she fed him while she ate hers. Not the mother/son moment she ever imagined, but it was an experience that she'd never forget. They watched an episode of The Big Bang Theory and were on the second re-run when Carson said, "Were you ever happy with Dad?"

"Of course. We had some great times, especially when we first met because it was new and exciting."

Carson turned to his mother, his eyes not quite focusing on her. "Like what?"

Rae thought for a moment. "Your dad and I had been seeing each other for about six months when we went on a camping trip to Tahoe. One of your dad's good friends lived up there and invited us to dinner. I remember sitting in this small, dark cabin with your dad, Tom, his wife and their baby, eating at a window ledge. They didn't have a dining room table. They barely had a kitchen. After dinner, Tom rolls this humongous joint and starts pouring us peppermint schnapps. We played Trivial Pursuit and cards. We had a blast. By the time we left, it was around two in the morning. We were still drunk and stoned. We walked outside and it was totally foggy and cold. Your dad wanted me to drive because he was too messed up, so I got behind the wheel and drove so slow that we both couldn't stop laughing. Finally, I had to pull over. Visibility was nil and I was wasted to boot. I find this spot where we can pitch the tent. It takes us twice as long to set it up. The whole time we're cracking jokes and having a blast. The next morning, I wake up to the sound of cars. A lot of cars. I look out of the tent and discover that we're on an island in the middle of a major thoroughfare!"

Carson laughed and then grimaced. "It hurts to laugh but that is so funny. What did you do?"

"We got out of there as quickly as possible, before a cop discovered us and gave us a ticket. We were both hung over, so that wasn't the fun part of the story, but I'll never forget it. Your dad and I had a lot of good times. I think that over the years our differences became more pronounced. After a while, we drifted apart."

"Can I have another popsicle?"

"I'll go ask the nurse." Rae got up and went to the nurse's station. When she came back to the room, Stuart and Jeff were talking to Carson.

"The nurse said she'd bring you another Popsicle, so you're set. I'll see you tomorrow, sweetie."

Rae kissed Carson goodbye and walked toward the exit. It was hard to imagine that the man she described in the story was the one she divorced so long ago. The one that was standing in their son's hospital room. Less than a year after they met, while lying in bed together, Stuart announced he wasn't attracted to Rae. It was a recurring event in his relationships with women and he asked Rae to stick it out until his feelings returned. In the meantime, he wouldn't touch her and avoided going to bed until she was asleep. It was difficult for Rae not to be able to reach out and hold Stuart's hand or spontaneously kiss him or put her arms around the man she loved, but she had to refrain. It was that or be subjected to his rebuff. As the days and weeks went by, Rae's self-confidence began to wane. Her first instinct was to end the relationship but she had fallen in love with Stuart and kept hoping that his feelings would change. They did a few months later. Even though Rae was happy that the romance was back on track, she feared it could happen again. It did a few more times in their twelve years together. If it weren't for Carson, Rae would have regretted staying with a husband who was able to turn his attraction for her on and off.

As she drove away, Rae still felt like she was in an altered universe. Instead of touring college campuses, she was having dialogues with spine surgeons, discussing Carson's insurance coverage with his provider, dealing with the motorcycle insurance and on and on. At least she wasn't talking to a mortician. She had to remind herself to be grateful. Carson's alive. He'd be walking soon. He'd have a huge scar that he could proudly show off to his friends. She wouldn't be surprised if he had a tattoo built around it. Maybe a serpent. No, he already had a rattlesnake wrapped around his left calf, poised to eat a rat. It was hard to believe that Carson used to be a vegetarian. Rae always thought he had more of a leader personality than a follower, but when it came to food, Carson lined up behind the majority of the population, breaking rank with Rae and the vegetarian lifestyle. Rae's thoughts were interrupted by her cell. She put on her headset and answered. It was Darlene.

"Glad to hear Carson's out of surgery."

"He may be out of surgery, but he's not out of the woods. Those two screws close to his spinal cord are not good. Anyway, he's resting now and Stuart is there with his friend, Jeff. Hopefully, Stuart's not getting all paparazzi on him like he did the night of the accident, taking gruesome photos. Enough hospital talk. Whatcha doin'?"

"Glad you asked. I just got off the phone with Peter and he's got this friend." Darlene waited for the objection, but didn't get one, so she continued. "He told him about you and we kind of, sort of set up a double date."

Rae was going to tell Darlene that she didn't want to meet anyone right now, but then she thought about it. The stress of the accident and the boredom of work should be interrupted by good conversation and a nice dinner. She loved Peter and told Darlene many times that she would appreciate a clone of the boy wonder, vegan-style. Maybe a friend of his would be a close second. "Sure. Why not?"

Darlene practically fell out of her chair. She knew Rae's last date went awry and her last relationship was eight years ago. Seventeen years her junior, Darlene wondered if that ennui would happen to her if she and Peter ever broke up.

"I'm stoked! That's great. So, let's work around your schedule since Carson screwed up your free time. Get it?"

"Yeah – funny broken back humor. So, tell me about this guy."

Darlene began. "His name is Steven. He works with Peter as an attorney. He's cute. I only met him once but he had a nice vibe to him, you know, not the typical 'I'm an attorney and I'm smarter and richer than you' attitude. He's around your age, maybe a little older. He has hair – yeah! He lives in San Francisco, not sure where."

Rae said, "You forgot to mention the deal breaker for me."

"Height?"

"Nope."

"Weight?"

"Uh-uh."

Darlene thought a moment. "Oh, his teeth! Nice teeth. Not crazy crooked or brown or yellow. So, did he pass, Cleopatra?"

"I do believe so. I'll call you when I get home so I can look at my calendar. Tell Peter thanks for thinking of me or maybe I should wait until after I meet Steven."

"I'll tell him now. This will be fun. We've never double dated. I have a good feeling about this."

"Okay, then. I'll talk to you soon."

Rae hung up the phone and already regretted her decision. She couldn't think of one blind date that went well, except for the Navy man she was set up with many years ago. He was in town for a couple of nights before being shipped to San Diego. He wasn't her type physically but by the end of the date his generosity, charm and pure heart had her wanting to go out with him again. Unfortunately, he left the next evening and was eventually stationed overseas. She never saw him again. As for the other dates, she could tick them off one by one, citing irreconcilable differences: breath that smelled like rotten eggs, marathon talker, too tall (six-foot-five), nose picker, crotch grabber/scratcher. She had to stop thinking about them or she would cancel the date. Her mind wandered to Granger. If he wasn't a rancher, he would be exactly Rae's type with his long legs, lanky body and those adorable vertical smile lines like Sean Connery's. She pushed him out of her mind. Reluctantly.

13

Hammerhead and Fin tagged along as Allie headed to the cow barn to begin her chores. It rained the night before, so she wore her rubber boots, purposely stepping in puddles and mud. She took in a deep breath, reveling in the scent of the damp ground mixed with hay. At this moment, there was no place she'd rather be. Tending to the animals was more than enjoyable to Allie. She fed them and sheltered them but the cows and sheep and chickens gave her so much more in return. They fed her soul. With every encounter, Allie was enriched: a nuzzle from a cow, the gentle head butt of a sheep or the way the chickens walked around Allie's leg and pecked at her shoes. They didn't want anything in return. There was no motive, no passive/aggressive behavior. Their emotions were diaphanous. Their love unconditional.

Allie broke apart the hay bales with a crow bar and spread them out in front of the barn. Then she filled the troughs with fresh water. Opening up the double doors, she walked inside the large barn. "Morning boys." As if on cue, Hammerhead and Fin stood on their hind legs and opened the stall latches. Allie had taught them how to unlatch the doors and always got a kick out of watching them. She made a beeline for Rodney's stall. He was now standing on his injured leg. He walked over to Allie and nuzzled her. "Well aren't you the handsome one, huh? The leg is looking better, Rods." She took a closer look and noticed a few flies dining on the sore. She swatted them away and, grabbing a cloth and the ointment the vet gave them, she wiped the area clean and then applied the ointment. Rodney pulled away slightly. "It's okay, boy. I'm almost done." Finished, she gave the steer a pat on the behind and he walked out to join the others. Luckily, Allie didn't have to clean the stalls. That was the students' job. There had to be some benefit to being the rancher's daughter.

Next stop was the horse stable. All seven horses were rescues. DeLinda, Jeeves and Harley were retired race horses. They weren't winning races which meant they were no longer paying for their room and board. Granger happened to be at the auction yard the day the three were being sold. Upon realizing that a killer buyer was interested, he got into the bidding war and won, paying twice their value, but to Granger it was worth it. The three shared the stable with Tuscany and Agave, Granger and Allie's horses. Lenore was the latest resident. Her story made the front page in the local paper. Her owners claimed that it was too expensive to feed her and thought she'd be able to forage on the land, but they failed to check on the chestnut-colored horse. The three-year-old gelding was skin and bones when the Humane Society found her in a pasture. She had been lying there for days and they thought she'd have to be euthanized. One of the volunteers knew Angel Lago, Granger's farmhand, and suggested they call him and get his opinion. When he lived in Mexico, Angel used to raise horses so his knowledge of them was extensive.

As soon as he got the call, he told Granger and they both headed over to where Lenore lay dying. When Angel saw Lenore's emaciated body lying on the hard, compacted earth, he began to cry. He got down on the ground and put his head next to her heart. He spoke gently to her in Spanish, stroking her matted mane and moving his hands over her protruding ribs. "¿por qué alguien haría esto a usted? Yo lo sanaré. Te cuidaré de ti "(why would someone do this to you? I will heal you. I will take care of you). Lenore's eyes showed a glimmer of hope where before they were dim, barely open. She tried to stand, but Angel stopped her. He looked up at Granger and claimed he could save her. With delicacy, they loaded her onto bedding in the horse trailer. Angel sat by her side on the trip back to the ranch. For weeks, he devoted his time to restoring Lenore back to health. He slept with her in the stable so he could monitor her breathing. He made special food for her: a mix of vitamins, grains and fruit and hand fed her. Three months later, a gorgeous mare emerged from where before there was a pitiful, gaunt horse. The transformation was astounding. Lenore would follow Angel as he worked on the ranch. She was patient, standing quietly while Angel swept the grounds or fed the chickens. She reluctantly went to her stall at the end of the day. She was the last horse Angel groomed and he spent a little extra time with her, singing a song he wrote while nursing her back to health.

Allie gave each horse their breakfast before she set them free to wander the pastures and hills. She loved watching Lenore race outside with the other horses. Her life could have ended tragically. Instead, she lived with people who loved her and animals who bonded with her.

Two down and two to go. The sheep barn was the next stop and, for some reason, Allie loved the sheep the most. Whether it was their rectangular, horizontal pupils that fascinated Allie as far back as she could remember or the astounding beauty and delicate features of a lamb, Allie would groom the sheep for hours. When they bleated, she would return their bleat, getting a kick out of the look on their faces. Some days, she would go to the sheep barn and read. Most of the sheep grazed on the hills but a few would stay in the barn. As she lay against them on the hay beds, they would nuzzle Allie's neck and nibble her fingers. The thirty sheep had belonged to a farmer who could no longer take care of his flock of eighty. His health was failing and he decided to move back east and live with his son's family. Granger heard about his predicament from a friend and offered to buy them all at top value. By the time the farmer received Granger's offer, he had already sold off fifty of his flock to another sheep rancher, so Granger ended up with the remaining thirty.

Allie used the bent wire comb, brushing Harriet's wool coat. "Someday, I'm going to learn how to weave and I'll make a blanket for you, Harriet." An old family friend, Margo Mayfield, had a sheep ranch in Bodega Bay. She also had a gift shop where she sold her woven items: blankets, sweaters, throws, shawls, scarves, and slippers. All were unique and the wool came from pampered sheep. Margo had given Allie an open invitation to her studio and lessons in sheep shearing and weaving. It was one of the many items on Allie's to-do list.

Opening the back door, the sheep went on their way to the fields. Her last stop was the chicken coop. In a structure that resembled a small hacienda, twenty hens lived in relative harmony. As with the sheep and horses, all the hens were rescues, taken from an abandon factory farm where the egg layers lived six to a cage no bigger than 12" x 12". They were de-beaked as chicks and spent their lives cramped and in constant anxiety. Unable to sustain the business, the owners of Aunt Ruthie's Eggs, took off in the middle of the night, leaving the hens. By the time they were discovered, many of them had died of starvation. The surviving hens were divided up between four ranchers. That was four years ago and out of sixty hens rescued by Granger, twenty remained. Granger had built the coop to look like a Mexican hacienda, complete with a bell tower. He thought it would be fun to design and build and it gave the normally banal chicken coop design some character. The 'girls' had ramps and nesting boxes, even a small pond for drinking. The fenced in area was surrounded by shrubs and plants, including borage, peppermint and lavender, all planted for their dining pleasure. There was a special area that Allie called the playground. It was a rectangular patch of dirt where the hens regaled in their ritual dirt 'baths.' Scratching and pecking out a spot to sit in, the hens used the dirt to get rid of parasites in their feathers.

Allie raked the grounds, refilled the feeding bins and made sure they had enough water. As she opened the hacienda's three doors to release the hens, her cell phone rang. She didn't recognize the number.

"Hello?"

"Hey beautiful. What are you doing?"

"Hanging with the chickens…who is this?" Allie said.

"What? You don't recognize my voice? I'm crushed."

"Sorry, but I don't have a clue."

"It's Chris. Chris Welke."

"Oh, hey there." Allie's heart beat a little faster.

"Are you in school?"

"Hanging with chickens? No. I'm working on the ranch right now. Just letting the girls out of their hacienda, then I was going to go horseback riding. Want to join me?"

"I wish. I'm in the quad. I just wanted to say hi and see if you'd like to go to dinner this Friday."

Allie was thrilled. "That sounds great."

"Cool. You still live off Bodega?"

"Yup. You can't miss it. Bowden Ranch is on the left, about six miles from downtown."

"Pick you up around seven?"

"I'll be ready."

"Okay then. See you Friday."

"Great. Bye Chris."

"Bye Allie."

Allie hung up the phone and let out a yell of joy. It scared the flock and some of them went running for cover.

"Sorry ladies. I didn't mean to scare you but I got a date with a gorgeous guy!"

Heading back to the stables, Allie saw Angel. He had his toolbox in one hand and a ladder in the other.

"Hola," Allie said as she waved to Angel.

"Hola, Allie-oop. Como esta?"

"Fantastico! Are you fixing the roof on the sheep barn?"

Angel nodded. "I can't put it off any longer."

Allie said, "Better you than me! I'm going to take Agave out for a ride."

"Okay. See you later."

As Allie saddled up Agave, she couldn't take her mind off of Chris. She wondered where he'd take her. Would he dress up or be casual in jeans and a hoodie? Would he try and kiss her? She hoped so.

Agave took off at a gallop toward Cougar Pond. It was one of Allie's favorite spots. The horse knew exactly where they were going. Granger had bought Agave for Allie when she was seven. She begged her dad to take her to the auction yard, wanting to get a horse that needed a good home, kind of like going to the animal shelter and saving a rescue dog or cat. Lydia, Allie's mom, was willing to spend thousands of dollars on a thoroughbred that a friend of hers was selling, but Allie wouldn't hear of it. She sat with Granger for the better part of an hour before Agave was walked into the bidding arena. A ten-year-old Arabian, he belonged to a young girl who wanted a faster horse. Agave liked to dawdle and didn't take instruction well, but he was a handsome steed. The bids were low and, without a lot of finesse, Granger was able to buy him for $350. Allie and Agave bonded quickly. He seemed to recognize her kindness and respect for him. He galloped faster than he ever had with his previous owner and instead of having an acre to live on by himself, Agave relished the vast amounts of land he could graze on with his fellow equine.

It was overcast and windy, not Allie's ideal riding conditions. She tied her long chestnut brown hair back in a ponytail and zipped up her jacket.

April was a magical month in Sonoma County. The fruit trees were in bloom, their white, pink and fuchsia flowers emitting a sweet fragrance. When the wind blew, their petals were released into the air. It was the closest thing to snow Sonoma County would see. The grasses were starting to grow and scrub dotted the landscape. Boulders and rock formations indiscriminately jutted out of the earth, creating a landscape similar to the Irish countryside. Some were the size of sheds while others were as large as houses. Allie rode to one of her favorite rock formations, a combination of large and small irregular-shaped boulders, trees and shrubs. She tied Agave's reins to the branch of a gnarled oak and climbed to the top of the structure. Eyes closed, she sat there listening to the hawks crying out in the distance. A slight breeze rustled the grasses below. Not long ago, Allie finished reading a book for her American Indian studies class called, *Power Animals: How to Connect with Your Animal Spirit Guide.* Sitting on top of the rock, she felt an overwhelming desire to try the technique she learned, even though it involved drumming. She closed her eyes, tuning out the sounds of nature. Breathing deep, she stilled her mind and then saw herself diving down into the rock, through the cracks and crevices and into the earth. She continued along the root of an oak tree growing out of the rock, watching for signs along the way. It wasn't long before she saw something moving to her left. She 'turned' and came face to face with a turkey vulture. It blinked three times then flew away, leaving a long, black feather. Allie picked up the feather in her mind, turned around and followed the path back up through the ground, up the cracks and crevices and back into her body. She opened her eyes half expecting to see dirt on her clothes, it felt so real. She gazed up at the sky and flying above her was a turkey vulture with a wing span of over six feet. Gliding on the hot air currents, it circled the rock a few times then flew off. She was disappointed. She had hoped her spirit/power animal was a horse or a cougar, something majestic; an animal that embodied grace and beauty; not one that dined on dead bodies. The bird was definitely impressive with its black and silver wings but its bald, blood-red and black head was ugly. It looked like a burn victim except for its pistachio-white beak. And they were scavengers, living off carrion. She made a mental note to talk to her professor about her experience. Maybe she didn't follow the procedure correctly and ended up with the wrong power animal. As she descended the rock, she found a feather embedded in one of the cracks. Plucking it out, she put it in her pocket. It was then that the name Iker came to her, so she named the rock formation, Iker.

When Allie got home, she googled turkey vulture. First, she scanned the images, then watched videos. The more she studied them, the more admiration she felt for the two and a half foot tall bird. Despite their size and scary appearance, they're not aggressive animals. When threatened, they throw up semi-digested food and the awful smell deters their provokers. They also don't perspire, so they urinate on their legs to cool off. At first, she was disgusted by their looks and characteristics, but then Allie decided that she was proud to have the turkey vulture as her power animal. The feather she found looked just like the feathers on a turkey vulture's tail in the pictures on Google images. Allie tied a string around the tip and hung it from her bedroom mirror. Then she googled 'Iker' since she'd never heard the word before. She discovered that Iker was a Basque boy's name. It meant 'visitation.' People with the name tend to be mystics, philosophers, scholars, and teachers. Perhaps Iker Rock would be her teacher. It already helped her attain her spirit animal. She wondered what else it had in store for her.

14

Rae watched Carson's chest rise and fall. He was still in ICU, but his recovery was going so well that they planned to switch him to a regular room within the week. Nurse Sandy Carver came into the room holding a small plastic device. It had a mouth piece and a tube with a yellow ball at the base of the tube. She smiled at Rae.

"Your son's doing great and he's so polite!"

"I keep hearing that but it's hard to believe. At home, he's anything but civil to me."

"That's because you're his mom. Wait until he moves out, then he'll treat you with respect."

"Can't wait," Rae said. Nurse Carver raised her eyebrows. Rae added, "When he's fully recovered, of course."

Carson opened his eyes. "You talking about me again?"

"Only in the loveliest of terms," Rae replied.

"Hi Carson. This is called an inventive spirometer. It'll help strengthen your lungs. What I want you to do is take a deep breath and then blow into this tube and try to raise the yellow ball as high as you can."

She handed the device to Carson. He examined it and then said, "Where's the carburetor?"

"What are you talking about? This isn't an engine, silly."

Rae rolled her eyes. "He thinks it's a bong. The carburetor is the little hole at the bottom of the pipe."

Nurse Sandy laughed. "And you know this how?"

"Uh, well," Rae sputtered, "I saw it on the Discovery Channel." Rae turned to Carson. "Just blow into it, honey. You're trying to increase not decrease your lung capacity."

Completely oblivious, Carson did as he was told, forgetting his question.

Rae was still very curious about the patient in the next room. Sometimes, she would hear him moaning and thrashing around. Another time, she saw one of the doctors talking to a policeman outside his room.

"I know it's none of my business, but what happened to the man next door?"

Nurse Carver said, "We're really not supposed to talk about the other patients due to privacy, but just between you and me..." she lowered her voice, "his wife sliced his hand open after he beat her up and threatened to kill her. As soon as he's well enough, they're carting him off to jail."

"Too bad she didn't aim lower."

As if on cue, the man starting yelling. They couldn't see him but it sounded like he was trying to break free from the restraints on his hands and feet. Nurse Carver stood quickly. "I'll be right back."

"Who's yelling?" Carson said as he laid his head back down on the pillow.

"An asshole."

Carson closed his eyes. The pain in his back was dull thanks to the morphine snaking through his system. He sensed the rods and screws in his body but couldn't actually feel them. It was a strange sensation, like a small pebble in your shoe. Not quite right. Breathing into that apparatus tired him out. He reached for his mother's hand for comfort and strength. In a sterile environment with machines as your company, it felt great having flesh and blood next to you. "Tell me a joke," Carson said.

"Really?" said Rae. She was the joke queen and prided herself on remembering jokes she heard when she was twelve years old. "Okay. What category?"

"Bar."

"Mild, bawdy or downright nasty?"

"What's bawdy mean?"

Rae smiled. "Vulgar."

"Give me that."

Rae thought a moment, then began. "A man walks into a bar and sits down at the counter. He looks to his left and there's a woman sitting at the end of the bar just finishing up her drink. The guy says to the bartender, 'I want to buy a drink for that douche bag at the end of the bar.' The bartender says, 'Sir, that's not very nice. You don't even know that woman.' The guy says, 'Buddy, just let me buy the douche bag at the end of the bar a drink.' The bartender goes up to the woman. 'That man over there wants to buy you a drink. What would you like?' and she says 'Vinegar and water.'

Carson had a blank expression on his face. "I don't get it."

"You know what a douche is?"

"Yeah, kind of."

"I picked the wrong joke for you. How about another one?"

"I'm tired. Maybe later." Carson closed his eyes but kept a tight grip on Rae's hand. With her free hand, she grabbed VegNews magazine and absently flipped through the pages. She started reading an article on the bile farms in China. Her chest constricted and tears welled up in her eyes as she learned how bears are imprisoned for life in small cages, tubes crudely attached to their stomachs to extract the bile, believed by the Chinese to be medicinal. Her first inclination was to do something, like start an online petition to outlaw the practice but reasoned that the Chinese wouldn't listen to a bunch of Americans. She could write the Chinese ambassador, but would it make a difference? She could post it on her Facebook page so others would be aware of the practice, but her friends were bombarded on a daily basis with causes. And then, like every other time Rae got outraged over injustices to animals, the enormity of the abuse overwhelmed her and instead of doing anything, she would do nothing. Cruella would castigate her for being so lazy. She argued that she had a lot on her mind with Carson's injury and the stress of working with Zoe. But then Cruella would retort, saying she had plenty of time to do something, anything instead of sitting on her butt. Her internal dialogue played like a loop, always criticizing and condemning.

Instead of continuing the 'conversation' Rae flipped to the recipe section and started reading about Cambodian cooking, vegan style.

Nurse Carver came back in the room. "That wasn't fun."

"Didn't sound like it," Rae said.

"I still have to take Carson's vitals. You can stay if you like but it will take a while. I also have to check his incision."

"That's my cue for taking a walk. I get queasy when I see blood and stitches. I don't know how you do it."

Rae extricated her hand from Carson's. He woke up with a start, eyes half-mast.

"Where are you going?"

"Sorry, kiddo, but you're going to be poked and prodded. I'll be back in…?"

Nurse Carver said, "Give me a half hour."

Rae kissed Carson on the forehead and left. She could only stay a little while longer because she had to get ready for her blind date with Steven the attorney.

15

Rae tried to read while waiting for Darlene and Peter to pick her up. She was anxious, worried that Steven would think she looked old. They were the same age, but fifty-eight on a woman looked worse than fifty-eight on a man. At least that's what her sexist attitude explained to her on a daily basis. She hated the marionette lines below her mouth and the upper lip lines drove her to distraction. She always felt that Botox or collagen fillers would rectify any facial imperfections, but she soon learned that they weren't the magic bullets they purported to be. Botox successfully eliminated forehead lines and crow's feet but below the eyes, it proved ineffective. Enter facial fillers which plump up the lines around the mouth but leave the upper lip looking like a beige shelf. Rae was surprised an entrepreneur hadn't created miniature vases and picture frames to sit atop the plumped-up lip. The honking of the horn pulled her out of her funk. She grabbed her purse and jacket, turned on the porch light and got into the back seat of Peter's Lexus.

"Ready to be wined and dined?" Peter said.

"Why yes I am."

"You look so pretty, Rae."

"Thanks Darlene, so do you. I love your necklace."

"You gave it to me!"

"I know. So, where are we eating?"

Peter said, "You're in for a treat. I made reservations at Chris's, the best steak house this side of the Mississippi."

"Very funny said the vegan. You're kidding, right? Tell me you're kidding."

"Shit, I forgot you were a vaygen!" Peter said.

"It's vee-gan and how could you forget?"

Peter and Darlene laughed. "I told you she'd freak out," said Darlene. "Of course we're pulling your leg. In your honor and with Steven's approval, we made reservations at Millennium."

Millennium was a gourmet vegan restaurant in San Francisco. It was lauded as one of the best restaurants in the city. Rae had been there a handful of times.

"Now we're talking. Even if Steven and I don't hit it off, at least we'll have a fab meal."

An hour later, the three of them walked into Millennium and were greeted by Steven. He and Peter shook hands, he hugged Darlene and then introduced himself to Rae. Darlene described him perfectly. He was average height and weight, and had a full head of salt and pepper-colored hair, more salt than pepper. When he smiled, he proudly displayed a beautiful set of straight, white teeth. They were a little larger than average, giving him a slight overbite.

Once they were seated, the waiter gave them all wine lists and as they perused the selection, Steven turned to Rae. "Peter tells me that you work for a financial company?"

"Yes. I'd been in media advertising for years and got sick of it, so I took a job in Petaluma working for a financial planner. And you must be the lawyer they've been talking about."

"That's me."

The conversation was light which was perfect for a first date. They ordered a bottle of wine and decided to partake in the four course prix fixe local & seasonal menu at $55 per person. As the wine was being served, another waiter brought over their first appetizer. They were devouring and waxing poetic about the fried oyster mushrooms when Rae glanced up and watched as three men and a woman were being seated across the room. It took her a little while but she soon realized that one of the men was Granger. He was wearing black jeans, a pale green long-sleeved shirt with a bolo tie and cowboy boots. He pulled the chair out for the woman. Rae guessed it was his mother, since she looked about tweny-five years older than him.

"Would you rather sit with them?" Steven said, his voice sounding a little irritated.

"Oh, I'm sorry. See the man in the light green shirt? It was his ranch that my son, Carson, had the motorcycle accident in front of. It's strange seeing a cattle rancher in a vegan restaurant. He must have been bribed or lost a bet."

Darlene said, "Maybe he's a vegan cowboy."

"Isn't that an oxymoron?" said Peter.

"When was your son in a motorcycle accident and is he okay?" Steven asked.

Rae recounted the April fool's day disaster and watched at Steven's eyes grew larger with every description.

"Wow. I think you could use more wine." Steven filled Rae's glass up to the top.

"You trying to liquor me up?"

Steven smiled. When he did, he reminded Rae of Steve Martin.

Rae glanced over at Granger's table. Granger was perusing the wine list and happened to look up and see her. He said something to the others and then got up and came over to their table. Rae got so nervous she had a hot flash. Her face turned red and perspiration collected on her forehead. She prayed no one noticed as she took off her jacket. Granger said, "Fancy meeting you here." He saw they were eating the fried oyster mushrooms. "Those are amazing, aren't they?" The group nodded in unison.

"Everyone, this is Granger, the good Samaritan who found my broken son. Granger, this is my friend Darlene, her boyfriend Peter and Peter's friend Steven."

"Nice to meet you all. How is Carson doing?"

"Good. They want him to get on his feet as soon as possible, with a walker, of course. According to the spine surgeon, walking is the best thing he could do."

"That's great. Tell him I say hi. Well, I should be getting back to my table. Enjoy your dinner."

"Thanks. You, too." Rae watched as Granger walked away. At that moment, she couldn't imagine a sexier man. The black jeans hugged his body and his tailored shirt accentuated his broad shoulders. He had soulful eyes, the color of dark gold. And that smile. So warm and sincere.

"He seems like a nice guy," Steven said.

"For a rancher," Rae replied.

"A fucking hot rancher," said Darlene.

"Darlene!"

Peter cut in. "That's okay. If my baby likes cowboys, I'll just have to buy me a lasso and some spurs."

"I'll drink to that," Darlene said as she hoisted her glass. The other three joined her, thoroughly appreciating the bottle of Sapphire Hill Pinot Noir.

By Rae's second glass of wine, she was nicely inebriated. It felt so good to shed her 'mothering' skin, not having to think about Carson for a little while. Steven was smart and funny. On more than one occasion, he would touch her arm or shoulder. She didn't mind at all. As they shared a second bottle and moved onto the second and third courses, Rae didn't notice that Granger was glancing her way more than a few times. He took a sip of wine and watched Rae as she bit into a slice of chocolate almond midnight mousse cake. The look wasn't lost on his mother. She tapped him on the shoulder. "How long has it been, dear?"

Granger snapped back from his reverie. "How long has what been, Mom?"

"Since you've been attracted to someone. By the looks of it, you're all but smitten."

Granger's brother, Dale, agreed. "If you had your horse, I can just see you now, riding up to the table and snatching little miss vegan away and riding off into the sunset."

Frank said, "Actually, he would be riding off into the Tenderloin District and would probably get shot or robbed."

Dale gave Frank a kiss on the cheek. "You can tell who the romantic is in this relationship."

Granger held up his hand. "Excuse me, but can I speak? Yes, I find Rae attractive and it has been a while since I've, you know, been with a woman, but I don't know if I'm smitten."

Without hesitation all three said at the same time, "You're smitten." It was loud enough that some of the other diners looked over at their table, including Rae. She couldn't quite make out what they said because their table was at the other end of the dining room, but her eyes locked with Granger's. She smiled. He smiled too, then looked away.

"It's a good thing Steven went to the restroom. You're blushing up a storm, woman. Admit it, you like him." Darlene took another bite of her dessert.

Rae said, "It's a hot flash and I'll admit that he's cute but he's a rancher. You know, the guys that raise cows for food? If you hadn't noticed, I'm diametrically opposed to that form of animal exploitation."

Peter joined in. "Leave her alone, Darlene. So, what do you think of Steven?"

"He's nice and very funny. And would you get a load of those pearly whites? They're almost perfect." Rae saw Steven coming back to the table. "Dummy up. Here he comes." Steven sat down and noticed how inordinately quiet it was.

"Were you guys talking about me?" he asked.

Peter said, "As a matter of fact, Rae was commenting on how nice your teeth are."

Steven smiled broadly. "On behalf of my parents, who paid a fortune for this smile, I thank you but I have to admit, these teeth were made to chew meat. This food is great but I don't know how you live without chicken, steak and pork ribs."

Darlene sucked in her breath, anticipating a biting reply. She knew Rae was a passionate ethical vegan and hadn't eaten animals for almost twenty-four years. She also wondered why Rae never tried to persuade her to adopt a plant-based diet. She reasoned that it was a topic as emotionally charged as religion and politics and broaching the subject could only add friction to their relationship.

Rae took a sip of wine and then looked directly into Steven's eyes. "My food choices are based on the fact that factory farmed animals lead the most horrific, painful and disease-laden lives of any creature on this planet. I cannot look at a piece of meat without seeing misery and hearing the screaming of the animal that was slaughtered, be it a cow, a chicken or a pig. My taste buds used to dictate my diet. Now my heart does."

Steven shifted uneasily in his chair. "So, you don't miss it, eh?"

Rae said, "Not one little bit."

Peter quickly chimed in. "Who's up for a vegan night cap?"

16

Rae stood in Carson's bedroom. He hadn't slept in his bed for almost two weeks. Gone were the sounds of teenage boys swearing, laughing, talking about their next tattoo or about girlfriends, past and present. The PlayStation II wasn't spewing out rapid gunfire, screaming commandos or screeching car tires. Under normal circumstances, Rae would have relished the solitude. She sat on the bed and put Carson's pillow up to her face and took a deep breath. There was a faint mixture of sweet, salty and human scents compared to his hospital 'fragrance,' a mix of antiseptic, gauze bandages and that accumulated smell of living amongst hospital fixtures.

Rae lay on the bed, wrapped in the faux fur throw that Carson loved. It was a deep chestnut brown and supposed to imitate the fur of a mink. It was a far cry from the real thing but it was soft, polyester soft. Rae stroked her face with its corner. It felt comforting.

As Rae got up to leave, she glanced over at Carson's desk. Sitting in the middle of the desk along with school books, pens and pencils was a sketch pad. It was open to an unfinished illustration of a skull, Carson's favorite subject. One eye socket held a shiny 8 ball, the other housed a very bloodshot eye. The cranium was cracked and Carson was starting to draw a whiskey bottle coming out of the top. The jawbone was nearly complete with a row of gold teeth. Rae didn't care for the subject matter but she had to admit that her kid was a talented artist.

The detail was impeccable. And then a thought occurred to her: What if Carson had died or became a quadriplegic? What if the accident left him brain-damaged? The drawing would remain half-done, incomplete. His life would have taken a cruel diversion and the 'new' Carson could never finish the illustration as originally planned. Her feelings of heart-break for her son touched a raw nerve with her own life. She saw her dreams unfinished because of her lack of drive. She could continue to plod through life, working at a dead-end job, continually repressing her desire to make a difference, but what if her life ended quickly? What if she was in an accident and became badly disabled?

Rae practically ran up the stairs, infused with a sense of purpose. Now was the time to make the change in her life. She made herself a cup of green tea, got into her sweats and, after grabbing a pen and tablet, sat at the dining room table. She started writing down everything she'd need to do before quitting her job. For the first time in a very long time, Cruella didn't say a word.

There were so many ways that Rae could help animals. Living in Sonoma County, the area was filled with dairy farms, cattle and sheep ranches, and egg farms. Petaluma had a poultry processing plant, an auction yard and a slaughterhouse. Exposing factory farming in her backyard was the logical choice and she was deeply passionate about the animals' plight. She had a video camera but it was almost twenty years old, making it an antique in the world of electronics. She wrote down 'new camcorder' on her list. Next, she took an assessment of her funds. She had an IRA, a savings account, a couple of stocks that her father bought her when she graduated college, and a deferred com-pensation account from a previous job. If she had to, she could live off her savings account and the IRA for about one year. That could give her the time to compile, film and edit the documentary. She didn't want to start living off her deferred comp account, but there was enough in it to give her a couple of more months without putting a sizable dent in the retirement fund.

Rae always had ideas floating around in her head about exposing factory farming but she rarely, if ever, wrote them down. If she did, it was usually on a scrap of paper. After languishing in her purse, in the car or on her office desk, Rae would find it and, for lack of initiative, throw it in the recycle bin.

There were already some excellent documentaries on factory farming: *Peaceable Kingdom*, *Earthlings*, *Forks over Knives*, and *Food Inc.* What would make Rae's film different than the others, more explosive, create a bigger buzz? Those questions would normally put her in a brain fog but not this time. She was ready for the challenge and welcomed it. Her only dilemma would be enduring the pain that she experienced looking at factory farmed animals and the conditions they lived in. The images clogged her mind for days. When Rae closed her eyes at night, they took turns revealing themselves until Rae could turn off the horror show and fall asleep. 'Poor dear,' Cruella lamented. 'You get upset because of their suffering. Suck it up and help them. You have the power. They don't.' Cruella could be such a bitch.

Rae began listing every idea that entered her mind, even if it was inane or banal or even hackneyed. She knew that she had to throw enough ideas against the proverbial wall so at least one would stick; that one gold nugget was all she needed.

Two hours later, somewhat satisfied that she made some headway, Rae got up to stretch. She raised her arms high and stood on her toes, then bent over and touched the floor. She repeated it a few more times, but that didn't satisfy her craving for movement. She put on Michael Jackson's *Greatest Hits* CD. Without Carson's protestations, she jumped, gyrated, danced and even attempted the 'moon walk' to *Billie Jean* and *Beat It*.

17

Allie hated when she ran out of tampons. She knew she'd be using them for at least a few decades and couldn't figure out why she didn't buy a supply to last her a couple of months, minimally. She also hated just buying tampons, so she walked up and down the aisles of Petaluma Market, searching for other items to buy along with her feminine hygiene purchase. One loaf of Rosemary and Meyer Lemon bread, four organic oranges and a jar of raw, virgin coconut oil later, Allie was standing in the checkout line. When it was her turn, she placed her items on the conveyer belt along with a reusable canvas bag, walked up to the checkout counter and found herself face to face with Francisco Santiago. When Fran saw her, he gave her a big smile.

"You're in my Communications class, aren't you?" said Fran.

"I am. How are you?" Allie said as she watched her tampons move closer to Fran's hands.

"Great." Fran scanned the bread, then weighed the oranges. The coconut oil was scanned next. When he got to the tampons, he faltered for an instant. Then he scanned them. Allie blushed.

"We sell a lot of these," he said, trying to lighten the mood.

"That's, um, nice to know."

"Okay, moving right along, your total is $28.16."

Allie swiped her debit card while Fran put her purchases in the canvas bag.

"So, you're a vegan?"

Allie glanced at her tattoo. "Gee, how did you guess?"

"I'm the smartest in my family."

"Can't wait to meet your family." Allie laughed. "It was nice seeing you…" She looked at his name tag. "Francisco."

"You, too." Fran glanced at the receipt. "Alison."

"Call me Allie."

"Only if you call me Fran."

"Deal. See you in class tomorrow." Allie grabbed her bag and left, leaving Fran with a smile on his face and a little twinge in his heart. Vegan shmeegan, he liked her.

"Hey Pop, I'm home and embarrassed!"

Granger was in the kitchen fixing lasagna and a salad for dinner. He was barefoot, wearing his faded blue jeans and an old white t-shirt. The shirt accentuated his tanned arms. "Talk to me, sweet pea, and tell me what you did this time."

"I bought tampons at Petaluma Market and the checker is a kid from my Communications class."

"Oh, the horror!"

"It's so stupid, I know. I mean, everyone knows that women have their period and we need tampons but it was still awkward."

"Yeah, I can see that. Are you going to transfer to another Communications class to avoid his stare?"

"Very funny. You want me to feed the dogs?"

"That would be great."

Allie went out to the porch and pulled the rope on the large bell. "Fin! Hammerhead! Food time!" Within seconds the dogs came bounding through the fields, racing into the house.

"Didn't you visit that kid who was in the accident today?"

"His name is Carson and I'm visiting him tomorrow. He's been out of the hospital for about a week."

"Why have you taken such an interest in him? You had nothing to do with the accident."

"The first time I ever saw him, he was lying in the ditch, broken. I'd like to replace that image with a better one. A healthier one. Does that make sense?"

"Sure. You're a good man, Granger Bowden. You have a big ass heart."

Granger turned his head and looked down. "At least I don't have a big ass."

The sun was setting over the hills as they sat down to eat. The sky was a pale shade of pink with patches of thin, wispy clouds. Allie was telling Granger about her day. He tried to listen but his mind kept returning to the approaching visit with Carson and his mother. He was looking forward to meeting Carson and talking to him, but the thought of seeing Rae again lifted his spirits and made him feel like a high school kid with a bad crush. When Rae gave him directions to their home, he discovered that she lived less than six miles away, off Bodega Avenue. He wanted to tell Allie about Rae but thought better of it. He decided to open up to her if the visit went well. A flock of geese flew by in a perfect v-formation. The leader let out a distinguishing honk and a few of the followers replied. He never tired of the sight or the sound. He wondered if Rae enjoyed rural Petaluma as much as he did.

18

"What the hell are you doing up there?" Carson yelled from his downstairs bedroom.

Rae had been vacuuming. Before that she was dusting and before that she cleaned the windows for the first time in, well the first time since they moved there six years ago. Rae put the vacuum away and walked downstairs.

"I was just vacuuming. You weren't sleeping, were you?" Carson shook his head. He was lying in bed, playing a video game. Sitting on the floor next to his bed was a full bottle of urine. Rae picked it up and took it to the bathroom and flushed it down the toilet. She washed it out and put it on the nightstand, ready to use again. Next to the bottle was a full container of Percocet. Sports Illustrated's swimsuit issue and a Car & Driver magazine also graced the table.

"Do you want to walk a little bit before Granger visits?"

"Sure."

Rae grabbed the clamshell, Carson's plastic vest for the next four to five months. It consisted of two pieces of thick plastic that had been custom fitted for him. The back piece had six long, black two-inch strips of Velcro on either side. The front piece had six loops where the Velcro circled through and was secured on the back. At first, Rae was nervous prepping Carson for wearing the brace because she had to turn him on his side, secure the bottom half under him and then place Carson on top of it. She was afraid of hurting him, terrified of jarring the two bolts close to his spinal column, but after two to three times of performing the maneuver, she never gave it another thought.

With his brace securely in place, Carson slid into his plaid slippers, grabbed the handles of the metal walker and tentatively stood, a little shaky. He moved slowly across the room, into the hallway and outside to the patio. Rae was right beside him, ready to catch him if he lost his balance. Carson walked in a large circle on the uneven pavement. He would impatiently wiggle his walker to push over a crack or swear when a wheel would get caught on a weed. Rae was quick to pull the weed. She'd then look for any other impediments to her son's stroll.

"This patio sucks!" Carson said.

"Wait right here and I'll re-pave it for you. It won't take long at all."

"Great." Carson stood there, waiting.

"I was kidding. How the hell am I going to re-pave this patio, son? You must be on drugs."

"Drugs? Did I hear you say drugs?" Neighbor Kevin appeared on the other side of the fence.

"Hey Kevin," Carson said.

"Except for being high on drugs, you seem to be doing better. I love the brace. Very stylish."

"You can borrow it, if you like, but I'll have to break your back first," Carson said.

"Maybe another time. So Rae, after you finish re-paving your patio, will you do mine?"

"I'm on it, Kevin."

"I have something for you, Carson. When can I come by and visit?"

Before Carson could answer, Rae said, "How about later this afternoon, around four?"

"That works for me. Later, you two." And with that, Kevin disappeared.

Carson walked around the cracked and weedy patio for another five minutes before returning to his room.

Lying down, he undid the straps. Rae turned him on his side and pulled out the back. She lowered him onto his back and grabbed the front piece.

"You did good, kid. Walking for ten minutes is great." She glanced up at the clock. It was 1:55. "Granger will be here at two. Do you want anything to eat?"

Using the remote, Carson turned on the television. Louis C.K. was on Comedy Central, performing his routine on the trials of raising two daughters.

"No, but could you give me some more water?"

"Sure." Rae grabbed the glass on the nightstand and went upstairs to the kitchen. She was hoping that Carson didn't notice how nervous she was. She chided herself for feeling this way. Of all people to be attracted to, a cattle rancher wasn't on her list, but there it was, that undeniable draw.

Rae checked herself in the armoire mirror one more time. She was wearing her faux leather cowboy boots with faded jeans and her favorite light blue t-shirt. She turned to the side and sucked her stomach in just as the doorbell rang.

Taking a deep breath, she opened the door. Granger stood there with a bouquet of white roses in one hand and a paper bag in the other. If it was possible, he looked even more handsome than when she saw him at the restaurant. He held the flowers out to Rae.

"Hi and thank you so much. They're beautiful. How did you know that white roses are my favorite?"

"Lucky guess."

Granger walked into the living room and then stepped back. "Do you want me to take my boots off?"

"No! With two cats, I tell people to leave their shoes on. You never know what you might step on or in. I was just getting Carson a glass of water. Would you like something to drink?"

"Water would be great, thanks." Rae went to the kitchen, saying to herself 'He's a rancher, he's a rancher, he's a rancher' hoping the mantra would break the spell.

"Carson is downstairs. Follow me." She handed Granger his water and he took a big gulp as they walked down the stairs.

"Hey guy. How are you feeling?" Granger went over to Carson's bed.

"Okay, I guess. Lot of pain, but the Percocet helps."

Granger handed the bag to Carson. "I brought you some goodies. Snacks that I thought you might like. I recruited my daughter to help me pick things out. I think you two are close in age. She's twenty."

"I'm eighteen." Carson stuck his hand in the bag and pulled out an assortment of candy bars, gum and ten lotto scratchers. "Thanks."

"You're welcome." Granger glanced over at the clamshell. "How long do you have to wear the brace?"

"They said around four to five months. I can't get out of bed without it. It sucks."

"I bet." Granger was about to ask him another question when Carson said, "You look really familiar. Wait a minute. I know you. I went to your ranch when I was in Mr. Fischera's class. You have that animal sanctuary."

"Yeah, that's me."

"You're the guy who turned your cattle ranch into a sanctuary? I remember Carson telling me about it." Rae said.

Carson said, "Didn't you call yourself the vegan cowboy?"

"Uh-huh. That was when people didn't even know what a vegan was."

"I've been vegan for three years and was a vegetarian for twenty," said Rae.

"Are you vegan?" Granger said to Carson.

"Hell no. Mom raised me vegetarian until I was nine. As she puts it, I went to the dark side. Full on carni, but your ranch, I mean sanctuary, was cool. You still have all the animals?"

"We have more. When you feel up to it, come visit. I'll give you and your mom the exclusive tour, minus the horseback riding."

"Give me a couple of weeks to master using my walker."

As the conversation continued, Rae excused herself and went upstairs. She grabbed the black vase with an art deco sailboat etched in gold and arranged the roses in it. She thought she was past getting excited about a man but her newfound knowledge of Granger overwhelmed her senses. She felt light-headed and unsteady, like someone replaced her knees with elastic. Rae liked to joke about meeting a vegan cowboy but she never really believed he existed. Yet, here he was in her home talking to her son, living up the street.

When Rae went back downstairs, Granger was just saying good-bye to Carson. He extended his invitation to visit the ranch again and then followed Rae upstairs. Back in the living room, Granger said, "Carson looks good. It's amazing how resilient kids are."

"I know. So, you have a daughter?"

"Yes. Allie is twenty."

"Is she a vegan?"

"Since she was eight. She's the one who showed me the light."

"A cattle rancher turned vegan. That must have been tough. What happened to all your rancher buddies? Did they threaten to throw you on the grill?"

"They preferred to slow cook me on the rotisserie. Seriously, they thought I was nuts and most of them distanced themselves from me. They couldn't understand why I would turn a thriving cattle business into a non-profit animal sanctuary. It was hard for me because I didn't want to hang out with people who raised animals for slaughter anymore. Ending the friendships was mutual."

As Rae listened to Granger, she assessed him. The way he stood, confident with a slight lean to the left. Perhaps an on-the-job injury. She guessed he was around her age, maybe younger. His face was weathered but in a Marlboro man way, not a Keith Richards way. Rae glanced at his boots. They looked like leather, but vegans eschew all animal products, including leather. Granger caught her staring.

"I know what you're thinking and you're wrong. They're not leather. A lot of the vinyl cowboy boots aren't sturdy enough for ranch work, so I commissioned a vegan shoe company to make me cowboy boots that were extra sturdy so I wouldn't wear them out in a few months."

"I wasn't going to question you...well, maybe I was. They look so authentic. I half-expected to see you sporting spurs."

"Never was a spur man."

"Be careful you don't say that too fast."

Granger said it quickly under his breath, then blushed. "Very funny."

"Hey, I'm not the one who said it." Rae glanced over at the coffee table and, to her horror, saw that she had left a small pile of toenail clippings in the bottom right corner. Granger started to look in that direction, so she walked in front of the corner, hoping to block the view. "It looks like you need more water."

"Thanks, but I need to get back to the ranch. It was really nice talking to you."

"You, too, and thank you again for the roses."

"I'm glad you like them." Rae walked Granger to the door and they said their good-byes.

Rae cleaned the clippings off the table, then she went downstairs to check on Carson. He had fallen asleep watching TV. She turned it off and was putting a blanket on him when the doorbell rang. Rae ran upstairs and answered the door. It was Granger.

Rae said, "Did you forget something?"

"Yeah, I did. What are you doing next Friday?"

"Are you asking me out?"

"I am. With very little finesse. I apologize."

"Granger, you could ask me standing on your head and I wouldn't mind. Come on in and I'll check my calendar." Rae went into her office/ guest room where her yoga calendar hung on the wall. "Shit," she said when she discovered that she had already made plans.

"Are you talking to me?" Granger said. Rae came back into the living room. "No, I was jabbering to myself. I'm busy on Friday." She paused, then said, "But I'm free Saturday."

"I'm not. Hold on. We're going to set a date or I'm not leaving."

"Geez, you vegan cowboys sure are aggressive. Who would have thought?"

Granger took out his iPhone and went to his calendar. "Okay, how about the following Friday, May third?"

"Don't move."

"I won't."

Rae went back to the calendar and to her delight, she was indeed free. She yelled, "It's a date! I'm inking you in. What time are you coming to pick me up on your trusty steed?"

"How's seven?"

"Perfecto." Rae came back to the living room. She hadn't felt this giddy in a long time.

"If I was wearing my Stetson, which I do have by the way, I would tip it and wish you a good day."

"And a good day to you, Mr. Bowden." Rae closed the door and immediately grabbed her cell and called Darlene. The butterflies that she thought long left her stomach had just taken a siesta. They were once again wildly flapping their wings.

"You're not going to believe this, but Granger isn't a cattle rancher anymore."

"That's good news," Darlene said.

"He asked me out to dinner. Our date is in two weeks. Darlene, he has an animal sanctuary. He's a vegan. I am in heaven! Oh, and get this. He brought me roses and he put together a bag of snacks and lottery tickets for Carson. What a sweetheart. And he has a daughter around Carson's age and did I tell you he lives up the street?"

"Yes you did. I'm sorry it didn't work out with Steven but I don't think you can get any better than Granger. I'm so happy for you, my dear. I hope he's as good as he sounds."

Their phone conversation was interrupted by Carson yelling for Rae. She finished up her call and attended to her demanding son, practically floating down the stairs. Suddenly, being his maid and nurse and chef didn't seem bad at all.

19

Granger couldn't stop smiling. He must have looked like a fool grinning from ear to ear but he couldn't help it. They were going on a date in two weeks. It seemed so far off. He'd have to figure out a reason to call her before then. Maybe he'd stop in and visit Carson again. He liked her son. Granted, he was on pain medication which probably made him a little more subdued than normal but he had a genuineness to him that Granger detected.

There was something about Rae's energy that made Granger light up inside. He felt buoyant. He couldn't wait to show her the sanctuary and introduce her to Allie and the rescue animals.

Granger pulled into the driveway, parking his truck next to Allie's Prius.

"Pop! Over here!" Allie yelled from the cow barn. It was located west of the house about five hundred yards away. Allie was standing in front of the barn in the enclosed area. One of the steers was standing next to her. Granger quickly walked down the hill. As he approached the barn, he recognized Rodney. Allie was massaging him on the flank where his injury used to be.

"Look at this. Rodney's infection is gone. You can barely see where it was. I'm just rubbing some salve on the spot in case there's any trace of infection left. He's a strong boy. Aren't you a strong boy, Rods?" Rodney turned to look at Allie. He moved his head side to side. "No Rods. It's this way. Up and down." She nodded but Rodney ignored her. "So, how was the visit with Brokeback Carson?"

"Very funny. It was great. He liked the bag of goodies and I gave you credit. He's unable to sit up without wearing a brace and I noticed a walker folded against the wall. The kid has a long recovery ahead of him. I invited him and his mother to the ranch when he felt up to it."

Allie noticed that her Dad was more animated than usual. She raised her eyebrows.

"What?" said Granger.

"You tell me. You're glowing in a good way not a radioactive way."

"I'm going out to dinner with Rae, Carson's mom." Allie hugged her Dad.

"That's great, Pop. You haven't been out on a date since I had braces or it seems like it's been that long. So tell me about her."

"She's around my age, maybe younger and in good shape. She's funny and…oh she's a vegan."

"Get out."

"Really. What are the chances that the mother of a kid that has a motorcycle accident in front of our ranch is vegan? It has to be fate," Granger said.

"Don't tell Brokeback that. What does her place look like?"

"It's a small bungalow-type house. Probably built in the fifties. Clean and neat. She has a lot of antiques mixed with modern furniture."

"It's called eclectic."

"I know what it's called, Miss College Student."

"Well I'm happy for you, Dad. This sounds promising."

"Quick question: Is it okay if I call her before the date, just to talk? I don't want to look too needy."

"Your date is in two weeks. I say call her in a couple of days and talk her ear off. You have my blessing." Allie hugged her dad once more. She hadn't seen him this excited about a woman in a long time. Tears of joy filled her eyes. She quickly wiped them away so he wouldn't see. She felt silly for getting emotional but she knew her dad was lonely and wanted to share his life with a woman. Her parents had divorced twelve years ago and he dated only a few times since then. To say he was picky was an understatement, but she figured he didn't want to make the same mistake he had with her mother. All the traits that Granger embodied; warmth, compassion, empathy, generosity, understanding; Lydia lacked. She was self-absorbed, materialistic and greedy. Allie was eight when she came home from school and announced to her parents that she was not going to eat meat anymore. Granger was a cattle rancher at the time and a successful one at that. Lydia forbade Allie from becoming a vegan, but Granger sat his daughter down and asked her why. She explained that one of her classmates' mothers came to speak to the class about animal rights. She revealed to the class how animals were raised and slaughtered. She talked about factory farms and the crowded conditions the animals live in. Allie said that she raised her hand and told the mother about the cows on their ranch and how they're treated well and then are sold so they can feed hungry people. The woman was understanding and agreed that some food animals are raised humanely, but the cows still go to the slaughterhouse which is not a nice place.

Allie was crying, asking her dad if it was true that all their steers ended up in a slaughterhouse. Granger couldn't lie. He had shielded his daughter from many of the practices on the ranch and Allie knew that the steers were sold so people could eat but she obviously didn't make the connection. All the ambivalence that Granger felt when he inherited the ranch from his father came bursting forth in his daughter's newfound compassion for animals. He had wanted to get out of the cattle business but every time he brought it up, Lydia talked him out of it. She came from a ranching family and loved every aspect of the lifestyle. She couldn't imagine living any other way.

Granger had contemplated selling off 10 of his 550 acres to a developer and Allie's newfound eating habits solidified the decision, much to Lydia's mortification. What made the whole experience even worse for Lydia was Granger's decision to become a vegan, too. At first, she thought he was kidding, but Granger had told her about his childhood and how the ranching business was such a peripheral part of who he was, regardless of the fact that it was his livelihood. He grew emotionally attached to the cattle. Selling them was always painful. The relief and joy that Granger felt after he decided to quit cattle ranching was negated by the grief he got from Lydia. Despite her vehement protests, Granger sold ten acres to Harriband and Sons, an environmental development company that built five custom homes with every eco-friendly bell and whistle while retaining the integrity of the land. The homes weren't visible from the Bowden estate. The developer planted a row of willow tree hybrids and within three years, the homes had complete privacy from Bodega Avenue and their neighbors. Everyone was happy with the arrangement except Lydia and she made Granger's life hell, despite the fact that the sale of the land made them very wealthy.

A year after Allie's revelation, Granger and Lydia divorced. He was tired of listening to her bitch about their vegan diets, the sale of the acreage, and keeping the cows as, she liked to call it, pets. As inevitable as the separation seemed, Lydia was shocked at Granger's decision to end the marriage. If there was any love left between them, it was in hiding. Granger acknowledged that his lifestyle change was drastic but he expected Lydia to respect his decision rather than fight him on a daily basis, just as he accepted her decision to continue to eat meat and dairy.

It was Allie's idea to turn the ranch into a sanctuary, declaring the fifty head of cattle the first sanctuary members. She had heard of a place called Animal Haven, located south east of Petaluma. She called them and told the sanctuary manager their plans for converting the ranch into a safe place for animals and any guidance would be helpful. The manager was only too happy to help and suggested that they come up for a day where they would be given a tour of the sanctuary and advice on how to start their own Animal Haven.

On the drive up, Allie asked her dad why he became vegan. It was such an easy decision for her after learning about the animal suffering but Granger was a rancher, imbedded in the lifestyle of raising animals for food. How could he make up his mind so quickly?

Granger had never talked to Allie about his childhood. He had given her some sound bites from his past, careful not to tell her the angst he experienced at the hands of his father. His mother would tell her granddaughter stories, but only the good ones, the happy ones. Since they had over three hours in the car, Granger decided to illuminate his life to his only child. He began to unfold the years of pain he felt living on a cattle ranch. When he finished, Allie was silent.

"You okay?" Granger said.

"Is that why Uncle Dale is gay?"

"What do you mean?"

"Well, did Grandpa make him do so many horrible things to animals that he turned gay?"

Granger tried not to laugh. "No, honey. Dale was born gay. He didn't choose to be a homosexual, just like you and I didn't choose to be heterosexual. Dale never liked living on the ranch and he was a lot stronger in his stance with our dad. He refused. I felt obligated but I hated it, too."

"I think Mom is mad at me for being vegan. She said I turned you against her."

Granger pulled off at the next freeway exit and parked the car. He turned to his daughter and looked straight into her innocent eyes. "Don't ever believe that. Your courage to become a vegan gave me the strength to do it, too. Your mother is angry and I understand that. I turned her comfortable world upside down, but it was her world, not mine. I didn't want to live a lie anymore. Someday, she'll understand that. Okay?"

Allie nodded. "I love you, Daddy."

"I love you, too, Al."

When they left Petaluma that morning, it was overcast, a thin layer of grey clouds covering the sky. By the time they arrived at Animal Haven, it was starting to drizzle. In anticipation of inclement weather, Granger and Allie brought raincoats. They wore their usual outfits: cowboy hats and boots, looking very much like the ranchers they used to be. Up the road, Granger spotted the sign for the sanctuary. He passed under an arch with 'Animal Haven' written in bright blue letters. Lining the driveway were animal sculptures including a hot pink horse on its hind legs, two cobalt blue dancing pigs and a bright orange duck flapping its metal wings. Allie loved every one of them and imagined them gracing her new sanctuary. They pulled up to the main building, a small brown ranch-style home converted into the sanctuary offices and animal hospital. Allie clamored out of the car as soon as it was parked. She ran up to the front door just as Lara Hiteman, a young woman in her early thirties, walked out the door to greet them. She was wearing a baseball cap over short-cropped hair. Her jeans were tucked into rubber boots.

"You must be Allie Bowden."

"I am." Allie held out her hand and shook Lara's. Granger stepped out of the car and walked up to Lara.

"Granger Bowden. We appreciate you showing us around."

Lara introduced herself. "I can't tell you how excited we all are that you're starting an animal sanctuary, especially in Petaluma. With all the ranches and dairies, it's so badly needed. Come on inside so you can meet our founder."

Walking into the offices, Granger and Allie were introduced to Jean Lowenberg, a middle-aged woman with long grey hair and an easy smile.

"I wouldn't mind meeting ranchers turned sanctuary owners all day long. It's a pleasure, Granger and Allie."

Granger said, "Same here."

"I can't wait to have a lot of animals living at our ranch. It'll be so much fun," Allie said.

"It's fun but it's also hard work. Many of the animals that live here have come from pretty bad places. Some of them adjust quickly and others, well, they need time to heal either physically, emotionally or both. Lara is going to give you a tour of the facility and then I'll meet you back here."

Granger said, "That sounds great. I'm sure I'll have a list of questions for you."

"Bring it on!" Jean replied. Just then, two snow white geese waddled in from another room, honking. As they got closer, Allie noticed that each had a 'wing cast' against their bodies. They started pecking at Allie's boots. Instead of being afraid of them, she thought it was funny and started laughing.

Jean said, "Who let Amos and Andy out of the infirmary?" She turned to her guests. "These two came to us last week. Some boys at the park started shooting the geese with bb guns. Amos and Andy took the brunt of the assault. It looks funny but their bound wings are held in place using sticking plaster. Hopefully, their broken wings will set correctly and they'll be able to fly again. If not, Amos and Andy will become permanent residents."

A young woman came over apologizing for the interruption and escorted the geese back to their cages. Allie turned to Lara and said, "Can we see the sheep first? They're my favorite animal."

Granger said, "I thought horses were your favorite animal."

"Can't I have more than one favorite, Daddy?" Lara stepped in. "Of course you can. All the animals here are my favorites. I love them all equally. Let's go to the goat and sheep barn first."

The drizzle turned into a light rain as the three of them walked outside and headed toward the animal housing facilities. Animal Haven was set on ten acres but most of it was contained in the area behind the office.

As they passed the hog enclosure, one of the hogs spotted them and trotted up to the fence. He was enormous, weighing over 400 pounds. He pushed against the fence, trying to get closer to them.

Granger said, "The pigs are laying on the hay out of the rain. I thought they liked to roll around in mud." He pointed to a muddy spot near the fence.

Lara shook her head. She went over to the hog and scratched his neck. "That's one of the biggest fallacies about pigs. Everyone thinks they're dirty and messy. Humans are called pigs if they're rude, someone scarfing down food eats like a pig, and a messy room is a pig sty. Pigs don't have sweat glands so they roll in the mud to cool themselves off. They're not overeaters but when they eat they snort and, believe it or not, they love sleeping on a bed of fresh, clean hay. This is Hedge. He's our oldest resident hog and a sweetheart, aren't you Hedge?"

Allie asked, "Can I pet him?"

"Of course. He loves being scratched under the chin."

Tentatively at first, Allie started scratching Hedge under his chin. His skin was tough like a callous and thick, white errant hairs sprung out in all directions. Hedge closed his eyes and made soft grunting noises. Allie said, "I think pigs are my favorite animals, too."

"Where did you get Hedge from?" Granger asked as he joined Allie and rubbed the hog's back.

"It's a harsh story. Are you sure you want Allie to hear it?" Granger looked at his daughter.

"I better get used to it since we're going to take in abused and neglected animals."

Lara said, "About six years ago, we got a call from the Highway Patrol. A truck carrying hogs to slaughter overturned. When we got there, many of the hogs were injured, some dead. The trucking company sent out another truck and they were moving the injured animals into it, using electric prods, kicking them to get them up. It was heartbreaking. I was glad that some of them died. They wouldn't have to experience the pain of being put on another truck bound for the slaughterhouse. Hedge was one of the few that they left for dead. He had two broken legs and wasn't worth the trouble. We brought him and five others back to Animal Haven and nursed them back to health. Hedge is the only one left. He's eight years old and that's old for a pig." Lara looked over at Allie who had tears in her eyes.

"Why were they so mean to the pigs?" Allie said.

"It's a business, Allie, and these poor creatures have the distinction of tasting good. That's the bottom line and they're treated accordingly. Are you okay?"

"Not really. It makes me very mad and sad." Allie gave Hedge a kiss on the head. "I love you, Hedge."

Above the door to the sheep and goat barn was a hand-painted sign that said, 'Billy Goats and Bo Peep Sheep' surrounded by large, colorful flowers. Lara brought them over to a stall where two sheep lay next to each other. Lara said, "These two lovely ladies are Dottie and Madge. We adopted them from a family that wanted to shear them and make clothing from their wool. Unfortunately, they weren't prepared to take care of sheep. They lost interest and brought them here last year."

Granger said, "If you have the land, how tough can it be caring for sheep?"

"There's the rub. Having the space so sheep can graze is crucial. There's also a skill to shearing a sheep. They thought they could use their electric razors." Granger looked at her like she was kidding. "I'm serious! Don't ever underestimate the power of stupidity. Anyway, Dottie and Madge lived in the family's little backyard. Even given enough feed, they ate almost every flower and shrub on the premises. When we went to the house to pick them up, the backyard looked like someone took pruning shears to everything that grew out of the ground. Needless to say, the family was very relieved to send Dottie and Madge packing."

Allie and Granger were introduced to Henry, a Nubian goat. He had a dark chocolate brown coat with small, irregular white spots. His floppy ears hung from his head, resembling a basset hound. He walked up to Allie and nuzzled her shoulder. She rubbed his head and Henry looked up and stared at Allie.

"Whoa! His eyes are so weird." Allie was referring to Henry's horizontal rectangular pupils.

"Goat eyes seem to freak some people out. They actually have very good vision and acute hearing skills, too, don't you Henry? Henry Higgins came from a defunct goat milk farm. It was us or the slaughterhouse. Our other six goats are also from that farm."

After meeting an assortment of other animals, they returned to the office. By then, the rain had dissipated and the sun came out, washing the refuge in a light that illuminated the land. After finishing up some paperwork, Jean got up from her desk and went over to Granger and Allie.

"Do you still want to open an animal sanctuary?" Jean said.

"More than ever!" Allie replied. "And we're going to have pigs and sheep and goats and…"

"Horses and whatever else comes our way," Granger said. "I know it will be a huge undertaking but it's more than worth it."

"That's good to hear. Tell me Granger, why did you decide to become a sanctuary owner?"

"Raising cattle was my life but I never liked it. Allie's conversion to becoming a vegan gave me the strength to follow my beliefs and my heart."

"Some of our most ardent animal rights people came from similar circumstances." Jean pointed to one of the office workers and whispered, "Used to own a McDonald's."

"The harder they come, the harder they fall," Granger said. "What made you start Animal Haven?"

Jean sat back in her chair and put her feet up on the reception table. "Most people assume that I was always involved in some way with animal rescue, but that's not true at all. About fifteen years ago, I got a DUI. Instead of paying the fine, I was given one hundred hours of community service. I lived in Chico then and one of my options was serving my 'time' at the Animal Sanctuary in Orland. I was never a huge animal fan. I ate meat and dairy, but I was not prepared for what I saw. They had pigs and sheep and cows. Some of these animals had been through horrible experiences but they all had this enormous capacity for love and affection. And some of them had the most amazing personalities. I had no idea farm animals, food animals, were like that! They had rescue turkeys whose feet were badly deformed from the weight of their huge chests. Why were their chests so inordinately large? Because humans like turkey breasts, so they were bred that way but the turkeys' legs and feet couldn't sustain the weight. After I performed the obligatory hours, I continued to volunteer for them. It wasn't long after that I became a vegan. A few years later, my husband was transferred to this area. I decided then to start Animal Haven. We're going on twelve years." She handed Granger a manila folder. "I've compiled some information that will help you get started. Of course, please don't hesitate to call me if you have any questions."

Granger said, "Thank you so much for your time and this information. I really appreciate it." He put out his hand and Jean shook it.

"My pleasure. When do you think you'll be able to accommodate animals?"

Granger thought about it for a moment. "Three to four months but I'll let you know when it's official."

"Sounds great." Jean turned to Allie. "It was so nice to meet you. Come back any time."

Allie went over to Jean and hugged her hard. "I hope my dad and I can help the animals the way you have." Jean looked down at this young girl with a big heart and tears welled up in her eyes. She said, "I don't doubt for one second that your sanctuary is going to be amazing. Send me pictures, okay?"

Allie said, "Sure."

20

Driving home, Granger and Allie were throwing out ideas, thoroughly excited about the prospect of creating their own animal refuge. Allie wanted to accept all animals, even dogs and cats, but Granger knew that, with the number of abused and abandoned animals, their sanctuary could get too large too quickly. They settled on farm animals only.

Throughout the years the sanctuary took in horses, chickens and a flock of sheep that were abandoned when the rancher became insolvent. Stray and feral cats ended up living in the barns. Allie became a pro at trapping them so they could be taken to get neutered or spayed.

With Granger's help, Allie became the assistant manager of Bowden Ranch. Every new animal was vetted through her checklist. After Granger and the veterinarian conducted a health examination, Allie would come in with her hot pink clipboard and the Bowden Family Form. With an orange sparkle pen in hand, she would introduce herself to the newest member of the sanctuary and then write down their markings, unusual characteristics, history and then give them a name, if they didn't already have one. If they came with a name, Allie would change it slightly. She wanted their new life to come with a new identity. Allie's first entry was Delilah, a rescued race horse. At only four years old, Delilah was put out to pasture because she wasn't winning races. She came from racing stock, but the filly didn't have the speed needed to win. Delilah's owner kept her for his daughter. At first, the girl rode every weekend. Then it became every other week until finally she grew bored with horse-back riding and Delilah became more of a financial burden than a companion. When she was eight years old, Delilah was taken to the auction yard. Granger bought her and brought her to the newly reno-vated horse stables. She joined Granger's horse Tuscany and Allie's mustang, Agave.

Allie sat on the stable fence and observed Delilah as the thorough-bred walked around the enclosed grounds. She sniffed the ground, then pawed it. Allie noticed how Delilah's right eye was slightly closed. She wrote it down. Sensing that she was being watched, the horse came right up to Allie and nudged her, almost pushing her off the fence. Once she righted herself, she rubbed the horse on her soft nose and then gave Delilah an apple from her backpack. While Delilah was munching, Allie gave her the name, DeLinda.

After DeLinda, they took in Jeeves (originally Jingles), Harley (Henry), and Lenore (Leonie). Despite some personality clashes, the horses were civil toward each other. It was as if they sensed that they were going to be treated well and, like a family, knew they had to get along.

As the brood grew, Granger realized he needed help running the sanctuary. He commissioned the same builders who bought the ten acres to build three eco-cottages in the northwest corner of the prop-erty. Each cottage had solar panels, a tankless water heater, a composter and gray water hookup. The toilets were low flush, the low flow shower heads filtered the water, and Granger even installed ceiling fans and skylights. The floors were recycled redwood and the windows were all double-glazed for heat efficiency. He encouraged the occupants to com-post and have a vegetable garden. Sometimes, Granger would visit The Seed Bank, an heirloom seed store that took over the Sonoma County Bank building, constructed in the 1920s. It had over 1,200 varieties of heirloom seeds and Granger was like a kid in a candy store, picking out the most unusual vegetable seeds, like Japanese Pie Squash, Purple Beauty Pepper and the Ozark Pink Tomato, for his garden. He always bought extra seed packs for the 'cottage people.' Currently, college students lived in two of the cottages. They worked and lived on the ranch rent-free, receiving college credit while being paid a fair wage. Angel Lago lived in the third cottage.

Angel was forty-two when Granger found him hanging out on the corner of Howard and Bodega at the Shell gas station. It was a popular place where ten to thirty Mexicans spent their day, trying to get part-time work. Granger spotted the heavy-set man with shoulder-length hair sitting on the curb, head down and hands moving. As he got closer, he saw that Angel was carving a piece of wood with a small switch blade. His rough hands deftly turned the wood, working quickly and intensely. In Granger's broken Spanish he asked him what he was making. Angel replied in Spanish that he was making a doll for one of his friend's daughters. Granger complimented him on his abilities, then asked him if he had any construction experience to which Angel replied that he did.

"In between carving, you want to work on my animal sanctuary? You'd be tending to the animals and doing repairs on the barns and other structures."

"For how long?" Angel asked.

"If it works out, for as long as you want."

That was twelve years ago. Angel took to the work with such an intensity and love for the land and the animals that Granger asked him if he wanted to live there. Angel graced the property with his carvings. He took great pride in his work. As he created a piece, he would wrap himself up in the subject. If it was a sheep, he imagined the animal as a living, breathing being. He made up songs and sang them aloud as his switchblade skillfully cut into the wood. What emerged was more than a carving. It was imbued with Angel's love and energy.

Jake and Lucy lived in one of the cottages. They were going to Sonoma State University. Both majored in viticulture, the study of wine. They had a vegetable garden and a quarter of an acre of pinot noir grapevines. They converted one of the bedrooms into a wine room and after a few misses, they produced some decent tasting wines.

The last cottage was occupied by Stephanie Benjamin. She was one of Allie's high school friends. After graduation her parents kicked her out, declaring that eighteen years was long enough to be living off of them. Allie suggested that she work and live at the sanctuary. At the time, Stephanie would have lived in the cow barn since she had nowhere to go, but she ended up loving the work and she couldn't imagine being anywhere else. It fit her ambition level perfectly.

21

"You're late," Zoe said to Rae without looking up. Her shoulder-length hair sported light green highlights. It would have looked edgy on a teenager, but on a fifty-year-old, it just looked pathetic.

"Sorry. I was on my way out and Carson needed me to empty his urine bottle."

"That's gross. I didn't need to know why."

"Sorry. It's such a normal part of my life now, I don't even realize how obscure or disgusting it is to other people."

Rae sat down at her desk. She still needed the income while she worked on compiling the information for her animal rights documentary. After number crunching, she realized that she could live off her IRA and sell what was left of the stock, but it wouldn't take more a year before she depleted her financial resources. She wasn't sure how long it would take her to complete the documentary. And after it was done, Rae wanted to promote it. Her inclination was to find another job but she made the decision to put all her energy and time into the film instead of job hunting.

"How's Carson doing?"

Rae said, "Much better. He still needs to use the walker but his pace is faster."

"That's good." Zoe picked up the phone and dialed. Soon, she was talking to one of her kids. Rae couldn't tell which one. She had three, two sons and a daughter.

"Don't forget that I have my manicure after work, so please feed the dog, then do your homework...Okay. Tell Daddy to defrost the meatloaf." Rae pulled up the window blinds behind her desk extra fast. Zoe gave her a discerning look. "I'll make a salad when I get home. No television until you do your homework. Bye."

Before Zoe could admonish her, Rae got up and went to the storage room, grumbling to herself as she grabbed some staples. "Would it kill her to open my blinds?" She took an extra-long time, staring into the supply cabinet, not looking at anything in particular. Finally, she sat back down at her desk.

Around 3:30, Zoe came over to Rae and handed her some files. "I need to have these files transcribed by tonight."

"I'll do my best. I have to leave at five to take care of Carson. Stuart will be picking him up tomorrow morning and then I'll have three days to myself and can stay late."

"So you're saying that if it's not done, you have to leave anyway?"

"Zoe, I'll take it home with me, okay? Carson can't get out of bed without his brace and he can't put it on by himself."

"Who's with him now?"

"His friend, Jarod, who has to go to work when I get home."

"Fine." Zoe left the office and Rae, hoping she wouldn't turn around, gave her the finger. She opened the first file and started transcribing.

The first thing Rae did when she walked in the door was plop down on the couch next to Jarod. She put the office files on the coffee table. "How's our patient?" Rae said to Jarod.

"Except for trying to sell me some of his Percocet at an outrageous price, he's fine."

"Tell me you're kidding."

"Of course. Carson's at his dad's for three days, right."

"Yes sir," said Rae. "Thanks so much for helping out, Jarod. You're a doll."

Jarod left and Rae went downstairs to Carson's room. "How are you feeling, honey?"

"Like shit. This sucks!"

"If my magic wand wasn't at the dry cleaners, I'd wave it over you and you'd never feel pain again. Did you take a Percocet?"

"I just did."

"I'll make dinner soon. By that time, the drug will have kicked in and you'll feel better. Do you want your brace on?" Rae said.

"Why would I want that fucking thing on when I'm in pain? Think, Mother."

Rae took a deep breath. "Breaking your back does not give you the right to be an asshole. Apologize."

"Sorry, but you don't know what it's like to have a fucked up back."

"You're right, I don't. But you don't know what it's like feeding, bathing and catering to someone who doesn't appreciate it. Between you and Zoe, I'm ready to drive north to Canada and never return."

"Before you do, can you give me the remote to my stereo…Please?" Rae grabbed the remote and tossed it to Carson, accidentally hitting him in the head.

"Ow!"

"It took your mind off your back for a second, didn't it?"

As she ascended the stairs, Led Zeppelin's *Whole Lotta Love* blasted from below. Robert Plant's raw voice dripping with sex stirred something inside of her. She stood on the stairs listening to Plant's moaning and telling her that 'way, way down inside, honey you need me. Gonna give you my love…' while Jimmy Page's guitar riffs grabbed her libido and made it vibrate. She closed her eyes and absorbed every note. For five minutes she didn't think about anything else, not Zoe or Carson or fixing dinner, but Granger's image easily intermingled with the tune.

22

"Meja, will you set the table?" Lornita asked Fran. He nodded and grabbed the mismatched, chipped plates from the cabinet and placed them on the bleached white tablecloth. The water glasses were next and the silverware and napkins last. Fran stared at the table, imagining what Allie would think. He wasn't ashamed of his family but when he looked at their home and belongings, he saw broken, worn and threadbare furniture intermingled with hand-me-downs. He saw inexpensive and cheap. But he also saw a loving, supportive family. Lornita stopped spooning the rice into the casserole dish and walked up behind Fran, putting her arms around her middle child. She didn't say anything. She didn't have to. Fran was used to her bouts of affection and always welcomed them.

With a new perspective, Fran observed his family eating fried chicken and shredded beef. He never thought twice about eating meat, but since he met Allie, his views shifted slightly. He watched Dario pull apart the chicken breast, separating the meat from the small ribs. It didn't look as appealing as it used to and Fran loved fried chicken.

"Dude, stop staring at me," Dario said.

"Sorry."

"How's school, Francisco?" his father, Ernesto, asked.

"Good."

"Any hot babes?" said his older brother, Luis.

"One. Her name is Allie. She's in my Communications class."

"White?" Luis said.

"Yeah."

"You gonna ask her out or what?" Luis said.

"Maybe. I don't know. She came into the store the other day. She's cool." Fran could see her face and that hot body but his mind always went back to the VEGAN tattoo. His diehard carnivorous family would have a fit if he started seeing a vegan. She might as well be an alien. He stuck his fork in the shredded beef and put it on his plate.

Three days alone. No one yelling for food or help with a brace. No cleaning out urine bottles or shampooing hair that wasn't hers. Rae felt light, as if someone unlocked the ball and chain from her ankle. Work wasn't too bad today. She only gave Zoe the finger twice. It was 6:00 p.m. She just finished dinner and was deciding which Netflix movie to watch when her cell phone rang. It was Granger. Her heart jumped.

"Hello?"

"Hi there. It's Granger."

"How are you?"

"Just dandy. How's your patient?"

"Carson's doing really well. He's with his dad for the next three days. Yea!"

"That is good news. I'm going out to a friend's sheep ranch in Bodega Bay and I was wondering if you'd like to join me. Don't worry. The sheep are used for their wool only."

"That sounds like fun. I was going to watch a movie but I like your plans for the evening better."

"Great! Can I pick you up in a half hour?"

"Yes, you can."

"Okay. I'll see you soon. Bye."

"Bye." Rae went over to Pierre and gave him a big hug and kiss. He let out a slight squeak, stretched and went back to sleep. She was about to hug Rita but when she saw Rae coming, her eyes got bigger than normal and she darted off before Rae could grab her.

"Why do you look at me like I'm going to hurt you? I give you food. I give you shelter."

Rae's first inclination was to call Darlene and then Rebecca and tell them she was going on her first date with the vegan cowboy but she hung up the phone mid-call. She loved and trusted her friends, but she also knew that they would give her advice and she didn't want to hear it. At her age, she should know by now exactly how she wanted to be treated and take no less. Rae was determined to follow her gut no matter how much her awakening libido might try and mislead her.

Rae stared into the make-up mirror. She had a love/hate relationship with it. It magnified her face so she could accurately line her eyes and apply blush but it also illuminated every pore, blemish and wrinkle six times its size. She studied her lip line and detected a small, black hair. Grabbing the tweezers, she deftly pulled it out. "Don't you dare show your hairy little body on my face again." As she added more mascara to her eyelashes she said, "Listen to me, Rae O'Brien. You're fifty-eight years old…young. The only man in your life that you need right now is one who respects you. No respect. No man. Got it? No pussying out." Rae burped really loud and then laughed. "Aren't you a peach?" She used a lipstick pencil and outlined her lips, then filled in the rest with rose-colored gloss. She smiled at her image, blew herself a kiss and then waited in the living room for the man she was hoping would be the one.

She was standing in front of her living room window when Granger pulled his 1967 Chevy truck into her driveway. The truck was faded blue and rust with too many dents to count. Rae had assumed that running an animal sanctuary didn't exactly bring in the big bucks but she had to admit that she would rather see him behind the wheel of a vehicle other than a beater. At least one with a decent paint job. "You can't have everything," she said to herself.

Rae watched as Granger got out of the truck. When he closed the door, it made a rattling noise. "Lovely," Rae said. She opened the door just as Granger walked up to the front porch. "Hi there."

"Good evening," said Granger. "I think you should bring a warmer jacket. Margo's ranch is on a bluff a few miles from the ocean. It gets mighty cold at night."

"Hold on." Rae went over to the antique armoire in the living room and grabbed her Eddie Bauer jacket with the hood. It wasn't sexy but neither were blue lips.

Granger headed west on Bodega Avenue toward Bodega Bay. As he switched gears, the truck lurched forward.

"Sorry about this truck. It was the only one available, believe or not. The others are being worked on."

"No problem." Rae could only imagine the condition the other vehicles were in, but when she looked over at Granger, she envisioned him rescuing animals. Decrepit trucks or not, she was still smitten.

"Why did you want me to come with you tonight?" Rae said.

Granger took a deep breath, adjusted his baseball cap and said, "Our official date is over a week away, right? I was going to call you so we could talk but then I had this brilliant idea that it would be so much nicer to talk to you in person and what better circumstances than driving on one of the most beautiful country roads in the world, or at least in Sonoma County."

"That *is* a brilliant idea. Do you come up with these often?"

"I try. So, tell me. What movie were you going to watch tonight?"

"It was between a Danish film called, *A Royal Affair* and Ang Lee's *Life of Pi*." The 'old' Rae would have asked Granger if he wanted to come back to her place and watch one of them but the 'new and improved' Rae stopped herself.

"I haven't seen either one but didn't *Life of Pi* win an Academy Award?"

"Ang Lee won for best director. Do you watch the Academy Awards?"

"Sure. My daughter and I watch them every year."

"It sounds like you two are very close."

Granger nodded. "Do you and Carson get along?"

"That depends. When he's sleeping, we are totally in sync with each other, but when he wakes up we're a bit of a train wreck. I think he told you that he was a vegetarian until he was nine. Peer pressure and my ex-husband pushed him to change his eating habits. When he started eating meat, I became the enemy. The grass-munching, tree-hugging hippie. I stopped fixing him dinner a few years ago because he would ridicule my meals. He's been eating what I fix now because he has no choice and, of course, he loves it. His favorite lunch is a veggie sandwich I make with tomatoes, avocado, lettuce, pickles, mustard and a sprinkle of Spike. I have to admit, it is delicious."

"It took a motorcycle accident to bring back family dinners."

"If I had only known, I would have caused it sooner." As soon as she said it, Rae regretted it.

"Huh?"

"Since this is our unofficial first date, I don't want to get too heavy, so I'll just say this and we can move on to more positive topics. My ex-husband blamed me for Carson's accident. He implied that I never should have allowed him to get a motorcycle."

"That's crazy. You know it's not true, right?"

"I do, but it doesn't stop me from playing it over and over in my head. Enough of that. Tell me about where we're going."

Granger said, "Are you sure you don't want to talk about it? You'll just owe me one heavy conversation about my ex."

"Another time. Talking about exes is way too drama-laden. Tell me about this sheep ranch where the sheep live long, happy lives."

Granger glanced over at Rae. He stretched his right arm along the top of the seat, careful not to get too close to her shoulder. He wanted to touch her but knew it was too soon.

"Margo Mayfield is an old family friend. She's an amazing woman, running the ranch, helping shear the sheep and selling what she weaves, like blankets, sweaters, socks. Her husband, Robert, died a few years ago. After he passed, she decided to stop selling the sheep. Allie and I must have made an impression on her. Anyway, the ranch sits on a bluff with an ocean view. It reminds me of Ireland."

"You've been?" said Rae.

"No, but I've seen pictures and I'd like to go. Have you?"

"Once, back in 1982. I hate to use a cliché, but it is magical. You should go. I think you'd love it."

"Then it's settled. I'm going."

Small talk took up the rest of the conversation until they arrived at Mayfield Meadows. The sun was setting over the ocean and the sky was slate gray. The air was tinged with saltwater. The temperature was at least twenty degrees cooler than Petaluma and the wind was strong.

Margo Mayfield's ranch-style home sat on the edge of a small hill. Her view was nothing short of magnificent. You couldn't hear the waves but you could see them building up and falling two, three at a time. The ocean was choppy and a dark, dark blue. As Rae and Granger were walking to the front door, Margo shouted, "Over here!" Partially hidden by the house, they could see Margo sitting in a lawn chair on the bluff about two hundred yards away. They walked past a small grove of cypress trees, their weathered trunks and branches permanently leaning away from the ocean. Two chairs were next to hers and they surrounded a round table. A picnic basket sat on top.

Bundled up in a scarf, overcoat, sunglasses and a wide-brimmed hat, Margo reminded Rae of Greta Garbo in her 'I vant to be alone' stage. She was more weathered but still had a strong jaw line and high cheek-bones. She greeted them, first hugging Granger and then giving Rae a welcoming hug.

"So nice to meet you," said Margo with a faint accent.

"You, too."

"I have a bottle of merlot that I've been waiting to try with you, Grange. I think you're going to lose."

Granger turned to Rae and said, "Margo and I love reds. We're always trying to outdo the other's selection. Last time I was here, I brought a 2005 Cakebread Merlot."

"It was marvelous, but I found a better vintage."

"Break it out, Margo," Granger said. Margo pulled the wine bottle from her basket and handed it to Granger with a corkscrew. He read the label, "Kingston Estate Merlot 2008."

"It was a great year for merlots," Margo said.

"We'll see about that." Granger opened the wine while Margo took out the wine glasses. It was chilly but Rae barely noticed. She was watch-ing Granger, trying to be discreet. She was also trying not to fall for him. So far, everything about him was perfect, from his tanned, ruggedly handsome face to his gentle sense of humor and laid back attitude. Rae knew he had imperfections: personality bruises and emotional warts, but she had yet to witness them. She would have loved to command him to expose all his flaws at once; get them all out and over with; but she knew that was impossible. Besides, if it was conceivable, she would be forced to do the same and that was not something she would be willing to do. Instead, Rae was satisfied enjoying the 'perfect Granger,' aware that it would end at some point. Margo went over to her basket and pulled out a small jar. "What goes great with red wine?"

At the same time, Rae said, "Chocolate" and Granger said, "Pot." Margo shook her head. "Rae's right and you're a bad boy. I discovered these at Whole Foods. They're raw, vegan chocolate truffles covered in crushed espresso beans." She opened the jar and held it out to Rae, who took one while Granger poured the wine.

With wine glass in one hand and a truffle in the other, they toasted. "Skoal," Margo said. She took a sip, swirled it around in her mouth and swallowed. "Mmm. Nice. I taste black cherry, plum, a little mint." She took another sip and swirled. "Vanilla, rose."

Granger looked at Rae. "Care to comment?" Rae took a sip and held it in her mouth for a few seconds and swallowed.

"I could taste the plum and the mint but I also detected some forest floor."

"Forest floor. Really?" Granger said.

"No. I read the description at Gary Ferrell Winery and have always wanted to use it." They all laughed. It was Granger's turn. He sipped, he swirled and he spoke.

"Definitely plum, a hint of mint and rose. I think this is better than the Cakebread. How do you pick them, Margo? This is your third win in a row." Granger took another sip and then bit into the round truffle. It melted in his mouth.

"Woman's intuition. Right, Rae?"

"Absolutely. Margo, could I use your restroom?"

"Of course. The front door is open and the bathroom is to your left."

"Be right back." As Rae walked toward the house, Margo said to Granger, "I like her. She has spunk."

Granger took off his cap and ran his fingers through his hair. "I like her, too. I feel so comfortable around her. She has nothing to prove, you know?"

Margo nodded. "Time will tell, but I do believe she's a keeper. It took you long enough, kid."

"I'm a slow learner."

"I consider two years slow. Six years is downright retarded."

"Margo, you are so politically incorrect."

Margo said, "I don't care. Who am I going to offend, the sheep?"

"How about me?"

"It takes a lot more than that to offend you, Grange. Living with your dad toughened you up plenty."

"Unfortunately, you're right."

Rae returned to the bluff. "Margo, your house is so lovely. I bet you wove that gorgeous blanket on the wall."

"I did indeed and thank you. Does weaving interest you at all?"

"Not really. It seems so tedious."

Margo said, "It's my meditation. Once I get into a rhythm, I can weave for hours. When Granger was a young boy, he expressed an interest in weaving, so I told him I would give him lessons."

"How did he do?"

Granger said, "I never got the chance. Once my father found out, he was adamant that no son of his was going to be a weaver. It's ironic because my brother Dale gave our dad a rug for Christmas that he had made in his weaving class in college."

"Does Dale still weave?" Rae asked.

"No, it was just an elective. I think he took it just to piss Dad off."

"Is he also in Petaluma?" Rae asked.

Margo said, "He's a doctor in San Francisco. Lives with his partner, Frank, in Pacific Heights."

"The irony is not lost on me," Rae said.

They sat on the bluff as the sun set, enjoying a great merlot, espresso truffles and inimitable company. Rae watched with admiration as Granger listened to Margo talk about her husband Robert. His attentiveness and genuine love for her was endearing. It had been so long since

Rae held company with a man of Granger's caliber, this wine enthusiast, this rancher turned animal sanctuary proprietor. This vegan cowboy.

"Was Robert your first love?" Rae asked.

"He was. I met him in college. We had the same major: animal husbandry." Margo put her hand on Granger's shoulder. "When I think about what your generation is going through with multiple divorces and online dating, I feel so lucky that I found Robert. He talked to my soul and I knew his. We were so in sync it was scary. But I never doubted that we would spend our lives together."

Rae said, "I can't even imagine that scenario. I've been married twice and dated before and after each marriage, a lot. Oops, maybe I've divulged too much." She blushed but it was too dark out to notice. "Even out the playing field, Granger. Say something revealing that you'd never discuss on a first date."

Granger didn't say anything right away, leaving Rae to wonder if he was too irritated to answer or had to dig deep in the depths of his memory to pull out a nice tidbit. Finally, he spoke. "The night before my marriage to Lydia, I was going to call it off. I knew I shouldn't have been with her, but I was too afraid of the consequences. Her parents had paid a bundle for the wedding and I didn't want to cause that kind of disruption. And…here we are."

Granger had never said it out loud before. He felt an uneasy euphoria. It was like he released a helium balloon, stuck in his gut, waiting for its escape. It was his turn to feel self-conscious. "Was that too heavy?" he said.

Margo gave him a big hug. "I always knew how you felt, Grange, but it was nice to hear it." Granger looked at Rae, "Bet you've never had a first date like this before."

"Are you kidding? This happens all the time. Guy takes you to a sheep ranch overlooking the Pacific Ocean owned by a really cool woman. She provides truffles and wine and then, just at the precise moment, my date reveals a pivotal piece of personal information. If I had a dime for every time this has happened, I'd have a shit load of dimes."

Margo smiled. "I like this girl."

Granger put his arm around Rae. "Yeah, she's a keeper."

Leaning back in her chair, Margo looked up at the dark sky filled with stars. "What if you both had the chance to experience a once-in-a-lifetime relationship? Maybe a date or two before you met, but no one after that. Till death do you part. Would you do it?"

Rae raised her hand. "I'll answer that first, if that's okay with you, Mr. Bowden."

Relieved, Granger said, "Be my guest, please."

Rae took a sip of her wine. The merlot loosened her thoughts. She felt relaxed and uninhibited. "I've thought about this before. Being the casualty of two failed marriages, a few ill-fated relationships and more bad dates than Carrie on *Sex and the City*, I would much prefer one true love for life. Let me preface my decision. I'm not talking about a partner who I've journeyed with through a drug or gambling addiction or alcoholism or infidelity and came out the other side in one slightly tattered piece, finally living in harmony and bliss. I want a Robert. A man who loved and respected me from day one and wouldn't dare deceive me. A man who was my rock, my support. Keep in mind, I've already gone the dating, relationship and marriage route. I know that it's not 'all that.' I may feel differently if I was with Mr. Marvelous, wondering what it would be like to be with someone else." Rae turned to Granger. "Your turn."

"While I agree with you on many points, I wouldn't change my life. Allie was instrumental in my change to becoming vegan, but I also think that Lydia's resistance fed my urge to oppose her and totally upend our lives. Lydia was anything but my true love but the marriage and divorce has brought me here and I'm really liking where I am right now."

"You both had great answers. Thank you for indulging me."

It was nearly ten o'clock when they said good-bye to Margo. The wind had picked up, dropping the temperature even lower, making it bitingly cold. In the truck, Rae said, "Are you okay to drive?"

"I'm fine. So what did you think of Margo. Is she amazing or what?"

"She's pretty amazing. Where's she from? I couldn't place her accent."

"She's originally from Stockholm but she came to America when she was a young girl. That's why her accent is faint."

"She reminds me of Greta Garbo. I bet she was beautiful when she was younger."

"She was and she's still is a beauty at seventy-five."

Rae nodded. "That was really fun. Thanks so much for inviting me."

"The pleasure was all mine. If you'd like, we could come back during the day and you can see the sheep. I'd also like to show you Margo's studio. Her loom is really impressive."

"I'd love that. Next time I'll bring the wine and you can bring the pot."

"I was wondering if you danced with the ganga."

"Ha! I dance, sing and play with the ganga, mon. Wait. That makes me sound like a stoner. Actually, I get high only about once a week and hardly ever during the week unless it's a holiday."

"Sounds like you come with operating instructions. Do you deviate much from the booklet?"

"Very funny. Getting high is a treat for me, like drinking. I can't remember the last time I had a glass of wine or beer by myself. How about you?"

"I don't mind having a beer or two after dinner. I get high about two to three times a week. Sometimes, I won't smoke for a month. Is that a lot?"

"I think that's acceptable behavior without going into the addictive personality category. Not to change the subject, but I'm going to. Tell me about the sanctuary."

Granger loved talking about the animals and their stories. He described their personalities and habits. He told Rae how much they enjoyed interacting with the school children when busloads would visit on their field trips. By the time he dropped her off, she had to refrain from throwing herself on him. Granger walked her to the door.

"Thanks again for a perfect evening," Rae said.

"I was going to say the same thing." Granger leaned over and gently kissed Rae. It was just long enough to feel his soft lips warm hers. Then he gave her a hug. Granger took a deep breath. "Sleep well."

"You, too. Good night," said Rae. She was euphoric. And for the first time in a very long time, she was terrified of the prospect of falling in love.

23

"You really don't eat any of these guys?" Chris asked Allie as they walked through the field of cows. It was a warm spring day and they were both in shorts and t-shirts.

"Chris."

"I'm kidding. It's a joke. Laugh."

"It's not funny."

"Where's your sense of humor?" Chris said as he ran up to one of the cows and kissed it on its side.

"Now, that's funny."

"So vegans do have a sense of humor. I was starting to worry."

Allie said, "I don't think there's anything funny about looking at another being as food. They want to live as much as you do."

"Then why do they taste so good?"

"Humans taste good, too, according to the Korowai tribe. Cannibals."

"Okay, now you're getting gross."

"We're all animals, Chris."

"I bet you taste good." Chris grabbed Allie around the waist and kissed her. "I was right."

Allie took Chris' hand and brought him to a spot far from the cows. "I want you to sit down and close your eyes. Just sit there, quietly." Allie sat down about twenty feet away and closed her eyes.

Chris complied. He sat with his eyes closed and tried to empty his mind. It was hard to do because his thoughts revolved around Allie. Slowly, the cows started to congregate around Allie and Chris, but two minutes into it, Chris got antsy and opened his eyes. As he got up, the cows scattered. Chris went over to Allie and kissed her. She returned his kiss and lay down on the grass as Chris kissed her deeply. His hands moved over her breasts and down her back.

"Moo!" Granger yelled.

They shot up and saw Granger walking toward them, wearing his tool belt and holding a tool chest in his right hand.

"Am I interrupting?" Granger said as they rose, Allie combing her hair with her fingers and straightening her shirt.

"Hey Dad. I'd like you to meet Chris Welke. Chris, this is my dad, Granger."

The two shook hands. "Nice to meet you, Mr. Bowden."

"You, too, Chris."

"Allie told me that you found Carson Tenman after the accident. I remember Carson from high school. He hung out with the stoners. Wasn't part of my group."

"Well, right now he's recovering from a broken back and ribs, so he won't be smoking pot for a while." Granger turned to Allie. "Angel and I will be fixing the roof on the cow barn. Holler if you need me."

As he walked away, Granger felt a tightening in his chest. He didn't like Chris and it wasn't because he caught the two in a pre-coital embrace. It was more instinctual than that. He didn't like the kid's energy. It was immature and ego-centric. Granger knew if he offered Allie his unsolicited opinion, she would be defensive, so he decided not to say anything. Hopefully, Allie would discover Chris' faults sooner than later.

Angel was on the roof when Granger arrived. Granger glanced at his watch. "Do you always start on time?"

"Are you always a few minutes late?" Angel replied. "Not usually." Granger steadied the ladder and climbed up on the roof. He walked over to where it needed patching. It was a hole about six inches wide. Granger bent down to examine the irregular shaped opening. "What could have caused this damage?"

Angel said, "Beats me. I saw you talking to Allie and her friend."

Granger smiled. "He's a punk but Allie likes him."

Angel opened the tool chest and extracted a sheet of tar paper. "She's a smart girl. It won't take her long to figure out he's a jerk."

"I hope you're right." Granger turned in the direction of where Allie and Chris had been but they were gone. Before his imagination got the better of him, he turned back around and started helping Angel with the roof.

"Are you expecting someone?" Angel said.

"No, why?"

Angel pointed in the direction of the parking lot. A truck pulled in and parked. The driver started honking the horn. Granger slipped off the tool belt, raced down the ladder and quickly walked over to the truck. The woman behind the wheel stopped honking and got out of the truck. She was tall and stocky with severely short strawberry blonde hair. Granger guessed she was in her early forties. In the back of the truck, grunting noises could be heard.

"This your place?"

"It is. I'm Granger Bowden." He extended his hand and she shook it.

"Pamela Truesdale. I'm hoping you can help me." She walked to the back of the truck and motioned for Granger to follow her. She pulled the truck bed cover back and there, laying on a blanket, was a pig, an American Yorkshire, the most common of the American breeds. Its back and front legs were tied together, the back left leg had an open wound and its head was covered in blood. Except for the soft grunting, it didn't move. Granger took out his cell and made a call.

"Doc, it's me, Granger. Someone just brought an injured pig to the ranch. It looks like it has head trauma. When's the soonest you can get here?" Granger listened and then said, "Great. I'll see you in a few minutes." Granger hung up and turned to Pamela. "What happened?"

"My neighbor was going to slaughter it. The jerk didn't know what the hell he was doing and was hitting this poor pig over the head with a baseball bat. I heard it screaming and came outside. I told him to stop or I was going to shoot his ass." Pamela pointed to the rifle in the gun rack. "My son came here on a field trip a few weeks ago, so when he helped me put the pig in the truck, he told me how to get here and here I am, saving the day for a pig. I knew Bob had farm animals but I didn't think the idiot would try to slaughter them himself. Isn't that against the law?"

"Yeah, it is. Let's take a look at this poor fella."

As Granger got closer to the injured animal, he spoke very softly. It wasn't even four feet long. He guessed that it weighed about eighty pounds. Its breathing was labored and when Granger put his hand on its back, it barely moved. He untied the pig's legs and then gently stroked its back while trying to assess the extent of the injury, but it was hard to tell because the blood covered his entire head. Granger took a corner of the blanket and pulled it over the pig's back.

By this time, Angel had come down from the roof and joined Granger behind the truck. When he saw the pig, he suggested that they move it into the cow barn, since it was the closest structure. While Angel readied a stall, Pamela and Granger grabbed the sides of the blanket and carried the pig into the barn. They laid it down on a bed of straw. It looked so small and frail on the ground. Angel knelt down and laid his hand on the pig's back.

Rodney, followed by another steer, walked up to the stall and stared at their new roommate. They had never seen a pig before and were clearly bemused. Rodney started to walk into the stall but Granger stopped him. "Hold on there, Rods. One false step and you can crush our newest resident."

Pamela clearly hadn't been so close to cows before and stepped back to give the two room. "They're huge! What do they weigh, about a thousand pounds?"

"Close," Angel answered. "More like twelve hundred but I don't think Rodney would hurt a fly. Granger, let him come over."

Reluctantly, Granger moved out of the way. Rodney slowly walked up to the little pig. He stopped a foot away and bent down, took a few sniffs then nuzzled the little snout. Opening its eyes, the pig made a few grunting noises and then closed its eyes. Angel, who was still sitting next to her said, "It looks like he's smiling."

When Rodney moved out of the way, it did indeed look like the pig had a contented grin on its face.

Pamela said, "Well, I'll be. It took a cow to get a reaction out of him. By the way, you can keep the blanket. It's too stained with blood. You know, my son loved coming here with his class. He kept talking about petting the cows and sheep and how nice they all were. I wonder if he met Rodney. The kid wouldn't eat meat for a week. After seeing this poor guy getting beat on, I don't know if he'll eat pork again."

"I'm glad he enjoyed the sanctuary. If he'd like to come back and visit, just have him call." Granger closed the door to the stall. "I think I just heard the vet pull up."

Granger greeted Dr. Nicols as he grabbed his medicine bag from the passenger seat. "I believe this is your first pig. Am I right?"

"Yeah, but I don't know if he's going to make it. Some idiot tried killing it by bashing its head with a bat. These backyard butchers are cropping up everywhere and a lot of them sound like sadists."

Granger introduced Pamela to the veterinarian and they followed him back to the barn. Angel was singing softly to the pig and Rodney was sitting next to him.

"Nice song, Angel."

"Gracias. My mother would sing it to me when I wasn't feeling well. The animals seem to like it." Angel got up and stood by Granger and Pamela but Rodney didn't show any inclination to leave the pig's side.

The vet realized he could either try to move a twelve hundred pound steer and risk getting stomped on or let him stay and watch the examination. The second choice was safer, so Dr. Nicols sat down on the straw and part of the blood-stained blanket and opened up his medical bag. Rodney watched with great interest as the vet cleaned the blood off the pig's head so he could see the wound site and gauge the damage. He said, "The skin is broken and it's a deep gash, but I can't tell if she suffered a fractured skull and I don't think you want to pay for an MRI." He checked her heart rate and temperature. "Her heart rate is low and temperature is elevated. It's a sow, by the way. I'm guessing around two years old. I'm going to stitch her up and then give her a dose of antibiotics. That should help with the sore on her leg as well." Dr. Nicols gave the pig a shot to numb the wound. While he waited for the local anesthetic to take effect, he looked up at Pamela. "If you're not comfortable reporting your neighbor, give me his name and I'll do it. The man obviously doesn't have a license to butcher and what he did to this poor animal is against the law."

Pamela said, "My son called the police, but thanks. I never liked Bernie. He's a son-of-a-bitch. Treats his wife like shit, too. I hope he gets jail time." Pamela looked over at the pig. "Do me a favor. If she makes it, will you name her after me?"

"That's the least I can do. Give me your number and I'll keep you updated on her, I mean, on Pamela's progress," Granger said.

Pamela took a card out of her purse and gave it to Granger. He read it out loud. "Pamela Truesdale, electrician. Don't meet many female electricians."

"My dad was an electrician. He taught me the trade when I was young and I loved it, especially troubleshooting electrical appliances. It's like a puzzle."

"Next time I need wiring done or I have a broken appliance, I know who to call."

Granger walked Pamela out to her truck and watched her drive off, leaving behind Bowden Ranch's first resident pig. He went back into the barn while the vet was finishing up and called Allie on her cell. When she picked up, he told her about the pig. She was down at the barn in less than five minutes with Chris in tow. When she saw Pamela and Rodney lying next to her, she laughed. "Rodney, are you taking care of our new resident?" Rodney just stared at her with his large, brown eyes. He exuded love and even Chris could see that Rodney's concern for the pig was genuine. Allie knelt down beside the still-anesthetized pig and stroked her belly. Pamela made soft grunting noises as if to say, 'Thanks for your kindness.'

"I don't understand how people can be so brutal."

"Lack of empathy and compassion, right Chris?" Granger looked over at Chris who was standing outside the stall with his arms crossed.

"What? I guess. You know, the guy was just trying to feed his family. He went about it the wrong way, though."

Allie looked up at Chris. "Would you raise animals and then slaughter them for food?"

All eyes were on Chris. He knew his relationship with Allie was going to be determined by his answer. "Hell no!"

Granger tried not to look disappointed. His gut told him that the kid wouldn't hesitate killing an animal for food or pleasure, but this wasn't the time to push him for the truth.

Allie said, "I didn't think so." She got up and wiped the straw off her pants and gave Chris a big hug. "Dad, I'm glad you want to keep Pamela. I hope she's the first of many."

Granger said, "I guess it was inevitable. The sanctuary's been around for about twelve years and this is the first time someone has brought in a rescue pig." He looked down at Pamela, who seemed to be sleeping. It gave Granger deep satisfaction knowing that he was providing comfort and shelter to this abused animal. He was already formulating in his mind the best location for the pig quarters.

24

Rae was on her lunch break when she called Darlene.

"I have five minutes before I have to go to a meeting," Darlene said.

"I went out with Granger last night. He is an absolute doll."

"Tell me everything!"

"Can't tell you in five minutes. You want to come over tonight for dinner?"

"Sure. Is six okay?"

"Perfect. I'll just tell you that he took me to a family friend's sheep ranch in Bodega Bay. Another 'no-kill' ranch. This unbelievable woman runs it and I have to say that Granger was nothing short of amazing. I'm completely smitten."

"Remember our pact? No falling in love until I check him out, okay?"

"Yes, ma'am."

"Gotta go. I'll see you at six. I can't wait to hear the details. You didn't sleep with him, did you?"

"No! But he did give me a goodnight kiss."

"Ooh, how was it?"

"I'll tell you tonight. Bye."

"You're such a tease."

Rae called Rebecca. They had met over eighteen years ago when Rae was pregnant with Carson. Rebecca was Rae and Stuart's Lamaze instructor. With her quick wit and great sense of humor, Rae instantly bonded with her. She and Rae became friends soon after Carson was born. A few months ago, Rebecca moved from Petaluma to San Francisco, changing professions and selling her Victorian home on Kentucky Street to live in an apartment in North Beach, the Italian section of the city. It was a radical decision but Rebecca felt like she was molting in Petaluma. "If I want to date a married man or a man thirty years my junior, Petaluma is paradise. But I don't and it's not." Obviously, she never met Granger, but then meeting a vegan wouldn't be high on her list of attributes either.

Rebecca picked up on the first ring. "Cutie Pie. What's up?"

"The man of my dreams. That's what."

"Hold it there, gal. We have a pact. No falling in love until…"

"I know. Darlene already reminded me. Don't worry. I'm not going to elope. Can I tell you about our date last night?"

"I thought you were going out next week."

"We still are but he wanted to see me before then."

"I think somebody's fallen harder than you."

"I can be really charming when I want to be." Rae went on to tell Rebecca in detail about the evening she spent with Granger. She felt like she was back in high school, jabbering on and on about a guy.

Rebecca said, "I haven't heard you this excited about a man since… since Doug."

"What a creep he turned out to be. I had a feeling he was an asshole but I went out with him anyway."

"That's because he was such a good kisser."

"Yeah. They're so hard to find, but I believe I found another one. I have to get back to work. Thanks for listening, you amazing friend, you."

"Anytime. Before you go, did he ask you out again, aside from the impending date?"

"No."

"Good. If he does, say you're busy."

"You want me to lie?"

"Rae, do not make yourself too available. Trust me on this one. If he's the one, you'll have plenty of time to be together."

"I'm fifty-eight years old and he's around the same age. One of us could have a heart attack or stroke at any moment."

"You're vegans. You'll survive Armageddon. Okay, talk to you soon. Love you, kale sprout."

"Love you too, my little parsnip. Bye!"

Rae inwardly groaned at the thought of going back to the office. She hated doing paperwork and abhorred reading the financial reviews and summarizing them for Zoe. Then she reminded herself how grateful she should be for having a job, a son who survived an accident, a house that she owned and a new man in her life that could be a keeper. To help prop her up until the work day was over, Rae resolved to head over to Best Buy and pick up a camcorder for her documentary.

The clock struck five and, not wanting to leave on the hour, Rae dawdled for about five minutes, re-arranging files on her desktop, then she turned off her computer and left.

Returning from the electronics store with a small, light camcorder, Rae opened the box and took out the camera along with the instruction manual. Her cell rang and her heart jumped, thinking it could be Granger. She looked at the cell. It was Carson. "Hey sweetie, what's up?"

"Dad wants to know if you could pick me up tonight instead of tomorrow after work. He was invited to a dinner party in San Francisco."

Rae looked at the camcorder still in her hand. If she picked Carson up, she wouldn't be able to do what she needed to without interruption. He would be her focus.

"I wish I could, but I already made plans tonight. I'll see you around five tomorrow."

"Dad's not going to be too happy."

"Tell him to give me more notice next time. Talk to you later, son. I love you."

"Love you, too."

Rae marveled at how easy it was to operate the camera. She followed Pierre as he chased Rita around the living room, then went in the backyard and filmed a blue jay using the birdbath under the locust tree. This time of year the tree was blooming and the fuchsia-colored flowers were stunning against the feathery lime green leaves. Rae was sure that this was the same jay that bathed regularly. She practiced using the zoom as the as the bright blue and white bird cleaned its body in the birdbath, then flew to one of the low branches. Again, it returned to the birdbath to spritz, then flew to a higher branch. Rae steadied the camera and pulled back to reveal the blue jay jumping into the water for the third time. As it ascended to the highest branch, it cleaned its beak on the bark then flew away. Rae caught its departure as it flew over her neighbor's house, the one directly behind the yard. After coming back into the house and shooting some more cat play, she transferred the film onto her laptop and toyed with the editing function.

Rae had downloaded a book on making and marketing documentaries. One of the first steps in the process was creating a storyboard of the film. One wall in her office was perfect for setting up a timeline. She had just started writing down the scenes on large post-its when her cell rang again. Rae looked at the number. It was Granger. As much as she wanted to speak to him, she didn't want to stop working. Also, at this early stage of her project, she wanted to tell as few people about it as possible. The phone continued to ring. She stared at his name on the screen and willed herself to be strong. Like Rebecca said, be unavailable. When the ringing stopped, Rae waited to see if Granger would leave a message. He didn't.

Once again, Rae focused on the storyboard. She wanted her first shot to be of the Petaluma Auction Yard, where every Monday morning ranchers drove into the dirt lot pulling trailers filled with animals: horses, cows, day-old calves with their umbilical cords still attached, sheep and goats. It was one of the stops along a food animal's journey to the dinner plate. Rae wrote down 'Auction Yard' and stuck it on the board. She stepped back to look at her first scene on her very first storyboard. It was a start and it filled her with a sense of pride. "Okay, scene two. How about the veal calf farm on D Street?" She wrote it down and stuck it next to the first scene. In between scene one and two, she stuck a large post-it note with a quote from Nobel Prize-winning author Isaac Bashevis Singer: 'In relation to animals, all people are Nazis; for them it is an eternal Treblinka.'

For the next three hours, Rae worked on creating as many scenes as possible, though she knew some wouldn't make the cut. She was energized by the creative process. It wasn't until Pierre jumped on the table and grabbed her pen that she looked at the clock. It was after midnight. She suddenly felt exhausted. The storyboard was far from complete, but she got a great start. Rae compiled the loose papers and post-its into a neat stack, then placed a paperweight on it so Pierre wouldn't mess it up.

As she slipped into bed, she wondered if Granger was asleep. Conjuring up his image made her heart skip a beat. She couldn't remember the last time a man had that effect on her. Part of her welcomed back her libido but the other part was scared to death of bringing a man back into her heart and her bed. She had grown accustomed to her autonomy. Normally, the internal conversation would have kept her up but she was drained and fell asleep quickly. Only Pierre stayed awake, desperately trying to move the paperweight.

25

Luckily there was a seat available next to Allie. Fran sat down behind her. She turned around and smiled, "How's the checker business?"

"It's always busy at Petaluma Market. You'd think it was the only store in town. Do you have a job?"

"Kind of. I work on our animal sanctuary a couple of days a week."

"You live on an animal sanctuary?"

"Yeah. My dad converted his cattle ranch years ago. At first, we just had cows but have since taken in horses, chickens and sheep."

"No pigs?" Fran asked.

"One. Her name is Pamela. She was slated for backyard slaughter but the neighbor of the jerk who tried to kill her saved her and brought her to us. Her best friend is Rodney, one of our oldest cows."

"Are you ever tempted to eat any of the animals?"

Allie shifted in her seat so she was directly facing him. "Do you have any pets?" Allie asked.

"Yeah, I adopted a stray cat."

"What's his name?"

"It's a girl and I named her Latté because she's white."

"Are you tempted to eat Latté?"

"Eww, no!"

"That's how I feel about the animals at our sanctuary." Allie opened her laptop and began typing, ignoring Fran.

Professor Hawley called the class to order, cutting any further discussion short. Fran knew it was a stupid question right after he said it. Allie was a hardcore vegan. The tattoo was a strong indication of her commitment to the lifestyle. He felt like an idiot.

Standing before his students, the professor announced to the class that their final was going to be the creation of a fifteen-minute documentary with a twist on an existing documentary. He gave the example of taking Michael Moore's film *Sicko*, about America's healthcare industry, and either expanding on the theme or using the same theme to explore a different aspect of healthcare. If the students didn't have access to a camcorder or couldn't afford to buy one, they had the option of creating a PowerPoint presentation. The students were to work either in teams of two or three. Allie felt a tap on her shoulder. Fran said, "You want to be on my team?"

"I don't know."

"I'm really sorry for that crack earlier. I wasn't thinking."

"Do me a favor. Think before you ask a question like that. It's one subject I'm very sensitive about."

"Got it. So...partners?"

"Fine. We could get together at my place later, if you're not working."

"It's my day off, so what time?"

Allie wrote down her address and gave it to Fran. "How about 7:00?"

"I'll see you then."

The doorbell rang promptly at 7:00. Hammerhead and Fin started barking as they joined Allie at the door. She was wearing sweats, an oversized t-shirt and fluffy socks. Her hair was pulled back in a ponytail and she wasn't wearing any make-up. Fran couldn't believe how sexy she looked. And he couldn't believe how lucky he was to be able to spend time with her.

Allie didn't attempt to hold the dogs back. They were trained not to jump on people but it didn't stop them from sniffing Fran and nuzzling his hands, coaxing him to pet them. "Don't worry, the dogs are very friendly." She led Fran into the dining room where she had the project summary on the table along with her writing tablet and laptop. Fran set down his folder and new laptop and took a seat.

"You have a cool house."

"Thanks. You want the five-cent tour or the dollar tour?"

"I'm in a spending mood. Give me the dollar tour. If it's good, there's a tip in it for you."

Allie laughed. "Now there's an incentive. Let's start right here. This is the dining room, which is easily identified by the dining room table and chairs." Allie went on to show Fran the rest of the house, avoiding the upstairs since her dad was in his bedroom and she didn't want to disturb him.

Fran was impressed. He had never been in such a luxurious home before. His parents' apartment could fit into the living room and the cottage he rented was the size of their kitchen. He took $1.50 out of his pocket and put it on the table. "Excellent tour. Thanks."

"Wow, a fifty percent tip. Maybe I should be going to tour guide school instead of SSU."

"Definitely. And don't change a thing, including your uniform."

Allie looked down at her sweats and socks. "Very funny. Let's get down to business. Do you have any documentaries in mind?" Allie sat down in one of the chairs. Fran sat across from her.

"I was thinking about it on the way over. I've never been a big fan of documentaries, but I really liked the one about the stock market crash. I think it was called *Inside Job*."

"Yeah. Great film, but that subject doesn't interest me at all. Sorry, but I'd be bored to tears. Have you heard of the movie *Earthlings*?"

Fran shook his head.

"It's about factory farming. How food animals are raised in intense confinement, plied with antibiotics and then shipped off to the slaughterhouse."

Fran should have known that Allie would want to make a documentary on animal abuse. His first inclination was to say no, but then he realized that this would be a great way to get to know her better and if, in the process, he learned more about factory farming, then so be it. "Sure. Let's do it."

Allie was waiting for a protest, so she was taken aback when Fran said yes. "Are you sure?"

"Yeah. Why not? We already have an advantage because you're so passionate about the subject matter. So what if my family disowns me for hanging out with a vegan and making a documentary that's against everything they believe in. That's their problem."

"Are you being facetious?"

"A little. So, what's the twist?"

"I haven't thought of it yet. I'm hungry, are you?"

"I could eat."

Fran watched Allie walk to the kitchen, her ponytail swinging. He glanced through the French doors to the courtyard. The outdoor lights were on. They illuminated the fountain and plants surrounding the patio. Despite their apparent wealth, Fran felt very comfortable in the home. It wasn't showy and had an air of tranquility.

Allie returned with a platter filled with crackers, cheese and chocolate. Under one arm was a bag of popcorn. She set everything down on the table and then pointed to the cheese.

"In case you're wondering, it's vegan cheese made with cashews."

Fran cautiously picked up a cube, put it on a cracker and popped it in his mouth. He was prepared to hate it, but the flavor was surprisingly good, the texture smooth.

"Not bad. Not bad at all."

Allie pointed her finger at him. "You thought it was going to be horrible, didn't you?"

"Yeah, but it wasn't. I really liked it." And to prove it, Fran ate another one.

"What if," Fran said as he picked up a piece of chocolate, "we exposed factory farming from the perspective of factory farm workers? I'm sure it's a shitty job."

Allie thought about it. "That's good. Maybe we could interview a worker. There are plenty of egg farms in Petaluma and did you know we have a chicken processing plant, too?"

"I didn't."

Allie jotted down the idea. "We could also include stories of people who have gotten sick and died from tainted meat, like that two-year-old who got e-coli from eating a hamburger. Remember that a few years ago?"

"No, but I like that angle, too. What about mad cow disease?"

"Yeah and we can show the brains of people who have died from it. I googled it when mad cow was first discovered in humans. The brain looks like a rotting, fungus-covered cauliflower. Really gross."

"I think we have the makings of an informative and visually disgusting documentary. When is this due again?"

Allie said, "June 15th. This is going to be great! Are you psyched?"

"Yeah, I guess."

"Come on, Francisco. We can really change the way people view their food."

"I'm sure I'll get stoked when we start filming. Give me time."

"Okay, I'll be patient. Let's put together a quick outline." She grabbed her Communications notebook and tore out a page. On the top she wrote 'The Chain of Death.'

"Do you mind if that's the working title?" Fran shook his head. She could have called it 'Meat Eaters Suck' and he would have been just fine.

26

Almost to the minute, the rooster crowed. Granger opened one eye and looked at the clock: 6:01. He sat up, "How the hell does he know when to crow?"

After stretching, he began his run. Tonight was his date with Rae. His pace was faster than normal and he felt buoyant as he ran down the trail. He couldn't wait to see her again. He had called her a couple of times, but she didn't answer and he didn't want to leave a message. He knew he'd see her in a few days and now the day was here. His excitement was palpable. He relived the night at Margo's every day, seeing Rae sitting on the bluff. She was so easy to talk to and treated Margo like she'd known her forever. He now understood why people who had religious convictions insisted on being with those who shared the same faith. They were in synch without even speaking. Their core beliefs were the same. He was with his own kind and it felt comfortable, effortless.

Granger decided to take Rae to his favorite restaurant, Gracias Madre, a vegan Mexican restaurant in the heart of the Mission District, San Francisco's Hispanic neighborhood. It was a dubious location considering the Mexican culture relied heavily on meat and eggs and cheese in their diet, but there it was on Mission Street flanked on either side by a taqueria and a liquor store.

Granger ran through the thick fog. On either side of the trail were scrub brush and Manzanita, its mahogany-colored limbs twisted and smooth. He inhaled deeply, enjoying the scent of wild sage and rosemary. In the distance, he spied a lone wild turkey walking on the hill. It was an odd site because they normally travel in groups. This one seemed to be enjoying the solitude. No 'mates' gobbling in his ears or hurrying him along. "Where are your pals?" Granger shouted to the turkey. It looked up and let out a gobble as it watched Granger run down the trail that disappeared into a thicket of trees.

His gait was steady and his breathing easy. As he ran toward the pasture, he heard some rustling to his left. He turned and saw about eight wild turkeys scratching the dirt, searching for food.

The air was cooler under the oaks, but he didn't mind. He was warm from running and the drop in temperature felt good on his skin.

Granger came around the bend and headed for the house. As he looked to the left, his eye caught a swath of dirt surrounded by scrub. It was the spot where his dad castrated the calves. Granger was three years old the day his dad let him witness the castration of a two-month-old calf. Evan Bowden grabbed the calf from behind and flipped him on the ground. The thud made Granger flinch. Then he took the Burdizzo clamp and affixed it to the testicles. Before the calf could wail again, he cut its testicles off with a knife, drained out the blood, sliced the membrane around the testicle and popped it out. His dad released the squirming calf. It ran into the pasture, then fell and lay there panting. Granger ran toward him, wanting to hold and comfort the baby cow, but when the calf saw the little boy coming toward him, he forced himself to get up and run away. Still unsteady on his feet, he joined a group of steers.

"He's mad at us, Daddy," Granger said as he walked back to his father.

"Can't help that, Granger." He cleaned up the remains of the calf's testicles. He handed Granger the bucket. "Now go over to the trash and dump this for me."

It still angered Granger that his father forced him to discard such contents at his young age. Instead of getting used to the workings on Bowden Ranch, Granger grew to despise it. He maintained the financial records, fixed and repaired fences, buildings and equipment but delegated the undesirable tasks like castration, branding and visits to the auction yard to his staff. If it weren't for Allie, Granger wondered if he'd still be a rancher.

The waitress at Ciao Bella showed Rae and Darlene to the outdoor patio's corner table for lunch. They both ordered a glass of chianti. It was Saturday and they were celebrating Rae's approaching date. Rae closed her eyes and tilted her head toward the sky. The sun felt good.

"What the hell are you doing? Little tiny wrinkles are forming under your skin as we speak."

Rae looked at Darlene. "Really, twenty seconds of direct exposure?"

"That's what Mother Theresa said and look at her."

Rae said, "I would but last time I checked she died and she was like 130 years old."

"She would have looked a lot younger if she had worn sunscreen while tending to the poor, sick and crippled. So, what are you going to wear tonight for the big date with the big hottie?"

"I was thinking about…"

"Hold that thought," Darlene said as she picked up the menu. "Let's figure out what we want first."

"Yes, ma'am. You seem more nervous about this date than me."

Darlene put down the menu. "I just want Granger to be the one, you know? You've had such bad luck with men and I want him to show you that there are still some great guys out there."

Rae hugged Darlene and tears welled up in her eyes. "You're so sweet. I know there are many amazing men in this world. Peter's a perfect example."

Darlene looked down at her lap. "Sometimes."

The waitress brought the women their glasses of wine, then took their order.

"Is there trouble in paradise?" Rae said. She was about to take a sip of her wine but Darlene stopped her. She lifted her glass and Rae did the same. "To Rae and Granger. May they always have plenty of kale and tofu…and love."

Rae took a sip and put her glass down. "So, what's up with you and Peter?"

"We got into a fight the other night because I think he smokes too much pot. He said as long as it doesn't interfere with his work, he's fine. The problem is, it interferes with our relationship. He's an amazing trial lawyer but when he's home, he gets stoned and then I have 'Dude, Where's My Car' sitting on the couch eating potato chips and drinking beer."

Rae thought about her conversation with Granger the other night. Darlene must have sensed that something was wrong. She took a large sip of her wine and said, "You look strange. What's the matter?"

"It's nothing."

"A furrowed brow isn't nothing. Talk to me."

"Granger said he likes to get high and drink a few beers two to three times a week. Should I be concerned?"

"If he's telling the truth, I don't think it's a big deal, do you?"

"No. I'll keep an eye on it, though. So, are you still in fight mode?"

"Kind of. He doesn't get it and I don't want to spend my life with someone who thinks that the perfect night is watching testosterone-driven movies, like *X-Men-The Last Stand*, and taking hits from a bong. I feel like I'm back in high school. I don't know what to do. I'm verklempt."

"And here I thought that you two were the perfect couple."

"Ha! Is there such a thing?" Darlene said.

"I'll let you know. Stay tuned."

The waitress returned with two heaping plates of pasta primavera. As they ate, Darlene said, "Remember what you told Steven about why you don't eat meat?"

"How could I forget?"

"Why haven't you told me how you feel?"

Rae put down her fork and wiped her mouth with the napkin. "When I first read about how food animals were treated, I felt tremendously guilty for eating meat. I couldn't even fathom the hell they were going through and I was financing it. I figured that, once I told people what I learned, they would react the same way. I was in for a rude awakening. Most didn't want to hear about it and the ones that did distanced themselves from me. My sister-in-law took it a step further. She called me a fucking self-righteous bitch."

"No way."

"Yeah, she did. Even though I didn't deserve that title, I clammed up. I didn't want to isolate my friends or family. I hoped that my lifestyle would influence people to change their eating habits. To date, very few people I know have adopted a plant-based diet. That's why I haven't said anything to you, but now that you broached the subject, would you be open to knowing how factory farmed animals are treated?"

Darlene shifted uneasily in her seat. "I love meat and eggs and cheese. I love cheese, but yes, lay it on me. If I'm supporting the industry, I should at least know what goes on."

Rae almost started crying. "Thank you! You don't know what that means to me."

"I didn't say I was giving up meat...and cheese."

"I know but you're taking a big step and I thank you for it." Rae raised her glass. Darlene followed suit. "To the animals."

Darlene said, "To the animals."

An hour later, as the women were ready to leave, Darlene held up her hand and said, "You have some food on your front tooth."

Rae rubbed the tooth with her finger. "Is it gone?" Darlene nodded.

"As I get older, my teeth have become food magnets. No wonder I'm hungry all the time. Most of the food doesn't make it to my stomach."

Darlene laughed. "Calm down, missy. It was only a piece of...wait a minute, is that a tomato on your bicuspid? You're like a walking buffet. One more thing to look forward to as I age. Maybe it's a good thing that Peter's high around me. He won't notice me devolving into an old lady."

"Are you calling me an old lady?"

"No way. You know I think you're beautiful, magnet teeth and all. I was just saying that aging can be traumatic."

"You know what Bette Davis said? Old age ain't for sissies."

"Right on, Bette."

Granger was picking Rae up in half an hour and she was beyond nervous. Every time she passed a mirror she thought she looked older than the time before. Every insecurity she felt about herself was intensified. Her marionette lines seemed deeper, the upper lip lines more exaggerated and she didn't find anything amusing about her laugh lines. She needed an ego boost fast. As she got dressed, she attached the blue tooth to her ear and dialed Rebecca. Upon answering, Rebecca started singing a song from Westside Story. "*Tonight, tonight won't be like any night. Tonight there will be no shining star!*"

"Very nice, but I need to unleash a torrent of insecurities and get them out of my system before Mr. Gorgeous arrives."

"You got it all wrong. You're supposed to recite positive affirmations not negative crap, otherwise you'll greet him at the door feeling like Yoda. I'm sure you look beautiful."

"Hmmm, freaking out I am. He's going to see me and wonder why he asked me out. Maybe I should take one of Carson's Percocets. At least I'll feel better."

"Rae, darling, if I was there, I'd slap you and tell you to shape up, but since I can't, I want you to repeat after me, 'I am beautiful inside and out.' Say it."

Rae mumbled, "I am beautiful inside..."

Rebecca interrupted her and yelled, "Loud and clear, missy. Do it."

"I am beautiful inside and out!"

"Again."

"I am beautiful inside and out. I am beautiful inside and out. Okay, I can do this. I can go out with Granger, the sexiest cowboy on the planet and feel good about myself."

"Hallelujah and pass the butter...I mean organic non-hydrogenated margarine. Do you know where he's taking you?"

"He said it was a surprise."

"I want to be the first person you call tomorrow. Understand? I earned it."

"Definitely. I gotta get ready. You're the best."

"Bye, dumpling."

"Bye, my little rutabaga."

Rae put on her favorite earrings. They were small, multi-colored fleur-de-lis. Then she put on her amethyst heart necklace. Taking a deep breath, she looked at herself in the full length mirror. She adjusted her underwear, attempting to eliminate the panty line and then the doorbell rang. Rae's heart started to pound. She started reciting 'I am beautiful inside and out' in her head like a mantra. She felt her confidence increase slightly. When she opened the door and saw Granger, her heart almost stopped. She realized that he made a big effort to look this good. For her. He was wearing black jeans and a cream colored western shirt with pearlite snaps. His cowboy boots and bomber jacket were dark brown. He even had on a bolo tie.

"You look beautiful," Rae said.

Granger laughed. "Isn't that my line?"

"You can use it, too, if you like."

"Rae, I must say that you look beautiful."

"Thank you." She closed the door behind her and Granger opened the door to his car, a deep green late model Mercedes Benz. Surprised, she said, "Is this your car?"

"Yes and so is the truck. I also have a more reliable truck and a jeep that I drive around the property. Did you think that the beater truck was my good vehicle?"

Rae nodded. "Guilty as charged."

"And you still went out with me."

"I'm not a snob."

"Did it change your opinion of me at all?"

Rae re-positioned herself and looked directly at Granger. "I will admit that seeing you drive up in that faded blue, rusty truck was a little disappointing at first, but knowing that you're spending your life saving animals, you could have picked me up on a tractor with straw in your teeth and I would have been just fine, as long as you had all your teeth."

Granger shook his head. "You're going to have to stop answering like that."

"Why?"

"Because you're sounding way too perfect."

"Ha! That's a laugh," Rae said, thinking about her errant face hairs, flabby belly and thorough lack of self-confidence.

"Would you like to expound on that?"

"Another time. So, where are you taking me?"

"Gracias Madre in the city. Have you been there?"

"No, but I've heard great things about it. Is it true that their vegan flan is to die for?"

"I don't know. I've always been so full that dessert was out of the question. We'll have to try it tonight. You with me?"

"Absolutely."

"Good. How's Carson doing?"

"He seems to improve every day. He's close to ditching the walker and he's taken to wearing the brace on the outside of his shirt. I think it's his way of letting people know that his injury isn't permanent and that he's not mentally disabled as well. Boys and their testosterone. I bet if you looked at their blood under a microscope you'd see little guns and knives floating around."

"It's a good thing you don't generalize."

"Come on. Hollywood doesn't make action blockbusters for us gals."

"True, but not all men are like that." Granger turned to Rae and gave her a big Cheshire cat grin.

"How did you turn out to be so sensitive and compassionate growing up on a cattle ranch? What's your story, Mr. Bowden?"

"I'll give you the abridged version and if you'd like, I'll tell you more another time. It all boils down to growing up with a father who demanded his two sons work the ranch. Dale hated it and flat out refused to make it his livelihood. Becoming a doctor and living in the city with his partner, Frank, is about as far from cattle ranching as you can get. I also hated it. I couldn't stand seeing the cows suffer and being shipped to the slaughterhouse but I wasn't as strong as Dale, so when my dad told me to take over the ranch, I did. By that time, I was numb to the suffering. Then one day, Allie came home from school and declared she was never eating meat again. They had someone speak to the class about animal rights and factory farming. I saw the pain in my eight-year-old's face and her conviction was so absolute. Something inside me clicked. We both became vegan that day. I stopped selling the cows and eventually turned the ranch into a sanctuary. Lydia, my ex-wife, was the only creature who wasn't happy about the whole transition. She was miserable. A year later we divorced. And that's the way it is."

"I think what you've done is fantastic and Allie sounds like a wonderful person."

"She is," said Granger. "It's your turn. When did you stop eating meat?"

"I'm going to give you the super long version." Rae waited for Granger's reaction, but he just nodded. "I'm kidding. I'll try to make it as succinct as your story. Let's see, I was thirty-four when I read, *Diet for a New America* by John Robbins. I became a strict vegetarian while I was reading the book, so no animal flesh or eggs but every once in a while I would eat cheese or put milk in my coffee at a restaurant if they didn't have soymilk. Almost three years ago I couldn't ignore the dairy industries' treatment of their cows and the male offspring, so I graduated to becoming a vegan. When Carson decided to start eating meat, it was like a knife through the heart but I was powerless to do anything about it, especially since he was with his dad forty percent of the time."

"How long have you been divorced?"

"Twelve years."

"Did you re-marry?" Granger asked.

"Nope. And only had one boyfriend and that lasted six months."

"Your dating history is as scarce as mine."

Rae looked over at Granger. "What's our problem?"

"Who said we had a problem? Maybe we haven't found Mr. and Mrs. Right. Yet."

"I think you're right."

"I think you're right, too." Rae suddenly felt self-conscious. She changed the subject, asking Granger about growing up and living in Petaluma. They moved on to the topic of raising kids and before long, they were crossing the Golden Gate Bridge. Granger took Lombard to Van Ness and then made a right onto Mission Street. He had to slam on his brakes to avoid a car turning left right in front of him. At a light, the car he was behind decided to turn left. "I swear, it's like driving in a pinball machine." He finally found a parking space and they walked a few blocks to Gracias Madre.

The waitress seated them at a table in the rear of the restaurant. It was quiet and private. On the wall was a mural of the Virgin Mary, arms open, rising above the city of San Francisco.

Rae opened the menu and couldn't help but comment on how exciting it was to be able to eat everything at a Mexican restaurant. Granger laughed. "That's exactly how I felt when I first ate here. My favorite is the Quesadillas de Camote: sweet potato and caramelized onions folded into tortillas with cashew nacho cheese and pumpkin seed salsa. I'm also a fan of the Enchiladas con Mole: spicy mole enchiladas topped with mushrooms and cashew cheese. It also comes with sautéed greens and beans."

"I'm going to get the quesadillas."

"And I'll get the enchiladas. Do you want something to drink? They have Eel River Beer on tap. And it's organic."

"Very cool."

"Everything here is organic, vegan and blessed by the Virgin Mary."

The food was excellent. Rae and Granger never seemed to run out of things to talk about. She found him funny and irreverent. He asked her questions about her family and actually listened to her answers. When it was time for dessert, they split the flan. It was divine, with its delicate flavor and creamy texture. Rae was sure the night couldn't get any better.

Granger pulled up to Rae's house. She wanted to invite him in but she didn't want him to get the wrong idea. She was madly attracted to him but wasn't ready to have sex. It had been so long since she'd been with a man sexually that she was afraid her body would malfunction and this wonderful relationship would end before it even began. Still, she felt it would be rude not to ask him.

"Would you like to come in for a drink or a cup of tea?"

"Thanks but I have to get up super early tomorrow. Can I take a rain check?"

"You can take a rain and a sun check. Thanks so much for a lovely evening. I had a wonderful time."

"You're very welcome. Let's do it again soon." Granger leaned over and kissed Rae. It was tender and strong at the same time. Rae felt the same wave of energy travel down her body the first time they kissed, but this kiss was longer and she kissed him back. He cradled her head in his hand as his other hand moved to the small of her back. It had been so long since Rae felt anything for a man that she wasn't used to being aroused. She couldn't get enough of Granger's scent, his touch, his body. When they stopped kissing, they looked into each other's eyes and they knew. This was not bigger than both of them. This is what they'd both been waiting for and it only took fifty-eight years.

Granger said, "I'd really like to see you again."

"I think that can be arranged."

"I'll call you."

"Okay. Good night."

"Good night." Granger watched Rae walk up the stairs to her front door and made sure she got in safely before he drove away. It was as if every system in his body was on overdrive. His heart was pounding and his stomach was in knots, but he felt euphoric. The last time Granger felt this strongly about anyone was when he was in elementary school. His nine-year-old classmate, Susie Hepner, kissed him in the cloak room. He never felt this way about Lydia. He was in love with her but the connection was never this potent. He wondered if Rae felt the same way. He thought he saw it in her eyes, but wasn't sure.

Granger wanted to call his brother, his mother and Margo and tell them about Rae, but it was after eleven and instead of sharing in his joy, they'd be pissed. He was hoping Allie was still up. He had to tell somebody.

27

Rae didn't remember touching the ground when she left Granger's car. Instead, she seemed to float up the stairs and into her home. She was so smitten by him that she was terrified she would resort to her old self and get lost in his life, his expectations and his needs. She would comply so as not to upset him and lose his favor. 'Snap out of it!' Cruella yelled, jolting Rae out of her internal blabbering. From that moment, Rae vowed to be true to herself no matter what the cost. She had always prided herself on having a non-addictive personality but she realized, when it came to men, that wasn't true. In every relationship, she felt compelled to defer to her significant other. It wasn't going to happen with Granger, but she also knew she couldn't do it on her own. Rebecca and Darlene would be her 'evolutionary partners,' guiding her back to herself when she strayed into the co-dependent zone. Satisfied with her decision, Rae was now free to fantasize as much as she wanted about Granger. It was going to be a long night.

Stuart dropped Carson off at Rae's a little past nine the next morning. She was in the kitchen, reading the Sunday paper and enjoying Meyer lemon and rosemary toast and a mug of coffee when Carson walked in carrying a bouquet of irises.

"Happy Mother's Day. Dad bought these for me to give to you, just so you know."

"Thanks, sweetie." She gave Carson a tentative hug and kiss. "How's your back?"

"Broken," Carson replied.

"Shit! When did that happen?"

Carson gave his mom 'the look' and then grabbed her toast off the plate and started eating it. She shook her head and got the bread out of the refrigerator. "Didn't you say you were going to the beach with your dad yesterday?"

"Yup."

"How was it?"

"Fucking freezing, but we walked a little anyway. Then we ate at the Station House Café. I had a monster burger with bacon." He watched for his mom's reaction but he got none. Instead, Rae said, "I love that restaurant. They have great garlic fries."

"That's what Dad got. Boner's coming over to hang out." Slowly, Carson walked down the stairs to his bedroom. Rae watched him go and shuddered to think that inside her son's body were rods and screws holding his spine together. She was so grateful that he wasn't paralyzed and he didn't suffer brain damage. Their lives would be very different if he had.

After putting the irises in a vase, Rae settled back into her chair. She picked up the local section of the paper and started reading it when her cell rang. She was hoping it was Granger. She looked at the caller ID and smiled.

"Hi."

"Good morning," Granger said. "Did you sleep well?"

"Like a baby."

"I never understood that expression. When Allie was a baby, she woke up every night crying. If a fly got too close to her crib, she'd wake up."

"Carson, on the other hand, slept through a remodel. He took a nap while roofers used a nail gun over his room. So, did you sleep like baby Allie or baby Carson?"

"Baby Allie."

Rae said, "Poor baby!"

"I'm fine. My evening with you made up for it."

Rae blushed. "Thank you."

Granger intended to talk to Rae for a while before asking her out again but before he knew it, he was blurting it out. "Are you free tomorrow? I was hoping you and Carson could come by the ranch. I'd like to show you around."

"I have to work tomorrow but I'm off at five. Won't it be too dark by the time we have dinner and come over?"

"How about if I fix you dinner? You could come over around 5:30 and I'll give you the exclusive guided tour and then we'll eat."

"That sounds great. Hold on while I ask Carson."

Rae went to her son's room and asked him if he'd like to visit the ranch. Barely looking up from his video game, he nodded. "We're on."

"It's set then." They continued talking for another half an hour.

Rae walked into work fifteen minutes late. She was always punctual, but taking care of Carson brought up unexpected requests and chores that weren't part of her normal repertoire. Zoe was at the water cooler. She looked at Rae and then the clock.

"I know. I'm sorry. You don't want to know what I had to do for Carson. Do you want me to pick up where I left off on Friday, calling clients?"

"Don't bother."

"Okay." Rae walked over to her desk and turned on her computer. She noticed the blinds were up.

"Don't bother sitting down, either. I don't think this is working, Rae. I need you to be here on time and lately, that's not happening. When you are here, you seem distracted and scattered."

Rae was dumbfounded. She didn't see this coming by a long shot. She walked back over to Zoe.

"Zoe, Carson was in an accident a little over a month ago. I've been taking care of him, so if I seem distracted maybe that's why, but I've done all my work."

"Not on time and I've had to answer the phone until you get here, which is supposed to be at nine. I need your undivided attention when you're here. It's best if you leave now. Today would be a waste of time."

"I don't believe this. You're firing me without any warning? What's the matter with you?"

"I'm running an office, Rae, and I want it to run efficiently and smoothly and that's just not happening." Zoe went over to her desk and picked up an envelope. She handed it to Rae. "This is your last paycheck. Good luck."

Rae took the envelope and, without saying another word, she left. She was approaching the stairs when she turned around and walked swiftly back to the office. "I think you should know that working for you has been a miserable experience. You never showed any concern over my son's accident. He didn't break a leg, Zoe, he broke his fucking back. He can't get out of bed without my help. One of your clients that I've never met offered to fix dinner for me but you wouldn't lift a goddamn finger. I had my suspicions but you just confirmed it. You are by far the most realistic robot I've ever seen. Do the next person you hire a favor and open the blinds behind their desk. It's something humans do for each other." Rae walked out of the office again, for good.

Rae's mind was racing. It was hard for her to concentrate. Zoe's words resonated in her head: 'This is your last paycheck. Good luck.' The last paycheck. After three years of walking through that door and forcing herself to co-exist with Zoe, working on projects that bored her to distraction, she was free. It was a relief, but from a financial stand-point it was frightening. She berated herself for not attempting to find a man that was loaded and could take care of her for the rest of her life. Then she berated herself for thinking that way.

Instead of going home, she walked down the street to Evolution Coffee, ordered a tall almond milk latté and sat in the corner trying like hell to figure out her next move. She had taken an assessment of her financial assets when she decided to make the documentary. Rae figured she could live off her IRA and savings account for a little over a year, but she'd be penalized for withdrawing on the IRA too soon. Unemployment would help, but she wasn't sure if being fired disqualified her from collecting. If she was able to receive it, it would pay for a little over half of her expenses. If Rae started looking for another job, it would take away from the time and energy she wanted to expend on the documentary. On her wall in the guest room was a greeting card. Rae had taped it there two years ago because she loved the quote: 'Sometimes the only available transportation is a leap of faith.' It was a lofty goal for Rae since she made sure that, for every action she initiated, there was a safety net. However small, she knew it would catch her if she fell. But a safety net also caught her dreams, entangling them. Stopping them from even starting.

Rae sipped on her latté and perused the room. Most of the patrons were on their laptops, ear buds in place and fingers deftly moving over the keyboards, completely unaware of the person less than two feet away. Some were students and others possibly aspiring writers. She was envious of all of them. Well, except for the white kid with blonde dreadlocks. Each dread looked like a huge, hairy grub. And they were on his head. Disgusting. Rae re-focused. Her mind returned to the quote. She needed to believe in herself. She needed to trust her instincts. If not now, when? Rae borrowed some paper from a young girl sitting in front of her. She wrote down 'Eating Animals. Eating Agony: a documentary by Rae O'Brien.' Working title. It's what popped into her head. For the next three hours, Rae continued to plot out the film. She listed all the sanctuaries she knew of in the surrounding area, as well as the places animals were sold, slaughtered and rendered.

By noon, the initial shock of being fired started to wear off. Rae felt lighter, more receptive to her new identity: unemployed single female. It was as if a thin film was rubbed off her mind. It was time to use a new mode of transportation. She could tell Cruella was smiling, giving her the thumbs-up.

Carson and Jarod were in the living room watching *Caddyshack* when Rae walked into the house.

Carson looked up at the clock. It was 12:15. "What are you doing home?"

"I kind of got fired." Carson paused the movie.

"No way."

"Yes way, but don't worry. Everything's going to be fine. Do me a favor and don't say anything to Granger, okay?" Carson nodded.

"I never liked Zoe. She reminds me of a cyborg."

"I know. I told her she was the most realistic robot I've ever seen." Carson and Jarod laughed.

"What happened?" Jarod said. Rae recounted the conversation then she went into the kitchen and fixed them lunch.

As Rae approached Granger's driveway, they both instinctively looked over at the accident site. Expecting to see a bare patch where Carson had landed, the spot was alive with color. A white rose bush was surrounded by pink and white striped, purple, red and yellow petunias. Behind the flowers, on the fence, hung a wooden angel.

"Wow, it looks like one of those memorials when people put bouquets of flowers on the spot where someone died. It's kind of spooky, especially the angel," Carson said.

"I think it's a lovely sentiment. Wouldn't you rather see that instead of the barren site where you could have been paralyzed or killed?"

"I guess. Aren't white roses your favorite?"

"Uh huh."

"I think my Madre has an admirer."

Rae turned left onto Granger's property. On either side of the driveway were pine trees interspersed with buckeyes and purple azaleas. There were rose bushes displaying flowers in deep reds, yellows and oranges. Rae rolled down the window and drove slowly so she could take in all the scents. The long road continued up a hill and as she came around the bend, the sight of the Mediterranean-style home made her gasp. It was like entering a sub-tropical oasis: the two-story stucco home was off-white with dark brown shutters. The red tile roof sported four chimneys, one with smoke wafting out of it, the smell mixing with the star jasmine, lilies and gardenias. "So this is what paradise looks like," Rae said as she parked the car next to a date palm tree.

"Yeah, it's sick," said Carson as he slowly got out of the car, the brace forcing him from making a graceful exit. The view was panoramic. Rae could see an outcropping of buildings she guessed were the animals' quarters. She turned to her left and caught a sweeping view of the valley and rolling hills.

They walked up to the Mexican tile entryway, a grouping of five palm trees to their right and a seven-foot fern to their left, its fronds lightly sweeping an azalea bush. The double wide antique oak door had two wrought iron knockers in the shape of iguanas. Rae grabbed one and knocked. "I'll get it," Allie yelled. Seconds later, she opened the door and welcomed them inside.

"I sure have heard a lot about you two. I'm Allie."

The entryway was the size of Rae's dining room, opening up to a spacious living room on the right and a stairway directly in front. Each riser had different patterned tiles and the wrought iron banister was topped with dark walnut. Aztec-style rugs covered the floors. Directly above them was a wrought iron chandelier, adorned with candles. Rae half expected to see Granger ride up on a steed, wearing his black Stetson and stellar smile, but instead he walked down the stairs looking every bit as handsome as she remembered. She would have loved to give him a big hug and kiss, but thought better of it.

"Nice entrance, Mr. Bowden. Have you been practicing?"

"All day long."

"I've got to tell you, your home is exquisite. I bet you even have a courtyard in the middle," Rae said.

"As a matter of fact..." Granger pointed the way and they followed him through the living room and French doors into a lush outdoor courtyard, surrounded by the house. In the middle of the patio was a fountain in the shape of a lotus flower. Copper patina lily pads came out of the sides of the flower's stem, water cascading over them and into the pool where more copper lily pads floated on the water. A turquoise café table and chairs sat on the flagstone patio. There were large pots of ferns, impatiens, petunias and dinner plate dahlias in deep red. One side of the house was covered in passion flower vines. Rae was in awe and even Carson was impressed.

"So gorgeous. By the way, we really like the flowers you planted where Carson had the accident."

"I'm glad you like it. I thought it might look too much like a memorial."

Carson said, "I thought so, too."

Rae shot Carson a dirty look. Granger noticed. "Hey, he's right but it's a hell of a lot nicer looking at roses and petunias than a dirt patch where you busted up your back, right?"

"Totally. Where'd you get the angel?"

Granger said, "My good friend and employee who works on the ranch, Angel, is a wood carver. Angels are his specialty. Go figure. So, are you ready to take the tour?"

"Yes, but I have this urge to stay right here and drink an espresso," said Rae.

Granger laughed. "You can do that later, I promise. First you have to go on the tour. I thought we could ride in the Jeep. The ranch is pretty big and some of the paths aren't paved. I think it would be too much walking for you."

Carson agreed. They followed Granger out to the side of the house where the Jeep was parked.

"Is this the house you grew up in?" Rae said.

"Yes, but I had it remodeled about ten years ago. I've always admired the Mexican-style architecture. This house used to be a ranch-style. It took about two years to transform it."

"You lived through a two-year remodel?"

"Thankfully, no. Allie and I lived in one of the bungalows on the property. One of my employees lives there now. Here we are."

As they piled into the Jeep, Hammerhead and Fin came running toward them and jumped into the back seat. Granger was going to kick them out but Carson insisted that they stay. He just had to make sure they didn't jump on him. Granger followed the driveway about two hundred yards, then made a left onto a smaller paved road. He drove past three bungalow-style homes on the right and came to a lot, where he parked as close to the first barn as possible.

"This is the cow barn where all the cattle from the original ranch live. The younger ones were bought at auction as calves." As Granger was leading them up to the gated entrance, a few of the cows that hadn't gone to the fields walked toward them. A trio of three calves came trotting up behind them.

Carson said, "Why did you buy more cows?" Granger opened the gate and walked in followed by Rae and Carson. Granger went over to the calves. They rubbed up against him and he stroked their backs.

"When males are born in a dairy they're of no use to the farmer, unless he also runs a veal calf farm, so he takes the day-old calves to the auction, sometimes they still have their umbilical cords attached."

"No way," said Carson.

"Unfortunately, it's true. Some of the babies don't make it and are thrown in the corner of the auction yard affectionately called the dead pile. If a calf survives and is auctioned off, they don't go for very much and if I'm there, I buy them."

It was obvious the cows loved Granger. It was as if they knew he rescued them. They nuzzled his legs and followed him as he took Carson and Rae inside the barn. Angel was raking hay into the stalls. He stopped when he saw them walking his way. Granger put his arm around Angel. "This is Angel Lago, wood carver extraordinaire. He does all the crap I don't like to do and more. Angel, this is Carson and his mother, Rae."

"You're the one who had the accident on Bodega, right?"

"That's me." Carson put out his hand and shook Angel's. "Your angel sculpture is really cool."

"Thank you. I'm so glad you're walking." He shook Rae's hand.

"Are you a vegan, Angel?" Rae asked.

"Not when I first started working here, but I am now. The animals are my friends. I don't eat my friends. Of course my other friends, human friends, think I'm crazy."

"That's the cross we vegans have to bear but it's getting a lot better. More and more people are becoming vegan," Rae said.

"Except my friends! It was nice meeting you both." Angel resumed his raking. Carson and Rae said good-bye and the three of them headed out the back of the barn. To their right was the chicken coop.

"I remember this when I came here with my class. Sick!" Carson said. The chickens were out front pecking at the ground and roosting under bushes. Carson walked ahead of them, eager to get a better look. Granger touched Rae on the shoulder, gently squeezing it. He spoke low so Carson couldn't hear.

"I'm so glad you came here today."

"Me, too."

"Granger, what do you do with all the eggs since you don't eat them?" Carson said.

"Good question. I donate them to COTS, the homeless shelter, but these hens are older and they don't lay nearly as many as they used to. We probably get five a day."

"Does Angel take care of the chickens, too?" Carson asked.

"Angel, Jake and Lucy live on the ranch and they all share the animal duties. Allie and I do, too. Stephanie, a student at SSU, was also working here but she just gave her two-week notice."

"Good timing," said Carson. "You can hire my mom. She just got the axe today."

"Carson!" Rae was mortified. She wasn't planning on telling Granger that she lost her job just yet. She wanted to wait until she had a succinct plan in hand.

"I'm so sorry to hear that, Rae."

"I guess it's for the best. I hated that place and planned on leaving but getting fired was totally unexpected. Can we talk about this later? I hate to ruin our tour."

"Of course," Granger said, but in his mind the wheels were turning.

From the chicken coop, they walked to the sheep barn and then the horse stables. By that time, Carson's back was getting sore, so Granger went back to get the Jeep. As he walked to the parking lot, he thought about the prospect of Rae working on the ranch. He would love having her there. He knew couples that happily worked together but he also knew how deadly it could be for a relationship, especially one as young as theirs. He'd talk to her about it after dinner, if he could get her alone.

Granger continued the tour by driving them on the property's paved roads so the ride was smoother. He took them up to Cougar Pond, along the creek and over the hills into another valley.

By the time they returned to the house, they were famished. Granger showed them into the dining room and then he helped Allie bring out the food: Salad, vegan eggplant parmesan and garlic bread. Granger poured a glass of merlot for Rae and himself. The conversation was light and the topic of Rae's unemployment wasn't brought up. For dessert, they had red velvet cupcakes.

"How am I going to top this when you two come over to our house for dinner?" Rae said.

"I'm sure you'll think up something amazing," Granger said. "And if not, I'll make Allie cook."

"You pimping me out, Dad?" They laughed. "Actually, I love to cook, so I wouldn't mind at all."

Rae looked over at Carson. He looked tired. "How are you doing, honey?"

"I'm kind of fading. It's been a long day."

Granger was trying to figure out how he could get Rae alone. Allie must have read his mind. She said to Carson, "Before you go, I think you'll like to see this. It won't take long, okay?"

"Sure." Carson got up slowly and followed Allie out of the room.

Rae walked up to Granger. "So, you finally got me alone. What do you plan to do with me in five minutes?"

Granger put his arms around her and gave her a big kiss. "I've been wanting to do that all day."

"So have I. Except for getting fired, this has been a fantastic day."

"About that. How would you feel about working here? I think you'd be great conducting tours for the school children."

Rae's initial reaction, her gut instinct, was to tell him that it was too soon in their relationship, but working with the animals in an idyllic setting and being able to see Granger all the time was very tempting.

"Why don't we talk about it later?"

"Sure, but think about all the espressos you could enjoy in the court-yard, surrounded by plants and me." Granger kissed her again and she felt her knees weaken.

"This is by far the best job interview I've ever had," Rae said.

Carson and Allie came back to the room. Carson said, "Allie showed me the sickest spider. It's like this big." Carson held his hands about three inches apart.

"Better you than me, kiddo. Well, I hate to say it, but we have to go. Thank you both again so much."

"Yeah, thanks a lot," said Carson.

"Anytime, right Al?"

"Sure," said Allie.

After Rae and Carson left, Allie said to her dad, "Well I can certainly see why you like Rae. She's so funny and pretty. Brokeback Carson is a nice guy too, or maybe it was the Percocet. Did you offer her the job?"

"I did. She wants to think about it." Allie gave her dad a kiss. "I still have some homework to do. Night, Papa."

"Good night, Al. Thanks for cooking a great dinner."

"My pleasure. Maybe sometime in the not too distant future, someone else will be cooking for us." She gave her dad a sly smile and went to her room.

Granger stacked the dishes by the sink. Hammerhead stretched his long body next to Granger's feet. The view from the kitchen was panoramic but this time of night it was all but pitch black. During the day, he would focus his attention on a lone oak tree. Some of its branches hung a few feet from the ground. It was a favorite spot for squirrels and lizards. The upper branches welcomed hawks, crows and other birds. Granger was particularly fond of a couple of blue jays that sat on the very top branch almost every morning. The jays would squawk for up to an hour. Their incessant, staccato shriek sounded like they were squabbling. He liked to think that they were old friends, indulging in their daily argument, not a married couple arguing about close to everything.

Granger missed Rae already. He enjoyed their repartee and her sense of humor. He admired her relationship with Carson, despite her frustration over his snarky attitude. He was a teenager, a typical teenager. Hopefully, he'd grow out of it.

Finishing the dishes, Granger sat down in the living room. He put his feet up on the coffee table, closed his eyes and bathed his senses in the music. He hadn't felt this content in a long time.

28

The timing was perfect. Rae was desperate to talk to a friend about her work dilemma and Darlene was free for lunch. They met downtown at Zazzle and, as soon as they ordered, Rae started telling Darlene about Granger's home, the sanctuary tour and the job offer.

"Very sticky situation, Rae. Do you want him to be your boss, telling you what to do? Think about it."

"I have thought about it. A lot." Rae pulled a sheet of paper out of her purse. On it, she listed the pros and cons of working for Granger. She started reading the positive aspects first. "I wouldn't have to expend the energy and time looking for another job, which would give me more time to work on the documentary. Did I tell you I bought a camcorder? It fits in the palm of my hand. It's so cute! Anyway, another plus is not living off my IRA or deferred compensation. I'd get penalized for early withdrawal and, if I do end up alone and extremely bitter, I won't have any savings. I'll probably have to move in with you."

"God forbid!" said Darlene. "Keep going."

"I'd be working with animals and giving tours. It would be a blast being surrounded by kids and teaching them about farm animals. I'd be working outdoors in one of the most scenic places in the world. Last pro, I could see Granger whenever I wanted and grab that sexy body, except in front of the children, of course."

"And chickens. They hate all that touchy feely stuff. Some good arguments for working there. By the way, I read the pamphlet you gave me from Mercy For Animals. I had no idea! I'm not turning vegan...yet, but I'm definitely cutting down on my meat consumption. Back to Granger. Hit me with the negatives."

"Darlene, that's great." Rae leaned over the table and hugged her. "Okay, I just met Granger and working with him five days a week at the beginning of our relationship could be too much too soon. If he's a lousy boss it could kill the relationship because I'd end up hating him. I might not be a good fit for the job and it would be really awkward quitting or, yikes, having him fire me."

"When Granger first asked you if you wanted to work at the sanctuary, what did your gut say?"

"Damn you, Darlene. I hate it when you ask poignant questions. My gut said no. But I didn't have a chance to think about it."

"That's the whole point of a gut reaction. You know that, right?"

"Yes, but..."

"You told me you were going to trust your gut from now on. Dare I ask, has your libido returned from the Hinterlands? How long has it been gone now, eight years?"

"Yes, my sex drive drove it back from the dead."

"It sounds to me like it's back in control."

Rae put her head in her hands. "Life was so much easier without it. I loved being alone. It made my choices immediate. Now, all I think about is Granger. I see his smile, his beautiful body, hanging out at the sanctuary with him. I imagine being in bed with him and kissing him and... damn it! My head was so clear and now it's all Grangerized."

Darlene put her hand on Rae's shoulder. "I know this is tough, my dear, but only you can make this decision. I promise to support you whatever you decide, because you're my buddy."

"Thanks, Darlene. I appreciate it. Speaking of buddies, how are you and Peter doing? Has he cut down on the ganga?"

"Yup. He realized I was right after he spaced out on attending a conference call the other night. The firm was not pleased."

"Did they know he was stoned?"

"Not a clue, but it scared him. When your goal is to be a partner in the law firm, you can't make mistakes like that. Peter promised to get high only on the weekends, if then."

"That's great," Rae said and took a bite of food.

While they were eating, a couple came into the restaurant. The man was wearing a black, mid-length cape. Darlene saw them first. She told Rae to turn around and then said in a low voice, "Would you go out with a guy who wore a cape?"

Rae cringed. "Absolutely not. There's a whole personality profile that goes with the cape and it ain't pretty."

"What if Granger wore a cape on your next date?"

Rae laughed so hard that people turned to see what was so funny. "I would tell him to return it to Zorro and hightail it out of there."

"You would not."

"No, I wouldn't. I do know that he's not a cape guy." Rae looked over at the man wearing the reviled piece of clothing. She shuddered. "Would you go out with a cape man?"

"That would be a negative, but a tutu would be fine."

"Yeah, a tutu is totally acceptable."

29

After finishing his American History homework, Fran got up from the desk. His first inclination was to take a walk and stretch his legs but he promised Allie he would have the research for their film done by their meeting tomorrow night, so he performed some cursory side bends, touched his toes a few times, then got on the floor and did some sit-ups. He stood up and opened the cottage door, letting in fresh air. He saw his cat Latté outside the door, rubbing up against a flower pot. He leaned over and picked her up, gave her some hugs and kisses, then dropped her on the couch. After going to the kitchen and grabbing a beer from the fridge, Fran reluctantly sat down at his desk. Latté jumped up on his lap. As he pet the snow white cat, he thought about the conversation he had with Allie in class the other day. "Don't worry, Latté, I'd never eat you." The cat looked up at Fran with her dark green eyes and meowed. Then she 'kneaded' his lap and lay down, nuzzling her head close to his stomach.

A search for 'factory farm workers' resulted in thousands of hits. He clicked on *Inside the Life of a Factory Farm Worker* and what he saw made his stomach turn. There was a photo of workers in a poultry processing plant, hanging fully conscious chickens by their feet and locking them upside down into shackles. The scene was grotesque and Fran was compelled to exit the page and find another article. Instead, he started reading about a worker named Stanley Ortega, a chicken hanger in a poultry slaughterhouse. He was required to hang about thirty-five birds a minute. In addition to the muscles in his hands and joints in his fingers becoming so sore that he could barely open and close them, the birds fought being hung in the shackles. They pecked and bit the hangers and, once secured, they emptied their bowels. "You wear hair nets, you wear beard nets, you wear goggles, you wear face masks, you wear an apron, you wear boots, but it doesn't stop the feces from getting into your eyes, your nose, your mouth, and your ears. The fecal matter hits you under your clothes, and you can feel it slowly running down your body. It doesn't matter how much clothing you wear or how much tape you use, it's still going to happen," Ortega said.

Fran stopped and looked away from the computer. He had no idea how terrifying it was for the animals and how revolting it was for the workers. He forced himself to continue reading. More photos accompanied the article. They left nothing to the imagination. Workers' injuries alongside photos of animals crammed into tiny living spaces was eye opening for the son of immigrants. The article revealed that almost forty percent of the workers are from outside the United States. Most are undocumented and don't speak English. They don't know their rights and the corporations that hire them keep them in the dark so they can get the most out of their employees for as little financial output as possible. He felt an anger surge up inside of him. The whole business was inhumane. The animals and the workers lived in fear, pain and misery. He went back to the search results and clicked on *The Most Dangerous Job in America*, an article about workers in meat packing plants and other food animal facilities. The article listed the titles of accident reports from OSHA (Occupational Safety and Health Administration). It read more like a horror movie than a government report: Employee Hospitalized for Neck Laceration From Flying Blade. Employee's Finger Amputated in Sausage Extruder. Employee's Arm Amputated in Meat Auger. Employee's Arm Amputated When Caught in Meat Tenderizer. Employee Burned in Tallow Fire. Employee Burned by Hot Solution in Tank. One Employee Killed, Eight Injured by Ammonia Spill. Employee Killed When Arm Caught in Meat Grinder. Employee Decapitated by Chain of Hide Puller Machine. Employee Killed When Head Crushed by Conveyor. Employee Killed When Head Crushed in Hide Fleshing Machine. Employee Killed by Stun Gun. Employee Caught and Killed by Gut-Cooker Machine.

Fran was coming to the realization that the whole food animal industry was replete with cruelty. The animals didn't have a choice but immigrants, once on American soil, might feel the same way after working for meat packing companies and slaughterhouses. These unskilled laborers were looking for a better life, leaving countries where they had no future. Fran printed out the two articles and accompanying photos. He secured them in his binder. He was starting to feel that what started out as Allie's passion for animal rights was becoming his passion for factory farm workers. He walked outside and looked up at the sky, taking in the night air. It was cold but he didn't notice. His mind was filtering through all that he read. He couldn't even imagine what it would be like to work every day in killing factories. The smell of freshly killed animals, the constant noise of the desperate creatures screaming above the sound of machines. He wondered how the factory workers washed the stench of death from their bodies. Would any amount of soap eliminate it? The poor animals' lives were cut short in the slaughterhouses, but the workers relived their hell day after day. It wasn't until he looked back at his home that he realized tears were running down his face.

30

"Al, we're going to be late!" Granger was waiting in the car. He and Allie were heading to Margo's for dinner and Granger wanted to be on time. Allie closed the front door and sprinted to the car. "Sorry Papa. Chris called as I was getting ready to leave." Granger pulled out of the driveway. He had only met Chris that one day, when he caught them kissing in the field, but there was something about him that made Granger uncomfortable. Maybe it was his cocky attitude.

Turning left onto Bodega Avenue, he glanced over at his land, past the cottages. The cows were still grazing in the north pasture. He loved watching them lazily graze without a care in the world. "Are you serious about this guy?"

"I guess, but it's only been a couple of weeks. He invited me to a party this Saturday. Hey, I was thinking about getting another tattoo right here." Allie pointed to her right shoulder. "What say ye?"

"I say it's your body. Do what you want, but I personally don't like them."

"I know. This one is going to be my spirit animal. A turkey vulture."

"Now you're just messing with me, right?" Granger said.

"No. I'm serious. I was on Iker Rock and discovered that the magnificent turkey vulture that pees on its legs to cool off is my spirit animal. I thought I could get a tattoo of its wing, not the whole body."

"That would definitely be easier to look at. Back to Chris. What is it that you like about him?"

"I'm getting a negative vibe from you. I should ask you why you don't like Chris but I don't want to go there right now, okay?"

"Fine."

Granger turned on the radio and they drove to Margo's in silence. Allie and Granger discussed almost everything and rarely fought, but Allie could tell that any discussion of Chris wouldn't go very well. She had to admit she had a feeling that Chris was hiding a darker side. In high school, he was brazen. Because of his great looks and charm, he won over a lot of girls. Allie had a crush on him back then but wasn't part of his crowd. Going out with him now felt like a coup. It fed her ego and he was fun to be with, but she was well aware that they didn't share the same values. Still, he intrigued her and she wanted to see how far she could take it. Talking to her dad about him would only weaken that resolve.

They arrived at Margo's with five minutes to spare. As they walked up to the front door, Granger put his arm around his daughter. "I love you, Al. I only want the best for you, you know that."

Allie gave him a kiss on his cheek. "Yup." She knocked on the door and Margo answered, dressed in her signature cable knit sweater, jeans and tennis shoes. Her silver gray hair was pulled back, revealing large hoop earrings.

"Well, aren't we the chic one?" Allie said as she hugged and kissed Margo.

"I try," she said.

"You look beautiful, Margo," Granger said as he hugged her. They took off their coats and sat down in the living room. Full of turn-of-the-century furniture with photos of the family on fern green walls and area rugs covering the hard wood floors, it was comfortable and familiar. Granger grew up visiting Margo's ranch and Allie crawled on these floors nineteen years ago. It was like their second home.

"I half-expected to see Rae with you," Margo said, as she set a tray of appetizers on the coffee table.

Granger grabbed a handful of almonds. "I was tempted to invite her. I'll be seeing her this weekend."

"She's a lovely woman, Granger. I'm happy for you. You know she's welcome any time."

"Thanks, Margo. I offered her a job on the ranch. I think she'd make a great tour guide along with taking on other responsibilities."

Margo sat down. "Don't you think it's too soon to be working together? Oh, what am I saying? Robert and I were dating for only a month when we got married!" She clapped her hands together and sat up a little straighter. "I'll never forget that day. Robert took me to Bodega Seafood for dinner. It's still there but so rundown. I think they have the same tablecloths! Anyway, it was a full moon and its reflection off the ocean lit up the horizon. No wind. That I remember because it always seems to be blowing. After dinner, we walked on the beach. This sounds so cliché, but back then it was very romantic. Robert said he saw something shiny in the sand. He bent down, picked it up and pretended to wipe it off. I asked him what it was and he held out a diamond ring and said, 'It's yours if you want it.' Then he got down on one knee and proposed. I was so happy I cried. We were married for fifty-two years."

"That was romantic and a little cheesy. I miss Robert," Allie said. "Me, too dear. So Granger, did Rae take the job?"

"She wants to think about it. Hopefully, she'll let me know this weekend. I didn't know you and Robert got married so quickly. He didn't knock you up, did he?"

Margo laughed. "No, we were just mad about each other. Back in those days if you wanted to have sex, you got married." Margo got up. "You two sit. I'll set the table."

"We're helping and don't say no," Allie said. She and Granger followed Margo into the kitchen. Allie grabbed the plates and utensils while Granger put out the hot plates for the casserole and steamed broccoli.

"Margo, I'd love to learn how to weave, especially on your loom. It's so beautiful," Allie said.

"I'd be happy as heck to teach you, Allie. Let me know when."

"I was thinking when school is out at the end of June. Does that work?"

"I have all the time in the world. June, July, November, December. It all works for me."

"Great!" Allie said. Granger looked over at Margo and smiled. He knew that Margo would love having Allie around. Her children were grown and lived too far to visit as often as she would like. Granger came by once a week and sometimes brought his mother along. Alda and Margo knew each other back when they were both newlyweds. Margo had friends in the town of Bodega Bay but she preferred to stay at home. She had daily contact with her two employees but it was more of a work relationship than a social one.

After dinner, Margo put the kettle on for tea. They sat in the patio. Up until ten years ago, it was an open room, but Granger insisted on enclosing it so Margo could continue to enjoy it during the winter months. A plush rug sat on the tiled floor. There was a couch, chaise lounge, a coffee table and two end tables. Granger hung speakers so Margo could listen to her stereo. He also installed heat lamps. Three walls had floor to ceiling windows. Two of them faced an expansive field and beyond it was a view of the ocean. There were nights when Margo would fall asleep on the chaise lounge while reading and wake up the next day, dappled sunlight peering through the blinds.

Margo said, "I can't imagine living anywhere else. I know that my children won't want to live here when I'm gone, but I want it to stay in the family."

"Don't think about that now, Margo. You're healthy and have years ahead of you."

"That's sweet of you to say, Grange, but tomorrow I could be dead. What if I slipped and fell off the bluff?"

"This is getting morbid," Allie said.

"Life can be morbid, Allie-cat. I just want my bases covered. Grange, promise me you'll help me with a living will, okay?"

"Definitely, Margo. In the meantime, don't stand too close to the bluff."

"Yes, dear." Margo took a sip of tea and began to tell her guests about the upcoming art festival in Bodega Bay.

31

As Granger drove to Rae's house, he pulled down the visor and quickly glanced in the mirror. He smiled, checking for errant bits of food. None were found, but when he glanced up at his eyes, he noticed a rogue eyebrow hair above his left eye. It was trying to escape from the rest of the hairs, migrating toward his nose. Granger pulled the truck over and unceremoniously yanked it out.

Back on the road, Granger wondered if Rae made up her mind about working on his ranch. Even though he was conflicted about having Rae as an employee, he was excited at the prospect of working with her.

As he pulled into Rae's driveway, he was suddenly struck with a bad case of nerves. What if she wanted to have sex? Granger hadn't been with a woman sexually in years. Should he make the first move? Would he be able to perform? And, if so, for how long? What if Rae wasn't ready? Granger grabbed the bottle of wine, flowers, and his courage and walked up to the front door. He knocked and as he waited, he heard classical music playing. It sounded familiar. Rae answered the door, looking radiant. Her hair was pulled back in a braid and her make-up was minimal. She wore small, green and black art deco earrings and a black onyx bead necklace. Her long-sleeved black t-shirt fell just below her belt and her faded blue jeans were tucked into dark brown boots. Granger handed her the bouquet of peonies.

"These are beautiful. Thank you. I'm going to put them in a vase. Why don't you open that bottle of wine? The wine opener is in the drawer to the left of the dishwasher."

"Yes, ma'am."

"I do believe that's the first time you've sounded like a cowboy."

"I can devolve into ranch talk any time you'd like."

"I'd like it better if you had a slight southern accent, you know, so I feel like I'm with a real cowboy."

Granger laughed. "So you're saying that only authentic cowboys sound like George Strait or Alan Jackson?"

"Yup."

Granger thought for a second, then said with a slight drawl, "I reckon I can tell you some ranch tales like this, little lady."

"I love it! Even the 'little lady' part. It's very sexy, you know."

"I didn't know. It'll be in my back pocket, ready to use in an emergency."

Granger's nerves evened out a little. Rae had a way of making him feel at ease. He found the wine opener and searched a couple of cabinets before he found the wine glasses. He looked around the kitchen. It was long and narrow with black Silestone countertops, stainless steel appliances, white cabinets, circa 1950s and a red linoleum floor. "Hey, your kitchen floor is the same one we had in my high school with the different colored flecks in it. It always reminded me of confetti. I haven't seen this linoleum in ages. It's very retro."

Rae put the vase of peonies in the middle of the dining room table. She inhaled the bouquet's soft scent one more time before she joined Granger in the kitchen. "Our school had the same pattern but in grey. Very industrial. This stuff will survive a nuclear attack."

"That's very comforting."

"I'm just saying."

Granger handed her the glass of wine. He raised his glass and Rae did the same. He said, "To tonight." Their glasses clinked and they both took a sip.

"Let's see. I detect sock monkey, frying pan and a touch of cat hair," Rae said.

"That's astounding. Your true calling is a sommelier."

"I know! Seriously, even though I hate getting serious, this is out-standing." Rae gave Granger a thorough once-over. "Who would have thought a cowboy could be a wine connoisseur?"

"Probably the same person who thought a cowboy could be a vegan. I love breaking the mold." Granger went over to Rae and kissed her. He felt light and air everywhere. He cradled her head in his hands and never wanted to stop touching her and feeling her body next to his. The oven timer buzzed and Granger reluctantly pulled away. "Foiled by the bell."

"Only temporarily," Rae said as she steadied herself and turned off the timer. She was conflicted over what may happen this evening. The last time Rae was intimate with a man was eight years ago and she was pre-menopausal. Once menopause hit, her libido all but disappeared. She had been attracted to men since then, but the longest relation-ship didn't progress past two dates. There were many reasons Rae lost interest: they were self-absorbed, geographically inaccessible, tight with money, or their kissing skills were nominal at best. She couldn't fathom why men who flicked their tongues in and out of her mouth like an iguana or stuck their fat tongues halfway down her throat thought that it was enjoyable. A bad kisser was a deal-breaker. But when they were great, like Granger, it only added to their appeal. She fantasized about what he would be like in bed and couldn't wait to see him under her covers, but then Cruella would cut the fantasy short by reminding Rae of her soft, marshmallow-like belly. Her daily yoga sessions slowed the aging process but her body had an agenda, and the once plentiful collagen and elas-tin in her skin was waning. In its wake, it left her skin slightly wrinkled and her muscles weakened. Rae was terrified that Granger would take one look at her naked body and sprint out of her house wearing only his Stetson. Despite the fact that she hadn't worn it in over eight years, Rae kept a see-through leopard teddy in the back of her bra drawer. She fantasized that one day she'd put it on and would look just as sexy in it as she did eight years ago. It could be tonight.

"What did you make?" Granger asked.

"Eggplant casserole. I also made a salad."

"Sounds delicious. I really like the music you're playing. Is it a CD?"

"Yes. It's from…"

"Don't tell me. It sounds so familiar." Granger went into the living room and turned up the sound. He stood in front of the stereo for a couple of minutes. "I got it! It's from the French film, *Moliere*. Good movie but great soundtrack."

Rae took the casserole out of the oven and placed it on top of the stove. She took the salad out of the refrigerator and put it on the dining room table. "Let me get this straight. You're vegan and own an animal sanctuary. You're a wine connoisseur, classical music fan, enjoy gourmet food AND you watch foreign films?"

Granger grabbed their wine glasses and put them on the table, then sat down. "I think that about covers it. Breaking the mold, baby. Breaking the mold."

"I'd say you broke the mother lode of all molds." She gave Granger a healthy serving of salad. He took a bite, then asked Rae what he had been wanting to ask since he arrived.

"Have you thought about taking the job I offered you?"

"I have," Rae said, and took a fairly large sip of wine. "Part of me thinks working for you is premature. I haven't known you that long, but another part of me would absolutely love to work at the sanctuary, surrounded by animals and your magnificent ranch and, of course, you."

Granger sat back in the chair and stretched his long legs. "So, which part are you siding with more?"

"Right now, it's a dead heat. I'm sorry but this is a tough decision. The last thing I want to do is mess up my relationship with you."

"I feel the same way. I'd be your boss. How's that for pressure? I have to admit, though, I'm one of the nicest bosses I've ever known. I've only had to fire nine employees."

Rae's eyes grew large. "Nine?"

Granger started laughing. "Just kidding. I haven't fired anyone…yet."

"Funny man. We should make a pact. If it doesn't seem to be going well, I'll leave."

"That's fair and very mature. Do you think we can be that mature?"

"In theory, yes. In practice..." Rae tilted her hand side to side. "So, let's say I do work for you. What would I do?"

"I think you'd be great conducting the tours. They're really a blast because a lot of these kids haven't been around farm animals, especially the cows. Everyone sees them when they're riding in the car, but up close, they're really massive creatures and so gentle. The kids love petting them. When you're not giving tours, you could help take care of the animals. That involves feeding, grooming and cleaning the stalls. Do you have any fix-it abilities?"

"I installed new outlet plates in the living room. And when my basement floor was leaking, I put a sealant on it."

"Okay, so feeding the animals, giving tours, gardening?"

"Sure, I can do that."

"Salary-wise, I was thinking $50,000."

"Wow. That's really generous for what I'll be doing. Are you sure?"

"You're the first person that's wanted less! You are too much!" Granger took Rae's hand. "You're worth a helluva lot more than $50,000 but that's my offer. What do you think?"

"I think I'm working at Bowden Ranch!" Rae got up and hugged Granger. "I hope we're doing the right thing. Are we doing the right thing?"

Granger looked Rae in the eyes. "Yes we are. We really are."

"Okay. This will be fun! I've always wanted to work at a sanctuary." Rae sat back down and dished out her casserole as they began discussing the various jobs around the ranch and what she'd specifically be doing. To Rae, it almost felt surreal sitting across from this man she hardly knew, listening to him talk about her new job.

When they finished eating and Rae was clearing off the plates, Granger said, "I brought a surprise."

Rae said, "More fun and frivolity from the Boy Wonder?"

"Come into the living room." Granger pulled a red and white striped joint out of his pocket.

"Is that Santa's joint?"

Granger laughed. "Peppermint-flavored papers. You want to partake?"

"Light 'er up." Granger lit the joint and took a deep hit, held it in and passed it to Rae. She took a hit and tried to hold it in, but the smoke expanded in her lungs, causing her to go into a coughing fit. Eyes tearing, she finally caught her breath and when she stopped, she was completely baked.

"Whoa. How did I get so stoned so fast?"

"Bowden Ranch special."

"Is your marijuana crop part of the tour? 'And this, kids, is really why everyone is always happy at our sanctuary.' Can cows get stoned?"

"I don't think so."

"Why not?"

"They can't hold a bong with their hooves." Granger started laughing and Rae joined in. Every time Rae caught her breath, she'd imagine cows in a field, standing upright, desperately trying to grasp a bong with their hooves, and start laughing all over again. That would set Granger off. Rae's mascara was officially gone and her eyes were puffy from crying. When they finally stopped, they were out of breath. They sat on the couch, exhausted. Rae said, "I was going to ask you if chickens can get stoned, but I'm not going there."

"Come on. Ask me."

"No!" Rae put her hand over Granger's mouth. He kissed it. Rae sighed and her heart started to pound. As she leaned into him, her hand brushed against her stomach. In her state of mind, it felt like a big ball of dough and she pulled back. She didn't want Granger seeing her stomach or touching it. As badly as she would have liked to have him completely engulf her, vanity won out. She took her hand off Granger's mouth. He looked up at her with concern and very red eyes. "Did I do something wrong?"

"Not at all. Everything you're doing is more than right. I'm just not ready to go there, you know?"

"I'm sorry. I don't want to put any pressure on you at all. We can take this as slow as you need it to be, okay?"

Rae nodded. "Thank you. So, you want to play cards or watch a movie?"

"I wouldn't mind talking."

Rae looked behind the couch. "What are you doing?" Granger said.

"I'm looking for your extension cord. You can't be a real man. Where's the power pack to your operating system?"

"I run on lithium batteries but I'm losing power. I can tell because my mouth is super dry. Could I please have some water, female human?"

"Sure cyborg." Rae got water for both of them. She marveled at Granger's temperament and his understanding. The last guy she told she needed time before they had sex said he'd get back to her because he thought about sex 24/7. She didn't give him a chance to think about it. Rae called him the next morning and said the relationship wasn't going to work. She was nervous telling him but after she hung up she felt empowered. It was a great feeling but not one she felt often.

Rae handed Granger the glass of water. "Thanks. Now tell me about yourself. Where did you grow up?"

Rae told Granger about being raised in Studio City, a Los Angeles suburb in the San Fernando Valley. Life there was close to idyllic, with a stay-at-home mom and a dad who was a civil engineer. Her younger sister, Ellen, still lived in Studio City with her husband and two daughters. Rae went on to relate her college years at California State University at Northridge. She worked at the university's radio station, KCSN, as an engineer and deejay, producing three programs: environmental issues, classical and rock & roll. She was about to tell Granger about her first husband, but stopped.

"Tell me about your childhood."

"What's there to tell? I was built by NASA in 2032 and then they put me in a time machine and sent me back to 2013 to find the perfect woman. And here we are."

"Well aren't you a charming cyborg? Seriously, tell me about what it was like growing up in Petaluma before the fast food restaurants, tract homes and strip malls debased it."

Granger was about to respond when Pierre walked into the living room with something bright green in his mouth. Granger said, "What is that?"

"It's a ponytail band. Pierre loves them. Watch what he does with it." Pierre went over to a corner of the area rug and pushed the band under the rug. He waited about four seconds, then tried retrieving the band. Once he got it out, he put it back in. "Is he a weird cat or what?" Rae said.

"He's a very strange cat. Quirky. Where were we? Oh yeah, so how long have you lived in Petaluma?"

Rae replied, "Twenty-six years. I moved here when the population was 34,000. Now it's 56,000, but I want to hear what it was like when you were a kid."

"First off, the freeway stopped in Novato and what's now Highway 101, was our main street. There were twice as many trucks as cars. This place was an agricultural mecca for dairy, beef, eggs and chickens farms but the operations weren't on the scale that they are today. Our big store was J.C. Penney. That's where my mom bought almost all my clothes until I was in high school: overalls, jeans, boots and the ever popular white t-shirt by Hanes. I was stylin' baby."

"I bet once you hit high school, you became a hippie with long hair, tie dye shirts and smelled of patchouli oil. Am I right? I am, aren't I?"

Granger took another hit from the red and white striped joint. "Did you watch Bonanza?"

"Sure. I loved watching the Cartwright boys ride around the ranch, especially Little Joe. He was so cute."

"Yeah, whatever. The point is, I was a rancher. Ranchers don't have long hair and smell of patchouli. I had short cropped hair and smelled like cows because I had chores before school and after school."

"Give me that joint." Granger held it up to Rae's mouth and lit it. She blew out the smoke and watched as it dissipated slowly in the air. She tried to imagine what Granger looked like as a teenager: tall, lanky, big beautiful smile. "Except for the smell, I bet you were adorable."

"Back then, Petaluma girls loved the rancher boys. We did okay. How about you? Were you one of the popular girls, fighting off the hippies and geeks and greasers?"

Rae let out a loud laugh. "Let me paint a picture of my high school years." Rae held up an imaginary brush and as she spoke, she made sweeping strokes. "I was pretty much a prude. Far from being savvy, I wore skirts and knee-high socks my freshman and junior years. Some guys liked me but I didn't return the sentiment. Instead, I fell for the bad boys and the inaccessible boys, the ones who were dripping in pheromones and had all the girls in a sexual tizzy. If there was a line, I was close to the back of it. These boys didn't even know I existed. I was briefly on the girl's tennis team but dropped out after my best friend, Simone Russo, left the team. She started dating a drug dealer and that was the beginning of the end of our friendship. Fast forward to the senior prom. I could have gone, but the only boy who asked me was John Conklin. A year earlier, he was in a bad car accident and it messed him up mentally. He walked around campus slightly off kilter and said bizarre, random things. I told him I already had a date. Big lie but there was no way I was going to be seen with him. I know, that sounds horrible, but I was a seventeen-year-old insecure square and didn't have the chutzpah to defray the taunts that I knew I'd get. So, I didn't go to my senior prom. Did you?"

Granger sat up a little straighter. "I'm sorry. I was re-charging. Could you repeat that?"

Before Rae could take a swing at him, Granger said, "Just kidding. Yes, I did go to the senior prom with Rose Hannigan. She was the Dairy Queen at the time."

"Did she smell like a cow, too?"

"Just a little. Funny, I thought you'd be one of the cool kids. When did you start to come into your own?"

Rae glanced at the clock on the wall. "Still waiting. Any minute now." She stood up and stretched. "Actually, it was when I went to college that I was able to be myself. The guys I found attractive returned the sentiment. Good times." Rae went into the kitchen. "I need more water. For some inexplicable reason, my mouth is really dry."

When Rae returned, she sat down next to Granger. He looked straight into her eyes and said, "Do you ever think of leaving Petaluma?"

"Ever see the movie *Roxanne*? It came out in the late eighties."

"Yeah, Steve Martin plays a fire chief with a huge nose, like Cyrano de Bergerac, right? Great film."

"It was shot in a small town called Nelson in British Columbia. I think about moving there every once in a while. I have this pipe dream of selling the house after Carson moves out and starting over in a place where I don't know anyone and anything's possible."

"I do remember really liking Nelson. It almost had a storybook quality to it. What's stopping you from re-inventing yourself right now? Right here?"

In her current mental state, it was easy to transport herself into the question and feel the answer. Rae saw her past and present colliding together in Petaluma, vying for attention, collapsing onto each other. It was messy and congested. "Too much baggage here."

Granger looked dead serious. "I'm here."

Rae was so used to being alone and fending for herself, she forgot that sitting next to her was quite possibly the man she'd be spending the rest of her life with, not to mention that his homegrown marijuana was quite potent. "I'm sorry. This pot is so strong. I feel like a hovercraft right now!"

"No offense, but you're starting to *look* like a hovercraft. Do you need some room to land?"

"Very funny. I'll survive. So, growing up with 550 acres at your disposal, I bet you have a secret place."

"I do."

"Have you ever shared it with anyone?"

"It wouldn't be a secret anymore, would it?" Granger said.

"Semi-sweet chocolate is still chocolate."

"Is this the kind of logic I'm going to have to put up with?"

"You bet your cute little cyborg ass." Rae leaned over and kissed him. She forgot all about her stomach and indulged herself, like eating a chocolate truffle with espresso cream filling. It was rich and sumptuous and she didn't ever want it to stop.

After a few minutes, Granger pulled back and said, "Do you want me to spend the night?"

Rae's mind was on overdrive. The pot magnified every thought and they were catapulting themselves off her brain. She saw herself having sex with Granger. She saw Granger disappointed in her body. She saw scenes from a movie that she watched the other night. She even relived her kiss with Brock Howard when she was eighteen. It was hard to separate the thoughts, but she tried. And then a small voice within her told her not to rush it. Take the time to know him better. She took Granger's hand in hers and said, "More than anything. But it's too soon and I'd regret it."

"Me, too," said Granger.

"Really?"

"Hell no!"

"Your cyborg days just ended, buddy. You are officially a man."

"Disappointed?" Granger asked.

"Not one bit. Can we still kiss?"

"Come here, you." Granger pulled Rae back into his arms.

It was close to 1:00 in the morning when Granger left. They decided it would be too tempting if he slept over, not because of Granger. He swore he had the discipline. It was Rae who said she wouldn't be able to resist ravaging him if he lay in bed beside her.

Rae's lips were pleasantly numb from kissing. She slipped out of her clothes, brushed her teeth but didn't wash her face. She splashed it with water and lightly toweled it dry. She wanted Granger's scent to remain. She wanted to fall asleep smelling that mix of sweet marijuana smoke and musk. As she climbed into bed, she stretched her arms and legs and took a deep breath. "Good night, Granger," she said softly and fell fast asleep.

32

Fran and Allie had the storyboards for their documentary assembled on the dining room table. So far, there were only twenty scenes, but tonight they were determined to double that. Various colored markers were strewn on the table as well as the first thirty-five pages of the script. Allie was putting the finishing touches on one of the storyboards when Fran said, "I just thought of a great idea. What if we interview some of the students on campus and ask them what they think of people who eat dogs and cats. Most will say it's disgusting and those people are cruel. Then we tell them that a pig's IQ is higher than many dog's and cat's. Why is it any less cruel eating a pig? Did you know that a pig has the intelligence of a three-year-old child?"

"Yeah, I did and I like that idea a lot," Allie said. "It would make great subject matter for the film and get the interviewees thinking. Do you want to conduct the interviews or do you want me to?"

"We should both do it. We'll get different reactions from people."

"True. We can get a nice diversity of answers, then pick the best interviews. Have you told your family about our film?"

"Kind of."

"What does that mean?"

Fran said, "They know I'm working on a documentary with you but I told them we haven't decided on a topic yet. Before you say anything, I want to remind you that I'm Mexican and our culture is so meat heavy that I was afraid I'd be skewered and roasted over a low flame if they knew what we were doing."

"I thought you had bigger cajones than that, Fran. You don't even live with your parents, do you?"

"First of all, no I don't live with them and second, don't talk about my cajones like that. They're growing slowly, but they're growing. I've never met someone who has a lifestyle like yours, someone who believes so strongly and passionately about something other than their own self-interests. A Mexican vegan is as common as a Taliban pacifist."

"You're right. I give you tons of credit for taking on this subject. I have a little prediction to make. I think that by the time this film is finished, you're going to be a vegan."

Fran laughed. He'd become a vegan on the spot if Allie would go out with him, but he was too scared to ask her. If she said no, they'd still have to work on the film and that would be beyond awkward. He would remain patient and, hopefully, he'd grow on her. The doorbell interrupted Fran's thoughts.

"That's probably Chris." Allie went to answer the door. Fran watched as Allie gave Chris a kiss. His heart sank and his first inclination was to leave. The only reason he chose Allie to be his partner was so he could eventually date her. Now, he felt like an idiot. He watched them walk into the dining room. Chris had just enough of a swagger to make Fran dislike him even more. He exuded confidence and it didn't help that he was so good-looking. He held out his hand to Fran.

"Chris Welke. Nice to meet you."

"Fran Santiago. Same."

"Allie told me what you guys are working on. Are you a vegan, too?"

Before Fran could answer, Allie said, "Not yet."

Chris said, "A Mexican vegan? Are you kidding?"

"It's not that far-fetched. Are you a vegan?" Fran replied.

Chris snorted. "Do I look like a vegan?"

Allie said, "What the hell is that supposed to mean?"

"Hey, chill out. I was just kidding. No, I'm not a vegan. But, if anyone could turn me into one, it would be Allie here. Are you guys done yet?" Chris ran his fingers through his thick, blonde hair.

"We have about an hour or so left. You can go in the living room and watch TV if you want."

"Cool." Chris left the room and a few seconds later, a sports announcer could be heard ticking off football statistics.

"Turn it down, Chris, we're trying to work," Allie yelled. She rolled her eyes and Fran shrugged. He wished Chris wasn't there, but he had to face the fact that he might be in Allie's life for a while.

"Let's put together the questions for the interview. First question should be, what do you think about other cultures' attitudes about eating dogs and cats?"

From the living room, Chris yelled, "They should be shot!"

Fran said, "Why?"

"Because they're eating pets!" Chris yelled back.

Fran yelled to Chris, "In those cultures, they're not considered pets. Did you know that pigs have the IQ of a three-year-old human and Americans eat 112 million every year?"

"That's because they taste so good. I couldn't live without ribs and bacon. Could you?"

Before Fran could answer, Allie yelled back, "That's what they say about dogs and cats. They supposedly taste great, so why is it wrong to eat a dog but not a pig or a cow or a chicken?"

Instead of answering, Chris started yelling at the game on TV. "That wasn't offsides! What are you, blind?"

"We lost him. Why don't you work on the questions and then we can role play and see how they sound?" Allie said. "Moving right along, do you know anyone who has Photoshop skills? I thought it would be cool to show a person who resembles an animal on the left side of the screen and then have the animal on the right side, then morph them together."

"I could do that," Fran said. "I could even use my Uncle Bernard. He looks just like a sheep. His face, not his body. His nickname is Wooly."

"Perfect. And poor Uncle Wooly!"

As Fran started writing out the questions and possible answers, Allie studied him surreptitiously. He wasn't a bad looking guy. He was slight and not too tall. His ears were on the large side, but he had beautiful mocha-colored skin and black straight hair that came halfway down his neck. He almost looked Native American.

Chris sneaked up on Allie, grabbing her from behind and kissing her neck. "Mmmm, you taste good. Maybe I'll start eating vegans. They're certainly healthy."

Allie released herself from Chris' embrace. "We're trying to work here. Go back to your stupid football game."

Chris ambled back to the living room and plopped down on the couch. He knew they wouldn't be done yet but, just like a dog, he wanted to mark his territory. He wanted to make sure that Fran knew who Allie belonged to, leaving no room for interpretation. Judging from the sideways look Fran gave him, he was sure the message was received.

33

"Let's get this over with as quickly as possible," Rae said to herself as she pressed 'play' on her CD player. The soundtrack from *Out of Africa* filled the room with the melodic sound of soft trumpets and violins. She needed forgiving music. She stood a few feet from the floor-length mirror on the other side of her bedroom door. The blinds were closed and her door was locked, in case Carson decided to pop in. Keeping her eyes on the mirror, she slowly undressed. As she did, she took note of her body, needing an honest assessment so she would feel more comfortable with Granger. Even with the lights out, she wanted to know how her body felt to the touch. She pulled her t-shirt off and observed her arms. They still had a nice shape. The shoulders were defined and when she flexed her arms in a he-man pose, the muscle was hard. As she relaxed her arm, she felt the underarm and cringed. It was like soft dough. She flexed again. Tight. "How the hell does that happen?"

The lush soundtrack continued to bathe the room as Rae took off her bra. Her size 36C breasts were still amazingly firm for her age. They sagged but kept their round shape. She smiled and waved at her breasts. "Thank you, girls. I knew I could depend on you."

Her upper back wasn't as unblemished as it used to be, but nothing about Rae's body was as it used to be. Satisfied that it was presentable, she took off her pants and grimaced at her stomach. Rae never had a flat stomach but after menopause she noticed it took on the shape of an oblong donut. She knew that in order to get rid of it she would have to exercise more and eat a lot less, but that wasn't a lifestyle she was ready to adopt. Thirty-five minutes to an hour of Kundalini Yoga every night was her comfort zone. Maybe dating Granger would give her the incentive to push herself harder.

Rae still had a waist, even though it wasn't the hourglass shape it used to be, but she was grateful that she hadn't taken on the contour of a soup can with legs. "Let the games begin," she said as she took off her underwear. Without elastic around her waist, her stomach didn't look as paunchy but when she turned to the side, her behind was almost vertical. Even though it was small, the definition was gone. It was hard to believe that, after enduring yoga poses that had her tightening her butt for a minute, there was nothing to show for the sacrifice. "Getting old sucks!" she yelled.

Rae stared at her naked body. She realized that she had two choices: never undress in front of a man again or let said man see it and deal with it. She closed her eyes and imagined her body burned and horribly deformed. She created images of herself missing limbs, having large, jagged scars. When she opened her eyes, her old body was replaced with one that was mature but still beautiful. It could run quickly and jump high, hug fiercely and love generously. Rae decided it wasn't Heidi Klum's body but it was a keeper. Granger had shown her that he was not superficial. If he couldn't accept her the way she was, then it wasn't meant to be. Besides, he was the same age as Rae.

Satisfied that she was fine just as she was, Rae dressed and turned off the CD player. Before she left her room she had remembered something she read on Louise Hay's website. Louise Hay, a self-help author and motivational speaker said, 'It's important to look at yourself in the mirror and say I love you and I always will. We're in this together. You're a wonderful person and no matter what you go through, I'll always be here for you.'

Facing the mirror once again she said, "I love you, Rae. You're the best. I'll always be here for you. Okay, gotta go and take care of my...of our son. I love you!" Strangely, it made her feel better.

Rae had a blast her first day on the job. True to form, Granger made her feel completely at home. His temperament was so soft and playful that no question she asked was dismissed as foolish. He had taken the time to write down her duties and they went through them one by one, beginning with the horses and finishing with the garden in the front yard. It was a mild sixty-seven degrees with a slight breeze. Granger was wearing shorts and Rae couldn't help but notice how toned his legs were. He told her he ran almost every day on his property and invited her to join him, if she'd like. She said she'd seriously consider it.

"Would you be interested in doing Kundalini Yoga with me?" Rae asked Granger as they relaxed in the courtyard, drinking beer and eating Bavarian pretzels.

"Isn't that the sex yoga?" Granger said.

"No. Everyone asks me that. I think you're confusing it with tantric sex. Anyway, kundalini means coiled serpent and it's the earliest form of yoga. It taps into and releases energy in the body. I love it but it's not for everyone. The poses can be repetitive and last anywhere from thirty seconds to over ten minutes. Almost all the exercises involve either long, deep breathing or breath of fire or…why don't I bring one of my DVDs by and we could try it."

"Sure, I'm game."

"Great. I'll bring one tomorrow."

The sun was setting over the hills, casting shadows on the golden slopes. The animals were lazing in the fields. It looked as if they were enjoying the last rays of sunlight before their feeding grounds were enveloped in darkness. Granger left the barn door permanently open, giving them the option to come in for the night. It was the same for the horses, but the sheep were brought back to the barn because of mountain lions and coyotes. At sundown, the chickens were escorted into their hacienda. They not only had to worry about coyotes and mountain lions, but raccoons. Those cute carnivores could get as big as dogs and, if given the chance, would rip apart a hen without thinking twice.

Rae took a long sip of beer. She glanced over at Granger. He was facing the sun and his forehead glistened slightly from perspiration. His aviator sunglasses made him look sexier than ever. Rae couldn't figure out how a Petaluma native, growing up on a cattle ranch, could be so cool. He loved classical music and was a wine connoisseur. He jogged and was willing to try yoga. Rae wouldn't have been surprised if this whole relationship turned out to be one big practical joke, perpetrated by the Cattlemen's Association. She laughed at the idea.

"What's so funny, Ms. O'Brien?"

"Just some silliness going on in my brain."

"Does this happen often?"

"Way too often. You know what would turn this great moment into a stellar moment?"

"A mariachi band?"

"Yuck, no. George Strait."

"You like country music?"

"Love it. Don't you?"

Granger shook his head. "I had to listen to it growing up and all the rancher's kids would have it blaring from their trucks as they cruised down the street. I love rock and classic rock, but you can have George Strait and George Jones."

"Well, knock me over with a feather. You just keep breaking the cowboy stereotype every time I turn around. Please tell me that you go to hoedowns and tractor pulls."

"No tractor pulls but the Occidental Volunteer Fire Department is having their annual country hoedown next week. Live band, beer and wine. I was going to bring some veggie burgers for the grill, since they'll be barbequing chicken. Want to go?"

"Yee haw. Count me in. So, how did I do for my first day? Be honest. I take criticism fairly well."

The air was getting cooler, so Granger got up to turn on the heat lamps. He also turned on the outside lights, including the fountain light. It came to life, giving the water a golden hue as it cascaded from lily pad to lily pad. Small foot lights under the plants made the gardenias and jasmine vines sparkle.

"You know you did great. You have a natural way with the animals. I think Rodney and Stucco are in love with you. Practice the script I gave you for the tours. You can shadow me until you're comfortable, but I may join you once you're settled in because I love connecting with the kids. They have great questions and I love seeing their eyes light up when they pet the animals. Would you like another beer?"

"Sure." Rae watched Granger go into the house. It was still hard for her to believe that she could be with someone who embodied everything she wanted in a man. She wondered if she should pursue the documentary. After all, working on the ranch was helping educate children on animal rights and she would be spending her off-hours with Granger as well. She hadn't been in a relationship with a man in so long, she forgot how wonderful it felt to be adored and held and kissed. She loved sitting and talking with Granger and couldn't wait to sleep with him, even though she still had trepidations. Granger returned with an ice cold beer. He handed her the bottle. "Thanks. Where's Allie?"

"I believe she's out with Chris, this guy she started seeing about a month ago." The way he said it gave Rae pause.

"Don't you like Chris?" Before Granger could answer, they heard the front door open and soon Allie and Chris were coming into the courtyard. Allie went over to her father and gave him a hug.

"How was your first day as a ranch hand?" Allie said to Rae.

"I loved it. I'm outside and can wear comfy clothes all day and you should see my boss. What a hunk." Allie laughed and then introduced Rae to Chris. They exchanged pleasantries, then Allie and Chris went inside.

After they were out of earshot, Rae said, "He seems nice enough."

"On the surface, but I'm getting a bad vibe from the kid. Call it a father's intuition."

"Or is it that no guy is good enough for daddy's little girl?"

"Please. I think you watch too many romantic comedies where the dads go to great lengths to try and disembowel their future son-in-law."

"Time will tell. Speaking of telling. Are you going to divulge your secret spot?" Rae leaned in closer to Granger. She could smell sunscreen mixed with the musky scent that was decidedly masculine and unique to Granger. It filled her senses and she suddenly wanted him. It was as if Granger read her mind. "Your timing is lousy, dear. Allie and Chris?"

"Carson isn't home."

Granger tenderly put his hand on her cheek. "Are you sure you're ready?"

Rae was never a big drinker. She was only on her second beer and already feeling the effects. The combination of the alcohol, the setting sun and Granger's essence created a trifecta of desire. She leaned over and kissed him. He tasted like salt and beer and pretzels. It was delicious. She wanted to continue kissing him but Granger pulled back.

"I don't feel comfortable doing this with Allie here. Are you okay to drive home right now?"

"I know I'm fine to drive, what is it, five miles, but I don't think a police officer would concur."

"I'll drive." They got up and took the bottles and pretzels into the kitchen, past Allie and Chris who were watching TV.

Granger said to Allie, "We're going to Rae's. You two have a nice night." They barely looked up from the television.

Rae and Granger walked in the front door only to find Carson sitting in the dining room eating pizza. He was wearing his brace outside his shirt. Rae was clearly puzzled. "What are you doing here?"

"It's nice to see you, too, Madre. Hi Granger. Dad got called in for overtime. You know how he is about working an extra shift. If he can make money, he'll get to the office faster than Ricochet Rabbit, bing bing biiing!"

"He could have called me." Rae tried not to sound disappointed.

"He left a message on your cell." Rae checked her phone and, sure enough, there was a message. Granger turned to Rae and said, "So, what's for dinner?" Rae smiled weakly. "I'll whip something up. You relax."

Granger sat down across from Carson and started talking to him about Rae's first day on the job. The two got along great. Rae was thankful for that. The last man she dated didn't relate well to children, especially hard-headed boys. Their relationship ended after Carson and Jeremy shouted expletives at each other during a one-on-one basketball game. Jeremy walked off the court fuming, expecting Rae to chase after him. Instead, she consoled her son who was only twelve at the time and didn't deserve to be yelled at by a fifty-five year old. Jeremy was the third and last house painter she dated. Rae was convinced that inhaling paint fumes for a prolonged length of time killed off millions, if not billions, of brain cells. Brains that clearly couldn't afford to lose any. The result was erratic behavior and spates of anger devolving into tirades.

Whether it was age or temperament or a combination of the two, Granger switched seamlessly from wanting to devour Rae sexually to thoroughly enjoying talking to Carson. He asked him about school, friends, even about his doomed motorcycle. He shared stories with Carson about his short-lived ownership of a Harley-Davidson, its demise resulting from an accident, too, but not nearly as critical as Carson's. Granger lifted his shirt revealing a five-inch scar below his right clavicle bone.

"I hate to break up this macho conversation, but dinner is ready. If you're still hungry, Carson, feel free to join us."

"Thanks but I'm stuffed. See you later, Granger." Carson slowly got up, pushing off the table with his hands and walked downstairs to his room.

"Dinner wasn't what I had in mind driving you home, but it's all good."

"Yeah, we'll work it out between our schedules and children. How tough could it be?"

Granger said, "A lot tougher than I thought."

"After dinner, you want to watch *Meet the Fokkens*? It's a documentary about twins from Amsterdam that became prostitutes."

"Sounds like a regular laugh riot. I'm in."

The dinner conversation was light. Both Rae and Granger didn't feel like tackling any heavy topics. They talked about the upcoming Farmer's Market in Walnut Park, the grocery stores they like to frequent and the demise of video rental stores. After the movie, which proved to be a fascinating expose on sixty-five-year-old identical twins who spent their adult life as prostitutes, Granger and Rae drove back to the ranch. Rae got in her car and started it up. She watched Granger walk to the front door and take a piece of paper off of it. After a few seconds, he waved the paper at Rae as he walked toward the car. Rae lowered her window.

"Allie is staying at Chris' tonight."

"You must not be too happy about that," Rae said.

"Yes and no." Granger looked at Rae and smiled. She immediately felt light-headed and anxious. Hours earlier, the beer had given her confidence. She was sober now and knowing that within minutes she could be in bed and naked with Granger, her insecurities were floating to the top of her mind and giving her pause. Granger looked so inviting, standing there in his shorts and t-shirt. His dark brown eyes filled with wanting. Rae had to take a stand with her inner critic. She didn't want her first night with Granger to be a mix of self-loathing and desire. She remembered a phrase that Rebecca made her repeat before she went out on her first date with Granger: 'You are a goddess like no other.' It sounded corny but it was a lot better than Cruella telling her that her stomach was flabby and her butt sagged. She started repeating the phrase over and over. She shut off her car and stepped into Granger's waiting arms. It was cold outside, but his kiss immediately filled her with warmth. They walked inside and, after Rae called Carson to make sure that he'd be okay for a couple of hours, she met Granger in his bedroom. The room was expansive with a sitting area off the main space. Granger's taste was exquisite. The white stucco walls complimented dark wood ceiling beams and shutters. A panama-style fan hung over the bed. The headboard had a simple wrought iron design and the duvet cover was white with faint turquoise stripes. A large oak armoire graced one of the walls and above the headboard hung an original oil painting. Its subject a grove of oak trees. The best feature in the room were the French doors opposite the bed. They opened to a deck overlooking the entire valley.

"Your bedroom is beautiful. You have great taste."

"Thank you. I'm glad you like it." Granger opened the French doors and turned on the outside lights. They walked out to the edge of the deck and Granger pointed to the right. "Over there? That's where my secret spot is. I'll take you there, if you'd like."

"Yes, please, but right now, I'd like to go to your other secret spot." Rae glanced over to the bed.

After Granger turned off the lights, they got undressed and slipped under the covers. Granger kissed Rae. His hand moved down her body and when it touched her stomach, he could feel her tense up. Granger said, "I know you're nervous. If it makes you feel any better, so am I. It's been…a while since I was with a woman."

Rae sat up on her elbows, the sheet sliding down to her waist. She grabbed it and pulled it up to her neck. "You don't know how nice it is to hear that. Eight years ago I wouldn't have had any hesitation, but now I feel so unattractive and out of practice. I really want to be with you but I don't want you to be repulsed by my body."

Granger sat up and looked into Rae's eyes. "Dear, sweet Rae. No matter what your body looks like, and it looks amazing for your age, I want to be with you. We're the same age and, believe me, I have the same concerns."

Rae looked at Granger's wide shoulders and defined arm muscles. His torso was toned and practically flawless. "Are you kidding me?" she said. "You put most thirty-year-olds to shame." She put her hand on his chest and played with his chest hairs. "I know I need to get over this insecurity and I'm sorry it's rearing its ugly, wrinkled flabby head right now, but at least we know we share the same anxieties."

Granger smiled and slowly pulled the sheet off Rae, exposing her breasts. "You have beautiful breasts." He kissed them tenderly, then moved down to her stomach and softly kissed it. As he continued to explore Rae's body, she relaxed and began to enjoy the sexual sensations she thought she'd never feel again. Granger took his time, caressing her as if she was something precious and cherished.

Afterwards, they lay in each other's arms. "I forgot how much fun sex could be," Rae said.

"Ditto." Granger lightly touched Rae's hair. "Except most of the time it wasn't *that* much fun."

"Are you going to tip your Stetson at me again? I wouldn't mind if you wore it to bed every once in a while. That's about as kinky as I get. Disappointed?"

"I'll let you know."

Rae looked at the clock. It was 12:30. She groaned. "I should go."

"Do you have to?"

"Yeah. I'm still uncomfortable leaving Carson alone."

"I don't blame you. When is he with his dad again?"

"I think it's in a few days. I'll check the calendar and let you know tomorrow." Rae got up and started to dress. Granger put his bathrobe on. "That was wonderful."

Rae went over to Granger and put her hands inside his bathrobe, "It was beyond wonderful. You're amazing." They kissed and Granger said, "I love you."

"I love you, too."

34

Fran was visibly nervous. He was never comfortable presenting an opposing view and he was about to approach students on campus and ask them how they felt about animal rights for the documentary. Standing in the quad, he was joined by Allie and her friend, Denise Pallowe, who volunteered to be the first interviewee. It was a warm day but Fran noticed that Allie was wearing a long sleeved shirt, covering up her VEGAN tattoo.

Allie said, "Let's do a test run. Are you ready, Denise?"

"Yeah."

"Fran?"

"Ready as I'll ever be."

Allie noticed the clipboard in Fran's hand was shaking. "You okay? You look a little pale."

Fran wiped the sweat off his forehead. "No, I'm cool. Let's rock and roll."

"Alrighty then." She turned on the camcorder and pointed it at Denise. "And we're rolling."

Fran looked down at the first question. "Hi, I'm, uh I mean, we're working on a documentary for our Communications class and I was wondering if I could ask you a couple of questions."

Denise nodded, so Fran continued. "How do you feel about people who eat dogs and cats?"

"That's disgusting! How can people eat their pets?"

"Dogs and cats aren't their pets. They're food, just like a chicken or pig or cow is our food."

Denise countered, "But dogs and cats are affectionate and they love people."

"Some can argue the same about our food animals. Did you know that pigs are smarter than dogs and dairy cows cry for their babies when they're taken from them to be sold as veal calves?"

"How sad."

"And cut." Allie stopped filming and hit the rewind button. "Nice work, Franny. Can I call you Franny?"

"Sure. Let's see how it came out." Fran and Denise stood behind Allie and watched the interview.

Fran said, "Good acting job, Denise."

"I wasn't acting. Allie didn't tell me what you were going to ask. I had no idea pigs were that smart, but you know, they're raised to be eaten, so what's the big deal?"

Fran looked at Allie. "Can I take this one?" Allie laughed. "Be my guest."

Fran went on to tell Denise how thousands of pigs live under one methane-filled roof, each pig in a small metal stall. If the piglets don't grow fast enough they're killed, usually by 'thumping,' a practice where the animal is grabbed by the hind legs and smashed against the concrete floor. If they're still alive, they're slammed again. "Employees have to wear protective oxygen masks working in the massive housing facility. I read about a guy whose mask fell off. He was overcome by the toxic fumes and died. Most pigs have respiratory disease by the time they're sent to slaughter."

"Enough! Please don't tell me anymore." Allie handed Denise a pamphlet entitled, *Compassionate Choices.*

Allie said, "Vegan Outreach prints them. They're a great way to learn more about your food choices. After each interview, I'm going to offer them one. If you're comfortable with it Fran, you can do the same."

"I don't see why not." Fran turned to Denise. "It was nice meeting you. Sorry for grossing you out. I had the same reaction as you but now I'm used to reading about the horrors of factory farming."

Denise said, "I don't how you do it but I'm glad you are. I guess if we're going to eat animals, we should know where they come from and now that I know about the poor piggies, I don't think I'll be able to eat bacon again and I love, love, love bacon! Okay guys, I have to get to class. See you later."

Allie gave Denise a hug and then turned her attentions to Fran. "Let's find our first interviewee."

Fran wasn't as tense when he approached a female student. His delivery was smooth and she gladly accepted the Vegan Outreach pamphlet. A few of the subsequent students weren't as receptive and one was particularly argumentative, but Fran took it in stride. It actually felt good creating a dialogue about food animals and educating people, many who were clueless about the rampant cruelty in factory farming. When it was Allie's turn to conduct the interview, she was a natural. Her passion for animals shone through and Fran could see how devoted she was, rattling off statistics and sharing stories from the sanctuary. She was only on her third interview when the camcorder ran out of memory, but by then they had gotten some great footage.

Fran said, "Do you have any pamphlets left? I want to give one to my mom."

Allie checked her bag and pulled one out, handing it to Fran. "Are you sure you want to do this? If your mom decides to cut down on meat or even nix it from the menu, it could cause world war three in the Santiago family."

"I know but I'm willing to take that chance."

"Good for you, Franny. Good for you."

35

Rae inserted the Kundalini Yoga DVD into the player. She chose one with easier workouts for Granger's first time. They moved the furniture in the bedroom sitting area out of the way. Yoga mats were placed on the floor. Rae reminded Granger to take it slow and if he couldn't strike a pose the first time, it was okay.

About ten minutes into the practice, they were instructed to lie on their back with their legs up in the air, spread as far apart as possible, then hold onto their thighs and do long, deep breathing. Eyes closed, Rae was performing the pose when she felt something on her leg. She opened her eyes to find Granger sitting up and staring at her.

"Are you okay?" she said.

"No, I'm not." He put his hand on her leg and gently massaged it. "I was right. This is sex yoga. I can't concentrate while you're lying there with your legs wide open breathing deeply. I have another form of exercise I think you'll like."

Rae put her hands on top of Granger's and smiled. He helped her up and, using the remote control, stopped the DVD.

For the next four days, Granger continued to train Rae on the ranch. She shadowed him as he gave tours to school children, learned how to groom and saddle horses, and she even got a lesson in tree pruning and landscaping. On Friday afternoon, they were in the horse stable cleaning the stalls. Granger said, "How'd you like to take the horses out for a ride before you leave?"

"I've been wanting to go horseback riding for a while. Are you asking so you can see my saddling skills?"

"That's part of it. I also thought you'd like to see the ranch from a different point of view. How long has it been since you've ridden?"

"When was the ice age?"

Granger laughed. "We'll make this a trial run. Any longer and you won't be able to walk or do other things, and I can't have that."

"No, we can't have that. Will you watch me saddle? I'm still not that confident and if the cinches aren't tight enough, it would be a bummer if the saddle dropped off the horse with me in it."

"No problem. Why don't you saddle DeLinda? She used to be a race horse, so her demeanor is quite gentle and patient."

Rae went over and brought DeLinda to the saddling area. Granger showed her the procedure a couple of days ago. They went over it a few times since then, but Rae was still not certain she could do it without instruction. She grabbed a saddle pad and was about to place it on DeLinda's back when Granger said, "Before you put the pad on, you need to groom the area where the saddle will sit to make sure there's no mud or other debris on her back."

"Right, right. Sorry! I'm not starting out well at all."

"Don't worry about it. This is only your second time. I'll make you a cheat sheet."

After about twenty minutes, Rae finished saddling up DeLinda. Granger checked the cinches, made sure they were tight enough, then he saddled up Tuscany, his six-year-old Arabian, and they rode off to the east, following a dirt trail as familiar to Granger as the front, back and side of his hand. Despite not riding for over thirty years, she felt at ease and comfortable. Perhaps it was being with someone as experienced as Granger. DeLinda was also a perfect companion, seeming to enjoy the ride as well. Most of the rangeland was wide open. The grasses were already tan and light brown, interrupted by a thistle bush with its purple spiked flowers or a spate of California poppies, their rich orange petals turning a patch of grass into a festive area. As they approached a large eucalyptus tree,

Rae asked Granger if they could stop. He gladly complied and they rode over to the ancient-looking tree. The trunk was about six-feet wide and the branches yawned and stretched from the trunk looking like human torsos with dark grey and taupe streaks. Knots and puncture marks that resembled enlarged pores sporadically marked the branches. Rae was enthralled. She sat under one of the branches, the bark peeling from it like skin. She pulled a piece off and studied it, marveling at its texture.

"How old do you think this tree is?" she asked Granger.

"My dad said it was here when he was a boy, so it's at least eighty years old. They can live to six hundred. Crazy, huh?"

"Yeah, it's a work of art. Wow, look at this." Rae crouched down and peered into a hollow area at the base of the tree. Its irregular shape reminded Rae of a clover. "I bet a leprechaun lives here."

"I wouldn't get too close. It could be a fox's den."

Rae quickly shot up. "Alrighty then. Shall we move on?"

Continuing past the hills and valleys, they came down into a semi-secluded area. At least fifty oak trees were scattered around a pond. A flock of geese had nestled on the side of the bank and a few ducks were going for a swim. Granger dismounted and Rae did the same. As her feet touched the ground, she could feel a slight soreness in her inner thighs, but she didn't say anything. They went over to the edge of the pond and sat down.

"How do you feel?" Granger asked.

"Fine." Rae lied.

"This is Cougar Pond, named by one teenager, Granger Bowden."

"And how, pray tell, did it get that name?"

"One summer night my friends Derek, Thomas and I camped out by the pond. We had one-man tents and pitched them next to each other. That evening we built a campfire and cooked our dinner. Afterwards, we got stoned and totally devoured a box of Twinkies and Ding Dongs. Derek and Thomas passed out, but I stayed up and just stared at that tree limb." Granger pointed to a large oak.

"It looks like a cougar crouching," Rae said.

"Exactly! Remember, I was stoned, so the more I stared the more realistic it became. I could practically see the whiskers. I imagined it watching me, like it was ready to pounce.

"I sat underneath the oak tree and studied the mountain lion, my eyes penetrating the wood, seeing the cat, sensing the cat. Then, I closed my eyes and got on all fours. I could feel my limbs turning into mountain lion's legs. I felt my long tail swaying back and forth. I licked my 'paw' and tasted fur, salt and damp ground. My thoughts were carnal and raw but I also felt this life-force pulsing through my body. I ran my tongue over my teeth, stopping to feel the large incisors, then let out a low growl and sauntered over to the pond. After a long, unhurried stretch from ears to tail, I jumped in. The water was cold but I felt totally exhilarated. I lay on my back, floating, eyes closed. I could feel my heart beating, slow and steady. I could smell wet fur. And then it was gone, shattered by a loud splash. Derek had jumped in the pond. The water suddenly felt icy cold and I started to shiver. I went to my tent, dried off, and quickly fell fast asleep. That night I had this dream where I was still a cougar. I traveled with thousands of other cougars across a rocky terrain. We ran and leapt over boulders, sometimes flying through the air, grazing each other's shoulders, flanks, even flowing into each other's bodies. It felt like we traveled halfway around the world. It was a transformative experience. The next morning, I named this little body of water Cougar Pond."

"I can totally see you transforming into a mountain lion. You have the grace and quiet power. Have you come back here to relive the experience?"

"I have."

"Is this your secret spot?"

"Nope. What is it with you and my secret hideaway?"

"I'm not sure. I think it has something to do with wanting to know all about you and seeing the place that you regard as sacred and private."

"If you want to see another aspect of who I am, go on vacation with me. I've been out of the state only twice in my life and have always wanted to travel, but I wanted to go with someone I love."

"That sounds great. It would have to be after Carson's fully recovered, of course."

"Sure. What do think about going to Italy?"

"Twist my arm. You're just full of surprises, aren't you?"

Granger gave Rae a kiss on her forehead. "I want to share everything with you."

"Including your secret spot?"

Granger laughed. "You're like a pit bull! You hold on and don't let go."

"So I've been told."

They mounted their horses and as he led them back to the trail, he said, "We better get going before it gets too dark and you won't be able to see my secret hideout, my man-cave."

"We can gallop, you know. I remember how."

Without another word, Granger yelled and Tuscany took off. DeLinda followed suit and to Rae's delight, they were galloping back through the valley, past the house and the animal barns, straight for the hills. After what seemed like half a mile, Granger slowed to a walk. They were riding into a wooded area where the hills intersected and the brush was dense. When it looked like they were approaching a dead end, Tuscany was directed to the right through eucalyptus trees and then up the mountain. Granger stopped and got off his horse. He went over to Rae and waited while she dismounted, then he tied the horses to a tree limb and started walking up the hill. After a few minutes, they came to a perfectly oval-shaped opening in the side of the mountain. It was about eight feet high by eight feet deep and ten feet wide. There were no signs of human encroachment, except for one of Angel's carvings above the entrance. It was a twelve-inch California Alligator lizard. Its olive green head was looking down at the cave's visitors as its tail whipped above its colorful body, the intricate design resembling a mosaic in tan, rust, black, grey and white.

"This is it. The place I go when I want to really get away from everything. Are you disappointed?"

Rae looked inside the cave. It was anything but inviting. The limestone walls were rough and the dirt floor looked a little damp. Rae walked inside. She felt the limestone. It was cool to the touch. She looked up, half expecting to see bats. It was the same as the walls. She sat down, closed her eyes and suddenly could feel the heart of the mountain beating inside of her. Her breath slowed and, if Granger wasn't there, she knew she could sit and meditate. She opened her eyes and smiled. "This place is magical. I totally understand why you love it here. Thank you for bringing me."

"You're very welcome. You can come here whenever you want. If you can find it again."

"Have I ever told you about my sense of direction or lack thereof? It's so bad that I have to leave breadcrumbs from my living room to my bedroom so I don't get lost."

"That's bad! We better head back before it gets dark."

Hand in hand, they walked back down the hill. Filtered sunlight through the trees gave the horses an ethereal appearance.

"This may sound new agey, but when I was sitting in the cave I could feel the mountain's heart beating inside of me. It was very powerful," Rae said as they rode home.

"I feel it, too. I first discovered the cave when I was in my early twenties. A couple of cows were unaccounted for, so I went looking for them. My search led me to the clearing where we tied up the horses. There they were, just hanging out. Instead of leading them back to the ranch, I had an urge to walk up the mountain. The cave wasn't as visible back then. I had to clear away some scrub and an oak tree blocked the entrance but it has long since died. I walked into the cave and sat down just like you did, in almost the same spot. When I closed my eyes, my heart started pounding but I realized it wasn't my heart, it was the mountain's. I can meditate there for hours. I've never told anyone about that or about this place because I thought they would think I'm nuts. Lydia would have had me committed."

"You're very spiritual, not crazy. I'd love to go back there sometime and meditate with you, if that's okay."

"It would be more than okay. The best way to get there is remembering that it's the trail behind the horse corral. You take it to the right when it dead-ends and go up the hill. Take a left when you come to the boulder that looks like a VW Bug. When you hit the clearing, walk up the trail. Can't miss it."

"Behind corral, right at dead-end, left at VW and up again at the clearing. Piece of cake."

They got back to the barn as the sun was setting, dyeing the clouds deep pink and purple. They streaked the darkening sky, giving the valleys and hills an aura of impermanence, as if the night would erase it all.

36

"What's it called again?" Fran's mother asked.

"Kung Pao *not* chicken," said Fran. He had been getting immersed in the documentary and, as a result, it was becoming more difficult for him to justify chomping down on a baby pig's ribs or cutting into a steak, especially when blood ran from the freshly sliced flesh. Fran always loved to cook, but between work and school and eating at his parents', he didn't have much time to indulge his hobby. Tonight, he took the time and prepared a vegan meal for his family. Allie gave him one of her favorite recipes. Kung Pao is a spicy Chinese dish made with peanuts, vegetables and chili, served over rice. She convinced Fran to make brown instead of white rice because it was healthier and to use organic peanuts. Instead of chicken, he bought Beyond Meat, a chicken substitute that was by far the closest in texture and taste to the real thing.

"Can't I just eat normal food?" said Dario.

"Your brother took the time to cook you dinner. Be nice." Lornita didn't care if it was vegan. She was ecstatic that someone besides her was cooking. She watched with pride as Fran gave everyone a serving of rice and then placed a generous helping of Kung Pao on top. Her middle child always was ambitious. He was the first in the family to go to college, a state university not a junior college. She didn't mind at all, unlike his father, that he was exploring a different lifestyle. A vegan in a

Mexican family was an anomaly, but they didn't live in Mexico. Petaluma was full of ranchers and farms but it also had its share of progressive thinkers and eaters.

"Dig in," said Fran. Dario was the first to comment.

"I thought you weren't using real chicken. I love the peanuts in it, too."

"That's fake chicken. Pretty amazing, huh?"

"I'll say."

"Franny, this is delicious," Lornita said.

His dad and Luis agreed.

"I thought I was going to get a lot of misery from you all. Where's the real meat? What are you feeding us?"

Luis said, "Did you get this recipe from your white friend?" Fran nodded.

"I thought so. It's not hot enough. It needs more chilies. So, what are you making tomorrow night?"

"Very funny. Maybe I'll cook dinner once a week. Is that okay with you, mom?"

"Take over my kitchen any time you want."

Fran couldn't wait to tell Allie. He imagined that she would be proud of him. How many Mexicanos make a vegan dinner for their family? Fortified with the knowledge of the farming industry, he knew that his friends would rile and chastise him for defending food animals. Working on the documentary opened a door into another world, an unspeakably cruel and hellacious world for the animals and the workers. That door wouldn't close. Too many facts kept it open. Fran knew he wasn't as handsome or charming as Chris, but he was hoping that Allie would see his compassion and a love for her that Chris was incapable of. He had about a month to convince her.

It didn't happen often, but when it did, the residents of Occidental savored it. Maybe twice a year the nights were warm, about seventy degrees. The usual sweater and jeans attire was replaced with t-shirts, shorts and sandals. The organizers of the Occidental Hoedown were thrilled. The event was being held at the high school's soccer field. It was a great location because the grassy field was surrounded by elm and sycamore trees. It gave the hoedown a genuine community feel. The warm, balmy night made for a good time, better than when a cold wind could end the festivities too soon. The volunteers were putting the finishing touches on the picnic tables, food stands and drink stations when Granger and Rae pulled up. After parking in the dirt lot, they walked over to Thomas Bono, retired fire captain and head of the Hoedown planning committee. Thomas was setting up the beer keg when Granger patted him on the back.

"Hey there, Granger. I'm glad you made it." Thomas looked over at Rae and smiled. "And who might this be?"

Granger put his arm around Rae. "Thomas Bono, meet Rae O'Brien." Rae put out her hand but Thomas came over and gave her a big bear hug, practically shoving Granger out of the way. Rae's arms barely circled Thomas. He was tall and had what could only be described as an ample beer belly.

"Nice to meet you, Rae."

"Same here, Thomas."

"I hope you two are in the mood to dance. We hired the Kentucky Flatliners. They play everything from country to funk. They'll be up on the truck over there." A large red flatbed truck was parked on the edge of the field. The crew could be seen positioning the amps, setting up the microphones, drums and other band equipment.

"I have to finish putting out the food and beer, but I'll catch up with you later."

"Sounds like a plan," Granger said. As they walked away, Rae rubbed her shoulders and said, "Isn't he a friendly fellow?"

"That he is. When he hugged you, you all but disappeared in his girth! I thought I'd lost you."

"Imagine how I felt, but he seems like a nice guy."

"I grew up with Thomas. Remember the story I told you about camping out with my friends and becoming a mountain lion? He was one of the friends. He moved to Occidental a while ago. The only time I see him is at the hoedown. You want something to drink?"

"An ice cold beer sounds great."

Granger grabbed Rae's hand and they walked over to a newly positioned keg. He gave the volunteer a ten dollar bill and in return was handed two glasses of Springtime Ale. He passed one to Rae. She raised it to his and said, "To a night of fun and frivolity."

"I'll drink to that." They clicked glasses and drank the rich, amber brew.

As the sun went down, it refused to take the warm air with it. The soccer field began filling up, coming alive with families, couples and groups of teenagers mingling amongst the beer and food. The mood was infectious and even though Rae only knew Granger, he made sure she felt welcome. He must have introduced her to a dozen people, all greeting him like a long lost friend. On their way to get another beer, Granger ran into an attractive woman named Irene Baker. She was a good six inches taller than Rae, partly due to her three-inch heels. Eventually, she would have to take them off because they kept sinking in the soft sod. After Granger made the introductions, Irene said in a low voice, "Don't look now but Lydia's coming our way. This is where I exit. Nice meeting you, Rae. Take care, Granger."

They said goodbye to Irene and then watched as Lydia made a bee-line for them. Granger turned to Rae. "Brace yourself, dear. You're about to meet my ex."

Lydia walked over to the couple with purpose. The five-foot-eight-inch blonde had a stellar figure and she knew it. Her cut off shorts barely covered her derriere and her breasts seemed to float inside her hot pink lace tank top. Rae could have sworn that Granger told her they were in the same high school class but Lydia looked about fifteen years younger. Her green eyes were flawless and there wasn't a wrinkle to be found on her beautiful face. Rae suddenly felt short, old and flabby. She sucked in her stomach and stood a little bit taller. Lydia embraced Granger, despite his apparent discomfort. She held on past the point of good taste until Granger gently disengaged himself from her grip.

"Hey stranger. Fancy meeting you here. And you must be Rae. Am I right?" Lydia blatantly gave Rae the once-over. She practically scanned her from head to toe.

Rae said, "That's me. Nice to meet you, Lydia."

"You, too." Lydia turned to Granger. "You still a vegan?"

"You still a carnivore?" Granger replied.

"Yes I am and loving it. Greg has bred the most amazing cattle. I've never tasted such tender steaks. So, have you met Allie's new boyfriend? Isn't he adorable? I just love him."

Granger said, "Chris? Yeah, I met the wonderful and adorable Chris."

"You don't sound sincere. Allie told me you had a bug up your butt about him. What's the matter? Is it because he's a meat eater?"

"No, Lydia. He didn't make a great first impression but if he makes Al happy, I'm fine with him. Is Greg here?"

Lydia waved her hand behind her. "I left him over there, talking to Bob Grohl."

Granger turned around. He nodded to Greg and Greg returned the silent salutation, continuing his conversation with Bob. Granger said to Lydia, "It looks like Greg is calling you over."

Lydia shook her head. "The man can't even have a conversation without me. You two have fun. Nice chatting." Lydia turned and walked away before they could respond.

As they watched her leave, Rae said, "She's really beautiful."

"On the outside only. It's a shame that plastic surgeons can't make people beautiful on the inside as well."

"I thought she had her face done. Her nose is way too perfect."

"Actually, she never had a nose job but she did get her lips plumped and a facelift."

"Geez, what I wouldn't give to have a nose like that. Maybe in another life. I'll tell you, if I had the money I'd do some nipping and tucking."

Granger looked thoughtfully at Rae. "Sweetie, you look wonderful. I wouldn't change a thing about you."

"Not even my flabby belly?"

"Not even your flabby belly."

"See, you think it's flabby!"

Granger's soft, brown eyes became softer and he looked at Rae with such love and affection that she thought she was going to cry. "When I think about you, I think of your incredible spirit, your warmth, sense of humor and compassion. And when I look at you, my dear Rae, I see a beauty that money couldn't buy. Your perceived imperfections are invisible to me." Granger kissed Rae passionately. It made her knees weak. When they stopped kissing, Rae noticed a few people looking, including Lydia and she didn't look happy.

"It appears that Lydia still has a thing for you. She's giving me the hairy eyeball."

"She doesn't want me. She's pissed because I divorced her. Egomaniacs can't stand rejection. Shall I kiss you again and see if I can unleash the horns she's tucked under her hair extensions?"

Before Rae could answer, the band started to play the Beatles', *Twist and Shout*. Granger led her onto the grass in front of the band and started dancing. He kicked off his sandals and she her shoes, feeling the warm grass between their toes. Granger started twisting and so did Rae. They synchronized their movements, laughing and singing along with the music. Within seconds, others joined them. Most were in their fifties and all seemed to know the words, singing at the top of their lungs. It was one of those moments where Rae felt a connection with them all, especially Granger.

After a half an hour of dancing, including the band playing a perfect rendition of the Ohio Players' *Fire*, they decided to get a drink. "This weather is unbelievable but it's making me hot. I'm schvitzing." Rae wiped her brow, then picked up her shoes and followed Granger to the beer table.

"I've built up a sweat, too, and that is why beer was made for nights like this. Let's drink it over at the far end of the grass." As Granger pointed to a spot at the opposite end of the field, Rae noticed something in his hand. "What you got there, Willis?" she said.

"Just a little grass of my own." He put the red and white striped joint in front of Rae's face. She grabbed it and headed over to the designated spot. When she got there, she lay on the warm grass and put the joint in her mouth. Obliging, Granger took out his lighter and brought the peppermint-flavored joint to life. After she took a hit, she handed it to Granger, then put her head on his chest. Looking up at the stars, Rae located the Big Dipper.

"I can always find the Big Dipper but where the hell is the Little Dipper?"

"I believe I can help you with that. See the ladle's upper right star? Follow it up to the North Star, the brightest star in the sky. That's the tip of the Little Dipper's handle. It looks like the little dipper is falling into the big dipper's ladle. Can you see it?" Granger pointed to the North Star. It took Rae a little while, but then she yelled, "There it is! Finally! You don't know how long I've been wanting to see the Little Dipper."

"Because?"

"Because I knew it was up there. Okay, so listen to this. Tonight was a night of firsts. I saw the Little Dipper, we danced together for the first time, my first Occidental Hoedown and meeting the ex."

Granger stroked Rae's hair. "I'm glad I was here to be a part of all your firsts."

"Couldn't have done it without you." Rae closed her eyes. The sound of Granger's rhythmic breathing combined with the rise and fall of his chest, put her in a hypnotic state. The band was on a break and the hum of the crowd was distant. Rae felt herself drifting off. Her body felt like it was floating above the field while her mind threw out random memories: seeing Carson in the emergency room, getting fired from her job, sitting on the bluff at Margo's sheep ranch. Granger interrupted her mental montage.

"What are you thinking about?"

"A lot." She pointed to her head. "It's like a whirling dervish in there. You?"

"How I'd like to make love to you right now."

Butterflies flew about in her stomach. "I'm with you on the first part but I think we should hightail it back to your place. I've only had sex in public places twice and got caught once. I Don't want that to happen again."

"Get out."

"Really. The first time was on a balcony at a hotel in Hawaii. The second time was late at night on the beach in Malibu. A surfer scared the shit out of us. At first I thought it was a land shark."

Granger laughed. "You're just full of surprises, aren't you? A bed *would* be a lot more comfortable than the grass."

Slowly they both rose and stretched. Granger took Rae's hand and they were walking to the car when the band took the stage and started playing Average White Band's *Cut The Cake*. Rae looked at Granger and said, "Sorry, Dude, but I love this song. One more dance, okay?"

"Sure. Lead me to the dance floor."

Most of the dancers knew the song but it was obvious by the blank expressions on the younger dancer's faces that they'd never heard of the all white band that played funk.

Rae and Granger reveled in their last dance of the evening. Out of the corner of her eye, she caught a glimpse of Lydia and Greg dancing, too. Without being obvious, Rae watched them. A huge smile appeared on her face. Granger said, "What's so amusing?"

"She may be beautiful but the woman dances like she just got struck by lightning. Does she know how ridiculous she looks?"

Granger replied, "Not a fucking clue."

37

The dining room table was filled with index cards, highlight markers, post-it notes in yellow, green and violet, a Pilot G-2 gel pen and a mechanical pencil. Rae stared at it all, her eyes glazing over. She had mapped out the first half hour of her film a few weeks ago, but tonight the creativity train had come to a grinding halt. There appeared to be a cow on the tracks. Or was it a huge chicken? Rae's mind was blank, except for a song that played on a continuous loop. She couldn't get Chuck Mangione's *Chase the Clouds Away* out of her head. It would only fade when she came up with an idea. But once Rae negated it, passing it off as redundant or over-used, Chuck's flugelhorn would begin blowing again, its soft melodic tune filling up her head and refusing to leave. She absently started to pick at her fingernails. Realizing one of the nails was now uneven, she eagerly went to the bathroom to get a nail file. When the nail was filed to perfection, Rae was thirsty. After pouring herself a glass of water, she wandered back to the dining room, glancing at the index cards. As desperately as she wanted to finish the documentary, she also resented the fact that it took up time. Time that could be spent watching a movie or visiting with friends. It was a counter-intuitive attitude but there it was.

After Cruella gave Rae a verbal wedgie, she forced herself to 'walk through' the film, from the beginning to where she left off, hoping it would jump-start her imagination. Fade in, a family eating at a fast food restaurant. The kids are eating chicken nuggets and the parents each have a hamburger and fries. All are sipping on extra-large sodas. One of the kids throws a nugget with ketchup on it at the other. A chicken clucks. The other child dips her nugget in a lot of ketchup and throws it at her sibling. The chicken clucks louder. As the kids laugh and continue to have a nugget fight, the scene transitions into a broiler facility where thousands of male chickens are packed into a huge building. The sound is deafening. The title comes onto the screen: *Eating Animals. Eating Agony*. The chickens fade into a Foster Farms commercial. Two unkempt chickens are driving in a filthy car to Foster Farms. They want to be Foster Farms chickens but the 'ultra-picky' company only accepts the cleanest, healthiest chickens. Cut to a chicken processing plant where the chickens are being yanked out of their crates and hung upside down in clamps where a conveyer belt glides them toward the station where their throats are slit. Cut to the 1983 Charlie the Tuna commercial for StarKist Tuna. Charlie's desire is to be caught on a hook so he can be a StarKist tuna and end up in a can. Cut to a tuna boat hauling in a net full of tuna fish. Show tuna gasping for air as the net hits the ship's deck. Cut to a cartoon clip of Porky Pig saying, 'That's All Folks' and cut to a pig farm where row after row after row of pigs stand in metal crates. As the camera pulls back, thousands are revealed. Cut to egg cartons from Judy's Farm, Uncle Eddie's Wild Chicken Eggs and Rock Island Farms. All show illustrations of free-roaming chickens, pecking at the dirt. Cut to the chicken 'bunkers' where thousands of egg-layers live indoors their entire lives. A small door is visible but very rarely do the chickens go outside. Most can't even see the opening.

Rae smiled. She hadn't begun compiling the scenes, but she liked how it started. Subconsciously, she started picking her nails again and accidentally ripped off her pinkie nail too close to the skin, causing it to bleed. She let out a small cry of pain, then sucked on the finger. Once it stopped bleeding, she applied a Band-Aid. Rae looked at her fingers. Every single nail and cuticle was affected by a habit she had as long as she could remember. She got it from her mother who, at times, had every finger covered in a beige Band-Aid, like wrapping them up hid her destructive habit.

Glancing up at the clock, Rae realized that one of her favorite sit-coms was on in fifteen minutes. She rarely missed *The Big Bang Theory* and, despite the fact that she could easily record it, she made a mental note to finish up her work, brew some tea and watch it. Cruella wasn't happy. 'It's a show for Christ sake. Record it and work on saving the animals. Remember them?' Okay, Rae told herself, dedicate a solid hour on the film and then watch Big Bang. "Thanks Cruella!" she said out loud. Sometimes, the hag was right. For the next hour, Rae poured every bit of concentration into the documentary. It wasn't easy. When Pierre jumped onto the dining room table and started pushing the pencil around, Rae grabbed him and rubbed his chin hoping it would calm him down, but he was too wound up. She put him on the floor and he took off like he was shot out of a cannon. By the time she positioned herself in front of the television, Rae had written four more scenes, uncovered a website full of animal rights material that was public domain and sent e-mails to five people in the movement that she wanted to interview. She congratulated herself for getting so much done and chided herself for not working at capacity as often.

38

For three weeks, Rae had been working at Bowden Ranch. She was giving tours solo now, which freed up Granger's time to tend to other duties. He and Angel always seemed to be fixing a roof or repairing a fence. She pulled into the lower driveway next to the stables and parked close to Granger's Jeep. She had an hour before the first busload of fourth graders arrived. Lucy was carting vegetables in a wheelbarrow, heading over to the chicken coop. Rae waved. "How's it going, Lucy?"

"Good morning." Lucy set the wheelbarrow by the coop's front gate and walked over to Rae. She was a pretty girl with short brown hair and blue eyes. She had a boyish figure, but working on the ranch gave her defined muscles and a flat stomach that Rae envied. She gave Rae a warm hug.

"You enjoying yourself on B Ranch?"

"It's the best job I've ever had. And believe me, I've had a lot of jobs."

"It doesn't hurt that you're sleeping with the boss."

"Lucy!"

"It's cool. I think it's great that Granger finally met someone. We all thought he'd be single forever. Time to dummy up. The boss man's coming." Lucy waved to Granger and then headed back to the coop to feed the chickens.

"Hi there Sunshine." Granger was wearing a Forty-Niner's baseball cap and his regulation work outfit: faded jeans, cowboy boots and a dark grey t-shirt. He walked over and gave Rae a big hug and kiss. "Ready for a bunch of fourth graders?"

"Yeah. I can't wait. Ten is a great age. So, what are you up to today?"

"Fence repair with Angel." Granger pointed to the hills. "A little past the ridge, about a swath of ten to twenty feet is down. Not many of the animals travel that far but we need to keep the fence line intact."

"Do you use barbed wire?" Rae said.

"Hell no. After I took over the ranch, I replaced all the barbed wire fences with wooden fences and poles. Barbed wire is cheap but it's inhumane. Years ago, I was out in the field with my dad when I heard a high-pitched yipping. I knew it was an animal in pain. We followed the sound and found a coyote, its leg caught on the barbed wire. Dear old dad told me to get the gun and kill it. It's one of the few times I didn't listen to him. I put on my gloves and slowly went over to the coyote. It was panting heavily and started to struggle violently to free itself when it saw me. I quickly grabbed the coyote's leg and lifted it off the barb. It dropped to the ground and lay there, exhausted. His leg was bloody but didn't look broken. I stood perfectly still, watching him, knowing he wouldn't let me get any closer to help him. As the coyote started licking its freed leg, I slowly backed away, leaving him in peace."

"What did your dad do?"

"I can't remember exactly what he said but it was something like, 'You should have shot the son-of-a-bitch. They're nothing but trouble.' I think they're remarkable animals. Their survival instincts are perfectly honed. They've adapted to living with humans in rural areas and even the suburbs."

"They do get a bad rap but I agree with you. They have amazing survival instincts. Here comes Angel."

Angel drove up in his truck. The bed was filled with fencing materials and a large box. Rae walked over to the truck, trying to peer inside the box. It was open but she couldn't see the contents.

"What's in the box, Angel, or should I ask?"

Angel said, "Of course you can ask. Check it out." Rae climbed up in the truck bed and her eyes widened. "Can I pick it up?" Angel nodded. Using both hands, she lifted up the most exquisite miniature home carved out of a hollow branch. The roof resembled a turkey tail mushroom with a stovepipe chimney. Standing a little over a foot high and six-inches in diameter, the home had four windows, each with its own turquoise shutters and ledge. A fairy peeked out of one of the windows. Another fairy sat on a bench made of moss-covered sticks outside the light green door, complete with hinges and a bronze dragonfly knocker.

"I am totally in love! Angel, you are so talented!"

Granger came around to examine the work of art. "It's beautiful, Angel."

Rae said, "I bet I know where you're going to put it. In front of the clover-shaped hole in the huge eucalyptus tree off the trail."

"Very good! I checked to see if it was occupied but no one lives there, so now the fairies do."

"We can install it on the way to the fence." Granger gave Rae a kiss and got into the truck. "You'll have to come see it this afternoon when we're done with the fence. Good luck with the kids – you'll do great."

"Thanks," Rae said, and waved good-bye.

At 10:00 a.m. sharp, the bus pulled into the parking lot. Rae walked up to the door and greeted Mrs. Klein and Mr. Fischera, the two fourth grade teachers.

"Hi, I'm Rae O'Brien. Welcome to Bowden Ranch. Mr. Fischera, do you remember Carson Tenman? He was in your class and came here about twelve years ago."

Mr. Fischera thought for a moment and said, "Wasn't he wearing black nail polish in those days?"

Rae laughed, "Regrettably, yes, but he's over that. Now he wears a tiara and red lipstick." Before he could react, Rae quickly said, "Just kidding. He's all boy. So I take it the kids have been briefed on the rules of the sanctuary?"

Mrs. Klein said, "Yes, but it wouldn't hurt to reiterate. Rules and regulations tend to seep out of their little minds like Slurpees."

"I know only too well."

Once the thirty-five fourth graders disembarked, they stood in front of the school bus with their teachers and the four parent chaperones and listened while Rae went over the rules. It only lasted a few minutes but some of the children were already restless. Two of the boys were talking to each other and exchanging kicks and hits. Rae pointed to one of the boys.

"What's your name?"

The boy looked up, surprised. "Henry."

"Hey Henry. Can you tell me what I just said about walking near the horses?"

Henry hemmed and hawed, then said, "Don't pet them?"

Rae smiled. "No. You can pet the horses. What I said was do not walk behind them. The calmest horse has the potential to hurt you if they get scared. They'll kick out their back legs and the result isn't pretty. Otherwise, they love to be pet. Okay then, are you all ready to meet the animals?" The kids let out a resounding yes. "Follow me over to where our first residents of Bowden Ranch live."

Rae had everyone come into the middle of the cow shed so they could get a good view of the stalls, equipment and supplies stacked up against the side of the barn.

"Most of our cows are Herefords, the brown and white ones. These guys have lived here for twelve years. They were originally part of a cattle ranch and were destined to end up in the meat section at your local supermarket, but the ranch owner and his daughter became vegans and these fortunate cows escaped death and now live in peace with the other rescue animals here at the sanctuary. The black and white spotted cows are Holsteins. They were rescued from the auction yard as day old calves.

One of the girls raised her hand. Rae said, "You have a question?"

The sixth grader replied, "Why are newborn calves at the auction yard?"

"When a male calf is born on a dairy farm it's useless to the farmer, so they bring the babies to the auction yard to sell. Some of them are so weak or sick, they don't make it and end up in a corner known as the dead pile. Bowden Ranch was able to save some of them but the stronger ones are sold and end up as veal calves or steers on a working cattle ranch."

"That's horrible," the girl said.

"Yes it is, but that's the industry. At Bowden Ranch these calves are safe. With a few exceptions, most of the fifty head of cattle live in the fields. They're always free to stay in the barn but our weather is so mild, even in the winter, they prefer to live outdoors." Rae noticed that the group was focusing on something behind her. Some were pointing and others started laughing. Rae turned just in time to see Rodney sauntering up behind her. She put her hand out to pet him and Rodney returned the gesture by licking her arm with a tongue the size of Rae's head. Rae tried not to look too grossed out. "This is Rodney, one of our oldest steers and definitely the most affectionate." Rae grabbed a towel nearby and wiped her arm.

The kids were delighted to get so close to a cow. Most of them viewed the 1,200 pound bovines in the fields, usually from a car window. Rodney was as tall as the children, standing a little over four and a half feet. "Does anyone else want a big lick from old Rods?" Predictably, no one wanted to get slobbered on but they were anxious to touch him, so Rae let them take turns petting a very willing Rodney.

"Before we leave," Rae said, "I'd like you to meet Rodney's best friend, Pamela." She directed the group to the far end of the barn with Rodney in tow. Pamela was in the last stall, laying on a bed of straw. She raised her head as if to greet her guests but when she saw Rodney, she stood up and went over to him, walking in and out of his legs. When she emerged from underneath him, Rodney gave her a kiss on the top of her head.

"Pamela came to the sanctuary in pretty bad shape. She was rescued from a backyard butcher, a man who thought he could raise and slaughter animals any way he wanted, so he took a bat to poor Pamela, cracking her skull. On her arrival, Rodney here fell in love. He'd never seen a pig before and now they share this stall. The veterinarian who took care of Pamela didn't think she'd make it but after witnessing her recovery, he's convinced that Rodney had a lot to do with it. While the other cows were having fun in the fields, Rodney was lying beside Pamela, keeping her warm and keeping her company." As if to further validate the story, Rodney began licking the fading wound on Pamela's head.

One of the children shouted out, "I want a cow and pig, too!" Other kids chimed in, requesting their very own star-crossed couple.

Rae said, "I don't think your parents will let you adopt a cow and pig, but you can all come by any time you want and visit."

Reluctantly, the kids said goodbye to Pamela and Rodney. From the cow barn, Rae brought the group to the horse stable and from there, they visited the chicken coop and finally the sheep barn. By that time, they were ready for lunch. Picnic tables were set up under a grove of walnut trees. The teachers had been instructed beforehand that no meat or dairy was allowed at the ranch. Some of the children had pasta in plastic containers, others had tomato and lettuces sandwiches, but most dined on peanut butter and jelly sandwiches. The sanctuary provided dessert, which consisted of vegan chocolate chip cookies or cupcakes in a variety of flavors, including red velvet, almond joy and chocolate butterscotch. A few years ago, Granger talked Flour Power, a local bakery, into making vegan cupcakes and cookies. He promised to buy at least six dozen a week. The bakery readily agreed.

Rae sat at the end of the table with the teachers and two of the parents, one an attractive mother in her mid-forties. As they were finishing their lunch, she moved closer and introduced herself to Rae.

"Hi Rae. I'm Sue." She pointed to a pretty blonde girl wearing a red and white-striped t-shirt. That's my daughter, Riley."

"She's adorable."

"Thanks. This place is wonderful. I had no idea animals were treated so cruelly. I'll be cooking less meat, believe me. So...what's Granger Bowden like?"

Rae could see where this was going. "He's a great guy. Friendly, generous, compassionate. I can't say enough about him."

"I hear he's really good-looking."

"Gorgeous is the word that comes to mind."

Sue bent toward Rae and lowered her voice. "Any chance you could introduce me?"

"I'll make you a deal. If we break up, you'll be the first to know."

Sue blushed. "Oh dear, I'm so embarrassed!"

Rae said, "Don't be. I'd be trying to get into his pants, too, if I wasn't already in there."

"I wish you the best, but in case it doesn't work out, here's my card." Sue reached into her purse and fished out a business card. Rae gave her an obligatory smile and looked at the card. Sue was the owner of *Just Leather*, a boutique that featured all things leather including, Rae had heard, a leather jock strap and matching thong. She chuckled to herself, wondering if Sue knew that vegans didn't wear animal hides. She put the card in her pocket and turned her attention to the group, instructing them to take their trash over to the bins and put the food, napkins and paper in the compost bin. Juice boxes and plastic went in the recycle bin and the remainder in the trash bin. When they were finished with the task, Rae said, "This is my favorite part of the tour because you have a chance to just hang out with the animals in the pasture. I'm going to ask you all to pretend you're guests in their house. This is where they live and we need to respect their space. Gentle petting is encouraged. Please remember not to sneak up behind any of the animals. Any questions before we go?"

A boy raised his hand. "Yes?" Rae said.

"Can we visit Pamela again?"

Rae laughed. "Of course! She would love it. Okay, follow me troupes. We're off to cavort in the country with the animal folk."

As the kids ran around the field and interacted with the animals and each other, Rae joined them, answering questions and occasionally scratching under a sheep's chin or rubbing a horse's soft, velvety nose. She delighted in watching the children's joy as they played. Even the adults enjoyed themselves. Except for the teachers who had been coming to the sanctuary for years, many of the chaperones had little contact with farm animals.

After one last visit to Pamela's stall, Rae handed each child a goody bag as they boarded the bus. It contained a vegan candy bar, a twenty-page cookbook for kids called *Good Eats* and a magnet with a photo of Pamela and Rodney lying side-by-side.

Rae waved to the bus as it left, thankful that she could relax for a little while before embarking on her other duties. She imagined Granger working on the fence, getting sweaty and hot. The image was turning her on and she considered calling him on his cell. Just then, her cell rang.

"Are you hot and sweaty?" Rae asked.

"As a matter of fact, I am," Granger said, as he wiped his brow with a handkerchief.

"I bet you look really sexy."

Granger laughed. "If you like dirt, sweat and torn jeans, I'm your man."

"Oh baby, I wish you were closer."

"So do I but Angel and I are only half-way finished. So tell me, how did the tour go?"

"It was great. The kids were wonderful. They adored the animals. The only gross thing was when Rodney licked my arm."

"He thinks he's a dog. A humongous, mooing dog. Did he follow you around, too?"

"He would have if we didn't stop in to visit Pamela. They've got some mad love going on there. It's so sweet."

"It is. Okay, gotta get back to work. I'll see you later."

"Bye, hunky sweaty guy."

From time to time, Rae would check in with her intuition, asking herself questions about Granger and listening to the answers. On the issue of her documentary, her gut told her to tell Granger but it also told her he'd disapprove. She was afraid he would tell her not to spend time on it and that her work at the sanctuary was enough. She didn't want to hear that, so she kept putting off the inevitable. When Rae wasn't seeing him, she worked on her film, plotting out the storyline, writing the narration and setting up the storyboards. She planned to start filming over the weekend, so if she was going to tell Granger, this was the week to do it. When the timing was right, she would casually let him know. Butterflies filled her stomach. Her insecurities started to pervade her confidence and she was terrified that she'd disappoint him or upset him. What if he broke up with her? Would she end the project or would she want to be with a man who didn't respect her passion?

Rae sat back, enjoying an iced tea in the courtyard. She was still going over the pros and cons of telling Granger about the documentary when Allie and Fran walked in.

"Slacking off are we?" said Allie.

"Please don't tell the boss. I don't want to get whipped again!" Rae put out her hand to Fran. "I'm Rae, hired hand."

"Fran Santiago. I go to Sonoma State with Allie."

Allie said, "We're working on a documentary for our Communications class."

"What's it about?"

"Factory farming and how it affects the employees as well as the animals."

Rae said, "What a great idea. You never hear about the workers and how poorly they're treated. I'm working on an animal rights documentary, too."

"You are?" Granger walked into the courtyard from the living room. Dust clung to his work clothes. His hands and face bore the result of working the land. From the look on his face, Rae knew she should have told him sooner.

"I kind of just started, really. I'll tell you about it after work."

"I'd like to hear about it now."

Allie felt a chill in the air even though the sun was beating down on the courtyard. "Fran and I are going to work on our project. See you guys later." They quickly left.

Granger sat down at the table. He took a handkerchief from his pocket and wiped his face, then his hands.

"I was going to tell you this week, I swear."

"How long have you been working on it?"

"About two weeks," Rae said.

"Why didn't you tell me when you first started?"

"I don't know. Part of me wanted to tell you and another part of me wanted to surprise you with it. I want the film to be groundbreaking. There are a lot of documentaries on factory farming and animal rights, but I want it to be different and, hopefully, change a lot of people's minds about eating animals."

Granger took his hat off and ran his fingers through his hair. He looked up to the sky for what seemed to Rae like a long time. Her heart was pounding. Finally he spoke.

"Were you afraid to tell me because you thought I'd ask you to stop?"

"Yes."

"You're right. You're changing the way kids look at food animals right here. You don't have to prove anything. I thought you were happy working on the ranch. What happens once you finish the film? How much time will you put into promoting it?"

"Granger, please. This is my dream."

"Then what am I? Sloppy seconds?"

"That's not fair. I started working on this before we went out." Rae stopped, realizing what she just said.

"We've been going out for over a month. You said you started working on it two weeks ago. Now you're lying to me?" Granger stood up and Rae did, too.

"I didn't mean it. I do want to be with you. I love you! I don't see why I can't do both."

"I don't think you can."

"Why not?"

Granger took a deep breath. He had to because he was having trouble breathing. His insides were tight, as if his internal organs were bound. His life was finally progressing, adhering to his goals. And now this.

"I'm at a point in my life where I can finally travel, something I've been wanting to do for a very long time."

"You can still travel. You…"

Granger interrupted harshly. "Rae, let me finish." He walked over to the fountain and stared at the water cascading down the copper lily pads. "Italy, France, Japan. I've wanted to visit them all but not alone. I wanted to share the experience with someone I love." Granger turned around and faced Rae. "You're working on a big project. You're not going to have the time to travel, especially after it's done."

"That's not true. I'll make the time."

"Really? Will you be entering the documentary in contests and film festivals?"

Rae said, "I guess. So?"

"So? There are thousands of them in the U.S. alone. You're going to be so busy submitting your film and attending these festivals, you'll have no time for me, let alone traveling."

"Granger, that's not true. In a year or two, I'll have the time."

"I don't want to wait that long and I don't feel like talking about it." Granger started to walk in the house.

"That's it?" Rae yelled after him.

"You women. All you want to do is talk something to death. It's clear what the problem is and that it can't be resolved." Granger turned to go. "I'm taking a shower."

Rae stood alone in the courtyard. She felt like crying but held it in. It was 4:00 in the afternoon and she still had work to do. She was thankful that Allie and Fran were in the dining room so she didn't have to see them. She was embarrassed and felt sick that she lied to Granger. The look on his face before he walked out only deepened her shame.

It was a little after 5:30 when Rae finished her chores. Granger never came down to the stalls to talk to her. As she got in her car, her sadness turned to anger. Once again, she felt that a man was telling her what to do, giving her the choice of being with him or following her dream. She should have told Granger about the film from the beginning and that was her fault but her fears were realized. She thought he was different than the others who wanted to control her and change her. And then she heard him say, 'You women are all alike…' It struck a nerve. Rae hated her actions being reduced to a generalization. It trivialized her point of view.

By the time Rae got home, she was livid. She knew Granger really wanted to travel but why was it so difficult for him to wait one, possibly two years? The ache in her heart wasn't as strong as her will to be her own person. She turned off her cell phone and home phone and played her favorite George Strait CD, blasting it as high as she could bear. Rae brought her folder filled with the elements of the documentary to the living room table. As she re-read her notes, she transferred them onto one piece of paper since they were written on various scraps of paper, including a napkin, the back of an envelope and the top of the front page of the *Press-Democrat*. She sang along with George at the top of her lungs, successfully pushing thoughts of Granger away.

It was after midnight when she got into bed, exhausted. She lay back on her pillow and closed her eyes. Instinctively, she felt for Granger.

"Damn it!" she yelled. "I used to love sleeping alone!" Before Granger, Rae relished having the whole bed to herself. If she wanted to read, the light was on. If she wanted to go right to bed, she didn't have to check with someone else or block the light with her arm so she could sleep if they wanted to read. It was her bed, her room, her choice. All that changed when Granger Bowden came into her life with his irresistible charm and compassionate personality. He made her feel so special and beautiful, a difficult thing to do. She wanted to hold him and feel his body envelop hers. There was a void and, right now, her documentary wasn't filling it. She had gone so long without a man in her life that she had forgotten how strong the bond could become when you made that emotional connection with another person. Rae forced herself to meditate. Granger's image kept interrupting her concentration but she persevered. Eventually, she fell asleep only to dream about being with the vegan cowboy.

39

Driving to San Francisco, Granger felt very fragile. His heart was bruised and his head ached. For the past month, he was the happiest he'd ever been. Rae was everything he wanted in a woman. She adapted to ranch life perfectly. She was funny and generous and attractive. And now, he couldn't imagine being without her. In his mind, he kept going over their conversation. He was mad that she didn't tell him about her documentary and that she lied about when she started working on it, but he couldn't understand why his love for her and working on the ranch wasn't enough. He always thought he treated women with respect and he had the highest respect for Rae, but he also knew that once the film was complete, she'd be spending time away from him. At the very least, she would be submitting the documentary to as many film festivals as she could for the exposure. Working on the ranch would be impossible. He also doubted that she would be able to travel to Italy in a year or two.

Granger pulled up to Dale and Frank's. He looked at the clock: 6:00 p.m. on the dot. Right on time. With a heavy sigh, he walked up to the front door of the English Tudor-style home, grabbed the large cast-iron door knocker in the shape of a fox head and banged it against the door. Shortly, Dale answered in his sweats and t-shirt. He gave Granger a big hug and walked with him into the living room where Frank was watching the San Francisco Giants play the Oakland A's. Beer in hand, he stood up and greeted Granger with an embrace.

"Dale told me about you and Rae. I'm really sorry."

Granger sat down on the couch with Frank. "Thanks, but it's not completely over until the fat lady sings."

Dale came back into the living room with two bottles of beer. He handed one to his brother. "I was under the impression that the fat lady sang, went home and ate a whole Tofurky. Something you're not telling me?"

"Not really. I haven't spoken to Rae in three days. I just can't imagine it being over."

"Then why haven't you called her and tried to work it out?" Dale said, sitting on the chair next to the couch.

"Why hasn't she called me? I'm the one who was slighted."

Dale took a pull from his beer. "Grange, don't get into who's right and who's wrong, especially when Rae didn't do anything that horrible."

"She lied to me. In my book, that's pretty darn horrible."

Frank was trying to watch the game and listen to the conversation at the same time. "Didn't she neglect to tell you that she was working on a film or something?"

"A documentary," Granger replied. "When it's done, she'll be entering it in film festivals and traveling all over the country to promote it. I'll never see her."

"Why don't you go with her?" said Frank. He got up and headed to the kitchen. "I'm listening. I want to get some chips and salsa."

"I like being at the ranch. It's peaceful and quiet."

Dale said, "Come on, Grange, you always wanted to travel. Now's your chance and you'd be doing it with a woman who is so well-suited for you. She's like your female counterpart, except for the height and weight and her apparent obsession with country music."

Frank came back into the living room carrying a bag of chips and a bowl filled with salsa. "Didn't know about the C and W thing. My condolences." He placed the chips and salsa on the coffee table. "Help yourself."

Granger stood up, clearly agitated. "I thought she'd be satisfied working at the ranch and helping animals through educating the school children, not gallivanting all over hell and back."

Dale said, "How did you feel when Dad told you that you were going to take over the ranch?"

"Dale, don't give me that therapy crap. You know how I felt. Powerless."

"Isn't that what you're doing to Rae? It's her life, Granger. If she chooses to produce a documentary and show it all over the country, shouldn't she be allowed to do that?"

Granger sat down and ran his hands through his hair. "Yes, she should. All I'm saying is that I want to be with a woman who is satisfied living in Petaluma, working on the ranch and traveling for fun, not work. I guess Rae and I just weren't meant to be."

Dale shrugged. "Maybe not. I'd never tell you to settle, you know that."

Frank tried to lighten the mood. "There's a really nice, single woman I work with. Her name is Gina and she's in her forties, probably mid-forties. Want me to set you up? We could go to Millennium."

"Thanks Frank, but I'm going to need some time. So, what's for dinner?"

"Veggie burgers with all the trimmings. I sautéed mushrooms and onions and also made home fries. Watch the game with Frank while I get everything ready."

"I can do that. What's the score?"

"Giants are up by three." Frank raised his beer bottle and Granger clinked it against his. Frank continued. "I've known you for a long time, Grange. You've always been an upbeat guy, but when you were seeing Rae, you positively glowed. It's like she turned on a beacon inside of you. I know you're hurt and I'm not trying to diminish it, but you really need to consider calling her and talking it out. Don't let the relationship die without at least discussing your differences."

"I'll consider it."

Frank looked over at the kitchen door and lowered his voice. "You and Dale have a lot more in common than you think. You're both generous and kind, thoughtful and the most stubborn sons of bitches I've ever known. It's not a good trait. While you're closing off your mind, blocking any room for compromise, you're turning away potentially amazing experiences and people."

"Thank you for your input, Dr. Kratchnic."

"Don't mention it."

Dale opened the kitchen door carrying plates to the dining room table. He put them down next to the utensils. "Dinner's ready."

Leaving the game on, Frank and Granger sat down at the dining room table. The view was amazing and it wasn't lost on Granger. Through the expansive picture window, he could see the Golden Gate Bridge. A few sailboats were gliding across the bay, their white sails barely visible through the fog. The hills of Marin County rose up behind the bridge in various shades of brown from wheat to golden to chocolate.

"I live in one of the most beautiful places in the world. I have no right to complain, you know?" Granger said.

Frank replied, "We live in one of the most beautiful places in the world. You live in Petaluma."

"Very funny but I'll drink to that because right now I just want to drink." The men raised their bottles of beer and toasted.

40

Rae woke up with a start, heart pounding inside her chest. At first, she thought it was an earthquake, then realized Pierre had jumped on the bed. She looked at the tuxedo cat walking toward her. He stretched and then laid down on the pillow where, up until recently, Granger lay his head. It was 2:12 in the morning. Her heart was still pounding. What if it was an earthquake? Petaluma was on the Rodgers Fault line. It could shift at any time. Rae had home insurance but not earthquake coverage. She had seen photos of houses knocked off their foundations, large cracks in walls, and collapsed roofs. One of her friends down in Los Angeles paid tens of thousands of dollars to repair her pool and patio when the '94 earthquake destroyed them. Rae's home was her only asset, aside from her retirement accounts and they weren't significant. If her home incurred damage, she could feasibly have to spend her retirement money repairing it. She would be financially ruined. Worst case scenario, she would have to move in with her ninety-year-old father. She could hear her father clearing his throat. It reminded Rae of a motorcycle revving its engine. His habit of recounting his life story whenever and wherever he felt like it, drove her to distraction. Now she was in panic mode, feeling completely helpless. Rae always felt independent. As long as she had a job, she knew she could handle whatever was thrown her way. But without that safety net, the one she depended on up until recently, she realized that a major disaster could fell her. Rae got out of bed and quietly walked through the kitchen to the outdoor patio. She stood in the dark, leaning against the railing, looking out over her backyard. The locust and plum tree's silhouettes against the dark sky were mildly comforting. They swayed in the breeze, changing the scenery with every move. She instructed herself to breathe deep. As she did, it helped calm her down but she still felt a pit in her stomach. She knew Granger didn't worry about money. He had plenty and it made her jealous. It didn't matter that he worked hard and made a lot of sacrifices to create his environment. He had financial stability and never had to worry about his comfort level being interrupted or snatched away from him.

Rae suddenly felt very vulnerable. She closed the porch door and started walking back to her bedroom.

"Mom?" Carson yelled.

"Yeah, sweetie?"

"You scared the shit out of me. What are you doing up so late?"

Rae walked downstairs to Carson's bedroom. "Sorry. I woke up and couldn't go back to sleep so I went outside to get some fresh air. How are you feeling?" Rae sat down on the bed and put her hand on Carson's forehead.

"My back hurts. Could you grab me a Percocet?"

Rae poured Carson a glass of water from the bedside pitcher and shook a pain pill out of the bottle. She handed it to him and watched as he popped it in his mouth and swallowed it down with water.

"Are you okay?" Carson said.

Rae thought about it for a minute. Was she okay? Not really. She broke up with a man who she thought was 'the one,' her fear of losing everything if a catastrophe struck had her paralyzed with a sense of foreboding, and she still worried about Carson's condition, even though he seemed to be healing beautifully.

"I have a lot on my mind right now."

"Like breaking up with Granger and not having a job?"

"Throw in your broken back and you win a stuffed animal."

"Don't worry, mom. You know, even after you and dad broke up and we were living in the kinda shitty neighborhood, I never worried. I knew you'd always take care of me. You'll find another job or your documentary will be a huge success. I can feel it in my bones, especially my back."

"Ah, so you have a psychic back now?" Rae laughed.

"Yeah. Don't worry, okay?"

Rae leaned over and kissed Carson on the forehead. "Okay."

"Good night, Madre."

"Good night, son. I love you."

"Love you, too."

Despite reassurances from Carson, Rae slept very little that night. It seemed as though she woke up every couple of hours. Her eyes stung from lack of sleep and her head felt dense. After breakfast, she decided to drive out to the coast. She always relied on the negative ions from the ocean to reinvigorate her mind and body. Carson was invited to join her but he had already made plans, so Rae packed a small snack, a bottle of water and a blanket and dragged herself to the car. As she headed west on Bodega Avenue, she popped in a Dwight Yoakam CD. Normally, she'd sing along but this morning she wasn't in the mood. A few minutes later, she was driving by Bowden Ranch. She slowed down and with a heavy heart glanced over at the pasture. As she watched the cows and sheep lazily grazing, she imagined Granger sitting in the courtyard, reading the paper and drinking his morning coffee. She hoped that he was as miserable as she was. Rae drove a good hundred yards past the entrance and pulled off onto the soft shoulder, driving over the uneven surface of weeds, stones and broken rocks. She was glad, for the first time, that her white Honda Accord was common and nondescript. Rae turned off the car, abruptly cutting Dwight off in the middle of *It Only Hurts When I Cry*, and looked across the road. A large buckeye tree towered over the fence, its conical white flowers resembling fingers pointed up to the sky. A group of cows sat underneath, thoroughly enjoying the moment. Some of them must have felt her eyes on them because they looked up from their comfortable spot and stared at her. She envied them. They didn't have to worry about bills and jobs and relationships. Unlike other cattle from neighboring ranches, they really didn't have a care in the world. They would die of old age. Nearby, a boulder jut out of the land like a whale breaching. Rae loved the ranch's landscape. She wanted to continue to give tours and work with the animals. She longed to be able to drive up to the house and park next to Granger's truck. She imagined him meeting her at the door and giving her a welcoming hug and kiss. She could feel his arms around her. She loved the way he made her feel safe. "This is ridiculous," Rae said aloud. She picked up her phone and speed dialed Granger, then immediately hung up. "What the hell am I doing? Why isn't he calling me? Probably because all us women are the same. Wrong." Rae started up the car and took off a little too fast, her back wheels skidding on the dirt.

Granger turned right out of his driveway as the white Honda swerved onto the road. "Stupid kids. All I need is another accident in front of the ranch." He watched in his rear view mirror as the Honda turned the corner and disappeared from his sight. His mind made a quick mental note that Rae drove the same car. He wished she would call.

41

There was a knock on his bedroom door. "Dad, are you in there?"

"Yes."

"Are you okay?"

"I'll be fine, sweetie. Don't worry."

"I just made dinner. You want to eat?"

"Maybe later, Al. Thanks."

"If you want to talk about it, I'm here. I love you, Dad."

"I love you, too."

It was close to 10:00 and Allie hadn't spoken to her father since dinner. She went to check on him, softly knocking on the door. When he didn't answer, she tiptoed in, in case he was asleep, but he wasn't there. She walked over to the sitting area. Next to Granger's cell phone was a small, black velvet box. Allie opened it. An emerald and aquamarine ring was neatly tucked into the casing. She felt a lump in her throat. Rae was the woman for her father. She knew it, but trying to convince him to call her and work out their differences was futile. She rarely witnessed her Dad's obstinacy and was perplexed as to why he felt the need to dig in his heels over this issue.

Allie went out to the courtyard but Granger wasn't there. She walked out front. The car and truck were parked next to each other. Panicked, she went back to her dad's room and called Rae on his cell. She picked it up on the first ring. Allie apologized for calling so late but told her she couldn't find her dad and was wondering if she could talk to Rae in person. Rae told her to come right over.

Less than ten minutes later, Allie arrived, looking weary. Rae showed Allie into the living room and they both sat on the couch.

"I know it's none of my business, but have you called my dad since the fight?"

Rae took a deep breath. She hadn't spoken to anyone about the fight because she was embarrassed. She had gushed about what an amazing man Granger was and how lucky she was to be with him. Then she discovered he was cut from the same controlling cloth as every other man she'd been with, and felt like, once again, she failed herself. Darlene and Rebecca would have been the two people she would have called first, but something inside stopped her. Perhaps it was her sense of pride.

"Maybe six or seven years ago, I wouldn't even be in this situation. But I've changed since then. I cherish my independence and at the same time, love being with your dad, but I don't like him telling me what to do."

"Dad really does want to travel and he wants to do it now before he gets too old. That being said, I totally understand why you want to make a documentary on factory farming. That's why I chose the subject for my film. It's not right for my father to make you choose. All I know is that he loves you so much and he's hurting really bad right now. Did he tell you about his marriage to my mother?"

"A little," Rae said.

"I love her but what a princess! I call her the heifer queen because she loves ranch life and all the prestige that comes with it. Living on one of the wealthiest cattle farms in the county was a huge coup for her because she was respected in the ranching community. When my dad and I went vegan and then, to my mother's horror, he turned the ranch into a sanctuary, she went ballistic. For a year, family life was like a bad reality show. That was over eleven years ago. I swear dad's probably dated only five or six times since then. When he met you, you totally rocked his world. Except for your hankerin' for country music, he feels he's found his life partner. I love George Strait, too. Just so you know."

Rae smiled and lightly touched Allie's arm. "Why can't he accept that I need to do this?"

"I think he's afraid of losing you," Allie said.

"I don't want to be with anyone else, but I'm so tired of men telling me what to do. I want his support not his condemnation. I wouldn't think twice about supporting his dreams."

"I promise I'll talk to him if you'll help me find him. He wasn't in his room and his car and truck are both in the driveway."

Rae thought for a moment. "I think I know where he is. Did you check the horse stable?"

"No. What would he be doing there?"

"I think he rode out to a place where he likes to think. His man-cave. I'll follow you to the house."

"What about brokeback Cars...I mean, your son?"

Rae laughed. "Very funny, but don't call him that to his face. He's a little homophobic. Right now, he's with his dad."

Rae parked close to the stables. It was a full moon and the ranch was illuminated in an eerie mist. Rae half-expected to see fairies and Leprechauns guiding her way to the horse stable. She looked up at the house. It was beautiful, the lights from inside giving it a warm glow. She loved hanging out with Granger there, whether it was watching TV or having her morning coffee in the courtyard. Allie met Rae inside the stable and, sure enough, Tuscany wasn't there and one of the saddles was missing. The thought of Granger sitting in his cave in the dark made her soul ache.

"I want to go out there and talk to him," Rae said.

"Do you know how to get there?"

"I think I can find my way. Do you mind if I take the Jeep?"

"Not at all but please be careful. It's really foggy out there."

Rae tried to remember the directions Granger had given her. She took off behind the horse stables and followed the road until she came to the dead-end and took a right. Nothing looked familiar, especially at night, but her desire to see Granger again took precedence over her fear of getting lost. She drove slowly, looking for the VW-shaped boulder. The headlights illuminated a boulder that kind of looked like a VW

Bug. In the light, it looked more like a massive tumor than the iconic car, but she went with her gut feeling and hung a left. A few hundred yards up the hill, an animal jumped out of the bushes and ran in front of the Jeep. Rae instinctively slammed on the brakes. Her heart nearly leapt out of her chest. She took a moment to compose herself, then continued up the hill. Within minutes, she came to the clearing and there was Tuscany, standing passively next to a tree, his reins tied to a limb. When Rae turned off the Jeep and cut the lights, it was almost pitch black. The moon's light was hidden by the thick cover of trees. As Rae sat in the dark, the reality of the situation became clear. Granger might be incensed that she came looking for him, invading his private place, his refuge. She started to panic. With her heart racing, she started the Jeep and backed out of the clearing, praying Granger was still in the cave. She looked in the rear view mirror as she drove down the hill, but saw only darkness. In her haste, she made a wrong turn. She drove for nearly a mile before she realized that she was going the wrong way and cursed her horrible sense of direction. Stopping the Jeep, she looked to her left and then her right, trying to identify a familiar bush or tree, but the fog was thick, blending the landscape into one blurry scene.

Granger rode toward the stable. As he approached the entrance, he saw Allie standing there, looking worried. He dismounted and walked up to her.

"What are you doing here, sweetie?"

"I was waiting for you and Rae. Did you guys make up?"

Granger looked back at the trail he'd come from. "What are you talking about? Rae's here?"

"Shit. She took the Jeep and said she was going to go to your mancave. You didn't see her at all?"

"No. Do you have your cell?" Allie nodded and took it out. She dialed Rae's number but her voicemail picked up immediately. Allie hung up.

"Dad, I don't think she has reception. You know how lousy it is closer to the hills. Do you want me to help you look for her?"

Granger got back on his horse. "That's okay, Al. There aren't a whole lot of places to look. I would think that once she hit the hills, she'd turn around. Hopefully, we'll both be back soon."

If the fog wasn't so thick, he would have taken off at a gallop but poor visibility and the prospect of crashing into the Jeep forced him to slow down. He wasn't too worried about not finding Rae, unless she veered off the road. After he passed the turn off for the cave, Granger began calling for her.

Rae looked at her cell phone. No bars. It was approaching 11:00 and she had no idea where she was. At least the heater worked, so she was warm. Rae was following the road, hoping she was driving in the direction of the barn when she started to drive up hill. "Son of a bitch!" she yelled. She stopped the car and was turning around when, out of the fog, she saw Granger riding toward her. She turned off the engine and got out of the Jeep. Taking a deep breath, she walked toward him as he got off the horse. He looked exhausted and she suddenly felt guilty for causing him so much pain.

Granger said, "Looks like I'm going to have to put a tracking device on you."

Rae said, "I came out to tell you that I'm sorry and I shouldn't have lied."

Granger came over and hugged Rae. He kissed the top of her head and held onto her as if she would disappear if he let go. Finally, he released her and they kissed.

Granger said, "I'm sorry, too. I have no right telling you not to follow your passion."

"Yeah, I know, but I'm not sure if my passion for you is stronger than my desire to create this film, so I've decided to put off filming until we've gone on at least one trip."

"Don't do it just for me, Rae. I don't want you to resent me."

"I'm doing it for me, too. I didn't think I'd be with a man again and, honestly, I didn't care. Then I met you. My internal landscape has totally changed. You're a part of it now."

Granger kissed her again. "So, where do you want to go first?"

"Back to the stables."

"I meant our first trip together."

Without hesitation, Rae said, "Italy."

"Italy it is. Now, let's go back to the stables."

The aroma of just flipped pancakes, soy sausages and coffee filled the air. The faint sound of classical music could be heard. It was the soundtrack to *Moliere*. The blinds were open and when Rae sat up, she was greeted with that amazing view of the valley against the softly sloping hills. It's a view she'd never tire of and hoped that, one day, she would wake up to it every day. The door opened and Granger walked in accompanied by Fin and Hammerhead.

"Good morning," Granger said, as he bent down and gave Rae a kiss. He was wearing his running attire. Rae looked at the clock. It was only 8:00 a.m.

"Good morning."

"Ready for breakfast? I made pancakes and soy sausage."

"Yum. Lead me to the kitchen. How was your run?"

"It would be better if you ran with me. Do you have any desire at all?"

"I'll be completely honest with you. I used to run and enjoyed it but getting up at 5:30 in the morning sounds horrid. I'm not a morning person. Never was and probably never will be."

"Okay. What if I ran at 7:00 a few days a week? Would you consider joining me?"

Rae lifted the sheets and stared at her belly. Yoga wasn't getting rid of it but it did keep it from enlarging. She smiled. "I'll give it a whirl but I'm going to warn you. I won't be able to keep up with your stride. I have baby legs compared to yours. I'm only five-foot-one and a quarter and you're what, six foot something?"

"I'm five-eleven and one-eighth. I can compromise my speed until you can keep up. And I'm not asking you to run with me because of your belly. I love your body, belly and all. I know once you start running, you'll love it. Now get dressed so we can gorge on pancakes and sausage."

"I'll meet you in the kitchen." Rae got out of bed and went over the sitting room where she put her clothes. As she leaned over to tie her shoes, she noticed a small black velvet box under the sofa. She reluctantly picked it up. Glancing toward the door to make sure she was alone, Rae opened the box. An antique engagement ring stared back at her. The setting held a solitary emerald with aquamarine stones cascading down the sides. Rae touched it but didn't take it out of the box. She felt light-headed and dizzy. She closed the box and set it back down on the floor, partially hiding it so Granger wouldn't know she saw it. She wondered if it was meant for her and, if it was, why it was under the sofa. After her second marriage ended in divorce, she vowed never to marry again, but what if Granger asked her? Would she agree to marry for the third time to someone she's known less than two months?

"Breakfast is getting cold!" Granger yelled from the kitchen.

"Coming!" Rae replied. She decided not to say anything but her mind was hungry for answers.

42

Except for the back brace and a prescription of Percocet in his backpack, it would have been difficult to detect Carson's injuries. He was caught up at school, thanks to his friends and sympathetic teachers. After almost two months of nursing him back to health, Rae welcomed her newfound freedom. If Carson continued to heal at the current rate, surgery would be scheduled for next month to remove the rods and screws.

It was the last weekend the Wayne Thiebaud exhibit was on display at the De Young Museum in Golden Gate Park. Rae enjoyed his paintings, especially the ones depicting desserts, like ice cream cones and petits fours. Rebecca had a print of his in her kitchen and was dying to see the original, so Rae picked her up and they headed to the museum for the day. On the way, they dropped off Carson and his friend, Jarod, in the Haight Ashbury neighborhood, in front of Amoeba Records. As soon as the boys shut the car door, Rebecca turned off the radio.

"Tell me the truth. Is Granger really the greatest guy in the world or does he pick his nose in bed, have hideous breath or smelly feet?" Rebecca said.

"He's pretty much perfect except for that blip over the documentary I was making."

"Have you really shelved it?"

"Yeah. I'll pick it up in the next few months or maybe I won't. I *am* educating a lot of school children about food animals at the ranch. This could be my destiny."

"Are you talking from your gut or your crotch?"

"Is it possible to talk from both?" Rae said.

"That's a big no. Rae, you're doing it again. You're sublimating yourself to a man. Don't fall under the spell of Granger's big brown gorgeous doe eyes. You'll regret it and then you'll resent him. Don't give up your dream, please."

"I'm afraid he'll leave me."

"Sweetie, if he truly loves you and not who he wants you to be, then he won't leave you."

"Sounds good in theory. I'll think about it. Thanks conscience. Did I tell you that I've been running with him in the morning three days a week? I can actually see a difference in my body. My belly fat is being jiggled away. I'm totally stoked. I told you about the ring, right?"

"Yeah."

"He hasn't said a word. Maybe it wasn't for me. Maybe it was his mom's and it needed repair and he just got it back from the jewelers."

"And maybe Big Foot lives in the mountains above his ranch. Hello? Of course it was for you. Just wait. He's going to ask you to marry him and you'll get to live in that gorgeous house and I won't be jealous one bit."

"Don't worry. I'll let you come over and clean the horse stables whenever you want, because you're my best friend."

"Gee thanks. Seriously, would you say yes?" said Rebecca.

"I would. I never thought I'd get married again but I also never thought I'd meet a man like Granger. Remember when we wrote down all the qualities we wanted in our dream man? I found that paper the other day. Except for two things, he was the guy."

"What did he fail to fulfill?"

"He's not a country music fan and he doesn't know German."

"What is it with you and German?" Rebecca asked.

"It's a very sexy language." Rebecca gave her a look of total confusion. Rae said, "Just let it go."

"It's gone. Turn left here. I can always find a parking spot on this street and it's not too far from the De Young."

Sure enough, a car pulled out of a perfect space as Rae was approaching.

It took them five minutes to walk to the De Young, one of San Francisco's premiere museums.

The exhibit wasn't that crowded, unusual for a Saturday, so the women didn't have to compete for space in front of the paintings. Rebecca was very happy to view the original 'Four Cupcakes' oil painting. As most exhibits do, this one ended in the gift shop. Rebecca bought the poster of Thiebaud's 'Big Suckers,' a composition of seven lollipops. Rae spotted a book on Matisse. She remembered Granger telling her it was one of his favorite artists, so she bought it for him.

After having lunch at the museum's café, the women spent the day walking around Golden Gate Park. They had tea at the Japanese Tea Garden and then went over to the Botanical Gardens. Because of its massive size, they decided to visit the Garden of Fragrance and the Ancient Plant Garden. By the time they finished touring, it was nearly 5:00. As they headed back to the car, Rae called Carson.

"Madre. What's up?"

"We're leaving the park and wondered if you wanted to join us for dinner." Rae could hear him asking Jarod.

"Where were you going to eat?"

"We were thinking Chinatown. We could walk up Grant and pick a place. How does that sound?"

"Let me ask Jar...oh shit. Hold on." Rae heard what sounded like firecrackers in the background.

"Carson? What's going on?" Rae could hear yelling, a grunt and then it sounded like Carson dropped the phone.

"Carson! Carson!" She turned to Rebecca. "We have to get over to the Haight, now!"

They ran to the car. Rae tried to put the key in the lock but she was shaking so hard, Rebecca took the keys from her and drove. Rae kept her cell on, listening to the cacophony of noise on the other end. She strained to make out the voices but it was too difficult to tell if Carson or

Jarod's voices were part of the mix, then the connection failed. Rebecca told Rae to calm down. She was sure Carson was fine. They heard sirens in the distance and as they got closer to Haight Street, the sirens intensified.

"What if Carson was hurt? It sounded like he fell. Rebecca, his back. He could be paralyzed." Rae started to cry.

"It'll be okay, sweetie. He probably dropped his phone and couldn't find it. You know Haight Street can get really crowded."

Two ambulances, a fire engine and a motorcycle cop passed them. Rae willed herself to stop shaking but she couldn't. Her fear was too intense. She tried calling Carson's phone but he didn't pick up.

"Don't you have Jarod's cell number?"

"Yes, but on the way to San Francisco he realized that he left his phone at home."

As they approached Haight Street, the police officers had a section cordoned off. Another policeman was re-directing traffic away from the epicenter of what looked like a crime scene. The two ambulances and fire truck were parked in the middle of the street. Despite law enforcement's efforts, a large crowd stood on the periphery. Rebecca was forced to turn away from the area, but before she did, Rae got out of the car. She told Rebecca to park and wait for her call. As Rae walked toward the scene, she tried once again to call Carson's cell phone. It went straight to voicemail.

There were too many people standing at the crime scene for Rae to get a closer look. She could make out paramedics crouching over a body, then putting him on a stretcher. When they lifted the stretcher, Rae could see the victim, his face partially covered in blood. It wasn't Carson. She took a deep breath and looked further down the street. Another body lay on the ground, obscured by the paramedics. Rae looked at the victim's feet. He was wearing black sneakers with a white stripe down the side. Carson was wearing the same sneakers. Panic rose up in her chest. She tried to walk past the police barricade but was stopped.

"I think that's my son! Please, let me through!" The officer tried to calm Rae down to no avail. He called another cop over and asked him to bring her to the other victim. Terror rose inside her as she approached the scene. She could now see the boy's pants: the same blue jeans that Carson was wearing. Before she got any closer, someone yelled, "Mom!" She turned around and saw Carson and Jarod walking toward her. Rae ran to them, hugging Carson a little too hard, his brace digging into her chest but she couldn't feel it. She hugged Jarod, too.

"Are you both okay? Carson, how's your back?"

"It hurts a little. This guy knocked into me."

"What happened?" Rae said.

Carson and Jarod started talking at the same time. Rae said, "One at a time, please."

Carson said, "I was on the phone with you when we heard these guys start arguing. I think there were three or four."

"There were four," Jarod said.

"Two of the guys ran right toward us. One of them knocked the phone out of my hand. Then this guy starts shooting at these dudes. It was totally insane. Jarod and I took off. I don't know where my phone is. The cops won't let anyone over where we were standing."

One of the ambulances took off, its siren blaring.

"At least one of the boys is still alive. I'm going to call Rebecca so she can pick us up. Why don't you ask the cop over there about your phone? Maybe he'd let you look for it or he could look for it. Make sure he sees your brace. He might feel sorry for you."

Carson rolled his eyes but he and Jarod went over to the cop while Rae called Rebecca. When she got off the phone, Jarod and Carson were still talking to the cop. Finally, they came back over as the officer walked away.

Carson said, "The brace totally worked. He asked what happened and it turns out he's a motorcycle cop. Pretty cool dude for a cop. He went over to look for my phone."

"Great, honey. I sure hope he finds it." A few minutes later, the policeman returned with Carson's phone. He was thanked profusely. The iPhone's face was cracked but it still worked. He found it under a planter in front of a head shop, 'The Ripped I.' The second ambulance left just before Rebecca arrived. There was no siren.

Rebecca said to Carson, "What is it with you and excitement? I thought your mom was going to faint when she heard the sirens."

Jarod said, "We were so scared. People say that gunshots sound like firecrackers but when you're that close, they sound fuckin' loud. My ears are still ringing."

"I know, dude. That was unreal. I can't wait to tell Boner and Jess. They won't believe it."

Rae said, "Shall we still go to dinner in Chinatown? My appetite is starting to come back."

Everyone agreed that Chinese food was the way to go, so Rebecca parked in the Stockton Sutter garage and they walked up Grant Street, Chinatown's main artery. Vendors on either side of the street had cheap toys and trinkets in bins outside the stores. The prices were very reasonable but the merchandise was poorly made, almost guaranteed to break within the first month of purchase. Still, Jarod and Carson had to stop in front of almost every store and check out the goods.

"Guys, look at these. Unbelievable!" Jarod was pointing at small, ivory-colored figurines in a shop window.

Rebecca said, "They're nasty netsukes." The figurines depicted women in various sexual positions. Some were with men but most were with animals. One woman was having sex with an octopus. Another was entwined with a tiger. Still another was 'doing it' with a monkey. They were very detailed and explicit.

Carson said, "These are so twisted. Why would anyone want to have sex with an octopus?"

Rebecca looked at Rae and she raised her eyebrows. Rae whispered in her ear, "You are one sick puppy."

After walking a few blocks, they decided to eat at Lotus Flower, a restaurant specializing in Hunan and Szechwan cuisine. Throughout the meal, Carson kept checking the local news for reports of the shooting. Toward the end of the meal, he finally found a link to the story. According to the report, the two boys that were shot had shoplifted drug paraphernalia from one of the stores and refused to share it with the other two. They argued and then, as the two shoplifters fled, the other two shot at them, seriously wounding one and fatally shooting the other. The boys were all between eighteen and twenty years old.

Carson said, "The kid that was killed was the one who pushed me. I remember looking down and noticing that he had the same shoes as me. He was also wearing a Giants cap like mine."

The boys became unusually quiet. The enormity of the incident sunk in. It was a strange feeling to have not only witnessed a shooting but to have had contact with someone who was killed.

The conversation on the ride home was subdued. After dropping Jarod off, Rae said, "We could go to the AT&T store tomorrow and get another phone, if you'd like."

"That's okay. I don't mind the cracked glass."

"If you change your mind, let me know."

Carson went straight to bed after they arrived home. Rae gave him a big hug and kiss. She wanted to tuck him in. Her only son. Her little boy who endured two traumatic events in less than four months. She knew she couldn't protect him from the outside world but at that moment she certainly wanted to try. She was closing Carson's door as Pierre ran into to his room, jumped up on his bed and curled up next to his right shoulder. Carson grabbed him and put him next to his chest, holding him close.

After Rae got into bed, she called Granger and told him about her day. He had seen the incident on the news earlier that evening.

"Honey, that must have been horrible. Do you want me to come over?"

"That sounds lovely. I don't know if I'll be great company. I'm starting to feel the effects of being so close to death. Can you de-shock me?"

"I'll give it my best shock, I mean shot. See you in a little bit. I love you."

"I really love you, too."

Rae hung up the phone and smiled. The warmth she felt in her heart was comforting. She had forgotten what it was like to be so in love with a man. She closed her eyes and put her hands over her heart.

"I am so grateful for the people in my life. I'm grateful for Rebecca and Carson. I'm grateful for Pierre, that little scamp and Rita the loner. I'm grateful for Granger, a man I only thought existed in my imagination. Thank you for these gifts. Thank you for my blessed life."

"No, stop!" Rae heard Carson shout. She ran downstairs and opened the door. Pierre bolted from the room, clearly freaked out. Carson was still asleep. Amazingly, the nightmare didn't wake him but his breathing was shallow and quick. Rae bent over her son and gently wiped the sweat off his forehead. She told him everything was okay and continued to gently stroke the top of his head. After a while, his furrowed brow softened and his breathing returned to normal. She thought about Jarod and hoped that he was coping better than Carson. The headlights from Granger's car came through the window. Satisfied that he was sleeping soundly, Rae jogged up the stairs. She got to the door just as Granger knocked. They embraced. She said, "Boy, are you a sight for sore eyes."

"How's Carson doing?" Granger said.

"He went to bed when we got home. Poor thing was exhausted. A little while ago I heard him yell 'No, stop!' and went downstairs. He was having a nightmare, so I stayed with him until he calmed down."

"This should make you feel better." Granger pulled a chocolate bar out of his overnight bag. He gave it to Rae.

"My favorite, dark chocolate with orange peel. Thank you. You want to eat it in bed?"

"Among other things," said Granger.

"You nasty cowboy, you." Rae grabbed his hand and led him to the bedroom.

After making love, Rae lay awake in Granger's arms. His breath was even and deep. She loved feeling it on top of her head. Normally, that would drive her to distraction but with Granger it was comforting. His arms enveloped her body, making her feel safe and loved. She stroked his arm, thinking again about the day. It was difficult to pull the scene of the injured boy out of her mind. He's somebody's son. His parents are in a hospital room right now, praying their son lives. It could have been Carson but it wasn't. But it could have been.

In a rare appearance, Rita jumped on the bed and curled up in the far corner. She looked at Rae, blinked a few times and fell asleep. Rae closed her eyes but as soon as she did, the images of the shooting aftermath started all over again. She gently extricated herself from Granger's arms, careful not to wake him but was unsuccessful. He opened his eyes.

"What's wrong, babe?"

"I can't sleep." She pointed to her head. "There's a war going on in here."

Granger sat up. "I have two remedies. If the first one doesn't work, I'll need a large mallet for cure number two."

"Very funny. Let's try the first one."

Granger instructed her to lie down, then he walked her through a guided meditation, starting with the relaxation of her feet and moving up her body. By the time Granger got to her neck, she was lightly snoring. Granger lay down next to her. "Good night, my love."

After procrastinating and postponing, Allie finally set up a date with Margo to begin weaving lessons, only to be usurped by a party with Chris. At first, she was hesitant because she wasn't crazy about some of Chris' friends. The party was at a house in the Petaluma hills. Derek, one of the boys who lived there, went to the junior college. The other two, Bobby and Adam, worked in construction. To Allie, they all typified the immature, testosterone driven teenage boy. They drank to excess, smoked way too much marijuana and spent hours playing video games. It took a lot of convincing on Chris' part but she agreed to go if he ate vegan for one week.

The three bedroom, one bathroom house was 1,100 square feet, filled with used furniture, dirty carpets and filthy windows. The walls were discolored from cigarette smoke and the kitchen's appliances were vintage avocado, not because the boys liked retro colors but because they were the original appliances from the 1960s when the house was built. The walls were pretty bare except for a few randomly-placed posters. When Chris and Allie showed up, the debauchery was in full swing. Rap music blasted from over-sized speakers and thick marijuana smoke hung in the air. Seventy plus kids were drinking, getting high, making out, and eating tortilla chips, salsa, popcorn and Oreos. Outside, the barbeque pit was shooting flames into the cool night air. Derek saw Chris and bounded over, Budweiser in one hand and a bong in the other.

"Dude, you made it. Hey Allie. Welcome to our hovel." Chris took the bong from Derek, grabbed a lighter from the coffee table and lit it.

He took a hit and handed the bong to Allie. She took a hit and handed it back to Derek. He pushed it away.

"I can't get higher. You two go forth and hit the ceiling but watch out for the fan. Beers are over there."

"Thanks, D." Chris took another hit but instead of blowing it out, he kissed Allie and blew it into her mouth. They made their way through the crowd to the cooler filled with beer. Chris grabbed one for himself and one for Allie.

"This is a sick party." Chris grabbed Allie by the waist and gave her a long kiss. They started dancing. Allie looked at Chris and smiled. He was fun and sexy. She loved the way he moved. She glanced over at a couple dancing beside them. The girl was all but ignoring her partner and practically drooling over Chris. Allie wasn't jealous. She enjoyed the attention Chris got. Allie took a swig of her beer. It was ice cold and was the perfect antidote to the hot, stuffy room. She took off her sweater and wrapped it around her waist. Allie glanced through the window to the backyard but couldn't see much, the windows clouded with dirt. She could hear some girls screaming and guys laughing. Chris looked too, then he grabbed Allie's hand and pulled her out back. He went up to a guy standing at the outer edge of a semi-circle.

"What's going on?"

"This dude cornered a fucking opossum. It's so sick. The possum's hissing and shit."

Chris and Allie pushed their way to the front and what she saw made her sick. An adult opossum was up against a wall, trapped. Some boys were poking it with a stick. It was hissing and trying to move but they wouldn't let it. Someone yelled, "Put it in the fire pit!"

"Yeah. Let's burn the ugly sucker!"

One of the boys tried to grab its tail and that's when Allie lost it. She got in front of the possum and screamed, "What the fuck's the matter with you? Torturing a terrified animal makes you happy? You sick fucks. Get out of here."

"Hey ve-gan. We're not going to eat it," A boy in the crowd shouted out. Some of the kids laughed.

Chris went over to Allie. "They're just having some fun. It's an opossum."

"What's that supposed to mean? It deserves to be tormented for our entertainment? Look at it. It's scared out of its mind. That's funny to you?"

One of the boys got behind Allie and tried to grab the opposum's tail. She grabbed the stick out of his hand and whacked him with it. "Chris, help me out here."

"Sorry. You're on your own." Chris walked away, leaving Allie standing there, but not for long. Two of the guys from the crowd stepped up next to her and told everyone to leave the animal alone. Losing interest, the revelers dispersed. Allie thanked the boys. She turned to the opossum who had practically become part of the wall. Once it realized that it was free to go, it scampered off into the brush. Allie dropped the stick. She looked around for Chris but couldn't find him.

"I think what you did was great. I wish I had the guts to stand up to those guys." The girl looked fairly familiar to Allie.

"Thanks. It's not hard to stand up for what you believe in. Try it sometime." Allie looked at her more closely. "Didn't you go to Petaluma High?"

"Yeah," she said. "I recognize you from school, too. I'm Deborah."

"Allie."

"I remember Chris, too. Great looking but kind of a dick wad. What are you doing with him?"

"You mean, what was I doing with him? I got wrapped up in the great looking part but just remembered what a dick wad he was. You didn't by any chance drive here, did you?"

"I did. You need a ride home? I'm ready to leave now. I don't feel like hanging with these idiots."

Without looking for Chris, Allie left. The house was quiet when she got home, but she knew her dad was there because both his vehicles were in the driveway. She wasn't in the mood to talk about what happened, so she walked down the hallway to her room as quietly as possible.

"Al?" Granger called out from his bedroom.

Allie sighed. "Yes?" She walked into his bedroom. Granger was lying in bed reading a book.

"You're home so early. Bad date?"

"That's a big yes." She told Granger what had happened at the party. "You were right about Chris."

"Sweetie, if you don't make mistakes in life, you won't know when you make the right choices, so don't beat yourself up, okay?"

Allie nodded. "What are you reading?"

"*Journey of Souls*. It's about reincarnation and the life of our spirit before human life."

"Wow, I can see your mind expanding."

"Very funny. I never believed in reincarnation but now I'm not so sure it doesn't exist."

"I bet Rae lent it to you."

"Wrong, smarty pants. She gave it to me. You want to watch a movie?"

"No. I'm going to bed. Good night."

"Good night."

43

Allie and Fran were behind schedule on their documentary, so they decided to spend Sunday afternoon working on it. Not the first choice for either of them, but the project was due in a couple of weeks and they had some catching up to do. It was an unusually warm day in May, so Allie opened the French doors to the courtyard. The light poured into the room and the sound of the fountain mixed with the song, *Be Healthy* played in the background. Allie thought it would be a good idea to listen to Dead Prez, a hip hop vegan group. The storyboards were almost complete but they couldn't decide on the opening shots and how they wanted the film to end. Allie's cell phone rang. She looked at the number and ignored the call.

Fran was trying hard to concentrate on working, but he was too distracted by Allie. She was wearing shorts and a crop top. Her hair was up in a crude bun with wisps of loose hair falling around her face. She smelled like peppermint soap and her skin was luminous. Even without makeup, she was beautiful. She had her hands on her hips, studying the storyboards on the table. The doorbell rang. Fran said,

"Is that Chris?"

Without looking up, Allie said, "Nope."

Minutes later, Rae walked into the dining room with Granger. Rae said to Fran, "You work at Petaluma Market, right."

"Yeah. It's a cool place to work."

Rae said, "I thought I recognized you the first time we met. I hope you get a discount. It's pretty expensive."

"I do but I still shop at Trader Joe's."

Rae laughed. "Smart boy."

Granger took her hand and was heading to the door when Rae said, "Mind if I look at your storyboards?"

Fran said, "Not at all."

Granger came up behind Rae and looked at the layout. After a few minutes of perusing the storyboards, Rae said, "Are you going to mention fish farms?"

Allie slapped her forehead. "I can't believe we totally forgot about them." Fran had a confused look on his face. Allie explained, "Last I heard, more than forty percent of all the fish eaten are raised on aquafarms. They spend their entire lives in cramped, filthy enclosures. Almost all of them suffer from parasitic infections, diseases, blindness. I could go on and on. We definitely have to add fish to the documentary."

Fran shook his head. "Are there any food animals that are treated well?" Allie, Granger and Rae just stared at him.

"You still stuck on a beginning and end?" Granger said.

"Yeah. We want it to start with a bang and end with one, but we can't agree on either." Fran smirked at Allie.

Rae said, "If you want to start with a bang, record the sound of the captive bolt pistol they use to stun the cow before it's hoisted upside down on a hook. Loop the track and then lower the volume and have a voice-over identify the sound and say something like, 'The captive bolt pistol is used to temporarily render a slaughterhouse animal unconscious before its throat is slit. In a typical slaughterhouse, workers use the gun every twelve seconds but there are, fill in the blank, number of slaughterhouses in the United States alone.' I think at that point you can have the sound of the gun go off like an assault rifle."

Allie said, "I love it! What do you think, Fran?"

"Brilliant! Thanks."

Granger said, "Every twelve seconds? I can't imagine the terror those animals feel before they even get to that point."

Rae said, "It gets worse. I read that it costs a penny per shot, so some slaughterhouses forgo using it. The animals are fully conscious when they're killed."

Fran said, "How much money are they saving? It's only a penny per shot."

"About 2,500 cows are killed per day. You do the math." Rae said, "By the way, I think it's a great idea to incorporate the food animal workers in the film. I know a lot of them are immigrants and are treated almost as poorly as the animals. How long is the film?"

Allie said, "Fifteen minutes." Her phone rang again but she ignored it.

Granger said, "How about showing children eating fast food and then cut to obese adults and have a narrator say something like, "One out of four Americans are obese and diabetes has reached record levels." He looked at Fran, "I think it's one in four. Can you look up the obesity rate in America?"

Fran nodded and went to his laptop. Within minutes, he had the answer. "You're wrong. It's more than one in four. Over one in three American adults are obese. That's crazy." He then looked up diabetes in America. "In 2012, almost twenty-six million Americans had diabetes. It makes total sense after doing research for the documentary and reading about the amount of sugar and fat the average American diet has in it. Working at Petaluma Market, I see all the crap people eat. It's disgusting, but what's worse is that I used to eat like that. I'm not vegan yet, but I've changed my eating habits a lot."

Allie's phone rang for the third time. She picked it up and walked out of the room. "Stop calling me. Now."

Fran said, "Is she okay?"

Granger replied, "I have a feeling she's about to read Chris the riot act, which he so deserves."

Fran could hardly contain his excitement. "What did he do?"

Granger filled him in. Rae was also hearing it for the first time. "What a jerk. He didn't stand up for the animal or his girlfriend. That speaks volumes about his character."

Allie returned. "It certainly does. I don't have to deal with him anymore. So, where were we?"

Fran said, "Diabetes, obesity, the plague, pestilence, Chris tossed in the garbage. Did Allie tell you her idea for the montage, showing people who look like food animals? I'll be morphing them together. Isn't that cool?"

"I love it!" Rae said. "What have you paired up so far?"

Fran said, "We have a lot of people who look like pigs to choose from and we're using my Uncle Wooly who looks like a sheep. I also found a woman who totally resembles a chicken, skinny legs and all."

Fran brought the pictures up on his laptop and they couldn't believe how much the humans resembled animals, especially Uncle Wooly. "There's a man who comes into the market and I swear he's a giant frog, but I don't know if he'd let me use him in our film."

Allie said, "If this was a French film, we could use him, but people here don't eat frog's legs."

Granger said, "Actually, you'll find live frogs in every Chinatown market in America. Why don't you highlight all the animals people eat worldwide and show the number that are consumed every year?" Granger glanced at Fran.

"I'm on it," Fran said, and googled the question. "Fuckin' A. Between 200 million and a billion frogs a year! That's nuts."

Rae said, "That's human's desire for eating animals. There are no checks and balances. That's why food animal production is polluting the environment and wreaking havoc on our health."

Granger looked at Rae. "You still want to go for a hike out to Cougar Pond?"

"Definitely. Thanks for letting us put our two cents in. I'd love to see the documentary when it's finished."

Allie and Fran both agreed that the input was valuable and when the documentary was finished, they were going to have a family showing, including Fran's parents and siblings.

Granger spread the blanket out near the pond. It was breezy, so he secured the corners with fist-sized rocks. He couldn't have been happier.

The weeks following his fight with Rae had been nearly perfect. Short of finishing each other's sentences, they got along better than ever. As he opened a bottle of Stag's Leap Sauvignon Blanc, Rae dug into her backpack and brought out the plates, crackers, dark chocolate truffles and a wheel of Kite Hill White Alder vegan cheese. Granger eyed the cheese suspiciously.

"I'm not a big fan of vegan cheese. Most of them vaguely resemble their dairy counterparts." He picked up the wheel, reading the label. "Does it really taste like brie?"

"I think it comes pretty damn close. The rind looks just like brie's but this is not as creamy and it doesn't melt."

Rae placed the crackers on a plate, surrounding the cheese. She cut into it, placed the small wedge on a cracker and handed it to Granger. He deliberately chewed it slowly, giving it the full benefit of the doubt.

"I like it. It has a tangy mushroomy flavor with a silky texture. Where did you find it?"

Rae said, "Whole Foods carries it in the artisan cheese section. They were giving out samples."

"That's a great find." Granger handed her a glass of wine. "To us."

"To us."

Rae lay on the blanket, looking up at the sky. The sun's rays filtered through the clouds. She could smell the smoke from a distant chimney. A crow was cawing in the tree above them. It sounded like he was announcing something. A party?

Rae said, "Growing up here would have been a dream come true for me. I'm glad I was raised in surburban San Fernando Valley but it was nothing like the beauty and splendor of your ranch."

"I guess it's all relative. As a teenager, all I wanted to do was leave the ranch and go away to college in a big city. My first choice was Chicago. Northwestern. I thought it would be a blast to live in the third largest city in the country. Did I tell you I wanted to be a veterinarian?"

"You did not. Do you regret it?"

"For a long time I did. Then Allie was born and she became my focus. If it weren't for her, I wouldn't have converted the ranch into a sanctuary.

I wouldn't have found Carson on the side of the road. I wouldn't have met you and I wouldn't have been able to ask you to marry me."

Granger took the engagement ring out of the black box. Rae sat up and stared at the beautiful, antique ring with a large emerald in the middle and aquamarines cascading down the sides. She looked at Granger who was barely holding it together.

"Yes, I'll marry you, Granger Bowden." She wrapped her arms around his neck and gave him a kiss. Granger put the ring on her finger. It fit perfectly.

"I want you to know something about me that's crucial to keeping me happy and loving and from turning into an apathetic hag."

"I'm all ears."

"You *will* be in about twenty years, but I don't want to think about that right now. I need reassurance on a fairly regular basis that you love me. I was insecure in my twenties, so you can imagine how my self-esteem has devolved and continues to as I age. Some days, some minutes I think I look great but there are more times than not that I look in the mirror and I swear my grandpa David is staring back at me. As I get older I watch helplessly as parts of my body that used to be cute and perky are now curdled and saggy. Am I grossing you out?"

"I'm a lot stronger than that. You shouldn't be so insecure. I'll love you no matter what."

"You can say that now because I'm still fairly attractive. But aging is a slippery slope and I've been trying not to fall too hard, so promise me, please, that you'll reassure me on a daily basis that I'm loved and adored."

Granger held up his right hand. "I swear that, no matter what happens to your face and body, I will reaffirm my love for you every day. But know that I would love to hear those words, too."

"Geez, you're so demanding. Okay, fine." Rae kissed him again. She looked at the ring on her finger. "Is this a family heirloom?"

"It's new. I designed it with a jeweler friend of mine in town. He uses recycled gemstones and gold. I knew you loved antiques and that your birthstone was aquamarine, so we incorporated those elements into the design. I'm glad you like it."

"I love it. Did you have a date in mind for the wedding?"

"No. I thought we could decide on that together. We should wait until after Carson's operation, then you can put your house up for sale, unless you want to keep it and rent it out. It's totally up to you."

"I think we should have cougar sex right here."

"O…kay. Where did that come from?"

Rae said, "I'm getting a really strong cougar vibe. We can talk about the wedding later. Right now, we need to have carnal, unbridled sex."

"How can I argue with that?"

44

Rae picked up her coffee order and sat down at the counter next to Darlene. She was wondering how long it would take her friend to notice the engagement ring on her finger. They'd been talking for nearly fifteen minutes and Darlene didn't have a clue. Finally, Rae put her hand to her face and left it there until Darlene noticed. When she did, she screamed, scaring half the patrons in the coffee shop.

"I don't believe it! Tell me everything. When did it happen? Where were you? How did he ask you?"

Rae filled her in, leaving nothing out, even the puma sex. She was beaming.

Darlene said, "Do you think you'll eventually work on your documentary again?"

Rae took a sip of her coffee. "I don't know. Did I tell you that his daughter and a classmate are producing a documentary on factory farming? They've put together some compelling stuff. The time and energy it would take for me to produce a full-length documentary would be exhausting, but for them it's part of a class assignment. Maybe it's time to pass the gauntlet and let the next generation change the world. The thought of traveling with Granger all over Italy makes me giddy. I'm almost sixty years old. Don't I deserve to relax and enjoy myself?"

"I totally get it," said Darlene. "You're retirement age, so retire. Show me that ring again." Rae thrust her hand into Darlene's face. "It's beautiful."

"Thanks. I hate to sound cliché, but I certainly hope third time's a charm."

"I can see you with Granger for a very long time. He's totally a keeper. We should celebrate. Why don't we all go out to dinner next weekend? I'll check with Peter and you check with your honey bunny or should I say, your mountain lion."

"Will do."

"I've got to say, before you met Granger I thought you were going to be single and celibate for the rest of your life. And I'm not saying it in a bad way. It's just that you were so content living your life, doing things your way without consultation or compromise. You found your vegan cowboy, Rae. How cool is that?" Darlene started to cry. She hugged Rae and kissed her on the cheek. She took out a tissue and blew her nose.

Rae said, "Now you're going to get me all teary-eyed." Rae wiped her eyes. "I'm so glad I had those years to myself. If I had settled, I never would have met Granger and what a tragedy that would have been. She took her last sip of coffee. "I gotta go. Stuart is dropping Carson off in a little while and I haven't told him yet. I have no idea how he's going to react. I'm a little nervous."

"Don't be, sweetie. That kid has had you to himself since he was six. Time to share mommy."

One last hug and kiss and the women went their separate ways.

By the time Rae got home, Carson had been there for an hour. He was in his room, doing homework. "Hey Madre, what's up?"

"Did you have a good time at your dad's?"

"It was okay."

Rae sat down on Carson's bed. She was feeling a little dizzy. Telling Carson about her engagement didn't seem to be such a big deal until she was ready to utter the words. "Can I talk to you for a minute?"

"I'm doing homework. Can it wait?"

"Not really," Rae said.

Carson put down his pen and swiveled on the desk chair, facing Rae. "Well?"

"Granger asked me to marry him."

"What? Really? I hope you didn't say yes."

"Why?"

"Mom, you've only known him for like two months. That's crazy."

"No it's not. We're not getting married until next year."

"So you said yes? I don't believe it. Big mistake. Big mistake."

Rae took a deep breath. "I have been single since you were six. That's twelve years, son. This is the first time, ever, that I feel right about someone. By the time we get married, I will have been with Granger for almost a year and I'll be fifty-nine. I don't want to wait any longer."

"Why even get married at your age? You're not going to have kids. Why not just keep dating?"

"When you get married, you're pledging yourself to each other. It's more of a commitment."

"Like with Dad? How did that work out for you? And your husband before that?" Carson gave her a condescending look.

"That was mean."

"Boo flippety hoo. If you're going to tell me something stupid, then be prepared for the response."

"We'll talk later. Finish your homework."

Rae walked out of the room and felt an uncomfortable anger. She loved Carson but wanted to slug him. Before she started ticking off all the reasons her kid should be forever grateful to her, she took a deep breath. Then she took another one. She knew his resistance to the marriage was due to jealousy. Despite their mercurial relationship, he was still her only child and never had to share her with a sibling or a man for any length of time. She had to remind herself that she was the adult and he was an immature eighteen-year-old who, a few months ago, almost lost his life or at least his mobility, to an accident.

By the time she started fixing dinner, Rae's anger dissipated and she resolved to let the subject of wedding and marriage and housing arrangements go unless Carson brought it up.

45

Allie was craving chocolate. And not just any chocolate. Margo introduced her to Ulimana's Salty Nut Truffles. One truffle and she was hooked on the creamy, intensely rich salted raw chocolate covered in walnuts. She was in the middle of homework but it would have to wait. The desire for chocolate trumped almost anything.

There were two jars left at Petaluma Market so she grabbed them. She was going to wait in Fran's checkout line, but it was too long, so she opted for the checkout counter three lanes down. While waiting, Allie was reading the cover of People Magazine. Mel Gibson was in hot water, yet again. And Britney Spears was pregnant. Again.

"This is all I have, man."

Allie looked up. A homeless-looking man was talking to Fran. His hair was filthy, his clothes worn and dirty. He was holding a canvas bag that had holes in it. Fran was speaking low, so Allie couldn't make out what he was saying, but his tone was friendly. Other patrons were listening, too.

"I'll put something back. No worries," the homeless man said, but Fran shook his head. He reached into his back pocket, pulled out his wallet, extracted a couple of bills and put them in the register. He said something to the man and pointed to some shopping bags for sale. The man took one and handed it to Fran, who promptly put the items in it.

"Miss?" the grocery clerk said.

"Sorry," said Allie.

"That's okay. It'll be $24.96."

Allie paid and put the truffles in her purse. She wanted to talk to Fran but he was too busy, so she left. It didn't surprise her that he would help out someone in need, but witnessing it made an impact on her. She got into the car and before starting the engine, opened the jar of truffles and took a small bite out of the donut hole-sized treat, letting it melt in her mouth. She closed her eyes and savored the flavor. The contrast of sweet cocoa and sea salt was heavenly. It took Allie a few minutes to finish the truffle. Satisfied, she started her car and pulled out of the spot. She saw Fran walking out of the store, so she backed up to where he was standing and lowered her window.

"Hi there. Are you on a break?" She said.

"Just got off. Leaving?"

"Yeah. I had to get my chocolate fix." Allie held up the jar of truffles. "Can you come over to the house? I want to show you something."

"Sure. I'll see you soon."

"Okay."

Back at the ranch, Allie put her purse in the house and then waited for Fran in the driveway. For the first time since meeting him, she was a little nervous. It felt out of place but there it was, nerves coming to the surface, creating an emotion that she hadn't experienced with her classmate.

Fran pulled up in his dark blue Honda Accord. Allie watched him get out of the car. He looked taller. His gait more confident. Or it was Allie's imagination?

Allie said, "You up for a little walk?"

"Sure. Where are you taking me?" Allie just smiled and started to walk toward the stables.

They hiked past the chicken coop, then Allie turned right into the field. The animals were grazing. Some of them looked up but most couldn't be bothered by the intrusion while eating the grasses and leafy plants.

"Rodney!" Allie yelled to one of the steers. He looked up and started walking over to her. Rodney rubbed his head on Allie's shoulder and she returned the favor by scratching his neck.

"I don't want to sound specist or anything like that but these cows all look alike. How did you know that was Rodney?"

Allie pointed to the scar on his flank. "Poor Rods had a bad infection a while back. We didn't know if he'd make it. Aside from the scar, Rodney has very distinct spots on his side." Fran looked at the marks Allie was referring to but all he saw was an irregular white blotch with a couple of little white spots around it.

"I give up."

"It reminds me of the solar system. The big blotch is the sun and that one over there is the Earth. See it?"

"Oh...yeah...no. Is this what you wanted to show me, a cow?"

"No, Fran, but check this out." She grabbed his hand and took him over to an open space, far from the animals. She instructed him to sit down and close his eyes. They both sat there very still for about five minutes. When they opened their eyes, five steers were staring at them from about two feet away.

"What a trip! Why do they do that?"

"They're picking up on our energy. Cows are social animals. They might not be the brightest creatures, but they're definitely one of the sweetest."

"I've heard bulls are really nasty. Look at what they can do to matadors."

"Oh boy, you've been sorely misinformed, but it's not your fault. Most people have no idea what's done to the bull before it even enters the ring. The bull is held in an isolation box. It's a small structure with a tiny ventilation opening in the top. He is deprived of light, food, water and he's injured with a harpoon-tipped ribbon that has been jammed into his side. When he's released into the bullring, he's disoriented from the sudden light, noise from the crowd and he's bleeding. Do you want me to go on?"

Fran shook his head. "What the hell's the matter with people?"

They got up and continued on their hike. They talked about the documentary and threw some ideas around. Fran told her he was nearly finished with the animal/human morphing sequence and she gave him an idea of how long it would take her to put together the first frames of the captive bolt montage. Finally, they came to a large structure consisting of boulders, trees and shrubs. Allie said, "This is Iker Rock."

"Wow. It's magnificent. What does the name mean?"

"I was meditating at the top one day and the name just came to me. I looked it up online. Turns out it's a Basque name meaning visitation. Want to climb up to the top?" Allie said.

"Sure."

As they ascended the small ecosystem, Fran noted the different kinds of plants that seemed to be growing right out of the rock. A display of deep orange California poppies clung to the side of the rock face, their petals a sharp contrast to the lichen-covered boulder. A blue-bellied lizard scurried past Fran's foot, disappearing under a rosemary bush. Allie rubbed her hand on the bush's leaves and inhaled deeply.

"They say that if you have trouble remembering something, take a whiff of rosemary."

Fran inhaled the fragrant leaves. "I just remembered I have class tonight!"

"Really?"

Fran said, "No, but I had you there, didn't I?"

Allie laughed. Upon reaching the top, they sat down. Fran could see the field where he and Allie were earlier. They didn't speak for a while, Allie allowing Fran to take in the serenity and splendor of the moment. Fran said, "This may sound a little crazy, but I can feel energy coming from the rock."

Allie put her hand on Fran's chest. His heart started beating even faster. Then Allie leaned over and kissed him. It felt so natural. Fran returned her kiss. Allie said, "You're a beautiful person, Fran. I don't know why it took me so long to see it."

"Me, neither." Fran laughed. "Hey look." Two turkey vultures were flying toward them.

"That's my power animal," Allie said, and explained to Fran how she found out. They got close enough so Allie and Fran could see their expansive wing spans and bald, red heads.

Fran said, "No offense, but dang they're ugly."

"They won't win any beauty contests but they're impressive birds." She told him about their habits.

"No way do they throw up to fend off attackers. You're making that up."

"I swear. I read it on Wikipedia. Did I tell you that I want to get a tattoo of a turkey vulture?"

"Hey, why don't you get a tattoo of one sitting on your shoulder and puking down your arm?"

"Very funny, Francisco. What I had in mind was the bird in full flight with just a smidgen of red for the head."

"That would be cool. Where are you going put it?"

"I'm not sure yet. Any suggestions?"

"Yeah. On your back, between your shoulder blades."

"I like that. Would you like to go through the meditation and find your power animal?"

Fran thought about it. "I'm tempted but what if I find out that my power animal is a gopher or a mole? How embarrassing is that?"

"What if it's a fox or an iguana?" Allie said.

"True."

"Did I tell you that my dad and Rae are engaged?"

"How do you feel about your dad remarrying?"

"I think it's about time and Rae is perfect for him. It'll be very strange having someone else living here, though, and I really don't know her son, Carson. He's not a vegan and Dad told me that he makes fun of Rae's lifestyle. Sounds like a bit of a prick. Time will tell."

The sun was starting to set, so Fran and Allie hiked down Iker Rock and back to the house. He left soon after. They kissed good-bye and Allie watched him drive away with a new perspective and joy in her heart. She thought about the first time she met him in her Communications class. With his large ears and small frame, she wasn't attracted to him at all but she did like his dark brown, almond shaped eyes. They were exotic look-ing. She flashed on Chris, the polar opposite of Fran in looks and atti-tude and bravado. Instead of recalling his good looks, he appeared ugly to her. When he called her the other day, he didn't apologize because he didn't feel that he did anything wrong. Quite the contrary. She put him in an embarrassing position. The last thing he wanted was to look weak in the eyes of his peers and she should have understood that. Allie calmly told Chris that it wasn't going to work between them and wished him well. She wanted to wish him compassion and empathy, but realized that wasn't going to happen any time soon.

"It's funny how things turn out, isn't it Fin?" Allie said, as she walked toward the house. Fin wagged his tail, hitting Allie on the leg.

46

"I think he's jealous, mon petit choux," Rebecca said. She was sitting opposite Rae on her lime green couch in her apartment. Lily was sitting on her lap. The little dachshund/terrier mix was Rebecca's pride and joy.

"He's eighteen years old. Why does he care? We were close until he became a teenager and then the hormones kicked in and kicked me out of his circle of confidantes. You'd think he'd be happy for me. The little shit." Rae poured herself more wine and replenished Rebecca's glass.

"Use some empathy here. Carson is recovering from a broken back. The healing process is slow and he needs strong drugs to help him manage the pain. He's lost his physical mobility, even though it's temporary, and now he's going to lose his mother to another man. He's too immature to verbalize it so instead he berates you, which is so fitting for an eighteen-year-old boy. And he's been hanging out with his papa more than normal. I'm sure Stuart isn't singing your praises."

"So you don't think he has a point, that we haven't known each other long enough to get married?"

"There's no formula and if there was it wouldn't be coming out of the mouth of a teenage boy, that's for sure. What's your gut telling you?"

"Honestly? My gut is telling me that, once again, I'm abandoning my dreams for a man, but it's also telling me that Granger is the one. I think my gut is bi-polar."

Rebecca laughed. "Honey, I think that Granger is so in love with you that if you put the documentary on hold for a while, you'd be able to pick it up again and he'd be fine with it. One dream shouldn't eliminate another."

Rae said, "Speaking of dreams..." She got up and went over to her purse. She rifled around in it and pulled out a little rectangular box. "La Belle Intensive Repair Serum. Works on diminishing fine lines and wrinkles. I read a great review online about it. Want to try it?"

"Why not, but I must say that I think all skin care products should include on their labels, 'If you're over fifty, this won't help. Get thee to a plastic surgeon instead.' Now that's truth in advertising."

"So, what's the big news you want to tell me?" Margo poured tea into Granger's cup and then Allie's.

"Rae and I are engaged," Granger said.

"That's marvelous! Congratulations!" Margo went over and hugged him, then hugged Allie. "How are you doing?"

"I couldn't be happier. Rae fits perfectly into our lifestyle. It's her son I worry about."

"Why?" Margo said.

"Carson strikes me as being too macho. Maybe once his back is healed, he'll tone down the posturing. He won't have anything to prove."

Granger knew Allie was speaking from her heart and not out of jealousy, but he also welcomed male energy into his home. Having a stepson was going to be exciting, even if he was an adult. As if Margo could read his mind, she said, "I think it will be nice having another man living at Bowden Ranch. You'll both be a great influence on Carson. Before we have dinner, you have to see something in the barn."

The three followed a trail behind the house to the sheep barn. On their way, they passed a tractor next to an old shed. The ancient machine was rusted solid. Half of the shed's roof was collapsed, sagging against the barely standing north side. Moss and grasses were growing on top of the roof and the wood was splintered and sun bleached. The tractor and shed were slowly turning into the landscape, their colors reflecting more nature than man-made creations. As they reached the barn, Margo instructed them to be very quiet. Slowly, they walked toward the far right corner. Margo had created a space surrounding the corner, free of equipment, feed and sheep. As they got closer, they could see a pumpkin-colored bushy tail with a white tip laying on a bunch of hay. Its face was obscured.

Granger whispered, "Is that a fox?"

Margo nodded. "With four babies."

As if on cue, the fox lifted its head and looked at the humans, then hissed.

Margo said, "Don't worry, we won't hurt you or your babies. I think this mama was being pursued by a coyote or mountain lion and came in here for shelter. Isn't she precious?"

"I want to see the babies," Allie said.

"You may be in luck. The vixen goes out in the evening to hunt. Let's come back after dinner."

They slowly walked away, the fox's eyes never leaving them, protecting her babies to the hilt. When they were out the barn, Allie said, "Do you think we have time tonight to go through a lesson on the loom? I'd love to get started."

Margo said, "I don't see why not. Granger, do you mind?"

"Not at all," Granger replied. "As a kid, I remember watching you weave, but I wouldn't mind sitting in on the lesson."

An hour later, after dinner, they headed back out to the barn. Sure enough, the vixen had left her pups to go hunt. She partially covered them with straw, but they were easily visible.

Allie bent down close to the bed. She was ecstatic. "They are so cute! They look like puppies. Can I pick one up or will the mom freak if she smells my scent on her baby?"

Margo said, "That's an old wives' tale. Mother's aren't deterred by another creature's scent on their children. I don't know where that fallacy came from."

Allie gently picked up one of the babies. It hissed at her, mimicking its mother, but it was clear that it posed no threat. Its coat was soft and fluffy and its markings were distinct with the light pumpkin coat, brown vertical 'eyebrows' and white chest. Large chocolate brown eyes stared into Allie's. In its eyes, Allie saw another being with a beating heart and vibrant soul. A being who wanted to live as badly as she did. There was no difference in the intent only the power that Allie had over this tiny creature's life. She stroked it a little bit longer then put it back with its siblings.

"Can foxes be domesticated?" Allie asked Margo.

Granger cut in. "Don't get any ideas, Al. We're not adding a fox to our brood."

"I was just asking."

Margo said, "One of the ranchers found an abandoned baby fox a few years ago and she raised it. She named her Suzy and she hangs out with her dogs. So I guess the answer is yes."

Granger said, "Let's go to your studio and check out the loom, shall we?" He started walking to the exit. His long legs strode swiftly. Another minute with those pups and he knew Allie would start badgering him to adopt one. On their way out, they passed the sheep, who were settled in for the night. Their stalls were clean and Margo made sure they had plenty of straw for their bedding so they would be comfortable. Her sheep were her children. Their normal life expectancy was about twelve years but some of Margo's sheep were fifteen and sixteen. A few sheep stood up and went to the edge of their pens when Margo walked by. She stopped to give them a rub on the head or a kiss on their muzzles.

Margo's weaving studio was built thirty years ago with oak from the property. The giant loom sat to the left, a partially finished blanket captured in the wool threads. Margo started working on it over a month ago. Beautiful rugs covered the hardwood floor and photos of past accomplishments shared the wall with blankets hung from dowels. The studio had a distinct scent: a mixture of lanolin and Margo's lotion, Vanilla Bean Gardenia. Allie went over to the loom and was dazzled by the work in progress. Margo's pattern was inspired by the Arts and Crafts era. Geometric designs with an American Indian theme was in the process of being created. Margo chose earth colors mixed with red, green and yellow.

Granger said, "It's beautiful, Margo. Really."

"Thanks, Grange. Okay, Allie. I want you to grab that chair and sit next to me, but before we do that, let me introduce you to Mollie, my loom. She's been in my family for over eighty years, before I was born. With love and care, she'll last forever."

Allie positioned her chair close to Margo's. As Margo began her tutorial, Granger noticed a spider walking up the side of the loom. He went over to the sink and grabbed a glass, then came back, knocked the spider into the glass and brought it outside. As he turned the glass upside down and shook it, the spider fell out and scurried away. Instead of going back inside, he walked toward the bluff. The nights were always cold out by the ocean and the winds made it colder, but breathing in the ocean air made it worth the discomfort. He buttoned up his jacket and put his hands in his pockets, trying to stay warm. Granger looked out at the ocean, watching the waves break on the shore. He heard rustling from behind and turned around to see the vixen hunting something in the grass. He stood very still as he watched her staring intently at one spot. Finally, she pounced and came up with a small rodent in her mouth. She looked at Granger and he could have sworn there was a moment of recognition in her eyes, then she walked away toward the barn. Granger turned back to the ocean when his cell phone rang. He looked at the number and smiled.

"I was just thinking about you," Granger said.

"What do you mean just? You don't think about me all the time?" Rae said in jest.

"That's what I meant to say. So, what are you doing?"

"Watching *Blades of Glory.*"

"Without me?" Granger said. "I love that movie."

"I own the DVD, so we can watch it together. I've already seen it four times."

"I never get tired of seeing Will Ferrell ice skating in a leotard."

"Legend has it that you used to work on the ranch in a bright red and sparkly pink leotard." Rae tried to sound as serious as possible.

"Sadly, it's true. Daddy never would let me ride into town with it on. I'll wear it for you though. As of last week, I can still fit into it."

There was silence on the other end of the phone.

"I'm kidding!"

"Whew. I almost called off the engagement. I wanted a vegan cowboy not a cross-dressing cowboy."

"Don't worry. The closest I get to a leotard are my bicycle shorts. Are we still on for dinner Friday night in Santa Rosa with your friends?"

"Yes, sir. They told me to pick the restaurant, so I chose John Ash and requested two vegan dinners. We're set."

"Sounds great. Margo is showing Al how to operate her loom. I'm going to join them so I'll see you tomorrow. You have two tours, all third graders. One is shorter, after the first tour's lunch. It should be fun. I love you."

"Love you, too. Tell Margo and Allie I said hi." Rae hung up and smiled to herself. Life was great.

"Mom! I'm hungry!" Carson yelled from his bedroom. Rae could hear the sound of gunfire and yelling. As virulently as Carson loved his Xbox games, she hated them.

"I'll make you a sandwich, my sweet son, but first I need to hear the magic word or you won't get jack shit."

"Please."

47

Granger and Rae were on their way home from dinner at John Ash with Sid and Felicity Stenback, Rae's friends from college. Granger fit right in with Rae's friends. He could joust with the best of them and, unlike some of Rae's past relationships, she wasn't anxious, anticipating an awkward moment or embarrassing verbal exchange. They were listening to Mozart's *Jupiter Symphony* when Rae turned it down.

"I love Sid and Felicity but I have to say, it bugs me that they can't even have one meatless meal when they're with us."

"Sweetie, they don't have the same view of animals that we do. When they think cow, they think steak, t-bone, burger, meatloaf. The animal doesn't have any other purpose than to feed them."

"But Felicity knows how the animals are treated. I slip some facts about downed cows and slaughterhouse abuses into our conversations every now and then."

"She doesn't care, period. Her taste buds are stronger than her compassion. I grew up with a father that looked at his steers as commodities. When he'd castrate the calves, they would cry and struggle to get free. He didn't hear their cries. He was doing his job because if he didn't, he couldn't continue to sell his cattle and keep up the ranch. I never heard him say a kind word about his cows. As a matter of fact he rarely, if ever, said a kind word about me either. But that's another story. What I find ironic is the attitude meat eaters have about animals, some claiming to love them. They don't even take food animals into consideration."

Just then, Granger drove up behind a truck filled with caged chickens en route to Petaluma Poultry Processors. The birds were trucked in at night so the least number of people witnessed the transport. Five cages high and six cages across, with at least six chickens in each small cage, it's the first time and the last time they'll be outside. As Granger maneuvered around the truck, Rae looked at the birds. They were packed so tightly that legs and partial wings stuck through the wire. Rae's heart constricted. She started to cry, quietly at first, then louder.

"This is so wrong. I can't stand it. I can't stand that these animals' lives mean nothing to Carson and Felicity and Sid and, shit, almost everybody. I have to help them. Granger, please take me home so I can get my camcorder. I'm going to go to the plant and tape as much as I can. I want to make my film."

"No." Granger was also upset. He had a pained look on his face as he began driving faster.

"What do you mean, no? I have to help. I can't live with myself if I don't try."

"You're not going to do this alone. Let's do it together."

"Really?"

"Yeah, really. I'm so disgusted with how apathetic our society is toward these animals. The misery is palpable and if I don't help you bring this into people's psyches, I'm as bad as they are."

"I don't know what to say. I have a really good feeling about this. I think we make a great team. I'd love to see Foster Farms go bankrupt. I hate those commercials of the chickens that want to be Foster Farms chickens but they're too messy. I want to scream but instead I turn the channel. You know that the Pork Producers of America have a coloring book for kids. It shows illustrations of happy pigs on a farm playing in the mud. I was so revolted by their propaganda that I called them and asked what percentage of pigs are factory farmed. The woman said ninety-eight percent, but she added that many people live in crowded conditions, too, like big families in small apartments. I told her that was true but the people can leave their apartments. She had no reply, so I hung up. What kind of rationale is that?"

"It's the rationale of the meat business. So, are you ready to blow the lid off the industry?"

"Ready as I'll ever be. Should we change into dark clothing and be all ninja?" Rae said.

"Let's not get carried away, dear. We're not breaking the law filming outside. We won't even step foot on their property."

"We met for a reason, Granger. I believe that. We're going to make a huge difference in animal welfare if we can break through the lies and deception. I think people's biggest fear is that they'll die without eating meat or get sick. With all the information out on the internet and in the media, it's obvious that people are healthier on a plant-based diet. We definitely have our work cut out for us. I'm up to the challenge. Are you?"

"Yes, partner."

"Am I being way too optimistic? Look at all the amazing documentaries about animal rights. *Earthlings, Forks over Knives, Food, Inc.* Can we make a better one? I know people that saw those movies and they're still eating meat. Is it hopeless, Granger?"

Granger pulled into Rae's driveway. He shut off the car and looked at Rae. Her eyes were red from crying. She looked so innocent and hopeful.

"Rae, let's make the best documentary we can and see what happens. More people than ever are looking into meatless diets. Our film could turn the tide. We won't know unless we try. I'm willing to take the chance."

"Let's get my camcorder."

When they got to Petaluma Poultry Processors, the workers were approaching the poultry truck. Granger parked across the street and they walked over to the far end of the facility's parking lot, partially hidden by trees. Rae filmed the morbid scene. Cramped and injured, the chickens looked dazed and in shock as the workers unloaded the cages, sometimes dropping one in their haste. Despite the overwhelmingly pungent smell and the helplessness she felt for the hundreds of chickens going to their deaths, Rae kept the camera steady and got some great footage. As one of the last cages was being taken off the truck, a worker pulled it at an angle, releasing the latch. Most of the chickens were too weak to leave, but a couple of them jumped out of the cage and took off before they could be caught. When the workers turned toward the facility, Rae stopped filming, and put the camcorder away. Granger took off his jacket and Rae did the same, then they ran in the direction of the escaped chickens. They found them hovered under a Manzanita bush, shaking. Their wings were all but featherless. There was no resistance as they were gently scooped up into the jackets. When they got to the car, Rae held the birds while Granger drove. Even though it was heart wrenching knowing all those birds were going to die, Rae felt a jolt as if a spark inside her was ignited. She was finally doing something to help the helpless. It was as if Granger could read her mind.

"That was depressing, but I feel a surge of excitement and hope. Even if one person is affected by our film, it will have been worth it." Granger glanced at the chickens. They seemed to be at peace, never knowing a kind hand. "It looks like they were battery hens from an egg-laying factory. What shall we name the sole surviving ladies?"

"How about Ethel and Lucy?" Rae said. She stroked their heads as her eyes welled up with tears. "I'm sorry. I usually don't cry this much, but I can't imagine how utterly horrifying their lives have been."

"Don't apologize. I totally understand. Let's get Ethel and Lucy settled into their new home."

Allie and Fran finished looking at the footage Rae filmed the night before. Ethel and Lucy, after being bathed, had been placed in a large cardboard box with plenty of bedding in a corner of the kitchen. Granger surrounded the box with a wire cage to keep Fin and Hammerhead from bothering them. Allie wiped away some tears. She had seen the poultry trucks every once in a while, but watching the cages being unloaded in such a cavalier and clumsy way, made her heart ache. Fran, the neophyte, was stunned. "That was brutal." He joined Allie, who was looking down at Lucy and Ethel.

"Dad, can we hold them?"

"Sure, sweetie. Just be real gentle. Their wing feathers will eventually grow back but right now, their wings are very sensitive. The one with more feathers is Lucy."

Allie removed the cage, picked up Lucy and gave her to Fran. He sat down and let Lucy settle in. She looked up at him, then buried her face in his lap. He stroked her and spoke to her, saying it will be okay. Allie put Ethel in her lap. The bird was missing an eye and her left wing hung at her side. She looked old, her feathers ripped and discolored but Allie knew she was only about two years old, a teenager for a chicken but used up for a battery hen.

Fran said, "Why don't we all work together on expanding our documentary into a feature film? Between the four of us, I think it could be stellar. Is that okay with you, Allie?"

"That's a great idea! Dad? Rae?" Allie said.

"I'm in," Rae said. "I think Bowden Ranch should be part of the film. Your back story is great. Who knows how many other ranchers feel the way you did?"

All eyes turned to Granger. He was staring at the table, eyes unfocused. "Dad?"

Granger looked at Allie. "Sorry honey." He stood up and walked over to the window. "When Pamela brought Pamela 2 to the ranch, she said something that's been bothering me ever since. She told me that, after going on the field trip with his class, her son didn't eat meat for a week. One week! It's almost pointless. I want to make more of an impression on people than that and I don't know if a documentary, even if it's amazing, will accomplish that purpose. Most people will see the documentary once, right? In order to have an idea sink in and take root, they would need to see it at least four or five times and that's not going happen."

Rae cut in. "What about a television ad? A thirty-second spot? I bet we could use some of the footage from both our documentaries."

Fran said, "Aren't TV ads expensive?"

Rae replied, "Depends. We could run them on off hours, like late at night or early in the morning and we'd start with local stations, not the networks. We could also use social networking to blanket the internet, like blogs and Facebook, YouTube, and animal rights websites."

Granger said, "Rae, if you could research ad rates, we can put together a budget. Fran, I'm assuming that the software you're using for the film is fairly easy to learn?"

"Piece of cake," Fran said. "You guys will pick it up in no time and I wouldn't mind helping you put it together. I think it would be really cool to produce an ad."

Allie put Ethel back in the cage and left the room. When she returned, she placed her laptop on the kitchen table and opened it up. "There's a YouTube video that reminds me of what you're talking about, Dad, but it's not hard hitting. I don't think it would convince a meat eater to go vegan, but it will give us an idea of what we need to do. Ah, here it is." She clicked on the link and the four of them watched the one minute video. When it was over, they all agreed that they could create a much more dynamic piece with footage they've already shot.

The atmosphere in the Bowden kitchen was electric. Everyone got caught up in the excitement, throwing out ideas and suggestions. Even Lucy and Ethel became more animated.

Rae got home a little after 5:00 in the evening. She felt liberated, like she could accomplish anything. Then she heard Carson downstairs and realized that one part of her life was still tenuous.

Carson looked up when Rae came into his bedroom. His drawing of a skeleton riding a motorcycle was nearly done.

"That's really good," Rae said. She sat down on his bed.

"Thanks."

"What you said about me and Granger getting married hurt but I also realize that this is a big deal for you. I am far from perfect and I've made some bad choices in my life and will continue to make mistakes, but right now I am madly in love with Granger and marrying him feels like the right thing to do. The wedding won't be until next year, so right now let's concentrate on you getting better."

"Fine. I still don't understand why you have to get married."

"You don't have to understand, but I would appreciate you respecting my choice. I love you very much, Carson."

Carson stood up and hugged Rae. "I love you too, Madre."

Granger sat very still on the cave floor. It was cool and slightly damp inside his sanctuary but as he meditated, he felt a warm glow emanating from his heart. As he fell further into a meditative state, images of Rae floated by along with those of Allie, the ranch, even Carson. He allowed them to appear and disappear. An image of his father materialized in his mind's eye. Instinctively, he wanted to erase it but this time he let it stay. He looked into his father's eyes and saw a profound sadness. He couldn't remember when he didn't feel disdain for his dad, but now he felt differently. Instead of anger, he felt sorry for a man who had such a difficult time expressing his love for his wife and children. Granger wasn't sure if his father enjoyed ranching or settled on the occupation because he didn't know how to do anything else. Maybe he was forced into it by his father. Suddenly, he saw his father drawing, his arm making rapid strokes on the paper with a charcoal pencil. At first, it was a blur. The activity was frenzied as if he was possessed. Granger watched in amazement, never even imagining that his dad held the slightest spark of creativity. When he put the pencil down, the drawing was revealed. It was a portrait of the Bowden family circa mid-seventies, when Granger was a teenager. They all looked so happy and serene, a family that didn't come close to the one in real life. The vision began to fade and, once again, Granger faced his father. He told him that he forgave him and that he loved him. His dad smiled and Granger felt his father's love reciprocated for the first time.

Upon opening his eyes, Granger felt complete, like the last piece of the puzzle was found and placed in its rightful position.

13793229R00161

Made in the USA
San Bernardino, CA
05 August 2014